Born in England in 1970, Santa Montefiore ~~~~~~ in Hampshire. She is married to writer Simon Sebag Montefiore. They live with their two children, Lily and Sasha, in London.

Visit her at www.santamontefiore.co.uk and sign up for her newsletter.

Santa Montefiore

The
DISTANT
SHORES

SIMON &
SCHUSTER

London · New York · Sydney · Toronto · New Delhi

First published in Great Britain by Simon & Schuster UK Ltd, 2021
This Paperback edition published in 2022

Copyright © Santa Montefiore, 2021

The right of Santa Montefiore to be identified as
author of this work has been asserted in accordance with
the Copyright, Designs and Patents Act, 1988.

1 3 5 7 9 10 8 6 4 2

Simon & Schuster UK Ltd
1st Floor
222 Gray's Inn Road
London WC1X 8HB

Simon & Schuster Australia, Sydney
Simon & Schuster India, New Delhi

www.simonandschuster.co.uk
www.simonandschuster.com.au
www.simonandschuster.co.in

A CIP catalogue record for this book
is available from the British Library

Paperback ISBN: 978-1-4711-9706-2
eBook ISBN: 978-1-4711-9705-5
Audio ISBN: 978-1-4711-9819-9

Typeset in Bembo by M Rules
Printed and bound by CPI Group (UK) Ltd, Croydon, CR0 4YY

To my dear friend Peter Nyhan

WHY

Please tell me, Lord, the answer to the
     question why
You put us on this Earth, to live a little
     day, and then to die.
We are born into this world – the fruit of
     Love and Pain
And live in suffering till 'tis time to
     leave again.
Alone we come. Alone we walk through
     Life. Alone we go.
And yet the purpose of it all we
     do not know.

ANON

Kitty

1980

I knew what to expect from death. I have always known. So
when it came it did not frighten me or surprise me. It came as
a friend, with its arms outstretched and its familiar face radiant
with light and love, just as I knew it would. I had completed
my life; it was time to return home.

I was a weary traveller at eighty, my heart ragged from the
love and loss that had filled it and shredded it in equal measure.
My body frail and my strength seeping away with each new
dawn that brought me closer to my release. I admit that a part
of me longed for it, this respite, like a runner approaching the
finishing line longs for the race to end. A part of me yearned
for repose.

When I was a little girl Grandma Adeline had told me that
being born on the ninth day of the ninth month in the year
1900 meant that I was a child of Mars and my life would be
full of turbulence. Well, so it was. War, betrayal, pain and
sorrow accompanied me on my journey like shadowy hounds
in constant pursuit. But I never allowed those trials to define
me or hold me prisoner. I never lost sight of my greater
spiritual purpose, of who I really was and from where I came.

I had been dealt a challenging set of cards, and yet within them was an abundance of hearts; I never lost sight of those, either.

Indeed, I have loved. I have *truly* loved. Yet when death came to carry me into an even greater love, I did not go. My attachment to my home was too strong, my love of the towers and turrets and stone walls of Castle Deverill too fierce; my rage at its loss all-consuming. How could I enter the Gates of Heaven with a soul weighed down with bitterness and resentment? I could not.

So I chose to stay.

I rejected the light, the promise of reunion with those I love and the rest in beauty and peace that I know is what lies ahead for those who deserve it; and I deserve it. I truly do. Yet, I am not ready. I might have completed my life, but I have not fulfilled it. God has extended His hand; it is with His gift of free will that I reject it.

Like my grandmother before me, I was born with the psychic ability to see the finer vibrations of spirit. Now that I am dead, I reside here as one of those spirits, in this shady limbo between the two worlds. I cannot go back to the material plane and I have rejected Heaven. But it is my choice and I don't regret it. Not for a moment. I have work to do and it must be done. You'd be surprised at the things spirits can do when they really put their minds to it.

You see, it is really very simple: I will not rest until Castle Deverill is returned to a Deverill. There, that is it, my work, my purpose, the reason I have chosen to remain. My grandmother did not mention how stubborn are the children of Mars!

My half-brother, JP Deverill, sold our family home. The home that, with the exception of fourteen unfortunate years when it was owned by the Countess di Marcantonio, had belonged to us since 1662, when King Charles II awarded my ancestor Barton Deverill with a title and lands in Ireland's Co. Cork as a reward for his loyalty. For over three hundred years that castle had belonged to my family. Three hundred years! As a symbol of dominance by the Protestant Anglo-Irish class the 'Big House' withstood centuries of menace by the Irish baying for independence; it survived rebellion, intrigue and fire, only to rise out of the flames like a phoenix along with my beleaguered family. It survived all that, and then one cold February day in 1976 JP signed it away. One sweep of his pen and it was gone.

Castle Deverill has been converted into a hotel and I am in it and will not remove myself from it. No, I will not. I will cause havoc, inspire fear, do all manner of terrible things in order to bend them to my will, these people who think they can profit from my family's history, from my family's pain. We Deverills have not suffered so that unscrupulous people can make money by turning our beloved home into a circus.

I am a child of Mars and I am ready to fight for what I love.

Castellum Deverilli est suum regnum is the family motto Barton Deverill carved in stone above the castle's great door: *A Deverill's castle is his kingdom.*

At least once it was.

I will not rest until it is a Deverill's kingdom again.

Chapter 1

As Margot Hart drove into the small town of Ballinakelly she slowed her little blue Beetle to a crawling pace. Thick fog had drifted inland from the sea, rendering it almost impossible to make out where she was going. The tarmac shimmered in the headlights, the windscreen wipers swept away the soft rain. A farmer with his sheepdog stopped outside O'Donovan's Public House to watch her pass, shaking his head at her imprudence, for wouldn't it be wiser to wait it out in the pub until the fog lifted? But Margot ignored him and motored on. After all, she had driven all the way from London, via a ferry across the Irish Sea, and wasn't about to let a bit of fog deter her. However, the fog seemed to condense the closer she got, as if the castle was deliberately hiding itself, as if it didn't want to be found. But it would have taken more than fog to put off Margot Hart. The sight of the old estate wall materializing out of the gloom injected her spirits with excitement and spurred her on. She was near. Very near. She took a deep breath then coasted along the boundary, until, to her delight, she reached the entrance, advertised by a bold green sign with elaborate gold lettering: *Castle Deverill. Hotel & Fine Dining.*

The black iron gates were just as she had seen them in old photographs. Splendidly grand with a pair of stone lions posing high up on pedestals either side of them, their teeth bared in readiness to defend this once stately home from intruders. But they were benign now, those lions, their ferocity no longer called upon, for the War of Independence and the civil war that followed had finally come to an end some sixty years before and peace had settled upon the Deverill estate. History was Margot's passion, especially the history of old castles. And history was why she was here, of course. As she drove through the gates and up the drive that swept in a gentle curve through thick rhododendron bushes, she smiled to herself and said out loud and with satisfaction, 'Here I am, Margot Hart, Writer in Residence.'

The first sight of the castle was arresting. After all, it was built to convey power, wealth and status. It was built to be magnificent. And magnificent it certainly was. Margot stopped the car a little ahead of the forecourt and gazed in wonder at the glistening grey walls and tall, crenelated towers and parapets, and was immediately struck by its sense of permanence, as if it had always been here and always would be. The sea mists would come and go, the sharp winter winds and gentle rain and the seasons, one after the other, but this castle would remain for ever, defiantly unchanged.

She took a deep, gratified breath for here she was at last, in the heart of the Deverill family history. In the place where it had all happened. She envisaged Barton Deverill, the first Lord Deverill of Ballinakelly, proudly mounted on his steed, with a plume in his hat and a sword at his hip, leading the hunt into the forests and fields that now belonged to him, courtesy of the King. She imagined the balls. Ladies in silk dresses stepping out of elegant carriages, gloved hands reaching for the liveried footmen in attendance, satin slippers gingerly feeling for the step. In her mind's eye she could see candle-light glowing in the darkness and hear music and laughter resounding from the ballroom with the clinking of glass as the Deverills and their friends toasted their good health and their even greater fortune. Life was good for the Anglo-Irish in those days. She lifted her eyes to the upstairs windows and wondered at the secret trysts that had taken place behind them, at the intrigue and skulduggery played out in the shadows. She would uncover it all. Every drama. What a fascinating book she was going to write.

Margot had signed up to spend nine months at Castle Deverill, which, to a twenty-eight-year-old girl shy of com-mitment, had initially seemed rather daunting. After all, she was always on the move, continually packing a suitcase, setting off for a new horizon, in a hurry to leave the old one behind. Yet, she had figured that it would take at least nine months to finish researching the subject and to write the book itself. The time would fly by, and it would be a pleasure because this was what she enjoyed doing most, burying herself in research and the written word. Initially, it had seemed like a coincidence that she had met the hotel's owner at a London cocktail party, but now she wasn't so sure: it felt more like Fate.

Margot had been fascinated by the Deverills since she was a child because of her grandfather's stories. Grandpa Hart had been wistful about his past, having grown up in Co. Cork and been a close friend of Harry Deverill. In 1919, when he was twenty-four, his family had sold their house and settled in England to escape the Troubles. He had never gone back. He had died recently, at the age of ninety, having lived many dif-ferent chapters in a long and varied life, yet it had seemed that *that* chapter of his youth in Co. Cork had been the most vivid and the most special, when the summers had seemed endless and the days idle and full of frivolity. His stories had become a little repetitive in the end. But there had been something compelling about the charisma, drama and sheer jauntiness of this extraordinary family that had never bored her. This book needed to be written and *she* was going to be the one to write it. She was just surprised – and pleased – that the Deverills' story hadn't been written before.

She motored onto the forecourt and parked in front of the big doors. As she turned off the ignition an eager old man in a black-and-green uniform hurried out with a golfing umbrella emblazoned with the hotel logo of initials and shamrock. He held it above her head and she stepped out of the car and onto the wet gravel.

'*Céad míle fáilte* to Castle Deverill,' he said in an accent as soft as Irish rain. ''Tis a day fit for the bed or the fire. You wouldn't turn a fox out of a henhouse. You must be perished. How in God's name did you find us in the fog?'

'It only got bad as I drove into Ballinakelly,' Margot replied, walking briskly towards the hotel entrance.

'Sea mist, I'm afraid, the devil's trick,' the man informed her with a shake of the head, then added brightly, 'As sure as there is an eye in a needle, the sun will come out tomorrow and burn it away as there was a ring around the moon last night.'

Margot stepped into the hall and gasped in delight at the splendour of it. To think that this sumptuous palace was once a family home. She swept her eyes over the hall in wonder, taking in the size and grandeur, and wondering what it would be like to live in a castle like this and have it all to oneself. A fire crackled cheerfully in a baronial fireplace, and above it a giant portrait of Barton Deverill, seated masterfully on a rearing stallion and dressed in bright yellow and gold with a scarlet plume in his hat, reminded her of the lost glory of this ill-fated family. How the local Irish must have resented the wealth and privilege of their Deverill masters. Even today, sixty years after the War of Independence, the impression of luxury was noticeably at odds with the harsh Irish landscape. The light was golden, the air lily-scented, the glint of chrome and glass opulent. It was like being welcomed into a parallel world of unbridled extravagance and comfort, while outside the grey fog swirled about the wind-battered cliffs and shivering hills, and the cold penetrated the bones of humble cottages.

The hotel was full of activity. A young couple reclined on purple velvet armchairs, drinking coffee out of pretty turquoise cups and studying a map. Three men in plus fours and guernseys loitered by the hearth, smoking cigars and guffawing loudly after what appeared, by the look of their florid faces, to have been a good day out on the hills, while the light clatter of bone china turned Margot's attention to guests enjoying tea in the dining room next door. She stood on the polished marble and took in the beauty of the staircase. It was quite the centrepiece, ascending gracefully to a wide landing before dividing into two elegantly curved arms that continued on up to the first floor. Crimson carpets, gilt-framed paintings, crisp white walls and glittering glass chandeliers gave the place the lavish feel of old-time glamour. She thought of Hubert Deverill then, who she could picture standing there on the landing, one hand in his jacket pocket, the other holding a whiskey glass as he surveyed the guests entering his home for the 1910 Summer Ball, and she smiled with pleasure, because here in this luxurious palace was where she was going to reside for the next nine months. Suddenly nine months didn't feel long enough.

As she crossed the marble chequerboard floor towards the

reception desk she overheard an elderly lady complaining to the hotel manager, a tall, patient-looking man in a navy suit and green tie with a sympathetic smile especially designed for moments such as these. The lady, in a tweed skirt and jacket and sensible brown lace-up shoes over thick brown socks, was anxiously wringing her hands, clearly upset about something. Margot, with the curiosity of a journalist in perpetual search for a good story, cocked an ear.

'I assure you the hotel is not haunted,' the man was saying, inclining his head and holding her fretful gaze with his cool blue one. 'It's an old castle and creaks a lot, especially in the wind, but you won't encounter any ghosts, I promise.' His Irish accent was especially reassuring, Margot thought.

'But I saw someone with my own eyes,' the lady explained, lowering her voice, fearful perhaps that the ghost might hear and take umbrage. 'A woman, elderly like me, in an old-fashioned maid's uniform, cleaning the room. I saw her clearly. As clearly as if she were a real person.'

The manager frowned. 'Cleaning the room, you say? If the castle were full of ghostly housekeepers, Mrs Walbridge, I wouldn't need to spend any money hiring living ones.' He laughed in amusement, displaying a set of large white teeth.

Mrs Walbridge did not appreciate his humour. She lifted her chin and stiffened her jaw, looking a good sight more formidable, and added, this time more confidently, 'I know you think I'm making it up, or was dreaming or hallucinating, but I assure you, Mr Dukelow, I was lucid. Quite lucid. I might be old but I have all my faculties, you know. Your hotel is haunted and I'm not staying another night. I would like a refund for the two nights for which I will no longer be requiring a bed. I will book in somewhere else tonight and return to England forthwith!'

Margot's eavesdropping was cut short by an efficient young woman with a black bob and blue eye shadow who was enquiring from behind the reception desk whether she could be of service. 'Oh, hello,' said Margot, reluctantly tearing herself away from the enfolding drama. 'I'm Margot Hart, the Writer in Residence.'

The woman's face lit up. 'Miss Hart, welcome to your new home. I'm Róisín.' She pronounced it Ro-sheen. Her crimson lips expanded into a pretty smile, revealing a wide gap in her two front teeth. 'I'll let the manager know you're here right away. Isn't it exciting? We've never had a Writer in Residence before.' She came out from behind the desk and went to interrupt the conversation between Mrs Walbridge and Mr Dukelow. A discreet word in his ear and Mr Dukelow was striding over to meet Margot, leaving the receptionist to lead a dissatisfied Mrs Walbridge to the dining room on the other side of the hall. Presumably she was hoping she'd persuade her to stay over a cup of tea and a scone.

'Miss Hart,' said Mr Dukelow, extending his hand. 'Welcome to Castle Deverill.' He shook her hand with gusto, relieved to be free of the irate Mrs Walbridge.

Margot grinned. 'I hope there are no housekeeping ghosts in *my* room!' she said, a twinkle in her eye.

Mr Dukelow laughed, already won over by her charm and good looks. 'I'm afraid we do get the odd strange complaint, but that's the first we've had about a ghost.'

'Perhaps a cunning way to get one's money back?' she suggested, guessing that Mr Dukelow had a good sense of humour and wouldn't object to her running with the joke.

'I'm afraid she believes she really *did* see a ghost. But fear not, Miss Hart, there will be no ghosts, housekeeping or otherwise, in your quarters. We have one of the finest suites of rooms for you. Mrs de Lisle was very specific. She wants you to be comfortable and to experience the best the hotel has to offer.'

Margot recalled Angela de Lisle at the cocktail party: short red hair, power suit, expensive gold earrings and pearl necklace, lashings of Rive Gauche perfume, an immaculate manicure and a facelift that looked as if it had been performed by an overzealous American surgeon. She was the sort of woman who clicked her fingers and expected mountains to move. Margot suspected that the mountains did move, unquestioningly and without hesitation.

'Let me show you to your room.' Mr Dukelow gestured for her to follow and made his way towards the stairs. 'I gather you've driven all the way from London. That's quite a drive, and on your own too.'

Margot smiled patiently; she was used to men patronizing her. Long blonde hair seemed to scream 'helpless'. But Margot was far from helpless. She'd driven from Buenos Aires to Patagonia without so much as a blink; the road and ferry trip from London to Ballinakelly had hardly posed a challenge. 'I figured I'd need my car, Mr Dukelow,' she replied coolly.

'Cork is indeed a beautiful county and there's much to see, especially for a historian like yourself. By the by, your biography of Eva Perón was very well received here. We have a copy in the library. Perhaps you'll sign it for us.'

Margot was delighted. Her first biography, which had taken three years to write, had been a bestseller when it was launched the summer before. She knew that she owed much of her success to Andrew Lloyd Webber's musical *Evita*, which had debuted some seven years ago and given her the idea for her book. Indeed, had it not been for the show, most people in the United Kingdom wouldn't even know who Eva Perón was. But Margot also knew that, in spite of that advantage, the book was good and deserved its success.

'Of course I'll sign it for you,' she said distractedly, running her eyes over the paintings in elaborate gold frames that hung on the wall. 'Were these here when Mrs de Lisle bought the castle?' She peered at one of the inscriptions, not recognizing the name of the young man in the gleaming suit of armour. Disappointingly, he was not a Deverill.

Mr Dukelow stopped on the landing and put his hands on his hips. 'I'm afraid, with the exception of Barton Deverill in the hall and Tarquin, his grandson, in the drawing room, the most valuable paintings were auctioned off by Lord Deverill before he sold the castle. Fortunately, Mrs de Lisle was able to purchase Barton and Tarquin, but the others are part of her own collection and on loan to the hotel. As I'm sure you know, she's an avid collector and a woman who takes great trouble with details. She wanted the castle to retain its authentic feel. They look like they're family portraits, don't they? But they're not. I couldn't tell you who they are of.'

'Might there be someone here who does know what the original features are and which are Mrs de Lisle's contribution? I'd love to get a feel of what the castle was like when it was a home.'

Mr Dukelow's veneer slipped a little and he looked unsure. 'The only person who really knows the castle is its previous owner, Lord Deverill. He lives in the old Hunting Lodge on the estate. I believe that was not part of the deal when he sold the castle to Mrs de Lisle. I doubt he'll want to speak to you, I'm afraid. He's a recluse.'

Margot wasn't surprised. 'It must have been hard selling his family home,' she mused. 'After all, it had belonged to a Deverill for over three hundred years. He must have felt great shame in being the Deverill who let it go. The Deverill who sold it to a de Lisle so that it could become one more hotel on their long list of luxury hotels. I wonder what the rest of his family think of it now that it's full of people like me tramping insensitively over their memories.'

Mr Dukelow looked at her, his face full of admiration. 'You do have a way with words, don't you, Miss Hart. I have never thought of it like that. I suppose it takes the mind of a historian to consider the people who lived here before. My mind is very much in the present moment and in the future. This is one of the finest hotels in the world and it's my job to ensure that it remains so. Mrs de Lisle will accept nothing less.' They continued up the stairs. 'There was very little artwork remaining when the castle was sold. But I believe the four-poster beds and some of the furniture was bought with the castle. Mrs de Lisle gutted it and renovated it, keeping what was good and getting rid of what was not. The project took six years to complete. The building was in very poor condi-tion even though it was rebuilt in the 1920s, after it was razed to the ground by a terrible fire. Mrs de Lisle is American, so she likes certain standards, which is why the hotel is such a success. You'll see, Miss Hart, how she has managed to retain the feeling of history and family while bringing it into the modern era.'

Margot smiled to herself as he spouted the company mis-sion statement. 'I can tell that already,' she said. 'Does Lord Deverill live alone?'

'He does,' Mr Dukelow replied.

'And the Hunting Lodge is close by?'

'Yes, you can try knocking on his door, Miss Hart, but I cannot guarantee he'll open it.'

'I'm not a woman who is easily put off when I'm on the

trail of a good story.' She was sure that she would inveigle her way into Lord Deverill's confidence somehow.

'The trouble is, it's *his* story and I'm not sure he'll want it published for all the world to read. However, there *are* people in Ballinakelly who have lived here for generations and would probably be happy to help you with your research. I can put you in touch with them if you like. It would be my pleasure. I know Mrs de Lisle would like me to help you in any way I can. We're honoured to have a Writer in Residence and want your stay to be as productive as possible.'

Margot's room was in the western tower, up a narrow flight of stairs. The atmosphere changed the moment Mr Dukelow lifted the latch on the heavy wooden door. It was as if they were entering the oldest part of the castle, and the most secret. She knew from her research that the castle had been burned down in 1921 by nationalist rebels and only a small part had survived. She imagined that this tower must surely be a portion of that fortunate part. It consisted of a sitting room, bedroom and bathroom, with windows overlooking the gardens. With its low ceilings, crooked walls, uneven floor and strong almost deferential sense of the past, it was enchanting. Margot didn't imagine there was a nicer set of rooms in the entire castle. The sitting room had a big open fire, which was glowing hospitably, and dark wooden beams in the low ceilings that sagged, betraying their great age as well as a weary satisfaction at having survived when all around them had perished.

'I love it!' she exclaimed, turning to Mr Dukelow. 'It's adorable. I couldn't be happier.'

'There's a desk in the sitting room, but we'd like it if you spent some time writing in the drawing room downstairs. The guests would be delighted to witness the great artiste at work.'

Margot laughed. 'Oh, you flatter me, Mr Dukelow! But of

course, you're right. I will work down there and fend off my fans with my ink pen.'

Mr Dukelow laughed. Margot's enthusiasm was infectious as was the sparkle in her olive-green eyes.

They were diverted by the sound of heaving and puffing and mutterings of 'Jesus, help me' coming up the stairs. Mr Dukelow went to hold open the door for the porter who was struggling with Margot's suitcase. 'I'm sorry it's so large,' she said as the elderly man, swollen-faced and sweating, heaved it into the room. 'It's all my worldly goods, I'm afraid.'

'What doesn't kill me makes me stronger,' the porter gasped in an Irish accent as rich as Guinness, arching his back with a groan. Margot was certain she heard a click. He was much too old to be doing such heavy work, she thought.

'That's the spirit, Mr Flannigan,' said Mr Dukelow, ignoring the man's discomfort.

'At least it won't need to go back down until September,' Margot added, hoping to extract a smile by giving him one of her most charming.

Mr Flannigan glanced at her suspiciously. 'Indeed, and if I'm spared, it won't be me who'll be lifting it. I haven't been this worn out since me wedding night, God help us.'

'Well, thank you for bringing it up all the same. It's a lovely room and as long as nothing goes bump in the night, I'll be very happy here.'

Mr Flannigan caught Mr Dukelow's eye. It was a subtle communication but Margot was much too sharp not to notice it.

'Would you like anything brought to your room? A cup of tea, perhaps? A light meal?' Mr Dukelow asked.

'I'll unpack and then come down and have supper in the dining room. I'm dying to see more of the castle.'

'In that case, we'll leave you in peace.' The two men left the room, closing the door behind them.

Margot sighed with pleasure. She couldn't believe she was really here, in Castle Deverill. She went to the window and gazed out over the lawn. The scene of so many garden parties in bygone summers when the Deverills would inspire loyalty in their tenants and employees with tea and cakes, carefully chosen words and gracious smiles, staving off rebellion with arrows of charm. Now it shivered, silver grey and sodden, the memory of its glory days lost in the fog. Plants hibernated in the borders, trees looked forlorn without their fine leaves, only an enormous cedar with inky green branches was constantly vigilant – a giant keeping watch over the castle like a devoted old retainer who has vowed to defend it to the last. Margot was pleased she'd get to see it in summertime when the borders would be full of flowers and the trees thick with foliage. Her grandfather had told her a great deal about the gardens. How they'd played croquet on the lawn during the day and devil's chase, which was the Deverills' version of hide and seek, in the evenings. He'd kissed a girl in one of the greenhouses, he'd told her with a gleam in his eye. 'Make sure you take a look at those,' he'd said. 'Like palaces they were, with jungles inside.'

Every year the Deverills had held a grand summer ball. All the Anglo-Irish in the region were invited. Margot's grandfather had talked about that more than anything else, even the hunt, which he'd adored. Margot sensed he'd been a real ladies' man, dancing with all the girls. The secret to his success, he'd told her, was booking them in early so as not to miss a single dance. According to her grandfather, the Deverills were as wild as snakes. Not only out hunting where they outshone the other riders with their fearlessness, but on the dancefloor too. Bertie Deverill, who was his father's friend and contemporary and would later become Lord Deverill, was the most dashing and all the young women wanted to dance with him. 'The trouble was he often foxtrotted the ladies on upstairs,' her grandfather told her, arching an eyebrow. 'It was because of that my father did not allow my sister Abigail to dance with him. Abigail minded terribly having to turn down the host, but my father was insistent and quite right too.'

Then Bertie had had his wicked way with a housemaid and got her pregnant. He later recognized the boy as his and, when his legitimate son Harry was killed in the First World War, Jack Patrick, known as JP, had become Bertie's heir. Margot couldn't see the Hunting Lodge from her window, but it was out there somewhere and JP, the present Lord Deverill, was inside it, keeping all the family secrets. She knew that, in order to research the last sixty years of his family's history, she was going to need to speak to him.

She unpacked her suitcase and put away her clothes, happily humming Jennifer Rush's 'The Power Of Love', which was number one in the charts and a constant on every radio station. She placed her typewriter on the desk along with her notebooks, which were already full of her grandfather's stories and accounts she'd found in old newspaper articles. The fire of 1921 had been widely reported in the English press at the time. There was a photograph of Hubert Deverill, Bertie's father, who had died in the fire, and pictures of the RIC picking over the still-smouldering rubble. The criminals had never been brought to justice. The authorities knew who was responsible, of course they did. It was the time of the Troubles. British castles and 'Big Houses', as they were known, were being razed to the ground all over Ireland by the IRA in their fight for independence. Margot had discovered that a staggering two hundred and seventy-five of these beautiful houses had been burned down or blown up between the years 1919 and 1923. The Deverills were not alone, but that was no consolation. The perpetrators were free to continue their purge of British dominance without restraint.

During her search through the newspapers, Margot had found an article about Celia Deverill, a cousin, who had bought the castle and rebuilt it at great expense. The photograph accompanying the article revealed a beautiful blonde in a fur coat and diamonds, standing alongside a somewhat chinless husband with a long, serious face. Celia, a 'bright young thing' of 1920s London, had caused a scandal when she had run off to Scotland with the best man on her wedding day. Margot's grandfather had told her that there was talk of Celia's father paying her husband Archie a fortune to take her back and it was with *that* money that Celia had rebuilt the castle. Then, just when things were going well for Celia and Archie, tragedy struck again. The Great Depression of 1929 wiped them out financially and Archie hanged himself on a tree right here in the castle grounds. Celia disappeared to South Africa and sold the castle to a mysterious Italian. Count Cesare di Marcantonio's wife turned out to be Bridie, the housemaid Bertie had impregnated, JP's mother. Margot patted the pile of notebooks with satisfaction. She'd barely begun to dig and she already had enough stories to fill most of the book. It was going to be a gripping read.

At supper in the dining room Margot was given a round table in the corner. From there she could see the entire room, and very impressive it was too. She imagined it must have been the original dining room where the Deverills had enjoyed family meals, served by footmen in red-and-gold livery. There were elaborate plaster mouldings on the ceiling, art deco chandeliers in frosted glass and chrome, and tall

windows hidden behind heavy velvet curtains in a rich shade
of purple. Instead of works of art there were enormous panels
of hand-painted landscapes. The effect was stunning and
Margot, who loved anything of beauty, was drawn into the
bright purple mountains and vivid green fields. She imagined
that those must have been commissioned by Celia Deverill
herself, because they were part of the bones of the castle and
could not be removed.

She had ordered a glass of wine and was just beginning to
enjoy it when Mrs Walbridge, the lady she had seen in the
lobby earlier, approached her table. She too had changed,
swapping her sensible walking shoes and tweed suit for a
scratchy blue skirt and silk blouse embellished at the throat
with a gold-and-amethyst brooch. Her grey hair was swept
off her face and tied in a soft bun, and her little brown eyes
were lively and intelligent behind spectacles, giving her
the air of an old schoolmistress. She smiled at Margot and
introduced herself. 'Forgive me for intruding,' she said, 'but
I understand you are the Writer in Residence here and I
wanted to shake your hand. Your book on Eva Perón was a
frightfully good read.'

Margot did not object to people talking to her, in fact, she
welcomed it. Most people possessed something of interest,
even if one had to dig a little to find it. She offered the old lady
a chair and a glass of sherry. 'I grew up in Argentina and was
in my fifties in the 1940s when the Peróns were at the top of
their game,' said Mrs Walbridge, making herself comfortable
and looking forward to that glass of sherry. At the mention of
Argentina in the 1940s Margot was able to place her accent.
It was the clipped, upper-class inflection of a dying breed of
Anglo-Argentines who lived in Hurlingham, Buenos Aires,
and only married within their small circle of British expats.

'So I have first-hand experience of that dreadful woman. You were very fair in your book, balanced, I would say, because although she was an ambitious adventuress to the British, to the Argentines she was a saint. Of course, there's an argument for both sides, one has to acknowledge that, and you handled it well, I thought.'

'Thank you,' Margot replied.

'I could have told you some damning stories about her had we met when you were doing your research. Perhaps then you might not have been so balanced.' She gave Margot a knowing smile. 'Pity, really, that we didn't meet before. What are you working on now?'

'The history of the Deverill family.'

Mrs Walbridge's eyes lit up. 'Ah, that's why you're here. They have an interesting history, don't they?'

'They certainly do.'

'Lots of drama. That's what you need in a book. Lots of drama, otherwise your readers get bored. Although I've never been very partial to a dramatic life myself. I prefer peace and tranquillity. I like the waters to be smooth.'

The waiter promptly brought Mrs Walbridge her glass of sherry and Margot watched her take a sip then smack her lips with pleasure. She decided to be bold. 'I hope you don't mind but I couldn't help overhearing you talking to the manager earlier. I thought you were leaving for England.'

Mrs Walbridge pursed her lips and lowered her voice. 'You are not wrong. I most certainly had it in mind to leave, and as soon as possible. I've spent two nights here already and have barely slept a wink on account of the strange occurrences in my room. But that Mr Dukelow has the charm of the devil. He managed to persuade me to stay by suggesting I move into a different part of the hotel.' She leaned forward and whispered. 'He hasn't charged me for the two previous nights. Isn't that good of him?'

'When you say strange occurrences, do you mean ghosts?'

She lowered her voice. 'I do, Margot.'

Margot laughed. 'I'm curious. What exactly did you see?'

Mrs Walbridge's face tightened. 'An old woman in uniform, black dress and white apron, bustling about my room.'

'Cleaning?'

'Well, I'm not sure she did much cleaning,' she said with a sniff. 'There was still dust beneath the bed in the morning.'

'I don't suppose Mr Dukelow believed you.'

Mrs Walbridge narrowed her eyes. 'If he didn't believe me, why then has he taken the first two nights off my bill?'

'Because he doesn't want you talking about it and upsetting the other guests.'

'Perhaps,' Mrs Walbridge conceded. 'Although I would guess that this is not the first time a guest has complained of strange occurrences in the night.'

'Well, you won't upset *me*, Mrs Walbridge,' said Margot. 'I don't believe in ghosts.'

Just as the words escaped her lips her glass of wine toppled over and spilled onto the white tablecloth.

Mrs Walbridge blanched. 'Did you see that?' she gasped. A hand shot to her throat.

'I knocked it with my elbow,' said Margot, picking up the glass and placing a napkin over the crimson stain.

'I didn't see you touch it. That glass fell over all on its own, I'd bet my life on it.' The old lady's eyes rolled slowly as she searched for the culprit in the air around her. 'It's here,' she whispered darkly. 'I can feel it. The air has gone cold. Can you feel it? That's what ghosts do. They turn the air cold.'

'Really, Mrs Walbridge, if it was the housekeeping ghost

she'd hardly make a mess she'd have to clean up.' Margot laughed carelessly. 'My fault entirely. Typically clumsy of me! Now, where were we?'

Mrs Walbridge took a gulp of sherry. 'You were just saying you did not believe in ghosts!'

Chapter 2

Margot did not expect to sleep much that night. The episode with the glass, and Mrs Walbridge's reaction to it, had put the wind up her. She did not believe in ghosts, but turning out the light and listening to the creaking and groaning of the castle made her feel oddly apprehensive. However, it had been a long drive and she was tired. Shortly after putting her head on the pillow, the exceedingly comfortable pillow – Mrs de Lisle had spared no cost – she sank into a deep and dreamless sleep.

In the morning she ordered room service and drank her coffee at her desk, reading through her notes and working out where she needed to focus her research. There were eight Lord Deverills: Barton, Egerton, Tarquin, Peregrine, Greville, Hubert, Bertie and finally Jack Patrick, the present Lord Deverill. As they were a high-profile family with political influence, at least up until Greville at the end of the nine-teenth century, Margot had managed to research the first five lords pretty thoroughly. They were all colourful characters and fabulously wealthy, with dark secrets, including the usual extramarital affairs and illegitimate children favoured by the aristocracy. Barton had been a tyrant, Egerton a bully and horrid to his wife, and the worst, Tarquin, had been cruel to his disabled son who had drowned on his tenth birthday in the ornamental pond in the castle grounds. It was rumoured that his father turned a blind eye and allowed it to happen, because the child brought shame upon the family name. Tarquin's wife died shortly after, of a broken heart.

The last sixty years were Margot's main focus now, from Hubert Deverill to the present day. But it was going to be challenging when so many of the leading personalities were still alive. There was JP, the current Lord Deverill, and his ex-wife, Alana, who had moved to America after their divorce. She had apparently taken him to the cleaners in the courts, leaving him with no alternative but to sell the castle. They had three children who were in their late twenties and thirties. Margot wasn't sure where they were. Then there was Celia Deverill and her second husband Boysie Bancroft who were in their mid to late eighties – they lived in Paris. And JP's twin sister, Martha, and her husband Joshua, who divided their time between California and Cork. If Margot wanted information she was going to have to be devious. It was unlikely that any of these characters would want to help her.

To Margot's relief the fog had cleared in the night, leaving a crisp blue sky and feathery white clouds. The lawn glittered with a sprinkling of frost. Some sort of animal had trotted across it in the night, leaving its meandering footprints as evidence of the fun it had had while the castle slept. Margot decided she'd take a look around the town. If she was going to write about the Deverills, it was important to put the castle into context. After all, the relationship between the family and Ballinakelly had always been an uncertain one. The family had inspired both hatred and loyalty in the Irish; it was important to give a balanced account, as Mrs Walbridge would say.

Excited to be in Deverill heartland Margot put on her bright red coat and bobble hat and hurried downstairs. Mrs

Walbridge was in the lobby, standing in front of the fire in a camel-hair coat and crocheted hat that resembled a tea cosy. 'Good morning,' said Margot cheerfully.

Mrs Walbridge's keen little eyes lit up. 'Good morning, dear,' she replied. 'Are you going out?'

'Yes, I'm heading into town.'

'Me too,' said Mrs Walbridge. 'I'm waiting for a taxi.'

'You can come with me if you like,' Margot offered. 'I have a car.'

'Oh, how very kind. I'm visiting a friend who lives just the other side of Ballinakelly, by the sea.'

'How lovely. I'll get to see more of the countryside. I'll ask them to cancel your taxi.'

A moment later Mrs Walbridge was putting on her gloves and following Margot out into the sunshine. 'Isn't it a beautiful day,' she gushed. 'Ireland is so unpredictable. One day you can't see further than your nose because of fog and the next it's like this. As blue as cornflowers.'

Margot unlocked the door of her Volkswagen Beetle, which was as blue as Mrs Walbridge's cornflower sky, and climbed in. Mrs Walbridge waited patiently as she gathered up the papers and magazines, crisp packets and cola bottles she'd left on the passenger seat and chucked them into the back. 'Ready for you now, Mrs Walbridge,' she called.

Mrs Walbridge climbed stiffly into the car, taking a while to settle into a comfortable position and to strap herself in. 'My name is Dorothy, by the way. You can call me Dorothy if you like.'

'Thank you,' said Margot, turning the key. 'I will.'

Just as they were about to set off a robin fluttered in front of the windscreen and alighted onto the bonnet of the car. 'Well, would you look at that!' exclaimed Margot in amazement.

'Oh, this happens to me all the time,' said Dorothy casually. 'I have a thing with robins. It's extraordinary. They're always trying to get my attention. I'm not sure what it means, but they seem to be drawn to me.'

'St Francis of Assisi – St Dorothy,' said Margot with a laugh.

The robin hopped closer then perched on the windscreen wiper and pecked at the glass with its sharp little beak. 'You see?' said Dorothy with a sigh. 'It's as if it's trying to tell me something.'

'Well, I can't drive away until it flies off,' said Margot, letting go of the steering wheel.

'Go on, little robin,' said Dorothy, leaning forward to tap the glass. The robin looked put out, stared at her for a long moment and then took flight. 'Extraordinary,' she repeated with a shake of the head. 'And only robins. The other birds couldn't care a fig about me.'

Margot put the car into gear and set off down the drive.

'I wonder, would you like to come with me?' Dorothy asked, keen to repay Margot for her kindness. 'I'm going to visit my dear friend Emer O'Leary. She's JP Deverill's mother-in-law although, since the divorce, the two of them have barely spoken. But being related to the family you're writing about, she might be helpful. You never know. It's worth a try.'

'Really? You don't think she'd mind me turning up with you, uninvited?'

'Oh no, this isn't England, dear. The Irish are very hospitable. She'd love to meet you, I'm sure. A famous writer like you.'

Margot couldn't believe her luck. She'd only been at the castle one night and already she had a meeting with someone close to the Deverill family. If Mrs O'Leary was angry with her son-in-law she might be happy to share some family secrets. As she drove down the winding lanes Margot felt happiness expanding in her chest. The day could not have started more positively.

This time she was able to appreciate the wild beauty of the landscape. There was no fog to obscure the green pastures and rugged hills, no drizzle on the windscreen to mar her view. Sheep grazed in the sunshine on wild grasses and heather and wandered carefree among the crumbling ruins of long-abandoned cottages and drystone walls. Red kites circled above, their vast wings spread, ready to swoop on an unsuspecting creature minding its business in the undergrowth below. There was a sense of drama in those hills that appealed to Margot's love of stories. A sense of history. As if the resonance of centuries of conflict lingered in the soil still. As if its stain could never be washed away no matter how much it rained.

The O'Learys' home was a modest white house with a grey-slate roof, nestled in a sheltered bay with a view of the sea. The tide was out, leaving the sand damp and teeming with small creatures for the gulls to squabble over. Even in the bleakest of winter months, the velvet green hills and jagged cliffs possessed a Gothic charm. 'What a beautiful place to live,' said Margot, more to herself than to her companion. A part of her longed for such isolation.

She parked the car in front of the house.

'Emer has a lovely life. She's lived all over, you know. In America and Argentina – which is where I met her – and, for the greater part of her life, here. I thought when her daughter moved to the States she'd go with her, but her husband is Irish to his marrow. I don't think he'd want to be anywhere but here in Ballinakelly. He fought for independence, you know. He was brave and passionate and terribly idealistic. Quite the romantic hero. You can't take that kind of patriotism out of a man like Jack O'Leary, and place him on the other side of the world and expect him to thrive. His heart would wither. He'd die of homesickness.' Dorothy paused a moment and sighed pensively. 'He's old now, nearly ninety, but he's still got an air of mystery about him, you'll see.'

Margot suspected that Dorothy was a little in love with Jack O'Leary.

She followed her to the front door and watched her give it a vigorous knock. A moment later there was a shuffling sound behind it and then it opened. An elderly woman with short grey hair and a gentle face looked from Dorothy to Margot and raised her eyebrows in surprise. 'I've brought my new friend to meet you, Emer,' said Dorothy. 'Margot Hart is the Writer in Residence at the castle. She's famous.'

Margot put out her hand and smiled bashfully. 'I wouldn't go as far as saying I'm famous—'

'Oh, but you are, Margot. I should know, I've read your book,' Dorothy cut in with a chuckle. 'She's a very good writer too. I'm a fan!'

Emer shook Margot's hand. 'You're very welcome,' she said, smiling in amusement at Dorothy's enthusiasm. She opened the door wide and stepped aside to let them pass. 'Any friend of Dorothy's is a friend of mine.'

The three of them went into the sitting room. Bright sunlight streamed through the windows and a fire crackled hospitably in the grate. Dorothy didn't wait to be offered a seat but sank into one of the comfy chairs with a sigh, quite at home. She smoothed down her skirt and smiled with satisfaction. 'What a delicious smell,' she exclaimed.

'I've been baking,' Emer replied. 'My grandson is coming for lunch today and he likes my apple pie. He's nearly thirty but he wants me to cook his favourite things as if he were still a boy. Now, would you like a cup of tea?'

'That would be lovely,' said Dorothy.

'Can I help you?' Margot asked.

'If you don't mind, you can bring the tray in for me,' said Emer.

'Now I'm down, I'll stay down,' said Dorothy decisively. 'It's lovely here by the fire. Just lovely.'

Margot followed Mrs O'Leary into the kitchen. It was a light, pretty room with a pine floor, worn in the places that had sustained the most traffic. An antique wooden dresser was pressed up against the back wall, a long refectory table in front of it, laden with newspapers. A wicker laundry basket had been left on a chair, overflowing with clothes waiting to be ironed. 'Do excuse the mess. I wasn't expecting company. Or rather, I wasn't expecting *famous* company.' Emer arched an eyebrow and Margot suspected that she was less easily impressed than Dorothy.

'Dorothy told me you met in Argentina,' she said.

'We did, many aeons ago. She's been a dear friend for years.' Emer moved unhurriedly about the kitchen, opening cupboards, taking down china cups and saucers and arranging them tidily on a tray. She poured milk into a jug and assembled biscuits in a semicircle on a plate. She was elegant yet unpretentious in a pair of trousers, floral shirt and long cardigan. Margot imagined her as a young woman. She was probably never a great beauty, but she possessed a certain serenity that imbued her face with charm. Her eyes were a delicate shade of blue, the expression in them kind with a twinkle of humour. She sensed Emer was a patient and intelligent woman, which was probably just what a passionate man like Jack O'Leary needed.

'So tell me, Margot, what are you writing up there at the castle?' Emer asked, standing at the stove while the kettle simmered.

Margot braced herself for Emer's reaction. 'A history of the Deverills,' she answered, then held her breath.

Emer didn't miss a beat. 'I suppose there's enough for a book,' she said, narrowing her eyes reflectively.

'I'm going right back to Barton Deverill.'

'And up to where?' Emer looked at her steadily and Margot sensed the suspicion behind her smile.

'I'll probably take it up to the Second World War,' Margot lied and then regretted it. She had every intention of bringing it right up to the present day and wished she'd been honest about it.

'That would be prudent.'

'My grandfather was Anglo-Irish and hunted with the Deverills back in the day. He remembered them fondly.'

This piece of information immediately diffused any awkwardness. Mrs O'Leary nodded and her suspicion evaporated behind a relieved smile. 'Oh well, that makes all the difference,' she said happily. 'You're friend not foe.'

Margot looked horrified and put a hand on her heart. 'Absolutely not foe, Mrs O'Leary. I'm a massive fan of the family and the castle, especially. It's really the history of the castle that I'm interested in writing.'

'It was my daughter's home for seventeen years and her children's home. It broke their hearts when JP sold it. But that's life. We can't always have what we want and we must make do. It's only bricks and mortar, after all. The truth is that home is where love is. And there wasn't much love left there. *That's* the real tragedy.'

'I'm sorry to hear that,' said Margot, curious to know more.

'Why don't you take the tray into poor Dorothy. She'll be wondering what we're doing in here while she's sitting in there on her own.'

Margot did as she was told. Emer O'Leary was a straight-talking, practical woman and yet her tone was gentle and wise. Margot believed that if she and her son-in-law, JP Deverill, were not speaking, it was because *he* didn't want to speak to *her*, not the other way round. Margot didn't imagine Emer to be a woman to bear a grudge.

She put the tray down on the table in front of the fire. A moment later Emer came in with the teapot. 'Tell me, Dorothy, did you sleep well last night? Did you see that ghost again?'

'I slept like a baby, Emer. Mr Dukelow, the manager, was kind enough to move me to another room.'

'That's very good of him.' Emer passed her a teacup.

'Oh, how lovely.' Dorothy sighed with pleasure. 'Mr Dukelow has taken my first two nights off my bill,' she added with a delighted smile. 'Fancy that.'

Emer poured tea into Margot's cup, then poured one for herself and sat down in an armchair by the fire. 'I would say that Mr Dukelow doesn't want you spreading ghost stories around. If people get wind of the fact that the place is haunted they might stop coming altogether.'

'That's what I said,' Margot agreed. 'Although I would have thought people would be more likely to come. Ghosts are all the rage, you know. I have a friend in London who's a medium. I'm not entirely sure that he really communicates with the dead, but it's big business.'

'I'd like the dead to stay dead,' said Dorothy with a sniff. '*I* certainly don't want any strange apparitions in *my* bedroom, if you don't mind. If I'd known the hotel was riddled with them, I would have chosen another.'

'I *did* invite you to stay here,' said Emer.

'Jack doesn't like visitors. Although he says he doesn't mind, I know he does. And I like to be independent and not to be a burden to anyone.'

'He'll be here shortly. He went out to take the dog for a walk.'

'That's why he's going to live until he's a hundred,' said Dorothy. 'The secret to longevity is taking lots of exercise.'

'And luck,' Emer added. 'But luck runs out in the end.'

The three of them chatted in the cosy, soporific atmosphere of the little sitting room. The cast-iron fireback radiated warmth while specks of dust danced like fireflies in the shafts of sunlight that spilled through the windowpanes. Margot finished her tea and ate a couple of biscuits and listened to Dorothy and Emer reminiscing about Argentina. Her eyes strayed to the photographs placed on the side tables in frames. Attractive, happy people, smiling for the camera. She longed to ask who they were, but didn't want to look like she was prying – or researching her book.

A while later the front door opened and a gust of cold air swept into the sitting room from the hall. A dog came into the room, panting. 'I hope you're not a *wet* dog,' said Emer reproachfully. Whether he was wet or not, the mongrel sniffed the guests then turned his back and trotted out into the hall to join his master. A moment later Jack O'Leary appeared. He wasn't a large man, but his charisma was powerful and filled the room. It suddenly felt too small for the four of them.

'Hello, Dorothy,' he said, acknowledging his wife's friend with a nod, as if he saw her every day and didn't need to bother with pleasantries. Dorothy gazed up at him, an expression of awe and delight igniting a little fire in her eyes. He then turned to Margot. She stood up and put out her hand. 'It's very nice to meet you, Mr O'Leary,' she said.

'This is Margot Hart, Dorothy's friend,' Emer told him. 'She's the Writer in Residence up at the castle. Imagine that, Jack, they have a Writer in Residence now!'

'That's grand,' said Jack in his gruff Irish brogue that brought to Margot's mind winds buffeting cliffs and wild waves crashing against rocks. Dorothy had been right, this man was as much part of Ireland as a shamrock.

Jack O'Leary might have been nearly ninety but Margot could tell that he was once a dashingly handsome man. His hair was grey, his face as haggard as that of an old fisherman who has spent his life in the elements, but his eyes were the colour of deep blue sea glass, unfathomable and full of secrets. Margot sensed that he had lived many lives, and suffered. His skin betrayed a lifetime of turbulence in the hundreds of lines carved into it. Most of all it told of loss.

'And what are you writing?' he asked.

'A history of the Deverill family,' she replied, holding his gaze and watching it intensify with interest.

'Are you now,' he mused and a small smile curled his lips. 'Well, there's more than enough to fill a book. Indeed, I'd say you could write a trilogy.'

Margot sensed that for some reason the idea of a book about the Deverills amused him. 'I need to speak to people like you who knew them in the early part of this century,' she added. It was worth a shot.

Jack chuckled. 'Aye, I knew them well enough and I've had my fingers burnt in the process. Now that our families are interlinked, for better or for worse, I'll not be speaking about the Deverills to anyone. But there are those that will. You only have to ask around. There are plenty that would shed light onto those dark and secret places.'

'Our daughter was married to JP Deverill,' said Emer. She

sighed regretfully. 'We thought it a good match. But people change over time and often they don't change together or in the same way. They drift apart.'

'But you have three lovely grandchildren from that marriage,' interjected Dorothy, who sensed a heaviness pervading the room and decided to lift it. 'And Colm lives right here in Ballinakelly. How lovely for you to see him so often.'

'Yes, we're very lucky, for sure.' Emer smiled. She turned to Margot. 'Our grandson is a vet like Jack was, Margot. We're lucky he chose to remain in Ireland. His sisters followed their mother to America. But Colm's like his grandfather. His roots are embedded deep in Irish soil. He'll not be leaving it.'

Jack went into the kitchen, his loyal mongrel trotting eagerly after him. Margot took a breath and felt her whole body relax. It was as if Jack had taken his oppressive energy with him, restoring the sitting room to its original cosiness. But as much as Margot listened to the two women's conversation, her attention had followed Jack as well. She was drawn to that dark charisma, sensing a story there if only she could get him to tell it.

At length Dorothy pushed herself to her feet and declared that she had taken up enough of Emer's time. 'I'm leaving tomorrow,' she said. 'But I'll be back shortly.' She turned to Margot. 'When my husband died I decided I'd treat myself and come to Ballinakelly as often as I wanted. You have to do all the things you want to do, in the time you're given, and no one knows how long that will be. So I'll be back very soon. I'm already looking forward to it.'

Emer showed them to the door. She embraced her friend with affection and shook Margot's hand. 'It was very nice meeting you,' she said. 'I hope you enjoy the castle. I'm sure the de Lisles have done a good job in restoring it.'

'It's certainly luxurious,' Margot replied.

Emer nodded sadly. 'It was luxurious when JP inherited it.' She sighed. 'The trouble is an apple doesn't fall very far from the tree.'

Margot wasn't sure what she meant by that but she nodded as if she did. 'Thank you for welcoming me into your home,' she said, then stepped into the cold and made her way briskly to the car. Dorothy lingered, exchanging a few words with Emer. At last she climbed in beside Margot and rolled down her window to wave.

The car set off up the narrow lane. Margot did not expect anyone to be coming the other way for the road ended at the O'Learys' house, so she let her concentration lapse. Her mind wandered to Jack O'Leary, wondering where he had disappeared to and why he hadn't appeared to say goodbye. She failed to slow down as she approached the bend. Suddenly, a muddy Land Rover roared round the corner, clearly not expecting anyone to be coming the other way either. Dorothy gave a cry of panic. Margot slammed on the brakes. The driver of the Land Rover skidded to a halt. They missed colliding by only a few feet.

'Good Lord!' Margot exclaimed. 'You okay, Dorothy?'

'I'm still alive,' Dorothy replied shakily. 'But I think I jumped out of my skin.'

The two drivers entered into a stand-off, neither wanting to give way to the other. But Margot soon realized that the Land Rover could hardly reverse back round a blind corner without endangering an oncoming vehicle. With a sigh of irritation she decided that *she* was going to have to be the one to move. Reluctantly, she reversed her car into a small lay-by and waited for the Land Rover to pass. As it did so she found herself staring stupidly at the surprisingly handsome man in the driver's seat who was raising his hand in gratitude and smiling at her without the slightest hint of annoyance. He drove slowly, careful not to scrape her car, and Margot's impatience evaporated in the disarming appeal of his smile. No doubt he was wondering who she was and why she was there. Then he recognized Dorothy and his smile broadened. He doffed his flat cap and Margot noticed the dark hair that curled beneath it.

'That's Colm,' said Dorothy, watching the Land Rover pass. 'Emer and Jack's grandson. He's the local vet? He's so like his grandfather.' Margot drove back into the lane. 'There, your first sighting of a Deverill. I'm going to be sorry to leave tomorrow. I'm curious to know how you get on. You might have to call me and keep me up to date with your progress.'

'How old is he, do you think?' Margot asked, injected suddenly with enthusiasm.

'I can tell you exactly. Aisling must be thirty-one, which makes Colm twenty-nine and his younger sister Cara twenty-seven.'

'And he's the local vet,' she mused.

'Yes, but one day he'll inherit the title. Sadly, he won't have a castle to inherit. I doubt he'll use the title. Sounds a bit silly being Lord Deverill, the vet!'

'Is he married?'

'Not yet.' Dorothy glanced at her. 'Quite a looker, isn't he?'

'Very.' Margot laughed. 'But I'm not looking and I don't mix business with pleasure,' she added, because Dorothy was smiling quietly to herself.

'I'll remember you said that,' she muttered.

Margot laughed. 'Fancy some lunch?'

'What a splendid idea,' Dorothy replied. 'I know the perfect place. It's called O'Donovan's and they do the best Irish stew.'

Jack O'Leary stood at his bedroom window and looked out over the sea. He thought of her then and something pulled at the tender place in his heart where she still dwelt. He put a hand there, but it did nothing to ease the constant ache of loss. There was something about the view of that far distant horizon – the blurred line where the sea meets the sky – which brought her back to him, as if she was there, in that place between earth and Heaven. As if she hadn't left, but was waiting for him as she had waited in life. He stared, and as he stared two grey eyes stared back at him. He spread his fingers wide on the windowpane. He had loved Kitty Deverill his whole life and now she was gone. He pressed his forehead against the glass and closed his eyes. She was gone and this time she wasn't ever coming back.

Kitty

Oh Jack!

I see you, searching for me at the window. Those are not *your* eyes staring back at you in the reflection, but mine. I have not left you. I will never leave you. If only you could understand that death is simply a moving from one dimension into another. A change, that is all. I am still me, Kitty Deverill, and I love you as I always have.

I see you, Jack, when you walk your dog on the hills. When you linger at the Fairy Ring, high up on the cliffs overlooking the sea, where my mortal remains are scattered. How often we found each other there, in the place that was ours and ours alone. Do you remember how, as children, we played among those giant stones? How we kissed, as teenagers, in their shadows. How, as adults, we argued and fought and made love, hidden by those megaliths, the guardians of our secrets. They keep our secrets still.

Do you remember how we swore that we would be true, that we would never love another? Do you remember our promises? The promises of two fools, blinded by love.

Everything was against us, wasn't it, my beloved, as if we were cursed never to live out our dreams. We didn't ask for much. Only that we could be together, free to love openly, to share our joy with the world. But in those days we were on opposite sides of every river. You were Catholic, I was Protestant; you were Irish, I was Anglo-Irish; you were poor, I was rich; you were an O'Leary and I a Deverill. Yet love knows no boundaries. It is only human beings, with their narrow-mindedness and prejudices, who fail to realize that we are all the same. That we have the same hearts full of longing, whatever side of the river we are from.

Do you remember the secrets we kept? The notes we slipped into the stone wall of the vegetable garden up at the castle were only the beginning of years and years of deception. Time and again we found each other when we should not have. Ours was a passion that grew into something neither you nor I could control. A passion that no earthly hand could quell, not even the hands we held in front of God as we vowed to love and cherish. And together we fought for freedom. You gave me courage. I remember with pride the times I carried guns from one safe house to the next because the Tans would never think that I, a Deverill, would side with the Irish in their fight for independence. But I did. I fought for what I believed in. With you. We believed in it together.

Do you remember when you asked me to leave with you and start a new life in America? But I could not. I could not leave my home. My beloved home. I could not leave Ireland. And I lost you, Jack. You see, you are not the only one who harbours regret.

I feel your regret, but you came to that too late, after I was gone. While I was alive, your ties to your family were too strong. We were both ill-fated. If we had found happiness together it would have been built on the unhappiness of those who loved us. I am glad that I am not responsible for that. When I move on, which I hope I eventually will, I will go with a heart free of guilt. My sin has not been in loving you, Jack – there is no sin in loving. My sin is in earthly pride and vindictiveness. I know it, yet hold on to them still.

Five years I have been dead and five years you have mourned me. Yet time has no meaning where I am. I am in the In-between, still me, yet as transparent as vapour. There are very few, like me and my grandmother Adeline, who have the ability to see the fine vibrations of spirit. I watch you mourn me, Jack, and yet you do not see me, so close that were I made of matter I could press my lips softly against yours in a kiss. If only you knew how love connects us to each other. How we will be connected for ever, for eternity. I am with you, Jack, and always will be.

I am not alone in the In-between, however. There are some, like me, who cannot move on, either because they do not wish to, or because they do not realize they can. Mrs Carbery does not realize she is dead. She was the maid who worked in the castle when I was a child. She used to sit in a little room upstairs and sew. She made all my childhood dresses and those of my two sisters, Victoria and Elspeth. Of course, I did not live in the castle in those days. My grandparents Hubert and Adeline lived there and I lived with my father Bertie and mother Maud in the Hunting Lodge by the river. But I spent most of my time at the castle because I wanted to be with my grandmother Adeline, whom I loved a great deal more than my mother. In the little workroom on the first floor Mrs Carbery used to share her biscuits with me and Bridie Doyle, the cook's daughter, who was my friend. We would hide out there while my governess searched for me high and low, and she would tell us stories while we played with the ribbon and lace. She had a wild imagination, full of leprechauns and fairies, and she'd weave wonderful tales while she sewed our dresses.

Mrs Carbery passed away just after the civil war ended. I remember it well because her son was killed in the last days of that terrible war that saw brother set against brother, and she was beside herself with grief. They were buried next to each other in the graveyard of All Saints Church in Ballinakelly and I made a wreath of poppies and wild daisies and placed it at her headstone. Being intuitive, I saw spirits all through my life, but I never saw Mrs Carbery. Now that I dwell in the In-between I realize that she has always been here, a lost and lonely soul, going about her work as if she still lived. A soul who, for some reason, never found her way to the light, or didn't trust it when she saw it, believing perhaps that it was the devil, playing tricks on her. Stuck in the In-between, she is mystified by the strange people who occupy the rooms and complains about them bitterly.

I want to encourage her to move on, because she is not here by choice. I want her to be reunited with the son she'd loved and lost. But I have to tread carefully. After all, how does one break it to a person that she is dead, when she believes herself to be very much alive?

Over the five years that I have been dead I have watched her wander about the castle, spooking those unfortunate enough to see her, unaware that she is spooking anyone. She does not trust me and does her best to avoid me. I, on the other hand, am aware of every impact I have on the world of the living. It's astonishing how many people dismiss my hauntings with an earthly explanation. They put it down to the wind, to the natural noises of an old castle, and those who want to be haunted find evidence where there is none. It amuses me and I need amusement for there is little to entertain me here. I am even a little bored of my own malice. It is too easy to drop a vase, rattle a doorknob or dim the lights, and what is the point of causing the hotel to close if there is no Deverill waiting in the wings with the means to buy it?

And then a young woman arrives who arouses my curiosity. She intends to write a book about my family. She claims not to believe in ghosts, but I sensed her fear when I knocked over her glass of wine at dinner. I will keep an eye on her. The universe works in mysterious ways and I intuit that there is no coincidence in her coming.

Chapter 3

The following morning Margot stood at the front door of the Hunting Lodge and waited. She did not like the house. It was austere and charmless with pointed gables that stabbed the sky and dark windows that glinted like mean little eyes in a hard grey face. The energy wasn't right, either, she thought, recalling her medium friend, Dan Chambers, because that was just the sort of thing he would say.

At length the door was unbolted and a woman's face peered through the crack. She looked at Margot with suspicious china-blue eyes. 'Good morning,' said Margot, giving the woman her sweetest smile. 'I've come to call on Lord Deverill.' She found that, if she exuded confidence, people usually assumed confidence in *her*. 'He's not expecting me. I'm the Writer in Residence at the hotel and my grandfather used to be a good friend of the family.'

The housekeeper looked her up and down, unsure whether or not to invite her in. Deciding, at length, on caution being the better part of valour, she instructed Margot to wait while she went to speak with his lordship. The door was closed and Margot was left shivering on the doorstep. At least it was sunny, she mused. She pulled her coat tighter about her and lifted the collar. It might have been dry but there was a bitter wind blowing in off the sea.

It seemed like a long time before the woman reappeared and opened the door. 'Please come in,' she said in a gentle Irish brogue. She wore a long black skirt and white blouse, and her dove-grey hair was tied into a soft bun, leaving a few strands loose to float about her wide, solemn face. 'Lord Deverill will see you,' she said.

Margot was surprised and felt more than a little triumphant. She looked forward to telling Mr Dukelow how Lord Deverill had not been reclusive to *her*. In fact, he had invited her in without hesitation. The housekeeper took her coat and hat and hung them in a cupboard. Margot smoothed down her hair, glancing at herself in the tarnished mirror that hung on the wall above a dusty old console table. Her cheeks were pink from the cold, her green eyes sparkling. She licked her lips for want of gloss. The house had a stuffy smell, as if the windows hadn't been opened in a very long time, and an empty feeling that gave a strong impression of loneliness. 'Come with me,' said the housekeeper and Margot followed her across the hall and down the dimly lit corridor. The shuffle of her slippers was the only sound beside the desolate ticking of a grandfather clock.

Lord Deverill was standing by the window looking out when Margot was shown into the library. He was wearing a shabby tweed jacket and trousers and did not turn round until the housekeeper announced her. When he did, eventually, Margot noticed that his ruddy face clashed horribly with his thinning, rust-coloured hair. He must have been in his sixties, but he could have been older. He had the crumpled, dishevelled appearance of someone who is no longer aware of how unkempt he looks, or how helpless. Margot felt sorry for him as she might for a neglected dog and suppressed an ugly memory that surfaced unexpectedly. She had seen this pitiful neglect before. 'I never knew your grandfather,' he said, moving unsteadily across the room to shake her hand. 'But it's nice to meet a friend of the family.'

'It's very nice to meet you too,' she said, shaking his hand, which was warm and a little moist. 'Grandpa told me so much about your family.'

'Not all bad, I hope.' There was a defensiveness in his eyes that suggested he was used to people thinking ill of him.

Margot smiled kindly. 'On the contrary, Lord Deverill. He was an admirer.'

Lord Deverill seemed relieved to hear it. 'Do sit down. Mrs B will make you a cup of tea.' While Margot settled into a worn leather sofa, JP asked the housekeeper to bring them tea. 'If there's any of that porter cake, we'll have some of that too,' he added.

'Very well, m'lord,' replied Mrs B, trundling off down the corridor at a slow and stately pace. Margot didn't imagine anyone or anything moved very fast around here, not even time.

JP groaned as he lowered himself into the armchair beside the fire, then shuffled about until he found a comfortable position. Margot noticed a book and a pair of reading glasses on the table beside him, along with a packet of Jacob's Cheddars cheese biscuits and Marlboro cigarettes. 'They have a Writer in Residence up at the castle now, do they?' he said.

'That's me,' she replied chirpily, but the bitterness in his tone had not gone unnoticed.

He reached for the packet of cigarettes. 'You smoke?' he asked, tapping it against his knuckle.

'No, I don't,' she answered.

'Ugly habit,' he said with a sigh, pulling one out. 'One of the many things I ought to give up.'

'I'm writing a history of the Deverill family,' she said, aware that the sooner she told him the better. He might take offence if she waited until she'd drunk his tea and eaten his cake.

He popped the cigarette between dry lips and flicked the lighter with a trembling hand. The end glowed scarlet as he drew in the air with a few short sucks. All the while Margot waited for him to respond. He narrowed his eyes and blew out a cloud of smoke. 'Then you're in the right place,' he said.

'I've been fascinated by your ancestors ever since Grandpa started telling me stories of their antics.'

'I'm sure they're exaggerated.'

'Perhaps. To Grandpa the Deverills were larger than life, so he may have embellished his stories to enhance the legend. I believe them, though.' She gave him her most winning smile.

'Is that why you've come to see me, because you need my help?' He shrugged. 'Not many of us around these days. Once we were a great number. A great family with a great house and a great history. Little great about us now.' He sighed with resignation. 'Every dog has his day.'

'I'd prefer to hear it from the horse's mouth, so to speak, rather than interviewing vaguely connected people who are only able to give me gossip. I want this to be an authentic history of one of Ireland's greatest families.'

'The rise and fall,' he said glumly.

'If you're speaking of the castle, I would say the rise and fall and rise again.'

'I'm speaking of us both. The castle and the family are one. Neither can exist without the other. It is only a matter of time before the castle is a ruin once again, as I am.' He chuckled joylessly.

'I don't think Mrs de Lisle would like to hear that.'

'*Castellum Deverilli est suum regnum.*' He spoke slowly and deliberately as if he were casting a spell.

'A Deverill's castle is his kingdom,' Margot translated.

'You know our motto.'

'You'd be surprised by how much I know already. I've done quite a lot of research.'

'There is a dark magic in that motto. Like I said, our destinies are intertwined. But Mrs de Lisle does not know that, otherwise she would not have put her money there.'

'And it all started with Barton Deverill, did it? This intertwining of destinies.'

'It was never just a castle to him. It was the seed which sprouted a beanstalk.'

'In which case I'd like to think of the Deverills as the giants at the end of the beanstalk.'

'Am I Jack, I wonder? The one who cuts it down and kills the giants?' He gave her another sorry smile.

Margot laughed sympathetically. 'No, Lord Deverill. You're one of the giants!' He laughed then too, both flattered and disbelieving, and she knew that he liked her. 'Come, I want to show you something.' Mrs B appeared in the doorway with a tray. 'Put that on the table, Mrs B. We'll be right back.' Mrs B nodded and moved aside to let them pass. Margot noticed a startled look on her face. She noticed, too, a deep sadness in her eyes.

JP led Margot to the other side of the house, near the kitchen, and unlocked a door into the cellar. 'This used to be full of wine,' he told her. 'Now it's a storeroom. Come.' She followed him down the wooden stairs. It was cold beneath the floorboards and smelt of dead mice and sour, stagnant air. Margot did not imagine Mrs B came down here very often, if ever.

'All those boxes contain family records.' He pointed at the two dozen cardboard boxes carelessly piled into unsteady towers. 'I'm not even sure what's in them myself. Diaries, I suspect, letters, newspaper cuttings, photograph albums. I brought them from the bowels of the castle when I moved. They were spared the fire, being underground. You might find some useful things. Of course, you might find a whole heap of rubbish. I suspect, though, that you'll find what you're looking for. Then you and I can talk.'

Margot couldn't believe that he was going to let her loose among all these boxes. He didn't even know her.

'Why are you helping me, Lord Deverill?' she asked.

'Because it will give me the opportunity to put the record straight.' He turned and looked at her directly. His grey eyes suddenly steady and determined. 'Do we have a deal, Miss Hart?'

'We do, Lord Deverill.'

'Good. When would you like to begin?'

It was late afternoon when Margot left the Hunting Lodge. The sun was a fiery coal, hovering above the horizon, setting it aflame with pinks and golds. JP watched her drive away then closed the door. He turned to Mrs B who stood in the hall, shivering in the damp that was rising off the water nearby. The damp that caused her joints to ache; however there was nothing for it but stoicism, a quality she had in abundance. 'Miss Hart will be a regular visitor from now on,' JP informed her. 'I'd like those boxes brought up to the games room. You can light the fire in there so it's warm for her while she works.'

'I'll ask the boys to do it tomorrow, m'lord,' Mrs B replied. The boys were Tomas and Aidan O'Rourke who worked in the garden, cut logs and saw to the general maintenance of the place.

'She's researching a book on the Deverills, Mrs B. I suspect all the family secrets are going to be brought into the light.' He raised his eyebrows and grinned. Mrs B had not seen him this animated in a very long time. He rubbed his hands together. 'A few cages are going to be rattled, Mrs B. A few noses put out of joint.'

Mrs B frowned. She wasn't sure whether to look disapproving or to mirror his gleefulness with a smile. She didn't have much to smile about these days. The house was oppressive, her master's misery infectious. The long days of nothing happening, depressing. Yet she had worked for his family for over sixty years. She remained out of a mixture of loyalty and habit, and there was always the hope that things would get better. That they might return to the way they were when they'd moved into the castle after Bridie Doyle, the Countess di Marcantonio, had left it to JP in her will. Mrs B had felt sorry for the Countess's other son Leopoldo, who had expected to inherit it. After all, he was the only child of the Count and Countess. But JP was a Deverill, the illegitimate child of Bertie Deverill and Bridie, the child brought up by Kitty Deverill, his half-sister, and the rightful heir. He had believed his mother had died when he was young because Kitty had told him it was so. What a shock it must have been to discover, only after she had died of cancer, that his mother had been living in the castle only a mile or so across the estate. He had never had the chance to talk to her, to get to know her, and she had never had the chance to put her arms around him, her lost child.

Mrs B's heart had broken for all of them. Leopoldo had much to be bitter about, but so had JP. No one ever considered that. They thought only of the blessing of that castle being restored to the family and the fortune that went with it, for the Countess had been very rich. But Mrs B knew the value of things. She'd watched JP's world disintegrate around him in the twenty-two years he had lived in that castle, and she was pretty sure she knew why. The Deverills had always put much too much emphasis on their family name and their illustrious history. But Mrs B knew there was no real value in a family name or a castle. She knew this because she had suffered loss, and once a person has crossed that bridge of sorrow things like castles and family names were like ashes in one's hand. That is what loss had taught her. But some people took a lifetime to learn that simple truth.

'Yesterday is history and tomorrow is a mystery. Is it wise to dig up the past, m'lord?' she asked gently. She was aware that he wasn't in his right mind, on account of his drinking, and felt it was her duty to guide him as subtly as she could.

'Oh no, Mrs B, it's not wise at all. But as you know, I've never been very wise, or lucky.'

'We make our own luck, m'lord, and wisdom is learned through experience and mistakes. You have had enough experience and mistakes to have learnt the wisdom of Solomon, if you don't mind me saying.'

'If you're worrying what the rest of the family will think, Mrs B, you know I don't care about them and they care even less about me.'

'Get away with you now, that's not strictly true and you know it,' she said and her face was full of compassion and pity, because he had brought most of his troubles upon himself.

'It's only a bloody castle!' he protested, striding off down the corridor.

'Bricks and mortar and a house full of trumpery,' she agreed, and yet she knew how much the loss of it had wounded him.

JP was pouring himself a large glass of whiskey and looking forward to an evening alone by the fire, watching the television, when Colm Deverill strode into the library. JP was surprised by this unexpected visit, because he didn't get many visitors these days. 'Colm?' he said, looking up from the drinks table, glass in one hand, whiskey decanter in the other.

'Hi, Dad,' said Colm. His son always made him think of his ex-wife, but in truth he'd taken the best from both parents. Dark wavy hair, eyes the colour of cobalt, a straight nose and a sensual, honest mouth.

'Fancy a drink?' JP asked, holding up the decanter to tempt him.

'No thanks. I won't be staying long.'

'I'd invite you for supper, but Mrs B has only left soup and cold meat for one.'

'It's fine. I'll be heading home.'

It was awkward, their conversation. Standing the width of the room apart, the air between them charged with both guilt and blame. It was hard to believe that Colm had once worshipped his father. But that was before. 'So, this isn't a social visit?' JP was making a joke, bitter though it was. No one visited him.

'I've come to warn you about a girl called Margot Hart. She's staying up at the castle and she's writing a history of the family.'

JP nodded. 'Yes, I've already had the pleasure.'

A shadow of anxiety darkened Colm's face. 'She's already been here?'

'Yes. In fact, you just missed her.'

'And what did you tell her?'

'I invited her in and gave her a cup of tea and some cake. I was very hospitable.'

'I hope that's all you gave her.'

JP took a swig of whiskey and gave a little shiver as the heat of it reached his stomach. 'She's a friend of the family,' he added.

Colm sighed, 'That doesn't mean she's going to write a glowing book about us.'

'I don't think she's very interested in *you*, Colm.'

Colm ignored him. Alcohol made his father mean. Colm was used to it. 'As good as her intentions may be, it will be impossible to write a history book without including all the bad stuff.'

JP raised his eyebrows. 'Well, we do have a colourful history,' he conceded.

'We do and as far as I can tell, it just keeps getting more and more colourful. So I'm giving you a word of advice, Dad. Don't talk to her. She can get tea and cake at the hotel.'

JP took another swig. 'Trouble is, Colm, I've already decided that I'm going to help her with her research. I don't want her getting things wrong.'

Colm put his hands on his hips. 'Dad, you have no right. You're not an island.'

'I have every right. I'm a Deverill.'

'What would Grandpa say?'

'If you're hoping to shame me, that ship has already sailed. I'm sure every Deverill from the past is turning in his grave at the sight of the castle having been converted into a hotel and blaming me for it. I like Margot Hart. She's got character. I think she'll do a good job. It's a history that needs to be written.'

'I can't believe you're allowing this to happen.' Colm shook his head. 'If you were sober you'd never speak to a woman like her.'

'Have you met her, Colm?'

'No.'

'I think you'll like her. She's about your age and she's a beauty too.'

'I have no desire to meet her.'

'Shame.'

'I cannot for the life of me think of one reason why you might wish for a book to be written which reveals our family secrets. Besides the hurt you'll inflict on us all.' Colm looked at his father in bewilderment, wounded suddenly at the realization that his father might wish to cause him pain. 'Is that why? To hurt us?' When his father didn't reply, he added, jaw stiff, lips taut, 'Don't you think you've hurt us enough, Dad?'

As Colm turned and walked out of the room, JP stared into his glass. 'And I've been hurt too,' he muttered. 'But no one ever thinks of that.'

Margot sat at the desk in her tower room and reflected on the day. It could not have been more extraordinary. Lord Deverill was allowing her to go through the contents of the boxes, but understandably he had not given her permission to take anything away with her. So she'd spent the entire day in the cellar, cold though it was, and Mrs B had even made her lunch. She'd opened the first box with almost uncontainable excitement to find photograph albums dating back to the turn of the century. She resisted the impulse to open all the boxes at once and concentrated on the albums. She'd have plenty of time to go through the rest, and she didn't want to rush. She wanted to savour every riveting piece of information.

The photographs did not disappoint. They were windows into the past. Through them Margot could see what people looked like, what they wore, how they lived. Characters with whom she was familiar due to her grandfather's anecdotes materialized in the photographs, no longer mythical, but people of flesh and blood who had lived their own stories, full of dramas, tragedy, loss, laughter and love. People who had completed their lives and passed away. It made her think of mortality and what it meant. It made her wonder what the point of it all had been. She found herself reflecting on her own mortality. *My life might be long and full like Elizabeth Deverill's was,* she thought, gazing into the face of JPs great-grandmother, *and yet one day I will be nothing more than a face staring out of a photograph as she is. Where will my consciousness be then?* That was an uncomfortable thought indeed. Margot turned her attention to the castle. Celia Deverill had done a very good job in rebuilding it, she mused, but how much more magnificent it had been *before* the fire.

Margot was so excited that she had met Lord Deverill himself, and been invited to go through the family records, that she telephoned Dorothy. She had no one else to tell, at least, no one who would be interested. 'Dorothy, it's Margot from Ballinakelly,' she said when Dorothy answered the telephone.

'Margot,' Dorothy exclaimed happily. 'What a lovely surprise. How are you getting on over there?'

'Extremely well. You won't believe it, but I met Lord Deverill today.'

'Did you?'

'Yes, he invited me in for tea, and guess what?'

'Well, that's a surprise in itself. I don't imagine he invites people in for tea very often.'

'He took me into the cellar where there are boxes and boxes of family records.'

'I don't believe it! I think I'd better sit down!' There was a shuffling down the line as Dorothy moved to a chair.

'He's letting me go through them all. Every one. Isn't that amazing!'

There was a pause while Dorothy teetered on the edge of feeling happy for her new friend and anxious for her old ones. 'You will be careful, dear, won't you? I mean, Eva Perón is dead. JP's family are very much alive. I'd hate for them to be hurt.'

'Please don't worry, Dorothy. I'll be tactful. I'm not in this to hurt anybody.'

Dorothy sighed. 'Of course you're not. But they have a rather colourful history, and airing it in public will cause embarrassment to those family members still living.'

'I'll give a *balanced* account,' Margot added with emphasis. 'And I have Lord Deverill's blessing.'

Dorothy was silent for a moment. Then she sighed again. 'Yes, that's what I'm worried about.'

Chapter 4

When Margot returned to the Hunting Lodge the following morning she found that the boxes had been moved up from the cold cellar into a room that Mrs B referred to as the games room. Mrs B had lit a turf fire, which gave out little heat and choked smoke into the air, but warmth came from the hard winter sun that pierced the windows, illuminating a billiard table covered in a dust sheet and the boxes piled upon it. 'How kind of you to bring up the boxes,' said Margot when Mrs B came in with a tray of tea and porter cake.

The housekeeper nodded solemnly and placed the tray on the console table at the edge of the room, beneath an old wooden scoreboard that still retained in white chalk the record of the last game of billiards. Margot wondered how long ago that was. The house felt as if it had been asleep for years. 'His lordship was concerned you'd get sick with all the dust downstairs,' said Mrs B in her melodious voice. 'Not to mention the chill.'

'Sweet of him to think of that. It was rather cold, I admit. I went back to the hotel and had a hot bath.'

At the mention of the hotel Mrs B hesitated. She was curious to know what it was like, yet anxious not to be disloyal to her master. Since he had sold the castle she had been careful never to mention it, knowing how much it had grieved him to lose it. However, residing in the Hunting Lodge as she did and rarely going out save to buy supplies and go to Mass, she had isolated herself from the town gossip, which she knew must contain little else. Indeed, it must be endlessly charged with stories of the guests and the formidable Mrs de Lisle. Mrs B lowered her voice, her curiosity outweighing her prudence. 'I suppose it's very beautiful, is it, the hotel?'

Margot went to pour herself some tea, aware that it would swiftly get cold in that room. 'It's opulent, Mrs B,' she said, picking up the china teapot. 'I imagine it's far more luxurious than it was when it was a home.' As she hoped, Mrs B was quick to enlighten her.

Mrs B's blue eyes widened as she relinquished her caution and allowed her memories to surface. 'It was magical, like a castle in a fairy tale,' she said quietly, her face softening in the afterglow of her past. 'I was eleven years old when fire took it, so I only have vague recollections of what it looked like before. But I remember the size of it most of all. To me it was a palace. How warm it was. Oh, I remember the warmth of those great fires. Me mammy was a maid and sometimes I went with her and sat quietly in the corner, winding up balls of wool or helping polish the silver. There was always something useful I could do and I was happy to do it because it was warm there, in the big house.'

'Do you remember the fire that destroyed it?' Margot asked.

'Remember it, you say? God save us, I do. Most of all I remember Mammy and Daddy's shock and horror. 'Twas the talk of town and country. Everyone was affected by it one way or another, not just those who worked there – the forge, the butchers, the fishermen and the coopers. It was the life blood of the whole town and beyond. The very heart that kept us all alive. Lord Deverill, the present Lord Deverill's grandfather, died in the fire and poor old Lady Deverill lost her mind with grief, God rest her soul. Only a very small biteen of the castle survived.'

'The western tower, I'm told.'

'That's it. The oldest part.'

'Which is where my room is,' Margot told her. She took a sip of tea. 'It's got the most marvellous atmosphere.'

'There were always ghosts in that room,' said Mrs B casually. She might well have been talking about the furniture for the nonchalant way she mentioned them.

'I don't believe in ghosts, Mrs B.'

'Oh, it's not a question of believing in them or not, Miss Hart. They're around us all the same. Me mammy used to tell me about the strange noises and goings-on in the tower. Bold, she used to call them. Not afraid of anyone or anything. Daring blackguards. Mammy would never venture there without her Holy Water and rosary beads.'

'What was the castle like after Celia Deverill rebuilt it?' Margot asked, keen to stick to facts rather than fantasy.

'Well, I was in me teens and we were all curious about the building work going on up at the castle. We'd sneak in over the wall and watch it develop year after year, because it took years, Miss Hart, to complete. The body of money that went into that adventure! People said she must have found Old Séanadh's purse. Séanadh was an auld fella in folklore whose purse would refill as soon as it was empty.'

She shook her head in wonder that anyone could be so rich. 'Indeed, it was an expense Mammy would have disapproved of, God rest her soul and all the poor holy souls, for she always said isn't it easier for a camel to go through the eye of a needle than for a rich man to enter the kingdom of God. But I thought of nothing but going to work there, in that beautiful place. I seized me chance when Mrs Mayberry, Celia Deverill that was, moved in and started hiring servants. I presented myself for employment straight away. I will never forget the first sight of her home. It was like paradise on earth. I'd never seen the like. Even in the days before the fire it was never so beautiful.'

Her solemn eyes grew lively then and her lips parted into a smile, and Margot realized that she must have been very pretty as a young woman. 'The marble floors were so shiny you could see your reflection in them. And the beauty of the furniture and the linen and Mrs Mayberry's fur coats, so soft they were. You'd have to run your fingers over them yourself to believe it. There were so many titled people coming in and out of the place that in the end we took no notice of them.' She sighed wistfully. 'Then it all came to an end when Mr Mayberry did away with himself in the garden, God save the mark.'

'That must have been dreadful,' said Margot.

'What a waste of a life. Nothing should ever be so bad that you have to kill yourself for it. A long-term solution to a short-term problem.' Mrs B thought then of her own sorrows. Her face fell with sadness and her blue eyes, a moment ago so lively, dimmed suddenly. 'We all have our own Calvary in this life, Miss Hart. Prince or pauper, we suffer the same, every one of us. But God is always by our side and He only gives us crosses that we are able to carry, doesn't He?' She inhaled deeply, letting out a loud sigh, expelling the heaviness of those sad recollections. 'I saw Mrs Mayberry leave for South Africa and I saw the Countess di Marcantonio move in with her boy, Leopoldo, and her husband the Count, so handsome he was and so charming. You've never seen a man with whiter teeth,

God rest his soul. He was murdered. Buried up to his neck in the sand and drowned by the sea when the tide came in. Another waste of a life, Miss Hart. Indeed, Ballinakelly has seen its fair share of horror. Some say there is a scamall or a cloud over us and we are cursed and yet we soldier on. Sure, what else can we do?'

'Do you know why he was murdered?' Margot asked, putting down her teacup.

Mrs B pursed her lips. 'There were many stories and auld piseógs, but you can never be sure of gossip, can you, Miss Hart? Poor little Leopoldo was the one who discovered him, dead in the sand, thinking he'd found a ball, God bless us. He was never the same after that. How could he be, poor little boyeen? He was only a young garsún.' Again she shook her head and lowered her eyes. 'I left the castle when Celia Deverill sold it to the Countess and came to work for Lord Deverill, Bertie Deverill, here in the Lodge. I've worked for that family for over sixty years.'

'That's a long time.'

'Indeed it is. I've been in service all me life.' She closed her eyes, suppressing the sudden upsurge of grief. It did that to her sometimes, assaulted her when she was least expecting it. 'This family have seen me through difficult times, Miss Hart. When me head wanted to sink below the water, it was this position, this house, this family that helped me rise above it. I have a lot to be grateful for. As they say, God is good and the devil isn't too bad either. It does no good to dwell on unhappiness.'

Margot wondered what unhappiness she was alluding to, but she knew it would be intrusive to ask. 'You're right,' she agreed. 'One must always try to be positive.' Margot knew that. She had had her fair share of unhappiness, after all.

'Now you might find happier memories in those boxes, because for sure there have been good times. I remember when young Master JP moved in with his new wife, after the Countess was buried. I moved with them, you see. I looked after those three children, Aisling, Colm and Cara, from the day they were born. Those were the happiest times. Indeed, they were blessed by God, Mr JP and his wife Mrs Alana. Before the weight of the castle and the title changed things . . .'

'Why did it go wrong?' Margot asked, keen to understand how JP got to the point of having to sell the castle.

Mrs B had said quite enough. She pulled herself up short, appalled suddenly that she had been so loquacious. 'I'll bring you a fresh supeen of tea, Miss Hart, and leave you to those boxes full of trumpery. If there's anything else you need, you will ask me, won't you? Perhaps another sod of turf or a stick on the fire?'

'I can do that myself, thank you,' Margot replied.

'Very well.' Mrs B took the pot and left the room, leaving the door ajar. Margot watched her shuffle off down the corridor. Perhaps in time, and with gentle encouragement, she'd manage to extricate the story she'd never find in a box of old family records.

Margot set about sorting through the papers, photographs and documents that were carefully stored in the boxes. There was a wealth of information. However, although fascinating to her curious mind, much of it was not relevant to her research. There were birth, marriage and death certificates, theatre tickets, Christmas cards, menus, shooting cards and hunting records. Ledgers of farming accounts going back to the mid-eighteenth century and lists of tenants and their rent. Then, of course, there were letters. Plenty of letters. It would take weeks to read them all. Presently, Mrs B returned with the pot of freshly brewed tea. She crept in quietly and placed it on the tray. This time she didn't linger by the door, eager to talk, but slipped out as discreetly as she had entered. Margot tossed another turf log on the fire and listened to the crackling sound it made as the flames licked its earthy surfaces, trying to get purchase. She rubbed her hands together and remained there a moment, warming herself.

That was where JP found her. 'I see you're making your way through those boxes,' he said, wandering into the room in the same shabby tweeds as he'd worn the day before.

'Thank you for getting them brought up from the cellar,' she said. 'It's a lovely room, this.'

JP ran his eyes over it. He had never thought of it as lovely. The whole house was an affront. A daily reminder of his failure. 'My father used to live here,' he told her. 'He liked to play billiards. I used to play, but I don't anymore. As you can see, the table is covered in a dust sheet. It's been like this for years.'

'I play,' Margot said with a grin. She arched an eyebrow. 'I'm quite good, actually, if you fancy a game.'

JP chuckled. The girl's enthusiasm was infectious. She was pretty too, he mused, taking in her long blonde hair, tied into a ponytail, vivacious green eyes and pink cheeks. She was wholesome and seemingly untarnished by the stain of life's vicissitudes. He wanted to linger, to bathe in her innocence, to forget his guilt. 'I haven't ever thought to go through these boxes,' he said. 'They've been here, gathering dust, for decades, yet I've never been in the slightest bit curious.'

Margot could smell alcohol on his breath even though they were more than a few feet apart, and an ugly memory surfaced again, this time more persistently. She did not want to remember her past. She was here to learn about JP's, and yet his very presence reminded her of things she'd rather forget. It was hard to imagine that JP had ever been the insouciant young man people spoke of. Hard to find lightness in the dark miasma of addiction that seemed to envelop him. She had seen it before, the unbearable change that came over a person when they ceased to be themselves. For a second she recalled that sense of helplessness. That feeling of utter impotence. Of trying so hard to rescue someone when they didn't want to be saved. She knew now that one can only help a person if they want to help themselves. She knew, because she'd once tried, in her own way, and failed. Why hold someone's head above water if they're doing their very best to go under? Perhaps JP did not want to help himself. Perhaps he had no reason to. If his family and friends had abandoned him, for whom did he have to get better?

'Let me show you some interesting things that I've found,' she suggested, lifting a red leather journal off the table.

'What's that then?' he asked, leaning forward with curiosity.

'It's Adeline Deverill's dinner party book. She wrote down the table plan of every dinner she ever had. Isn't that fun? You can see who they entertained, where they sat. She's even included some of the jokes told during dinner.'

'Goodness. She couldn't have been a very busy lady if she had the time to do all that!'

Margot laughed. 'I think you're right.' She flicked the pages until she reached the one she wanted to show him. 'Look at this. *12 July 1903*,' she read. '*In the presence of His Majesty, King Edward VII and Queen Alexandra.*' She glanced at him and grinned. 'Fancy that!'

'Fancy indeed,' he said, taking the book from her and running his eyes over the list of names.

'I found a photograph of the house party posing in front of

the castle in one of the albums. It's wonderful. The ladies in their long dresses and enormous hats, with their tiny waists and fur stoles, and the men in uniform, puffing their chests out like cockerels.'

He laughed. 'I'd love to see that. Where might it be?'

'Let me find it.' She dug about for the right album and found the page immediately. 'Here, do you know who these people are?'

. JP looked closely at the black-and-white pictures. 'Not a clue, besides the family. It was twenty years or so before I was born.'

'Doesn't the Queen look splendid?'

'She does, but I think my great-grandmother Elizabeth appears more regal. Look at the way she holds her chin. From the little I know, she was away with the fairies, so she probably believed *she* was the queen.'

'There's definitely a streak of eccentricity running through your family, as there seems to be in most aristocratic Anglo-Irish families.'

He glanced at her and a look of self-pity clouded his face. 'I fear I'm rather boring by comparison, but then my mother was an Irish maid, so only half of my blood is blue.'

'I would say that makes you more interesting and less inbred.'

He closed the album with a sigh and placed it on the billiard table. 'I'd like to be able to say what a colourful person Bridie was, that she allowed chickens to wander into the hall like my great-grandmother Elizabeth, but I can't because I never knew her.'

Was this at the root of his unhappiness? Margot wondered. Not knowing where he came from challenged his sense of identity and belonging. 'That must have been hard,' she said with compassion, hoping he'd elaborate, not for the book, but because she was curious, and because she found she cared. She couldn't bear to watch someone suffer.

But JP simply shrugged. 'Many have fared far worse than me. It would be ungrateful of me to complain when I was lucky, really, having been brought up by Kitty, my half-sister, and her husband Robert, who was like a father to me. I had two fathers, you see, Bertie Deverill and Robert Trench. Two when most children have only one, or none. How many boys can boast of that?'

'Fortunate, indeed,' Margot agreed, and yet there was a bitterness in his tone that implied something had been lacking, and that he felt resentment for that.

'Have you everything you need, Miss Hart?' JP asked, straightening up and gathering himself.

'I have more than everything. Thank you so much.'

'Good. You must give a shout if you need anything. It gets frightfully cold in this house, so don't let the fire go out.'

'I'm used to the cold, having lived in England.'

'Whereabouts are you from?'

'I live in London, but I grew up in Dorset.'

He nodded. 'By the sea?'

'Sadly not. Near Sherborne. Pretty countryside though.'

'Very,' he agreed.

'It pales when compared to here, though. I think Ireland is the most beautiful place I've ever visited, and I've been to many places. The light on the hills takes my breath away.'

JP looked at her and a spark of enthusiasm flared in his eyes. 'Do you ride, Miss Hart?'

'I do,' she replied. Her father had been an enthusiastic rider.

'Then I'll show you the real Ireland, if you'll permit me. Perhaps we can ride out over the hills sometime and you can watch the play of light on a bigger canvas. The views from up there are enormous. We'll pick a sunny day so you see it at its best.'

'I'd love that,' she replied.

'Then that's another deal. I'll leave you to your research for now. Mrs B is around. Just shout if there's anything you need.'

JP left the room slowly, as if determined to hide his unsteady stride. Margot wondered what he was going to do. He had the air of a man who did nothing but sit and brood. The whole house seemed to resonate with his brooding. But he had offered to take her riding. She couldn't wait. The last time she had been on a horse was trekking across the Andes a few years before with a rather attractive gaucho as her guide. She smiled at the memory of making love with him beneath the stars, then brushed it away and returned to her work.

That night Margot went to soak up the local flavour at the pub. O'Donovan's, where she'd gone for lunch with Dorothy, seemed to be the heart of Ballinakelly. She did not shy from going out alone. She did not shy from much. She'd lived in enough foreign cities to be confident on her own and was perfectly content to be so.

The pub was as one would expect an Irish pub in the centre of an old town like Ballinakelly to be: low, wonky ceilings, wooden beams, framed photographs of bygone days on the walls, leather bar stools, dark wooden tables, small windows with diamond-shaped panes and stuffy air full of cigarette smoke. Through the fug Margot could see wary faces staring at her with a mixture of curiosity and surprise, for it couldn't have been common for women to enter such a place unaccompanied. Indeed, it wasn't so long ago that women were not allowed in public houses in Ireland at all.

Margot was not put off. She was used to it. A decade of travelling solo had hardened her to the mistrustful looks of strangers. She shrugged them off and took a stool at the bar. The bartender was a middle-aged man with thick black hair and a few days' stubble. He grinned crookedly, sizing her up and liking what he saw. 'You're a bold girl coming in here on your own,' he said. 'What can I get you?'

Margot smiled. If he only knew how many bars she'd sat at on her own he would not have remarked upon it. 'Vodka, lime and soda, please. Surely, with the hotel nearby, you should be used to people like me popping in.'

'Oh, no one comes in here from up there,' he said, taking down the vodka bottle from the shelf behind him. 'They're much too grand for our humble pub.'

'What do you think of it, the hotel?'

He shrugged. 'I suppose it's good for tourism, though it's no good for us.'

'Did you know it when it was a home?'

'Aye, everyone in this place will have known it back then. It was only sold nine years ago.' He poured a shot of vodka into a glass. 'You from England?'

'I am,' she replied. 'I'm the Writer in Residence at the hotel.'

He arched an eyebrow. 'That's grand.'

'I'm writing a book on the Deverills and their castle.'

He chuckled. 'You've got enough to fill a library, I suspect. They're a wild family, they are. A cursed family.'

Margot frowned. 'Why do you say cursed?'

'They've had more bad luck than most, haven't they?'

'I'd just call that bad luck.'

'*You* would, but we Irish are a superstitious lot.' He finished making her drink and slid the glass across the bar.

She took a sip. 'Lots of castles were burned down during the Troubles. Are they cursed too?'

'Perhaps the Anglo-Irish are a cursed lot. Most of them acquired their land from Cromwell or King Charles II. Who do you think lived on that land before them? The Irish.' He shrugged again. 'You piss people off and it comes back to haunt you. That's what I'd say. You build your houses on stolen land and you'll never be lucky.'

Margot considered his words. 'Interesting,' she said.

He gave her a crooked grin, a flirtatious twinkle in his eye. 'You going to put that in your book?'

She laughed. 'Maybe.'

'Be sure to get my name right. Seamus O'Donovan.'

'You own this pub?'

'It's a family business going back to 1764.'

'You look younger than that.'

He enjoyed her wit. 'What's your name then?'

'Margot Hart.'

'That doesn't sound very English, I mean the Margot part.'

'My mother's French.'

'Father English?'

'Was.'

'Oh, I'm sorry.'

'Don't be. He died a long time ago.'

The door opened and a cold draught swept into the pub along with Colm Deverill, who Margot recognized from her near crash on the road from Emer and Jack's house a couple of days before. He was wearing a flat cap and jacket, a wool scarf and heavy lace-up boots. No sooner had he closed the door behind him than he spotted Margot perched on the stool at the bar. His face darkened as he recognized her. Margot was bemused. He had smiled at her in the car, but presumably that was before he knew what she was doing there in Ballinakelly. He must know now about the book she was writing.

Colm acknowledged Seamus with a nod, then walked straight past the bar to sit with a group of friends at the other end of the room, near the fire. Margot watched him for a moment, wondering whether she should go and introduce herself. She was sure she could win him over, given the chance.

'I guess the Deverills are none too pleased about your project,' said Seamus, putting a pint glass beneath the Guinness tap. Colm was a regular at O'Donovan's and Seamus knew what he liked to drink.

'Lord Deverill has invited me to his house and given me access to the family records, so I wouldn't go as far as saying *all* the Deverills are hostile to my book.'

'Lord Deverill is not in his right mind these days,' Seamus commented, not unkindly. 'JP Deverill was a golden boy, but he's turned into a tarnished man. That's what they say.'

'Sad, if it's true.'

'Aye, it's true. I hear his own family no longer speak to him.'

'What? Just because he lost the castle?'

'More than that,' said Seamus. He put the glass of Guinness on a tray and walked out from behind the bar. 'Much more than that.'

Margot watched him take Colm Deverill his drink. They exchanged a few words. Colm glanced at her and glowered. She held his gaze, which must have unnerved him for he looked away.

'And tell me, me lady, are the pleasures of Ballinakelly to your liking?' came a gravelly voice from behind her. She turned to see Mr Flannigan, the porter, his face swollen and red. In his rough hand he held a glass of stout.

Margot's heart sank. She did not care for drunk men. 'Very much, thank you,' she replied politely, looking over for Seamus, hoping he'd return and rescue her.

'Did ye bump into any dead fellas in the night?' he asked, grinning lopsidedly.

'No, all very quiet at night,' she answered.

He swayed and smiled in the way people do when they know something you don't. 'That castle is full of ghosts and dead fellas wandering around without a by your leave, you know. Don't let that Mr Dukelow tell you otherwise.'

'I don't believe in ghosts,' Margot said, an edge of impatience to her voice. She was tired of talking about the supernatural.

'You won't be so by September, girl.' Mr Flannigan laughed heartily, exhaling a puff of sour breath, and swayed again. She wondered why he didn't steady himself on the bar. Perhaps he wasn't aware of how drunk he was.

'I'll let you know if I hear anything.' She turned away.

'Indeed and you will, because they will put the heart crossways in you. You're in the western tower. Mr Dukelow doesn't usually put guests up there, but Mrs de Lisle insisted.'

'And why would she do that?' she asked, irritated.

'Because it's a meeting place for the dead, that's why, God save the mark.'

'Like I said—'

He cut her off. 'You will, as sure as me name is Flannigan, mark my words,' he added with absolute certainty, trying but failing to wink.

Margot decided she'd had enough of this pub. She was on the point of leaving when the sound of music rose above the drone of voices. A hush descended on the room. A band of five musicians began to play Irish folk songs. She'd like to have stayed, there was something very charming in the cliché. However, her haunted bedroom was more attractive than this bar with Mr Flannigan trying to scare her with stories of ghosts. *Ghosts indeed!* she thought as she left the pub. *What a lot of nonsense.*

Kitty

This Writer in Residence, Margot Hart – the woman who doesn't believe in ghosts – is staying in the western tower. The very place Barton Deverill inhabited when he was stuck in the In-between, cursed by Maggie O'Leary, whose land he built his castle on and who he had burned at the stake for witchcraft. As a child I used to spend a great deal of my time in that tower, talking to him, but he was a curmudgeon in those days and not much entertainment for a ten-year-old girl. He had been there for over two hundred years, so I suppose he had a right to be bitter. He was only released when Maggie forgave him. I realized, at that point, that the curse had never really been about land but about love. It was forgiveness that broke the curse and saw the two of them disappear into the light together.

I think of love and forgiveness as I watch my half-brother JP colluding with Margot Hart as she researches her book. I feel his resentment towards his family; it hangs about him like a fog. A fog of self-pity and reproach. Our father, Bertie, became a pathetic drunk when Mama left him. Now, it seems that the son is repeating the mistakes of the father. His wife Alana is gone and JP dulls the pain of rejection and loneliness with whiskey, his loyal friend. I suspected as much when I was alive, but now I know because I can watch him from where I am between worlds. I cannot help him, however. I could have done so during my life, but I chose not to. Even here, I resent him still.

JP sold the castle in 1976 and, in the four years that followed, I refused to speak to him. I cut him off, like a rotten limb. I did not ask him how it had got to this, I simply cast blame. I didn't try to understand him and I didn't sympathize with him. I was blinded by fury and frustrated by my inability to buy the castle myself. My husband Robert was dead, my father also, and not since the days of my childhood has my family had the wealth needed to rescue it, as Celia did. Now we have no wealth at all. How the mighty fall!

When Bridie died, she left JP the castle and a fortune. Where did that fortune go? I ask myself. Now he has neither. He lives in the Hunting Lodge where I grew up. A bleak and depressing house that is always damp from the river that runs past it and dark from the small windows that let in little light. He has infused it with his negative energy, so it is even more gloomy than before. Yet Margot seems not to feel the oppressive atmosphere, or if she does, it does not bother her. She is focused on her goal, which is to write a book about the history of the castle and the family whose lives have been shaped by it. I could tell her a few things, if only she could hear me. But I cannot tell her how JP lost it, or how he lost his wife and family. I cannot tell her that. I'm hoping that she will find out and enlighten *me*.

Margot is in the games room, sitting on the rug in front of the fire, surrounded by papers, when I enter. Of course, she cannot see me. I am as transparent as air. She is engrossed in our history, delighted by every new piece of information she finds, like a child full of wonder at the world. The papers are in neat piles, sorted into what is relevant and what isn't, in date order. She is pretty with long blonde hair, tousled by the drizzle and partly swept up and held fast by a pencil. Her eyes are intelligent and green, the colour of beech leaves. Even in reading glasses she is attractive. I admire her, for her energy reveals a young woman with ambition, drive and vigour. She is independent and feisty and yet I detect a loneliness there, buried beneath a happy-go-lucky façade and fiercely denied. She thinks she can outrun it, but she cannot. It is deeply embedded, from childhood, I believe. An unhappy childhood. She cannot hide that from me, for I can feel her vibrations. I was empathetic in life, but my senses are more acute here. Here in the In-between.

I am beside her now. I hover over her, so close I could touch her were I made of matter. But I am as vapour, so I propel a ripple of energy through the air and, like a wind, it sends the papers flying across the rug. Alarmed, she scrabbles for them, catching them before they float into the fire, and arranges them back into piles. She looks at the door, which is closed, then back at the windows, which are also shut. I know she is wondering where the draught came from. She does not think it is a spirit. She does not believe in them. By the time I am finished with her, she will.

I am about to amuse myself with some more tricks when the door opens and Colm stalks in. He hasn't even taken off his coat and hat, which are both wet from the rain. Mrs B is behind him, anxiously twisting her hands and explaining that his father has gone for a nap so perhaps he should return later. But it is not JP he wishes to see – it is Margot.

Margot turns round and stares at him. She knows who he is and that he does not come as a friend. Slowly, she gets up, but she does not extend her hand. This is not a social call. Colm's face is contorted with fury. His anger has been boiling since his grandmother told him about Margot and the book. 'Thank you, Mrs B,' he says politely. 'You can leave us now.'

Colm is so like his grandfather. He is tall, with the same dark brown hair, the same cleft chin, the same strength of character in his features. But unlike Jack, those features betray his honesty, his inability to lie. Jack was the best liar I ever met. When Colm is not furious he is charming, witty, mischievous and kind. All the qualities his father once had in abundance, before he lost them in the whiskey bottle. I wonder, what would it take to revive them? My father was rescued by his cousin Digby. Who is going to rescue JP?

'I'm sorry we cannot meet in more favourable circum-stances,' Colm says. It goes against his nature to be rude.

'I am too,' says Margot, looking at him steadily. Trying to find a way to win him over, no doubt.

'I've come about your book. To ask you not to write it.'

Margot is surprised. She tilts her head and narrows her eyes. 'Why do you think I'll agree to that?' she asks calmly. 'Why do you think I'll give up my project just because you ask me to?'

'Because I'm hoping you're a decent woman.'

'I'm a writer. This is my job.'

'Eva Perón is dead,' he says, and Margot is surprised that he has done some research of his own.

'Yet Argentina is full of people who view her as a saint. People whose lives she touched in a magical way. *They* didn't try to stop me writing about her.'

Colm puts his hands in his trouser pockets and glances at the ceiling, as if hoping to find a more persuasive argument there. 'Look, I know there's no reason why you should feel any sense of responsibility towards a family you've only just met. But my father is not in his right mind.'

'He drinks too much, but he is not a hopeless drunk. I know about those and he is not one of them.'

'I disagree. You're preying on a vulnerable man.'

Margot is affronted at the suggestion. 'I'm not preying on anyone,' she replies, and even I, a spirit impervious to her moods, feel the sharp edge in her voice and am startled by it. 'I'm writing a history of your entire family, going right back to Barton Deverill himself. Yes, I will be writing about your father and the loss of the family home. The selling of the castle is the end of the story. The place where the Deverill seat and the Deverill family part ways. If you think I'm going to leave him out of the narrative, you are deluding yourself. The book would be incomplete.'

'You are delving into people's pain,' he says. His face is twisted with hurt. He cannot conceal it. His parents divorced, that I know. But why, I do not know. What dark secret is he trying to hide, I wonder?

'I am not a monster, Mr Deverill. I am a writer and I will give a balanced account. I admire your family. My own grandfather was a friend of your uncle Harry's. Your family has suffered tragedy but it has shown great resilience. Your ancestors were flamboyant, colourful, daredevil and big-hearted. The castle had been in your family, almost without interruption, for over three hundred years. How many people can claim that?'

At this, Colm's face looks even more agonized. He is thinking of his grandmother, Bridie Doyle, who as the Countess di Marcantonio, bought the castle. The fact that she was once a maid there will not worry Colm, he has no airs, but she died without ever knowing her son, his father, and that worries him. He knows how much that wounded JP. I know too, although during my life I did not want to acknowledge it, because it was *I* who brought JP up believing his real mother was dead. It was *I* who forbade Bridie to meet him when she moved back to Ballinakelly from New York, and it was *I* who kept her a secret from him, her own son, even though she had settled into the castle only a couple of miles across the estate. I had to live with the consequences of those choices when she left him a letter in her will explaining everything. I thought we were enough for him, me and Robert, and our father, Bertie. I thought he didn't care to know about his biological mother because he felt secure enough in our love. But I was wrong. When JP finally learned the truth, it was too late. Bridie was gone.

'This book of yours is going to further divide the family,' Colm says, moving towards the door. 'I hope you realize that what you're doing will scupper any hope of reconciliation between my parents, my siblings and my grandparents. By digging up the past you will thwart any plans to put it behind us. It is bad karma and it will come back to haunt you.'

Margot shrugs. 'I don't believe in karma. Nor do I believe curses, leprechauns or ghosts.'

'What do you believe in, then?'

'My ability to make my own luck.'

'And how has that gone for you so far?'

'I'm doing very well, thank you.'

'Good.' Colm turns the brass knob and opens the door. 'I wish you a good day.'

He leaves and Margot remains by the fire, staring at the place where he stood, a frown furrowing her brow. She tries to get back to work, but she is filled with doubt and fury. Colm has rattled her. The biography of Eva Perón was easy because she was dead. Perhaps Margot should not write about the living.

Chapter 5

A few days later Margot drove into Ballinakelly in search of some action. She wasn't used to living in such a quiet, provincial place. She'd lived in Buenos Aires, Milan, Paris, Amsterdam and Oslo, all vibrant cities in constant movement. Ballinakelly, by contrast, was eerily still. She had too much time to herself and too much time to think.

She hadn't seen Colm since their awkward encounter in the Hunting Lodge. Angry at the suggestion that she was preying on a vulnerable man, Margot had lain awake most of the night, going over their conversation, inventing responses that she hadn't had the wit to think of at the time, and imagining what she'd say to him were she to see him again. But that didn't seem likely. She had avoided O'Donovan's on purpose so as not to bump into him, even though she'd like to have seen Seamus O'Donovan again. He had a rough magnetism that appealed to her. She hoped she wouldn't bump into Colm in town. At least there were no animals at the hotel that might require a vet.

Two more hotel guests had complained about strange noises in the middle of the night. Margot wondered why these so-called ghosts always seemed to come out at that time. Why didn't they appear during the day? Were they like sea urchins that hid beneath rocks during daylight hours and crawled out when it was dark? The whole idea was preposterous. But Mr Dukelow had taken the complaint in his stride, persuading the young couple that the castle really wasn't haunted. Mrs de Lisle had even hired a priest to cleanse it of any negative vibrations, he'd told them. Margot wasn't sure that was true. Mrs de Lisle did not seem like someone who believed in such nonsense. She was an upfront businesswoman with a sensible and practical head on her shoulders.

The couple hadn't been convinced, but they'd certainly felt they had been listened to and went off appeased. Margot wondered whether Mr Dukelow was beginning to worry that these ghost stories might put guests off coming. 'It's a creaky old castle,' he'd told her when she mentioned it. 'Who's listening out for ghosts in the daytime? No one. They lie in bed at night, ears straining to hear every squeak and groan. If they were as alert during the day as they are at night, they'd hear the same noises and think nothing of them.' Margot was inclined to agree with him.

She parked the car on the kerb and stepped into the sunlight. The sky had been washed to a sparkling blue and seagulls wheeled beneath it, the tips of their wings catching the light and flashing white. The high street was made up of simple, flat-fronted houses painted in a rainbow of colours, set against the dramatic backdrop of green hills and patchwork fields. The slate roofs shone with the last rain and rooks were cawing loudly from the chimney stacks. Locals wandered up the damp pavements, browsing in shop windows and emerging from doorways with their shopping bags full, and a trio of elderly ladies in headscarves sat gossiping on a bench while a fat fox trotted blithely up the street as if in defiance of the Deverills whose hunting days were now over.

Margot went into a boutique. She wasn't very interested in fashion, but something drew her in there. No sooner had she entered than she realized what it was. Emer O'Leary was talking to the saleswoman. When she saw Margot her smile faltered and an awkwardness filled the silence that ensued.

'Good morning, Mrs O'Leary,' said Margot with her usual ebullience, hoping to defuse the situation by feigning cheerfulness.

Emer wavered between her good nature and her support for her daughter and grandchildren. 'Good morning,' she replied tightly. She gave the saleswoman a warmer smile. 'Well, I better be going, Sheila. I'll see you later.'

Margot felt it was impolite to let her leave without saying something. After all, Mrs O'Leary had entertained her in her home. She followed her out onto the pavement. 'I want you to know I'm going to be tactful, Mrs O'Leary,' she said, realizing as she said it how lame it sounded. How could she be tactful writing about a family plagued by so many unfortunate dramas?

Emer stepped close and lowered her voice. 'I know you mean well, my dear,' she said, her pale eyes holding Margot in their steady, gentle gaze. 'But everything has a consequence. Everything causes a ripple and that ripple will go out into the world and either harm or heal. You know nothing about the Deverills. You may think you do, following your research, but you don't. If JP is going to enlighten you, he will only give you one side of the story. Think about that when you write the final chapters. And think about my daughter, Alana, and her children, who have suffered also. Not only did they lose their home but they lost their father too.'

'Why don't *you* give me their side of the story? I want to write a balanced account.'

Emer smiled in bitter amusement at the suggestion. 'That would be a betrayal, Miss Hart,' she said. 'Good day to you.'

Margot knew she'd get nothing from Mrs O'Leary.

Feeling bruised, she made her way up the street, her eyes sweeping either side yet seeing nothing. She hadn't considered the living members of the Deverill family when she had pitched her idea to her editor. Her editor had loved it and her agent had negotiated a high advance, following the success of her biography of Eva Perón. She would struggle to repay the money and she didn't have another idea were she to decide to write about something else. She had committed to nine months as Writer in Residence at the hotel; she couldn't very well back out of that either. She was stuck.

As she walked past All Saints Church Margot's bruised ego began to retaliate. Why should anyone tell her what not to write? she thought angrily. The Deverills weren't the first dynasty to be the subject of a biography and they wouldn't be the last. What about the British Royal Family? They were written about all the time and they never kicked up. If JP Deverill wanted to help her with her research, she wasn't going to stop him on account of his mother-in-law and son, whom she didn't know. Why should she have any loyalty to them? If anything, she felt a certain allegiance to JP, who had invited her into his home and allowed her to look through the family records. And besides, what did it matter? In nine months' time she'd leave Ballinakelly and never see any of them again.

As indignation burned in her chest Margot felt a growing sense of defiance. She quickened her pace towards O'Donovan's. Striding past what appeared to be a group of farmers in caps and boots and heavy coats, she pushed open the door. There were a few people inside, enjoying an early lunch. Seamus O'Donovan was behind the bar, talking to a young woman who was drying glasses with a tea towel. When he saw Margot he raised his eyebrows and smiled.

'I wondered when you'd be coming back,' he said, grinning at her.

The indignation cooled. 'It's too early for a stiff drink, but I need one. A lime and soda will have to do.'

He laughed. 'This is Ireland, girl. It's happy hour somewhere in the world, if that's any consolation.'

'Lime and soda. I'm working.'

'That never put anyone off. Sure, even old Father Leader is half cut saying morning Mass.'

'You're a bit of a devil, you are.' It felt good to laugh.

'Lime and soda coming up.' Seamus reached for a glass. 'You ran off the other night. Was it something I said?'

She could tell by the twinkle in his eyes that he didn't believe it was. 'I'd grown bored of being leered at by Mr Flannigan.'

He shrugged. 'He's harmless enough. The worst of him is from the mouth out.'

'The "enough" undermines your defence, Mr O'Donovan. I'd also grown bored of being glowered at by Colm Deverill.'

'That's another matter altogether,' he said, pouring lime into the glass, followed by soda. She noticed his big, masculine hands and strong forearms and felt a frisson of desire. 'Surely you didn't expect the family to welcome you with stories for your book, exposing their underbellies.'

'Of course not. However, I did expect them to be civil.'

'He's angry.'

'So am I.'

'Look, it's none of my business. I've known Colm since we were kids. He's a good man. But he's a proud man too and protective of his family.' Seamus pushed the glass across the bar and Margot picked it up and took a sip. 'He's unhappy that his father's talking to you.'

'I know. He told me himself. But I'm not going to be pushed about by anyone. JP Deverill's a big boy. He can look after himself. I was a journalist once. I'm used to pissing people off.' Margot shrugged. 'It's the nature of the job.'

'You look like you can handle yourself,' he said. Then he leaned on the bar and looked her dead in the eye. 'Fancy a quiet drink somewhere, just the two of us?'

Her gaze didn't waver. 'Sure, where do you suggest?' She couldn't very well invite him back to the hotel.

'I can escape in an hour. I could smuggle you upstairs.'

She grinned at his allusion to danger. 'We're consenting adults,' she said.

'But this is a small nosy town and tongues wag. You've only just arrived. You need to mind how you go.'

'You're not married, are you?'

He shook his head. 'Not married, in spite of my mam's nagging. Who would have me anyway?'

'Neither am I. So we're free agents.' Then she laughed. 'Are you worrying about *my* reputation, Seamus? How gallant.'

He laughed with her. He'd never met a woman with the insouciance of a man before. 'Have some lunch, then I'll be dessert.'

'That's an offer I can't refuse,' she said, turning her attention to the menu scrawled onto the blackboard. 'It's part of my research, after all.'

Later, in Seamus's bedroom under the eaves, Margot lost herself in the arms of a man she barely knew, as she had done so many times in the past. Men she could enjoy with detachment. Men she didn't have to get close to. Seamus was strong and masterful and smelt good besides – of woodsmoke from the fire and a spiciness that was all his own. He was funny too and they laughed there between the sheets as his hands brought her into the present moment with their surprisingly light touch.

'That was great,' she said with a sigh, playfully pushing him off her. 'You've done it before.'

'A few times,' he replied, rolling onto his back.

'Just what I needed.'

'Not angry anymore then?'

'No.' She stretched and sighed. 'In fact, everything is right with the world now.'

He turned to face her, his expression one of admiration and puzzlement, as if he were looking at a rare creature from another world. 'They don't make them like you down here,' he said.

'I should hope not. I'd hate to be like everyone else.' Margot smiled at him, basking in his appreciation.

'So, we can do it again sometime?'

'I'd like that.' She propped herself up on her elbow and gazed at him steadily. 'I feel like you're sleeping with the enemy, Seamus. Is that why you wanted to smuggle me up here?'

'No, I'm impartial, Margot. I promise. I've no sense of loyalty to the Deverills. If JP wants to talk to you, that's his business. If Colm doesn't want him to, that's his. Besides, I'd say I'm on your side now, if I had to take sides.'

'You're easily bought,' she laughed, running a finger down

his chest. 'But don't worry. I'm not going to put you in a difficult position. This is pleasure, not work.'

'So it is,' he agreed.

'Tell me about Ballinakelly. Your family have lived here for generations. This is where you grew up. Have you ever wanted to move away?'

'No, I've always been content here. I can't imagine living anywhere else. Besides, I'm running the family business now. Da's retired, Mam's a busybody so she's still involved. The only way she'll be leaving is feet first.'

'Siblings?'

'Five, but I'm the only one who's stayed.'

'What do you make of the hotel? Did you feel sad when the castle was sold? Over three hundred years of history gone, over. The end of an era, of feudalism—'

'The hotel employs many more local folk than the castle did as a family house, certainly in its final years. JP lost money in the divorce and, I heard, bad investments. He was never very good with money, so I hear. He didn't grow up with it, you know. That family lost everything in 1921 when the castle was razed to the ground. Since then, they've not been rich. JP suddenly inherited a castle and a fortune. It ruined him.'

'How did it ruin him?'

Seamus squirmed uncomfortably, but Margot's fingers traced the tender part of his belly, just beneath his tummy button. 'He had an affair, apparently. That's usually reason enough for divorce, isn't it? I suppose that's why the kids all sided with their mam. They blame him for the break-up of the marriage and for their mam's unhappiness.'

'I suppose it's hard hiding something like that in a small community like this one. Everyone knows everyone else's business. There's always someone who saw something or heard something. I imagine the castle was full of staff with their ears to the doors.'

'You're not wrong. I think if I'd worked up at the castle, I'd have been just as nosy.'

'Listen, there are always two sides to every story. JP had an affair, but perhaps he was pushed into it. Maybe he was unhappy too.'

'If you ask me, that castle has never brought any of its owners happiness.'

'Surely some were happy?'

'You tell me. You're writing the history.'

'Were Bridie and her count happy?'

'Well, there's a story. You need to talk to Bridie's brother, Michael. You know he lives in the farmhouse down the road. Must be in his nineties now. He comes in here from time to time and, after a pint or two he's given to talk. He'll talk to you. He's always had an eye for a beautiful woman.'

She smiled. 'Thank you, Seamus.'

'Don't mention it. If the stories are true, Michael did away with the Count. Buried him up to his neck in the sand and let the tide take him. A gruesome way to go. Sure, that castle is cursed.'

Margot had heard that story before, from Mrs B. 'I need to talk to Michael Doyle,' she said. 'But I don't believe in curses, only bad people.'

However, as she thought about it, she realized that Seamus might be on to something. None of the heirs had enjoyed peaceful, harmonious lives. They had sacrificed much for their home, perhaps too much. 'A Deverill's castle is his kingdom,' she repeated pensively. 'Do you think they've always put their family seat above the welfare of those living inside it?' But she didn't need him to answer. A rush of excitement coursed through her veins, waking her from her post-coital apathy. She sat up. 'I think that's the theme of the book. As long as they put bricks and mortar above love they will never be happy. The castle itself is not cursed, but their attachment to it brings bad luck.' She shook her head. 'God, I'm sounding like Dan.'

'Who's Dan?'

'A friend of mine who claims to be a psychic medium. He's into all that stuff like karma, a universal consciousness, universal law, feng shui, tarot cards and the law of attraction. Mad,' she added with a laugh. Seamus looked at her in bewilderment; he'd lost her after karma. 'But it doesn't matter,' she continued. 'I think I'm on to something.' She bent down and kissed him on the lips. 'Okay, enough work, this is meant to be about pleasure. Shall we do it again?'

Mrs B opened the door to the games room to find Lord Deverill standing by the fireplace, flicking through a red-leather-bound book, a cigarette smoking between his fingers. She was surprised to see him there. The games room was one of the many rooms he never went into. 'Hello, Mrs B,' he said when he saw her. 'Miss Hart didn't come in today, did she?'

'No, m'lord, she didn't.'

He looked up from the diary. 'Do you think it's warm enough in here? I don't want her working in the cold.'

'When the fire's lit, it will take the chill off.'

'And light enough?' He glanced at the big windows, framed by heavy green velvet curtains. 'It gets dark early now.' He sighed. 'Bleak in winter, this place. Always was.'

'I'd say there's good lighting in here. She hasn't complained.'

He took a drag of his cigarette and blew out a stream of

smoke. 'She's not a complainer. She's got an easy temperament. Cheerful. I like that. It's nice to have a cheerful person around the house, isn't it, Mrs B?'

'Oh, it is, m'lord. She's cheerful all right.'

He looked down at the book. 'Do you know what this is, Mrs B?'

'No, I don't, m'lord. What is it?'

'My great-great-grandmother's diary. Makes fascinating reading. I can understand why Miss Hart is gripped by history. It is rather intriguing learning about those who lived in the past. My great-great-grandmother Hermione rescued donkeys. She had dozens of them. They each had a different coloured ribbon tied to their ears so she could keep track of their names. She also had a Shetland pony called Billy who used to come into the dining room at breakfast and drink tea out of a china bowl.'

Mrs B smiled and her solemn face grew soft and pretty. 'That's grand, that is.'

'But her husband died young. He drowned and left her with five small children to bring up on her own.'

'Oh, that's very sad.'

'It is. But she was a tough Englishwoman and earned the respect of her tenants and employees and she ran the castle with the efficiency of a colonel. I dare say she was the sort of woman who built the Empire. Tough and unflappable in a crisis. When she died the whole town came out to pay their respects and her coffin was put on a cart full of flowers and pulled by a pair of her donkeys. Deverill men have a tradition of marrying strong women, it seems.'

'You may say your grandmother Adeline was some woman.'

'She was indeed.'

JP thought of his own wife, his *ex*-wife, then shunted the

image away before it could take hold with its painful grip. 'Do you think Miss Hart will be back tomorrow?' he asked, putting down the book. His whole body suddenly ached for a swig of whiskey. He made for the door.

Mrs B stepped aside to let him pass. 'I'm sure she will, m'lord.'

'Good. Give the place a dust and perhaps the boys can bring in some more logs. Proper logs, not turf. Only wood will warm this place up and I don't want Miss Hart to get cold.'

Mrs B watched him stride off towards the library, where she knew he'd help himself to a glass of whiskey. He wouldn't stop after one, but would pour himself another and another. Often she found him asleep in his chair, the fire down to dying embers, a chill pervading the room. She sighed and hoped Miss Hart would be back tomorrow. Lord Deverill cheered up when she was around.

That night Margot lay in bed, staring up at the ceiling. Outside, the moon was full-faced and glowing, a luminous ball in a sky of twinkling stars. The curtains were open a sliver, allowing the watery light to enter in a shaft, bringing the furniture and beams into eerie relief. All was quiet, apart from the intermittent hooting of an owl or the screech of a startled animal. Even the wind was still. Margot had a strange sensation that she was being watched. She knew it was absurd. There was no one in the room but her. She was quite alone. However, it was as if a presence was right beside her bed, watching her. She rolled over and tried to sleep. Dorothy had put ideas into her head. If it hadn't been for her and her stories of ghosts, Margot would never have thought of them.

As soon as she began to drift off, JP Deverill surfaced in her mind. A pathetic, lost creature. Overcome suddenly by a wave of pity, she opened her eyes. She did not want to feel compassion. She did not want his addiction to suck her in. She couldn't help him. Nor did she want to. She closed her eyes again and thought of Seamus. Yet JP kept bobbing to the top of her mind like a cork in water, persistent and pleading.

Chapter 6

Margot spent the following morning in the drawing room, which had been renamed the Lady Adeline Suite, although Margot would have liked to point out that Adeline was never a lady in her own right, so Lady Adeline was technically incorrect. However, she sat in there regardless, at a desk that Mr Dukelow had brought in especially for her and placed in front of one of the big windows overlooking the garden. The lawn was white with frost, gleaming like a thousand pearls beneath clear skies and a low winter sun. The trees, naked and shivering, were silhouetted against the blue sky in a latticework of spindly branches, their fine lines marred only by a noisy flock of inky black rooks that had settled upon them.

The drawing room was harmoniously proportioned, with pale green walls and damask green curtains lined with fringes and held back by big, shell-shaped sconces. The fire was lit, the cushions on the sofas were puffed up, the lights glowing richly. Everything about the hotel was luxurious, extravagant and of the very best quality. However, it all paled into insignificance beneath the arresting gaze of the formidable Tarquin Deverill, whose portrait hung above the fireplace on two heavy chains. Margot stood before it and examined it with interest. It was magnificent, as all Deverill portraits seemed to be. Yet, where Barton had a wide and handsome face, Tarquin's was long and thin and mean. He was posing in front of a faded landscape, in an indigo-blue velvet jacket, draped in crimson silk. His hair was a cascade of brown curls and on his chest he wore an enormous diamond star medal. At his throat was a white cravat that accentuated his lofty chin and scrutinizing gaze. On closer inspection, Margot noticed the nasty twist of his mouth and the flat, impassive look in his eyes which did not seem capable of great depth of feeling, certainly not of compassion or love. He looked every inch the lord of the castle and every inch a man capable of great cruelty. She could see him leaving his disabled son to drown in the ornamental pond and imagine his relief when the stain on his good name was removed for ever. The portrait exuded a dark energy. She stepped away and yet, as she did so, she could almost feel his eyes following her across the room.

Margot turned up at the front door of the Hunting Lodge in the early afternoon. The air was damp, the wind laced with ice. Behind the trees the sun burned like a distant coal. She shivered, looking forward to the games room and its crackling fire. Looking forward, too, to those boxes full of treasures.

Mrs B opened the door a crack. When she saw Margot she opened it wide and her face softened with a shy smile. 'Come in at once, Miss Hart. The wind has teeth today.'

'Thank you, Mrs B.' Margot watched her close the door, shutting winter out. She took off her coat and hat, stuffing the gloves into one of the pockets.

'You'll be wanting tea, I suspect. I'll tell Lord Deverill you're here.'

'Oh, please don't disturb him,' said Margot, following the housekeeper's quick footsteps down the corridor.

'He'll be happy you're here. The house has been as quiet as a tomb all morning.'

As they reached the library, JP was already coming out. His face lit up when he saw Margot. 'Ah, good, you're back.'

'Yes, I am,' she replied, surprised that he didn't consider her visit an imposition. She had deliberately left it a day so as not to be a bore.

'Mrs B lit a fire in the games room on the off chance that you would come. It should be nice and warm in there by now. It's been burning since nine o'clock.' Margot followed him. 'Now, I wanted to tell you, I've been reading my great-great-grandmother's diary.'

'Hermione Deverill?' said Margot.

'Yes, Hermione What interesting lives these people led.' They entered the games room together. 'You've rather inspired me, Miss Hart,' he continued. 'I spent all of yesterday in here, reading.'

There was a vigour to JP today which hadn't been there on her previous visits. An enthusiasm that replaced the pathetic, hang-dog energy he had exuded. It gave her pleasure to think that delving into his family history might have cheered him up. 'Would you mind calling me Margot,' she said, putting her bag on the billiard table. 'It seems ridiculously formal calling me Miss Hart all the time. It makes me feel like a character out of a Jane Austen novel.'

'Then you must call me JP,' he said.

'I will. Thank you, JP.' She noticed that another armchair had been placed in front of the fire. Now there were two. One for her and one for JP. There was something touching about it, something that tugged at her heart and made her feel sad. The whole house resonated with loneliness. Those chairs were like a small oasis of companionship in a desert of solitude.

JP opened the diary and read her a few extracts. 'Charming, don't you think?'

'Hermione had a lyrical turn of phrase, didn't she?'

'Yes, she loved poetry. She quotes a lot from her favourite writers. Charming,' he repeated.

Mrs B came in with the tea tray and placed it on the billiard table where there was a space among the boxes. She poured the tea and JP took his cup to one of the armchairs and sat down with a contented sigh. Mrs B cut him a slice of cake and handed it to him. He smiled up at her with gratitude and thanked her. She gazed down at him with affection. Margot observed their relationship with interest. It seemed as if Mrs B was the only person who cared for JP nowadays.

Outside, purple clouds darkened the sky. Inside, the electric lights shone golden. The grate glowed with a hearty fire. The flames licked the logs with crimson tongues and crackled with relish as they found pieces of moss on which to feast. Margot sat down in the armchair opposite JP. Like a pair of old friends they were, settling in for the evening.

'Where did you live when you were a child, JP?' she asked.

'In a big house on the estate with Kitty, my half-sister, and her husband Robert. Not far from here,' he replied. 'It was called the White House. It's still there, but I don't own it. That went when I sold the castle. The only place I retained was this house and a small bit of land to go with it.'

'Was Kitty alive when you sold the castle?'

'She was seventy-six. She died four years later. I'm afraid I broke her heart. She loved it more than anything in the world. Mrs de Lisle let her live on in the White House, paying a peppercorn rent. But we didn't speak to each other after that. She never forgave me.'

'That's very sad.'

He shrugged. 'We both had a lot to be bitter about.' Margot said nothing, aware that any question about his relationship with his half-sister might be considered intrusive. But JP wanted to talk. 'Kitty was a mother to me. As I told you, my real mother was a housemaid who caught my father's eye. Me and my twin sister . . .' He turned back to her. 'Did I tell you about Martha?'

Margot shook her head, her interest piqued. 'No, you didn't.'

'Martha and I were born in a convent in Dublin. Martha was adopted by an American couple and spirited off to Connecticut. I was stolen by my mother's brother before the same fate could happen to me, and left on Kitty's doorstep in a basket.'

'Like Moses,' Margot interjected with a grin.

'Well, that's where the similarity ends, Margot. My mother, Bridie Doyle, started a new life in America. She worked for a very wealthy woman who left her a fortune in her will when she died. She married the Count di Marcantonio and bought the castle, eventually moving into it in 1940, some twenty-three years after she had worked in it as a maid. I grew up believing my mother had died. Kitty told me it was so and I had no reason to disbelieve her. I only learned the truth after Bridie had died of cancer. She left two letters, one for me and one for Martha, who had come to Ballinakelly in search of her real mother.'

'Did you meet Martha?'

'We met by coincidence in a restaurant in Dublin and fell in love. We were both seventeen years old. Children, really.'

'You fell in love with your sister?'

'We didn't know we were siblings. We were not identical. A cruel trick of fate.' JP's eyes turned to her and they were glassy and sad. 'It was a terrible blow when my father told us. We didn't think there could possibly be any reason why we couldn't be together. But there was, and that was it.' He shrugged. 'That was my first disappointment. Life had been carefree up until that point.'

'How did you get over it?'

'By throwing myself into the war. I flew Spitfires and didn't care if I lived or died. I wasn't particularly heroic, but I was awarded a medal for bravery.' He chuckled, then lost his focus in the flames. 'You know, I have a strange memory from early childhood. Probably one of my first memories. I'm standing in the playroom and a strange woman leans in through the window and gives me a teddy bear. I take it from her, but step away. I don't know who she is and there's something about her that frightens me. She tries to grab me and I scream. I scream loudly and don't stop. She looks horrified and leaves as mysteriously as she came.'

'Do you think that was Bridie?'

'Yes, yes I do. I think that was my mother come to claim me.'

'Did you ever tell Kitty?'

'I can't recall whether or not I did at the time, but the memory only came back to me after I read her letter. I didn't mention it to Kitty at that point. I think I was just trying to understand it myself and didn't want to share my thoughts with anyone. I needed time.' He sighed and took a sip of tea.

'How did you feel when you read your mother's letter?'

'I thought little of it, to be honest. I had grown up with two fathers and a mother figure in Kitty. I was loved. In fact, I was adored. I had everything I ever wanted, except Martha, of course. I had married Alana, whom I loved deeply. The fact that Bridie was suddenly revealed as my mother made little impression on me at first.' He smiled grimly. 'But then the mind starts working on it, like a beetle in dung, rolling it into a bigger and bigger ball, until it's pushing this great big weight about, trying to make sense of it. That's when the feeling of betrayal began to seep in. The feeling of injustice and hurt. Of loss. I never knew my mother, you see. If Kitty had been honest with me . . . If my father had been honest . . .'

'You might have got to know her before she died.'

'Yes. I regret that. Very deeply.'

'You have a lot to be bitter about,' Margot agreed. 'But every choice that was made was done so with the best intentions.'

'The path to Hell is paved with good intentions,' JP added wryly.

'I don't suppose any of the secrets were kept to hurt you.'

'I don't suppose they were. But secrets have a way of coming out in the end and, like arrows, they wound.'

Margot smiled sympathetically. 'Your story beats Hermione's diary, hands down!'

'And you've only heard the beginning.' He stood up stiffly. 'Fancy another piece of cake?'

'I would love one, thank you. It's very good.'

'Mrs B's an expert. She's not economical with the Guinness, either.' He cut the cake and brought it to her plate. 'When I was growing up, there was always a porter cake in the kitchen.' He cut a slice for himself and returned to his chair. He hadn't enjoyed himself so much in years. Besides her good company, there was a warm light in Margot's eyes that lifted him out of the darkness. A compassion that promised understanding – and he wanted so much to be understood.

'Tell me about Bertie, JP,' she asked.

JP sat back in his chair and crossed his legs. He took a sip of tea. The fire sizzled, Margot listened. It was nice to have someone to talk to. He thought of his father. 'He was, in essence, a country man,' he began. 'Like all the Deverills, he had a daring streak and an eye for the ladies . . .'

Colm and Jack headed up the beach towards home. The night was drawing in early and with some haste. Bruised clouds gathered overhead, darkening the sea that roiled in anticipation of an approaching storm. Colm lifted the collar of his coat as he felt the first dollops of rain. His grandfather, bent against the wind, put his hands in his pockets. The dog, wet and sandy, trotted along beside them, sensing a good tea and a warm hearth were not far off.

'Live like your grandmother, Colm, and you will never be unhappy.' Jack would not advise his grandson to live like *he* had, full of uncontrollable passions. Emer had been the stabilizing force in his life. A consistent, unconditional love that put him to shame. 'She doesn't allow bitterness and resentment to vex her. Let them go.'

'While that woman is inveigling her way into Dad's trust and drawing out our family secrets for all the world to read, I cannot feel anything but fury.' Colm was speaking of Margot Hart.

'You asked for my advice. Well, I'd say you have two choices. One, you do nothing and give up your anger. Two, you do something about it. What you *don't* do is sit in the middle, doing nothing but stomp about letting your fury eat away at you. That'll get you nowhere.'

'So, what is this something I can do about it, then?'

'Try a different tactic. Appealing to her better nature didn't work and why would it? What does she owe you, who she doesn't know from Adam? Wouldn't it be better to get to know her? That way you can work on her from the inside, rather than from the outside.'

Colm laughed. 'That's the old spy talking!'

'You have to be sly about it, Colm. If you become her friend then, eventually, you may be able to ask her to leave certain things out. Indeed, you'll have more of an idea of what she knows. You'll be in a better position to do something about it.'

Colm strode on. The wind was picking up. They were having to shout over the roar of the waves. 'That's good advice, Granda. Although, it's not going to be easy pretending I like her.'

'You can do anything when you put your mind to it, Colm. If it gets you what you want, you can play any part you choose.'

Colm knew some of his grandfather's stories of when he had fought in the War of Independence and was aware of the many different parts *he* had played to get what *he* wanted. Of course the stakes had been much higher then. Colm felt a little foolish making such a drama out of a book. But then his grandfather didn't know what *he* knew. No one did. Only he and his father, and he couldn't rely on JP to keep that knowledge secret. As long as he was numbing his brain with whiskey there was a strong chance he would divulge the whole story.

'You're right, Granda,' he said as they trudged up to the house that glowed invitingly through the dusk. 'I'll make a friend of my enemy.'

'Kill with kindness, Colm,' said Jack. 'That's the way to get on in the world. Let your enemy think you're their friend.' Jack had done that enough in his life to know that it worked.

It was late when Margot returned to the hotel and raining hard. She parked her car as near to the front door as possible and dashed inside. Mr Dukelow was in the lobby. 'Miss Hart, I have exciting news.'

Margot couldn't imagine what that could be. Had he rid the hotel of the housekeeper ghosts, perhaps?

He stood before her and lowered his voice, assuming a deferential air as if he was about to speak of royalty or the Pope. 'The Countess di Marcantonio came in about an hour ago, asking to see you,' he said.

Margot frowned. She must be Bridie's daughter-in-law, married to Leopoldo. 'Did she leave a note?' she asked.

'She left an envelope at reception. Róisín will get it for you.'

He nodded at Róisín, who was filing her nails behind the desk. When she didn't react, he called her name. 'Róisín, the letter for Miss Hart, please.'

Róisín lifted startled eyes, dropped the file and swung round on her chair to retrieve the white envelope she had put safely in Margot's pigeonhole. 'She's a fine-looking lady,' she told Margot as she handed it over. 'Just as you would imagine a countess to be. Do you know her husband once lived here?'

'Yes, I do,' Margot replied, distracted now that she was opening the envelope.

Mr Dukelow wandered behind the desk and began to look busy, but he was curious to know what the letter said.

Margo pulled out the letter and unfolded it. Beneath an elaborate gold crest of three large bees, the letter was written by hand, in ink.

Dear Miss Hart

It has come to my notice that you are writing a book about Castle Deverill and the Deverill family. As you know, my

husband, the Count, grew up there – until his mother died
and chose to leave it in her will to her illegitimate son, JP
Deverill. I think I may be able to help you with your research.
I'd be very happy to meet you. I leave my telephone number
here for you to contact me. We divide our time between our
various residences, but at present we are at our townhouse in
Dublin. I'd be willing to come to you. I don't often get an
excuse to visit my husband's family home.

> *Yours sincerely, the Countess di Marcantonio*

Margot put the letter back in the envelope and smiled at Mr
Dukelow. 'Countess di Marcantonio wishes to help me with
my research,' she told him and watched his face beam. 'She
wants to come here. Is there a private room we can use?'

Mr Dukelow rubbed his manicured hands together at the
thought of being graced by aristocracy. 'Absolutely. Mrs de
Lisle's own sitting room will be the perfect place to have a
quiet tête-à-tête. Mrs de Lisle would want only the best room
in the castle for the Countess. I will let her know at once.'

'Thank you.'

'It's my pleasure, Miss Hart.' And he picked up the telephone, puffed out his chest and waited for Mrs de Lisle's office
to answer.

Margot went up to her room in the western tower. She was
curious to meet this Countess di Marcantonio. She had a sense
of her personality already from the little she had written in her
letter. The Countess minded, dreadfully, that her husband had
not been left the castle in his mother's will. Perhaps *she* would
shed some light onto those dark and secret places?

Kitty

Margot is like a truffle pig in a forest of hidden fungi. Once she has the scent in her nostrils there is no stopping her. She finds out from Seamus where Michael Doyle lives and drives there in her little blue car without any prior warning, armed with a crate of his favourite stout. This amuses me. I know that Michael, an old man now, living off the rotten remains of a dissolute life, will be easily bought.

He lives alone. He never married, but he did live for a short time with a woman called Grace, who moved in with him when her husband, Sir Ronald Rowan-Hampton, discovered their affair and kicked her out. After the humiliation, not to mention the fall, which was from a great height for Grace had been one of the most highly respected ladies in the land, she took to the bottle. Michael, who had been sober for a good many years, joined her. The two of them became a sorry, though touchingly devoted, pair. Grace and I had been uneasy friends once, but that is another story.

Michael comes to the door of the farmhouse where he, his sister Bridie and brother Seán grew up with straw for mattresses and cows next door for warmth. The very same house where he and Jack and the other rebels planned their raids and their ambushes in the kitchen over tankards of stout and cigarettes. The house was renovated, thanks to Bridie's money, but it is still much the same, only with running water, electricity and the sort of creature comforts most people take for granted. Michael is ninety-four and in surprisingly good health. After all the unspeakable things he did during the War of Independence and, I dare say after it ended as well, I would have expected him to pop his clogs long ago, but karma is not limited to this life alone. I have no doubt that he will pay his karmic debts in the afterlife he has created for himself.

He peers at Margot with an irritated expression on his face. He suspects that she wants to sell him something, even though local people know not to venture so far down this track. He looks her over and I can see the old glint of the Lothario brightening his murky eyes. Michael always did like pretty girls. He grins with one corner of his mouth, more like a grimace, or a leer. He's a bitter man these days.

'Mr Doyle, I'm Margot Hart. I'm writing a history book of the Deverill family and would love to talk to you, if you can spare the time.'

Time is something that Michael has in abundance. He has nothing to do all day but brood. He glances at the crate of stout and opens wide the door. 'Come in,' he says.

Margot is a brave woman. She does not hesitate. Mind you, Michael is not the threat he used to be. Back in the day he was tall and powerfully built, like a bull, with eyes full of menace and an imagination to match. He had a reputation in this town and those who wanted problems dealt with came to him. They knew the way he worked. Everyone knew, even the Garda. But no one messed with Michael Doyle. Now he is stooped and as thin as a reed. His muscles have wasted away and he has a tremor in his hands. Indeed, he is as feeble as a kitten as he approaches the end of his life. I wonder whether he looks back over the years and regrets the things he did. I wonder whether the black dogs that chased him throughout his life are now snapping at his heels. One way or another, the bad things we do catch up with us in the end. They must be close, those dogs. Very close.

He shows Margot into the kitchen. It smells of cigarettes and boiled cabbage. The windows are closed. I don't imagine Michael thinks of letting the air in. Margot puts the bottles of stout on the table, takes a chair and sits down. Michael shuffles over to the kettle and switches it on. 'I presume you drink tea?' he says.

'I do, thank you. Would you prefer a glass of beer?' She lifts a bottle out of the crate and holds it up. 'Is this any good? I wasn't sure and, as I'm not Irish, I didn't know which brand to buy. The woman in the shop was very helpful, however.'

He looks at it and I can sense him salivating. He'd always prefer a glass of stout over tea.

'So you're writing about the Deverills, are you?' he says, coming over and taking a bottle from her.

'Yes, it's a history of the family, from Barton Deverill to the present day.'

He grunts. He does not like the Deverills. 'You won't hear anything positive from me.'

'You're JP Deverill's uncle – and Leopoldo's, of course, who grew up in the castle.'

'I don't see Leopoldo these days and as for JP, I never saw him then and I don't see him now. I have no relationship with either. I fear you're wasting your time in coming here.'

'Have you met Leopoldo's wife?'

Michael pours the stout into a glass. He finds a clean mug and fills it with boiling water. 'A woman full of airs and graces, but Leopoldo's always been an eejit.'

Margot laughs. 'You don't mince your words, do you, Mr Doyle.'

'I say it plain, all right.' He downs half the glass in one go, then wipes his mouth with his sleeve. 'My sister and her blackguard of a husband spoiled him. Then Bridie denied him his inheritance and left the castle to her bastard. What hope did he have?'

He brings her mug of tea to the table, puts a half-empty bottle of milk beside it, and sits down opposite. 'It's a sad story,' she says.

'Nothing good ever comes of crossing paths with a Deverill.' He smirks. 'But you must know that already. How's it going, your research?'

'JP has agreed to help me.'

'Don't be fooled. None of them will thank you when the book comes out.'

She smiled sweetly. 'Well, what do I care about that? I'll be long gone by then.'

He nods, impressed. I admire the way she manipulates people to serve her end. If Michael senses that she might give the Deverills a pasting he'll be more likely to talk to her. I know him and how his mind works. He's bitter and vindictive and has nothing good to say about anyone. Although, it is clear to me now that of all the people he has come into contact with in his life he likes himself the least.

They drink and talk and Michael enjoys her company. He's alone most of the time nowadays. He'd forgotten what it feels like to have companionship. It feels good and that good feeling makes him garrulous.

'What happened to Leopoldo's father?' Margot asks and looks at him steadily.

Michael has lit a cigarette. He takes a long drag and blows

the smoke out of the side of his mouth. 'The Count was an opportunist. He married my sister for her money and then treated her like shite. He lorded it over the village, swaggered around like he owned it, and those that were taken in by his shallow good looks were eejits. But this village is full of eejits, isn't it?' He chuckles joylessly and takes another drag. His gnarled fingers are stained yellow from the tobacco.

'I've heard that it was *you* who did him in,' Margot suggests slyly.

'Like I said, eejits! But I can't say I blame the person who did it. Cesare was a fraud. Those bleeding Barberini bees he went on about, God save us!'

'Bees?' Margot frowns.

'The Barberini family emblem was bees. Cesare claimed to be descended from Cardinal Maffeo Barberini who became Pope Urban the whatever. He had as much to do with that Pope as I do. He even put bleeding stone bees above the castle door, though it gave me a certain satisfaction to watch them destroy the Deverill family motto. He was running off with Bridie's fortune and a young girl he'd managed to seduce, poor lamb, when they did him in. If someone hadn't done it, I'd have done it myself.' He flicks ash into an ashtray. 'A good end to bad news.'

'I was told he was buried in the sand up to his neck and left to die.'

'That's true. The tide came in and drowned him. It would have been slow. Very slow.'

'A horrid way to go,' says Margot with a grimace.

'Nothing less than the blackguard deserved.'

'Poor Leopoldo.'

'He was better off without him. So was his mother.'

'Still, I'm not sure how a person recovers from finding his father murdered, and in that horrible way.'

'Leopoldo never recovered from that, or from being disinherited, I don't imagine. He's a damaged man with a strident, self-important wife who dreams of being chatelaine of the castle her husband *should* have inherited.' He grins again and looks at Margot through the smoke that floats out of his nostrils. 'Are you married, Margot Hart?'

'No,' she replies. 'It's not something I believe in.'

He shakes his head. 'You'll find it lonely on your own.' Then, as if he reads her mind, he adds, 'Lovers come and go, Miss Hart. I'm far from wise when it comes to questions about the heart, but I'll tell you this: adventure, independence, selfish living is all very well, but in the end, you just want someone to care about you.'

As Michael Doyle approaches the end of his life, he realizes that no one cares about *him*.

JP looks forward to Margot's visits. He fusses about the fire, throwing on fresh logs, stoking it to prevent it from smoking, pausing to enjoy the sparks that dance about the flames like fireflies. He wants the room to be pleasant for her. He wants those boxes to keep her here indefinitely. He doesn't want her to stop coming. Then he waits. The grandfather clock ticks loudly in the hall, emphasizing with its hollow echo the emptiness in the house, for apart from that sound the place is silent. As silent as a crypt.

JP goes through the boxes, extracting documents and sweeping his eyes over them, trying to while away the time. Some he takes to the armchair where he sits and peruses them, but it is not the same without Margot to share them with. When she appears at last, parking her little blue car in front of the house, he jumps out of the armchair and heads down the corridor to meet her in the hall. His whole body lights up like a bulb. I wonder whether he isn't a little bit taken with her; after all, she is a striking young woman. He is old enough to be her father, of course, but that makes no difference. He is a man and he has always appreciated beautiful women.

I can tell that Margot is growing fond of him too. But perhaps that's because she feels sorry for him. He is a pathetic sight, admittedly, although I have noticed that he is taking more care over his appearance now. He spends a long time in front of the mirror, searching for the handsome young man he once was and wondering where he has gone. I could tell him where he has gone, but even if he could hear me he wouldn't listen.

Over the next week they settle into a routine, the two of them. Mrs B brings in the tea and cake. Margot rummages inside the boxes, pulling things out, while JP looks over items of interest that she passes him and tells her stories of his own. Margot is fascinated. She writes it all down in her notebook, and I am fascinated too. Much of what he tells Margot is new to me. And, of course, one's own experience is subjective. I'm hearing his story from *his* point of view for the first time and I realize how very different that view is to mine, like two sides of the same coin. All the choices I made for him came from my heart, I can honestly say that is true, and yet they were made from my standpoint, not from his. I told him his mother was dead because I didn't want to have to explain why she had not kept him. I never thought she would return to Ballinakelly. I never imagined she would buy the castle. I never, in my wildest dreams, thought she might have given

birth to twins. I hoped that JP would be satisfied with me
and my husband Robert and our father, Bertie. And he was,
until Bridie revealed the hole in his life that he never knew
was there.

After a few days their routine changes and JP asks Mrs B
to make them lunch. They sit together in the dining room, at
one end of the long table where I used to sit with my brother
and sisters when we were growing up, and talk like old friends.
Margot is curious about every aspect of his life and he is
keen to enlighten her. No one has taken any interest in him
for years. She asks him about my daughter, Florence, who is
married and lives in Edinburgh with children of her own. She
asks him about me, and he tells her about my heroism during
the War of Independence, which is greatly exaggerated,
about my love of horses and riding over the hills, and about
our family life with Robert. But will he tell her about Jack, I
wonder? That is one of the many sore subjects Colm will be
hoping his father will avoid. You see, when JP fell in love with
Jack's daughter, Alana, she discovered that I, his half-sister,
had been having an affair with her father and called off the
engagement. JP was devastated and blamed me for destroying
his chance at happiness. The truth was, Jack and I had loved
each other all our lives. When I backed out of our plan to run
away to America together, he went on his own and eventually
met Emer, whom he married. They returned to Ballinakelly
years later and I had to face the truth, that my decision not to
go with him had opened the door for him to find love with
someone else. And love her, he did. He loved us both.

But that wasn't enough for me. I wanted Jack's love and I
wanted it all to myself. I only had myself to blame, and the
regret burned in my heart like a piece of coal; it still does.

Emer is a better woman than I am. She forgave her husband,

and Alana married JP after all and moved into the castle. After that, JP and I never spoke about Jack again. I watched him from afar, this man I had always loved, hiding my true heart, pretending that the feelings I had once had had died like embers in a cold grate. I watched him commit wholeheartedly to his wife and give up the past, for good. But one cannot erase those kinds of experiences from one's soul. They are indelible. They make us who we are. Jack and I were as one and yet, in spite of that, he never looked at me again with eyes full of understanding and love. He turned his back on me in order to devote himself to his wife and his family and his future. It was a sacrifice he had to make. We both had to make it. JP and Alana's love blossomed and for a while their happiness was complete. Out of something broken flowered something whole.

I hover now as JP deliberates how much of my story to divulge. And then he puts down his knife and fork, wipes his mouth with a napkin and settles back in his chair. It is the position of someone making themselves comfortable in order to start a lengthy tale. I think of Colm. Colm, who wants so badly to protect his family from the hurt that will be inflicted if the ghosts of the past are unearthed.

'Kitty was a passionate, hot-headed woman,' he begins. 'She loved a man from the wrong side of the tracks who she couldn't have, so she married Robert Trench, who had been her tutor when she was a young woman. He was gentle and kind but had none of the flamboyance of the other one.' I know then that he is going to tell my story. The little he knows is enough to wound. I cannot allow that. For Colm's sake, I *won't* allow it. I send a ripple into the atmosphere and both wine glasses topple onto the tablecloth. Margot's breaks. JP's bleeds claret onto the white cotton. They both stare at the glasses in bewilderment. My story dies in JP's throat. Margot frowns. She, who does not believe in ghosts, tries to find a logical explanation for how it happened. I can feel her mind working, like a little mouse scurrying about a room in search of a hole. But there is no hole.

They move back into the games room, shaken but both of them trying to hide their fright. JP lights a cigarette. 'How would you like to go riding?' he asks, shunting the thought of ghosts out of his mind and turning his attention to more pleasant things.

'I would love that,' Margot replies.

'You know, once I loved riding more than anything else. It's in my blood, you see. I spent all the time I could spare in the hills on horseback. It was exhilarating.' He pauses and gets a faraway look in his eyes. 'I met Alana on horseback,' he adds quietly. 'I was out riding and saw, in the distance, a child wandering lost about the rocks. When I reached her, she was proud and didn't want me to know that she couldn't find her way back. But I could tell from the anxious expression in her eyes that she was afraid. I lifted her up and we rode back into Ballinakelly together. She was a little girl then. It was before I went off to war. When I came back she had matured into a young woman. A beautiful, formidable young woman.' He chuckles, but there is no mirth in it, just a bitter regret, and nostalgia for something prized in the past, now lost.

They are standing in front of the fire, which has burned down to ash and the last remaining piece of log, glowing crimson. JP lifts a fresh log out of the basket and chucks it into the grate. It sizzles and spits and catches fire. 'What happened with Alana?' Margot asks softly and I am struck by how bold she is to question him like that, fearlessly.

To my surprise, he doesn't object. He takes a long drag of his cigarette, scratches his head where his hair is thinning and takes a deep breath. I am curious. *I* don't know why their marriage ended. This time I remain very still. I send no ripples out to shake their world. I listen, grateful for her fearlessness.

At that crucial moment, Mrs B opens the door. 'M'lord, Master Colm is here to see you.' Mrs B has called him by that name since he was a boy.

JP looks at Margot and sighs. Margot smiles in that carefree way of hers, but I know she is disappointed. An opportunity to discover why he had to sell the castle is lost. She pretends she doesn't care. She pretends too that Colm turning up does not make her uneasy. 'I'm sorry, Margot,' says JP. 'I'd better see what he wants.'

'Please, don't apologize. I have plenty of work to do here.' She pulls one of the boxes towards her to show that she has already moved on from their conversation.

'We'll ride out tomorrow morning, if the weather is fair.'

'Lovely. I'll come prepared,' she replies. I wonder what she might have brought in her suitcase that is suitable.

JP finds Colm in the library. The drawing room is too big and cold to sit in. It is years since anyone has lit a fire in there. Years since it was filled with people. My father used to entertain regularly but JP is always alone. Only Mrs B with her duster braves the chill and the silence. The library, on the other hand, is warm and welcoming. Colm is standing by the window, looking out over the garden, when his father comes in. He turns and smiles. It is years since he has shown his father any warmth and it raises my suspicions at once. Here in the In-between my senses are sharp – I've had a lot of time to hone them.

'Hi, Dad,' he says.

'A drink?' JP asks, heading straight to the drinks tray to pour himself a whiskey.

'No, thanks,' Colm replies and watches his father fill his glass. He has endured too many years of witnessing JP's descent into alcoholism to be shocked by it. Instead he feels only a weary disappointment, and resignation, because there is nothing he can do about it.

'I don't suppose this is a social call?' JP says, but he is feeling good about himself today because of his lunch with Margot. He is not going to allow Colm's visit is deflate him.

'I've come to apologize.'

'Apologize?' This is a surprise to JP.

'I've thought about this book that that woman is research-ing and, well, perhaps I overreacted.' Colm puts his hands in his pockets and lifts his shoulders. I feel that apologizing does not come easily for him.

'Yes, well, perhaps you did.' JP swigs his whiskey. 'But we all make mistakes.'

Colm's jaw tenses. 'I'd like to see some of the things in those boxes, if it's all right with you. I thought perhaps I could get into the spirit of it, rather than condemning the project without knowing anything about it.'

'I think that would be a capital idea.'

Colm nods. 'Good. I was hoping you'd say that.'

'Why don't you come and meet Margot. She's in the games room.' He stubs out his cigarette.

'I've already met her.'

JP raises his eyebrows. 'You have?'

'Yes, and I wasn't very polite. Perhaps I should apologize to her too.'

'Yes, you should. She's a guest in my house and I'd like her to be treated as such.'

'Of course.' Colm is being very agreeable today. I wonder what he's up to.

Whiskey in hand, JP leads the way down the corridor to the games room. He knocks. Margot calls for him to come in. He turns the brass knob and pushes open the door. Margot lifts her head out of the papers and smiles. When she sees Colm, her smile freezes.

'I gather you two have already met,' says JP.

'I'm afraid Miss Hart saw me at my most hot-headed. I'm sorry for that,' Colm says. His smile is as superficial as Margot's.

She gets up off the floor where she has been reading in front of the fire. She doesn't know what Colm is doing here. She waits for one of them to speak.

'I would like to show Colm some of the treasures in these boxes,' JP says.

Margot is visibly relieved. I imagine she thought he had come to berate her again. 'If you like, I'll leave you to it and come back tomorrow.'

'No, please don't go on my account.' Colm is quick to detain her. 'You probably know better than Dad what's of interest and what's not.'

Margot has begun to make piles on the table. She walks round to show them. 'This is all in date order. Starting here with the deeds to the land, dated 1662.' She pats each pile, making her way up the table. '1700s, early 1800s, late 1800s, 1900–10, 1910–20 and so on.'

Colm is surprised to see such a vast quantity of information on his family. He has been so consumed with the history of his own lifetime that he hasn't considered the distant past. His interest is aroused. He goes to the first pile and opens an old, leather-bound ledger, embossed in gold with the Deverill family coat of arms. He gasps in wonder at the neat rows of handwritten accounts. The household expenses, from food to labour, and every item is written in black ink in the finest hand.

Margot's smile is warmer now. 'Isn't it fascinating?' she says.

Colm nods. He forgets his wariness of her as he is pulled into the past. 'It's amazing!' he agrees, flicking through the pages. 'Incredible to think that this was written over three hundred years ago.' He runs his fingers over the ink. 'It feels very real, doesn't it. Very immediate.' Then he reads out some of the entries he finds amusing. 'Darton enjoyed entertaining lavishly,' he says with a grin. 'He spared no expense. Imagine spending fifty pounds, which must have been a fortune in those days, on candles!'

'While those in Ballinakelly starved,' Margot adds wryly.

'I disagree. I suspect he kept the whole village going,' Colm argues. 'Who were the armies of footmen, servants, cooks, maids, gardeners and pageboys? Local people, of course. Before the castle they might have starved, certainly Cromwell's armies would have decimated them, but when Barton Deverill built his castle they must have been thrown a lifeline. I bet they were grateful. There's no evidence of conflict between the people of Ballinakelly and the castle, is there?'

'Only Maggie O'Leary and her rabble army who tried and failed to burn it down.'

'Maggie, my distant cousin, burned at the stake for witchcraft.'

'Yes, you have the blood of both in your veins,' says Margot thoughtfully. 'Who'd have thought that some three centuries after Barton took the O'Learys' land for his castle and sent them off to the swamps, his descendant would marry an O'Leary and unite the two families.' She smiles, enjoying the romance of it. 'It's a beautiful story.'

Colm glances at his father. It would be a beautiful story if JP and Alana had not ruined it. Still, Margot is right, Colm is the flower that grows out of the charred ground of Barton Deverill and Maggie O'Leary's battlefield. He would most certainly be a symbol of redemption if he lived in the castle. But he does not, because his foolish father lost his birthright. How *could* he?

I am gripped by a sudden burst of anger. I send a ripple through the air and pieces of paper flutter to the floor like leaves. Colm and Margot catch eyes. They are as startled as rabbits who have just heard the bang of the farmer's gun. They drop to the floor together to gather up the paper. JP goes to the windows where he sees the night falling early through the glass. 'It's draughty in here,' he says, but he knows there is no draught, certainly not one strong enough to disturb a pile of paper. I sense his suspicion as he draws the heavy velvet curtains. After all, he grew up with me and my sixth sense. He is familiar with earthbound spirits and ghosts and knows very well the difference. I wonder whether he suspects that I have not left. That I will not leave until the castle is returned to a Deverill – to Colm. I wonder if on some deep, perhaps unconscious, level he knows.

None of them mentions the word 'ghost', although it is what they're all thinking. Margot looks at her watch and declares that she must be going. JP reminds her that they will go riding tomorrow. Margot bids Colm farewell. Colm replies awkwardly. Now that he is not gazing at the ledger, he stiffens, as if he remembers himself suddenly and reminds himself not to let down his guard.

Margot leaves. She is at home here now and lets herself out. JP and Colm are left alone together. JP has finished his whiskey and is already twitching with the craving for more. The two men say nothing. They stand uncomfortably together in front of the fire. Then Mrs B comes in.

'Has Miss Hart gone?' she asks.

'She left a moment ago,' JP replies.

'Oh, that's a shame. I know she likes my porter cake.'

'She does indeed, Mrs B.'

'*I'd* like some of your porter cake,' Colm says suddenly.

His father did not expect this. 'You'll stay for tea?' he asks.

'Sure,' Colm replies. 'Why not? I haven't had Mrs B's porter cake for years.'

Mrs B smiles. Her face softens as she looks at Colm with tenderness. She knew him as a little boy. I suspect this family froideur has hurt her as much as it has hurt all of them. 'I'll bring it at once,' she says and disappears.

Colm turns to the billiard table. 'So what else have you found here that's interesting?'

JP gives him Hermione Deverill's diary. 'Back in a tick,' he says. Colm settles into the armchair and begins to read.

A moment later JP is filling his glass with whiskey and knocking it back. I feel a wave of sadness as he stares into the glass, deliberating whether or not to refill it for the second time. I feel, also, a sense of helplessness. There is little I can do to help him from here. I can only watch as he attempts to drown whatever feelings he has of guilt or regret – for it must be those noxious bedfellows that plague him. A person only drinks like that if they find little in themselves to love.

Chapter 7

Margot had come prepared for riding. She knew enough about Ireland, and the Deverills especially, to suppose that there was a good chance she would find herself on a horse. Her grandfather had been an adept huntsman in his day and, as a child, Margot had taken riding lessons. Her mother didn't care for the countryside but tried hard to fit in with her husband's lifestyle, at least at the beginning, which made her agreeable to Margot signing up for Pony Club Camp and the odd point-to-point. For her eighth birthday, her father bought her a pony called Sergeant Percy, which arrived with his best friend, a donkey called Charlie, and for a few years Margot spent happy hours plaiting her pony's mane, brushing him down, polishing the tack and mucking out the stable. Charlie watched the goings-on with mild interest, enlivening only when Margot took Percy out of the field. Then the donkey would bray frantically until his friend was returned to him. Margot was passionate about her pony, until she discovered boys. Then Sergeant Percy grew fat and idle in the field, and Charlie was blissfully happy.

Now she set off in her blue Beetle for the Hunting Lodge, dressed in a pair of navy jodhpurs and jacket, black riding boots and hat. When Mr Flannigan had lugged her suitcase up the stairs to her room, those boots and hat were what had made it so heavy. The last time she had ridden was across the Andes from Argentina to Chile, sleeping under the stars. Now she anticipated a glorious day on the hills around Ballinakelly. The weather promised to be kind, but it could change quickly on the coast, the sea winds picking up unexpectedly and blowing clouds inland to unleash their showers on the unsuspecting tourist. Right now the sky was the colour of washed denim. The sun was shining in all its glory, bathing the fields in a bright golden light, turning the grass an almost phosphorescent green.

JP was waiting for Margot in the hall, looking a lot less glamorous in a long, olive-green wax raincoat and tweed cap. He did not wear jodhpurs, but a pair of moleskin trousers, and on his feet were an old pair of lace-up walking boots. Mrs B had prepared a Thermos flask of tea and JP had filled a hip flask with whiskey, the prospect of which warmed him as if it were a hot potato in his pocket.

'You look quite the part, Margot,' he said when he saw her. Her face was pretty, heart-shaped, naked without her hair which was now pulled back and tied into a plait. She looked younger, too, without make-up.

'I didn't want to get it wrong,' she replied with a smile.

'You can't get it wrong in Ireland. Isn't that right, Mrs B?'

'Oh, yes, m'lord. We Irish don't always do the done thing.'

'I hope you've had a hearty breakfast?' he asked.

'As hearty as I can tolerate at this time of the morning.'

'I'll make a good lunch for when you come back,' said Mrs B. 'I'll do a pot roast pheasant.'

Mrs B was heartened to see JP so full of enthusiasm. His tone of voice was chirpy, his humour restored. *This* was the man she knew, not the gloomy, desolate stranger who had gradually taken him over this last decade. She watched them leave and then closed the door behind them and headed off to the kitchen to prepare the pheasant. It had been a very long time since she had felt so positive, there was even a small bounce in her step. As she put on her apron and took the pots and pans down from the shelf it dawned on her that she was actually looking forward to cooking this meal and thinking of ways to make it more interesting. Margot's presence was lifting the house out of the shadows and filling it with light.

Then Mrs B did something radical. Injected with optimism she went into the storeroom and took down the old wireless from the shelf. She blew off the dust, for it hadn't been used in years, and plugged it into the wall. She turned it on. At once the sound of classical music floated out and Mrs B stared at it in wonder. There was magic in the way it rid the place of silence, the dreaded silence to which Mrs B had grown so accustomed that she had ceased to notice it. It had become a part of her, this silence, like a sad, stagnant pool of solitude in the centre of her being where all her hurts lay buried. Now the music stirred it, sending ripples across it, inspiring her to wonder how she had endured it for so long. She turned up the volume and sighed with pleasure. Things were going to change; she could feel it in the internal shifts taking place within her. And she could feel it in the music. She wasn't going to allow that silence to invade her kitchen again.

JP led Margot to the stables, which were at the back of the house, beyond the kitchen garden. Nothing grew at this time of year, and the gardens had an air of wistfulness, as if they had once been lavishly cultivated and were now cut back, minimized and simply maintained. The vegetable plots lay bare, the chocolate-brown soil neatly raked. The greenhouse was empty, its glass cloudy with mildew, haunted by the same desolation that haunted the house. She didn't imagine JP went out much. She didn't imagine he took any interest in the gardens. Margot wondered what the place had been like when it had been filled with love.

They reached the stables and JP introduced her to Tomas and Aidan O'Rourke, who had saddled up the horses. Margot thought she recognized them from the pub. Brothers, dark and handsome, with clear blue eyes, thin, stubbly faces and canine teeth that were longer than the others, giving them a foxy look. Margot needed no help in getting into the saddle. She slipped her left foot into the stirrup and swung up with ease. JP, on the other hand, was less agile. Tomas positioned the horse beside a stone mounting block specifically built for this purpose and JP climbed on with a groan.

'It's been a while since I've ridden,' he said, taking hold of the reins.

'When you say a while, how long do you mean?' Margot asked.

He shrugged. 'Years.'

She was surprised. 'You have two beautiful horses and you never go out?'

'I have six beautiful horses,' he corrected. Then he slumped, defeated. 'I haven't had the will, Margot.'

'Who exercises them when you don't?'

'These lads,' he replied, nodding at Tomas and Aidan. 'They keep the place ticking over.'

'If I wasn't a writer, I'd like their job,' she said, watching them smile with pride. She imagined it to be a lonely one, however.

'We could always do with another pair of hands,' said Aidan with a grin, those fox teeth giving his smile a raffish charm.

'Aye, and one with a seat as good as yours, Miss Hart,' Tomas added. He patted her horse's flank. 'You'll have a fine morning up there. The weather's good. You'll not get wet.'

'If you're wrong and I get wet, you'll have to buy me a drink tonight in O'Donovan's,' she told him as she squeezed her ankles and the horse walked on.

'So, that's where you go in the evenings, is it?' said JP.

'I've been a few times. It's a good place to observe people.'

He chuckled. 'It's the heart of the town. Always has been. You know, when I was growing up women weren't allowed in there.'

'Well, they looked pretty surprised to see me walk in on my own.'

'I bet they did. Old habits die hard in places like this.'

They left the estate and set off up a path that meandered gently around the contours of the land, taking them into the open countryside. Soon, they were ascending into the hills – velvet green strewn with rocks, grazing sheep, drystone walls, long grasses and heather. From there they could see the sea. Sheer cliffs with horizontal layers like slices of cake rose sharply out of the water, waves breaking against them, bleeding clouds of foam. Gulls cried into the wind that carried on its frosty breath the scents of ozone and brine. Margot was suddenly injected with excitement. It felt exhilarating to be up there in the elements, in this wild, unbridled land. It released something inside her that caused her eyes to fill with tears. She thought of her father then. Instead of pushing him out she let him stay for a moment. She pictured his face, heart-shaped like hers, and his jaunty smile, and was surprised that the image her mind conjured up was a positive one. She took a breath, inhaling the rich smells of wet soil and heather, ingesting the taste of Ireland, allowing the ancient enchantment that is sown deep into the earth to rise up and find its way into her heart.

JP must have felt it too, for he turned to her and smiled, a smile so full of gratitude that Margot felt a sense of gratitude of her own, surging inside her like the upward swell of an ocean. 'Let's gallop,' she suggested.

JP turned his face into the wind. 'Follow me!' he shouted and set off, the thunder of his horse's hooves dying away as he left her behind. Margot clenched her jaw and kicked her horse's ribs. In a moment she was flying over the grass in his wake, the air cold against her face, the adrenalin coursing through her veins like fire. She laughed out loud, the mad, abandoned laugh of someone who has just discovered something inside herself that she hadn't known was there. In that moment of total freedom from restraint, she felt more alive than she'd ever felt before. Even riding across the Andes hadn't given her this thrill, for the delight was in the land, in the wind and in the rumbling of the waves. The wildness of it unleashed the wildness in *her* and she did not try to contain it but let it express itself freely. When she joined JP, who had drawn his horse to a halt and was waiting for her on the crest of a knoll, she was out of breath and smiling so hard her face ached.

He held out his hip flask. 'This will fortify you,' he said.

Margot took a swig. The whiskey burned all the way down her gullet to her stomach. 'That was incredible,' she gasped. 'I don't think I've laughed like that, ever.'

JP's eyes sparkled, his cheeks flushed pink. He looked a decade younger. No longer the shadow of the insouciant young man he had once been, but an older version of him, as was right. He lit a cigarette, shielding it from the wind with his hands as he flicked the lighter and sucked until the little end glowed crimson. Then he sat back in his saddle and gazed about him, taking in the beauty of the vast horizon, feeling small beneath the heavens yet not insignificant. He shook his head. 'I should have come up here sooner,' he said. 'If I had known it would make me feel like this, I would have.'

Margot handed him back the flask. He drained it. They both sighed with satisfaction. 'When you said you lost the will, JP, what did you mean?' she asked.

'I lost the will to do anything. To see anyone. To go any-where. I was overcome with a kind of inertia.'

'Because you sold the castle?'

'Because of the breakdown of my marriage.' He frowned and allowed his gaze to be drawn into the distant horizon. The sense of release he had found here in the hills now inspired him to share his pain. 'I felt terribly guilty, Margot. I hurt the people closest to me. The people I loved most in the world. Because of me they lost their family and their home. If it wasn't for me we'd be a family still and our home would still be our home.'

'Maybe the castle was too much for you? After all, you'd been brought up in a smaller house and without great wealth. Was it, in the end, an unbearable burden?'

He looked at her steadily and smiled. 'You're very sharp, Margot, aren't you? No flies on you.'

'I'm just curious. Not for my book, JP, but because we're friends.' She grinned playfully. 'We've shared a gallop.'

He laughed with her. 'That does make a difference,' he agreed. 'A gallop's a bond.'

'Look, the way I see it is this. You grow up without a care in the world. You're a Deverill, which is synonymous with "special". You are cherished and indulged and life is

uncomplicated. Then you meet your twin sister and your
world is turned upside down. All at once, the life you have
lived is a falsehood. You discover the truth about your mother.
The terrible truth. And the woman you have trusted above
all others, Kitty, has lied to you. What's more, her affair
with Alana's father nearly cheats you of happiness. Then you
unexpectedly inherit the castle. The family home that comes
at a price: the great weight of responsibility. This is not an
ordinary home. It's the very heart of the Deverill family and
it is up to *you* to keep it beating. If you don't, your family
will not survive. All those Deverill heirs will turn in their
graves and you will be damned. Isn't that right? *A Deverill's
castle is his kingdom.* But something's missing. The focus on the
castle is blinkered. That's all one sees: the castle, its legacy, its
future, its enormous significance. But it's just a castle. What's
more important is the people inside it. Were you, perhaps, too
absorbed in the castle and what it meant to the Deverills that
you neglected your wife and children?'

JP considered her words. Chewing on them as if they were
bitter, unpalatable truths. Blowing smoke into the wind. 'I
started drinking,' he confessed quietly. He took off his hat
and scratched his head. The wind caught tufts of hair and
blew them about mischievously. He said nothing for a while.
The shrill cry of a curlew rose above the drone of the sea and
Margot waited, sensing he needed to share his story, but wasn't
sure how to tell it.

JP sighed, letting the air out of his lungs in a loud whoosh,
as if it had cost him to admit his drinking habit and yet, at the
same time, liberated him from the burden of a dirty secret.
'We had three children, Alana and I. Three beautiful children.
But Alana wanted another one. An after-thought. By then
Aisling was fourteen and our youngest ten. I didn't want any

more. I was already struggling to cope with my past, but no one wanted to acknowledge that. No one wanted to know. No one *listened.*' His face flashed with fury. He took another gulp of air and shook his head. His lips thinned, his chin trembled. He and Alana had been divorced for fourteen years and still the gash it had made glistened with fresh pain. 'Alana didn't care,' he continued in a flat voice. 'All she thought about was the children. I may as well not have been there. My father sought relief in the bottle and I suppose I followed him down that road. I won't deny it. But Alana played me. She agreed that we wouldn't have any more children, but she only said that in order to get her way. When she told me she was expecting a baby, I didn't celebrate it as I should have. I reacted badly. I felt betrayed and furious. Hurt, she stopped talking to me. I withdrew. I isolated her, she and her unborn baby, and shut myself out.' He lowered his chin and his gaze dropped into his hands. 'I sought comfort in another woman.'

So the rumour was right. 'And Alana found out?'

'Only after she miscarried at six months.'

Margot sucked air through her teeth. 'Ouch!'

'Her father had an affair with Kitty, which cut her deeply.'

'Then *you* did it to *her.* I understand why she didn't forgive you. Who was it with?'

JP shook his head. He did not want to elaborate further. 'No one of any importance.' He put his hat back on and tossed his cigarette butt onto the grass. 'It's been a downward spiral ever since. I made a mistake. A grave mistake. A mistake I'll regret for the rest of my life, and there's nothing I can do about it.' He gathered himself. The wind had picked up and a wall of grey clouds was slowly making its way towards them, shutting out the sunlight and dampening the air. He sighed and Margot sensed he wasn't going to say any more. What more was there to say? 'We must get back for Mrs D's lunch,' he suggested. 'We don't want to keep her waiting.' He spurred his horse on and they headed off down the hill towards home.

'I'm sorry, JP,' said Margot.

He acknowledged her sympathy with a nod. 'I'm sorry too, but I've only got myself to blame.'

'Do you blame Alana for wanting another child?'

'I blame her for luring me into it under false pretences. I suppose she thought that she could win me over once she'd got pregnant. Once she'd lost the child she rejected my sympathy as disingenuous because I never wanted it in the first place. When I tried to comfort her she rebuffed me. I couldn't win.'

'The affair ensured that you lost,' said Margot.

'I couldn't come back from that.'

They rode on in silence.

Any guilt that JP felt at having confided in a woman he barely knew, who was writing a book about his family, was shunted aside with the justification that Alana had only ever considered *her* side of the story. She had told her family and their children her version of events, and no one had ever listened to *him*. They had been so quick to blame him, while only knowing half the story. Well, if they refused to hear his words, they could read them on the page, in black and white. If they didn't like it, they could lump it. He had nothing to lose; he'd lost everything already.

Margot ruminated on what JP had just told her. It was quite a story. Intimate and damning, yet so human. It was the story Colm did not want her to know. As she followed JP back along the path she wondered whether Colm had a point. She *shouldn't* know it. It was too personal. It made her cringe to think of it in print. Then she reminded herself that she must remain detached. If JP took it upon himself to tell his story, then it was her job to write it. She had no responsibility to anyone, only to herself. Her focus was to write the best book about the family that she could write, and allow nothing, including emotions and a misplaced sense of loyalty, to get in the way. This was her job. This was what she did. She told herself to keep her eyes on the story and not be distracted by her empathy for the protagonists.

Mrs B had cooked a delicious lunch, just as she had said she would. She had laid the table with care and lit the fire. JP consumed a whole bottle of red wine. Margot drank nothing. She didn't like to drink alcohol in the day because it made her sleepy, and it went against the grain to waste time taking siestas unless she found someone attractive to share them with. JP was elated by their ride and the wine and told Margot again how he had lived for riding as a young man. 'If I was unhappy, I'd head onto the cliffs on my horse. If I was happy, I'd do the same. My life was defined by it. It's what we Deverills did.'

After lunch they went into the library. JP took the top off the whiskey decanter. He had confessed to turning to the bottle for comfort when he had been unhappy during his marriage. He clearly did not recognize that he had a problem *now*. He didn't try to hide it from Margot, or from Mrs B. There was no embarrassment as he knocked it back and refilled his glass, no apology. Margot felt a sick feeling building in her stomach. She had seen all this before. She tried to detach, not to feel responsible, but it was becoming impossible because she had grown fond of him. She'd been in Ballinakelly just over two weeks, and yet, she felt she had known JP for ever. It wasn't just that she felt she knew *him*, the man, but that she knew their dynamic. She had lived it before, this pattern of alcoholic and saviour.

When JP sat by the fire she excused herself.

'You're off, are you?' he said, without getting up. Margot wasn't sure he *could* get up.

'Yes, I've got work to do.'

'Of course you have,' he said and he blinked at her sleepily, as if trying hard to stay awake.

'I'll be back soon. There's still lots to go through in those boxes.'

'Good. You can come whenever you like. Mrs B will look after you. Might be an idea to telephone her so she can light the fire. Don't want you to get cold. Can get very cold in there. Always did.'

'Thank you, JP.' She left him nodding off in the front of the fire.

She found Mrs B in the hall. 'The two of you had a whale of a time out there, didn't you?' she said with a smile. 'I haven't seen him this happy in years.'

'I think he's been lonely.'

'Indeed, he has, the poor old creature.'

'Of course, *you're* here to keep him company.'

'We both know it's not the same,' said Mrs B, looking at Margot with her gentle gaze. 'Blood is thicker than water.'

'I know. Of course it is.'

Mrs B shook her head. 'He needs to make up with his family. That's what needs to be done and I have me knees worn out praying for it.'

'Do you have family, Mrs B?' she asked.

The old woman smiled with tenderness. 'Lord Deverill is all the family I have now,' she said. 'Which is why I care, Miss Hart. God keep him safe and protect him from all harm.' She crossed herself. 'Though, I'm not sure even God can protect him from himself and the lure of the bottle.'

Margot left the house and Mrs B closed the door behind her and padded down the corridor to the library. There she found her master slumped in his armchair, snoring loudly. The crystal tumbler lay loosely in his hand, the whiskey decanter on the table beside him. Both were empty. She glanced at her watch. It had only just gone three and he had already passed out. Mrs B sighed. Anxiety squeezed her stomach with its habitual cold grip. It wasn't healthy to drink so much, but it was Irish. She knew many who had lived to a great old age in spite of consuming vast quantities of alcohol. Still, there were just as many whose lives had been cut short by it. Mrs B hoped Lord Deverill would be inspired to conquer the addiction, but it didn't seem likely; it had been years and so far inspiration hadn't come.

Leaving him asleep she took the radio upstairs into the attic where her bedroom was, small and tidy beneath the eaves. She plugged it into the wall and switched it on. Once again classical music filled her heart with its uplifting harmonies. The music was balm to her soul. It made her feel positive. She placed the radio on the chest of drawers then picked up a box of matches and struck one. In front of four black-and-white photographs in simple leather frames were four votive candles. One by one, she lit them, muttering a prayer for each departed soul. 'Until we meet again, may God hold you in the palm of His hand.' In turn the faces of her family were illuminated in the glowing candlelight. Her mother and father, her older brother who had lost his life in the civil war when he was only seventeen and her husband who had died of leukaemia some twenty-seven years ago. They had not been blessed with children, she and Alfie. She had done her best but her body had been unable to hold them. Twelve miscarriages. Twelve disappointments. Twelve souls who had tried and failed to come into the world. But God works in mysterious ways and perhaps she wasn't meant to have them. She was meant to look after other people's children. Deverill children.

Now she looked after JP.

She slipped off her shoes and lay on the bed. Then she closed her eyes and allowed the music to wash over her, rinsing away the pain, releasing anxiety's grip, restoring her troubled spirit. She missed her parents and her husband, but she missed her brother most of all. The golden-haired brother she had looked up to and adored who had been taken from her when she was only thirteen. She squeezed her eyes shut and felt a tear trickle down her temple into her hair. It still hurt after all these years. A wound that never healed. *If you can hear me, Rafferty, know that I love you. That I'll always love you, and one day, when I die, I'll join you in Heaven. Isn't that what the Bible teaches us? A cross in this life, a crown in the next?*

How soothing the music was. How wonderful not to have to endure the silence. She could almost see Rafferty now, in her mind's eye, standing beside her, taking her hand. She could almost feel it. His skin against hers, warm and soft and deeply reassuring. Just like it used to be when she was a child. The music played on and Bessie Brogan fell asleep.

Chapter 8

That night Margot felt strangely low. She had adored riding out over the hills, but lunch with JP afterwards had been depressing. It wasn't their conversation and it certainly wasn't the food. She didn't mind the lonely atmosphere in the house: there was a tranquillity about it that appealed to her. What had affected her was his slow decline into inebriation. He didn't behave badly, he just slipped away. At the end of the meal she knew she had lost him. He had shuffled into the library, staggered to his chair and sunk into a drunken stupor. She had been assaulted by a feeling of helplessness so familiar to her that she was left with no option other than to leave as quickly as possible. To run from it. To find someone healthy to hold on to.

Seamus was only too happy to oblige. In his arms she was brought safely into the present moment. The past receded, with all its associated unhappiness, and she felt herself once more the person she was *now*, the person she wanted to be.

Margot had arranged to meet Countess di Marcantonio the following morning at the hotel. She had telephoned her office a few days before and spoken to her PA. The meeting had been arranged, and the PA, a breathless young woman with a tremulous voice, had told Margot how eager the Countess was

to see her husband's 'family home' again. Margot had made all
the right noises and the PA had sounded relieved, confirming
the meeting for eleven o'clock.

Margot waited in the hall at 10.45. It was a quiet morning.
Outside, the fog had settled over the estate, muting the colours
and giving the hotel an eerie air. Inside, the fire crackled and
the electric lights shone warmly. Mr Dukelow was loitering,
his polished black shoes gliding smoothly over the carpet as he
pretended to be busy. Róisín was as alert as a watchful rabbit,
eyes sliding every few moments to the door to see whether
the special guest was arriving. Margot's gaze was drawn to
the portrait of Barton Deverill. She wondered what he would
make of his home now. At least Mrs de Lisle had done a good
job, she thought. It might not be the home he had intended it
to be, but it was still magnificent.

At last a shiny Mercedes drew up in front of the hotel.
A porter hurried outside to assist. The chauffeur, dressed
in a black suit, cap and gloves, stepped out briskly and held
open the rear passenger door. The Countess appeared to be
in no hurry. She gathered herself while the porter waited
patiently on the gravel and Mr Dukelow and Róisín watched
with nervous anticipation from the hall. Margot was curious
to see what the Countess looked like. Judging by the letter
and the assistant's reverential tone, she expected her to be
very grand.

When the Countess stepped out Margot was surprised to
see that she was a lot younger than she had imagined. In her
late forties, perhaps. A great deal younger than her husband
who must have been in his late sixties. She was wrapped in
a mink coat that reached below her knees and a matching
pillbox hat. Her face was long and angular with high, chis-
elled cheekbones and thin scarlet lips. Her black hair, as shiny

as a raven's wing, was visible beneath the hat, tied into an elegant chignon at the nape of her neck. She carried herself in a stately fashion. The porter opened the front door and she swept in. Mr Dukelow put out his hand and welcomed her in a gushing sequence of superlatives. Margot was certain he bowed. The Countess's thin mouth smiled graciously, her imperious slate-grey gaze sizing him up like a hawk with its prey. She was obviously used to this kind of reception and didn't find it in the least theatrical, nor did she feel inclined to be grateful. It was her due. Margot was unimpressed. The Countess had been a secretary at the Austrian Embassy in London before she had married Leopoldo, so had little to be arrogant about.

'You must be Miss Hart,' she said, reaching out to shake her hand. She slipped out of her coat and held it out for Mr Dukelow. She lifted her hat off her head and held that out too. Mr Dukelow gave both items to Róisín who had left the reception desk unattended in her eagerness to make herself useful to their distinguished guest. Her face was full of awe at the sight of this striking woman, who had the remote glamour of a Hollywood movie star. She was wearing an elegant black dress printed with white polka dots, a shiny black belt and a large pearl choker at her throat. Its central clasp was made up of three large gold-and-diamond bees. She pressed her hand to her bosom and sighed. 'I am moved,' she declared in a brusque Austrian accent, running her eyes around the hall. 'This was once my husband's family home. It would have been *our* home if things had been done in the way they should. But life isn't always fair, is it?' She smiled tightly at Margot. 'Well, where shall we go to talk?'

Mr Dukelow escorted them through the castle to Mrs de Lisle's private sitting room situated away from the bustle of the hotel. There were armchairs and sofas assembled neatly around a fireplace. A fire burned hospitably.

'Ghastly weather,' complained the Countess. 'Poor Roach had to drive as slowly as a tortoise to get here.' The two women sat down. The Countess on one of the sofas, Margot on an armchair, closer to the fire. Margot opened her notebook and held her pen poised.

'So you're writing a history of the Deverill family,' she began, fixing Margot with cool, unemotional eyes. 'When Angela de Lisle told me, I jumped at the opportunity to talk to you. It's important that you speak to everyone involved. That you don't just talk to the Deverills.'

So Mrs de Lisle told her, thought Margot suspiciously. She wondered what her motive was for doing so. 'I agree,' she replied. 'I do want to write a balanced account.'

The Countess's face hardened. 'My husband was cheated out of his inheritance by his mother, which cut him to the quick. Can you imagine your own mother doing such a thing? I'm sure you cannot.'

Having an inheritance to be cheated out of was something Margot couldn't imagine at all.

'JP was her first child, and a Deverill, so I presume she thought she was doing the right thing,' she said.

The Countess was quick to jump to her husband's defence. 'The Count's father, Count Cesare, worshipped him. Had he lived, he would never have allowed his home to pass into the hands of a Deverill.'

Margot narrowed her eyes. 'I don't wish to speak out of turn, but is it not true that it was Bridie's money that bought the castle?'

The Countess stiffened and she lifted her chin. 'Let me tell you a little about my husband's family, Miss Hart. Count

Leopoldo is descended from Cardinal Maffeo Barberini of Rome who became Pope Urban XIII in 1623. His grand-mother was a princess. The Barberini palace in Rome was completed by the famous Bernini in 1633 and is now *La Galleria Nazionale d'Arte Antica*. His family were illustrious and fabulously wealthy.' She placed her long fingers over the bee clasp at her throat. 'The family coat of arms is three bees. The famous Barberini bees, which are carved into architecture all over Rome, illustrating their power. This choker was one of the Princess's treasures, handed down the generations to my Leopoldo.' Margot wanted to point out that it had only been *two* generations, but she didn't think the Countess would appreciate her pedantry. 'Have you been to Rome, Miss Hart?'

'Yes, I have,' Margot replied.

'Then you might have seen the famous *Baldacchino di San Pietro, L'Altare di Bernini*.'

'St Peter's Baldachin,' Margot translated. She did not have the patience for pretentiousness, even though the Countess clearly spoke fluent Italian.

'Then you will know that there are four plinths that hold up the pillars of that magnificent canopy. On each of the two outer sides of each plinth are the Barberini bees. You cannot miss them. They are enormous and flamboyant, as is the whole *Baldacchino*. Those bees are there as symbols of the Barberini family's supremacy and influence.'

'Well, three hundred years ago. I'm not sure they have any influence now.'

'The point is, Miss Hart, and I'm surprised that I have to labour it, my husband's family is wealthy in its own right. As they say, money marries money. That was the case with the Count's parents.' Margot wished she'd just call him Leopoldo.

The Countess glanced at Margot's notebook. 'Are you writing this down?' she asked, looking put out.

'Absolutely,' said Margot, hastily scribbling onto the page the words *Barberini, Urban XIII, bees.*

'Going back to the inheritance and putting one's emotions to one side,' she continued, 'JP is a Deverill, so wasn't it right that he should inherit the castle? After all, it was built by a Deverill and had been in the family for nearly three hundred years.'

'Of course not!' the Countess retorted impatiently. 'JP is illegitimate. His father behaved atrociously. Bridie was only seventeen years old when he took her for his pleasure! If it wasn't for Bridie's brother, Michael, JP would have ended up in America and Ballinakelly and the Deverills would never have heard of him again. But he was spirited out of the convent and placed on Bertie Deverill's doorstep. You know the history, I'm sure. The point is, Miss Hart, Bridie left him the castle because she felt guilty. That's all it is, guilt. She was sick. Dying of cancer. At that moment, when her life was ebbing away, she decided to do what she believed to be the right thing. But she was not in her right mind. Goodness knows who turned her. My money is on Kitty Deverill. Why would Bridie disinherit the son she shared with her beloved husband? The son she had brought up from birth? In favour of the son she never knew, or held, or loved. How can you love someone you have never met? You can't. You love the idea, but that is not love, that is fantasy. You see, it was purely out of guilt that my husband was denied his rightful home, not to mention the fortune that went with it.' Her nostrils flared and her lips shrunk into a tight little line.

'Was he completely excluded from the will?'

'He was given money in a trust,' the Countess replied,

dismissing it as but a trifle. 'He had to ask his uncle every time he wanted it. Imagine? How humiliating! If you knew the Count you would understand. He is a proud man and his mother humiliated him.'

'Why would Bridie have given the castle and money to JP with *no* strings attached, but money in a trust to Leopoldo with *many* strings attached? Did she not trust him to manage his money?' Margot suspected she knew the answer but she was curious to hear what the Countess had to say.

'He was flamboyant. He liked to live the high life.' The Countess smiled and her eyes shone with a feverish sheen. 'My husband has more character than all the Deverills put together. They think they're so bold and fascinating but my husband puts them all in the shade, Miss Hart.'

'Perhaps it wasn't such a good idea after all, leaving JP the castle. He lost it *and* his fortune.'

'You're right,' the Countess replied vigorously, pleased that Margot understood. 'The Count would never have let it go. He would never have become an alcoholic and squandered all his money. Shameful! That's what it is. Shameful!'

'Your husband has clearly done well for himself. You have houses all over the world. You lead an enviable life. If he didn't inherit a fortune, he must have made one.'

'He is an entrepreneur, like his father and grandfather before him. Whatever he touches turns to gold.'

'Then why didn't he buy back his home when JP was forced to sell it?'

The Countess squirmed then and Margot sensed she had caught her out. The older woman gave her head a little shake, as if playing for time, or frantically trying to think of a convincing reason. Margot wasn't sure she was hearing much truth in the Countess's account. 'By the time the Count heard about the sale, Mrs de Lisle had already made her offer and JP had accepted it. Too late. *Tant pis.*' She shrugged and gave a little sniff. The kind of sniff one does after telling an appalling lie.

'Do you know JP, Countess?'

Again the woman lifted her chin and stiffened her jaw. 'I have met him. After all, he is my husband's half-brother. But I don't know him. The two men have never been friends. After Bridie left the castle to JP, my husband left Ireland altogether and settled in London.'

'But he bought a house in Dublin.'

'I persuaded him to buy it. He spent fourteen years of his life in Ballinakelly. It grieved him to leave it. We have kept one eye on his former home all these years. It has become something of an obsession. Understandable, don't you think, considering the circumstances?' She sighed regretfully and swept her eyes over the walls. 'Now it is a hotel. Angela de Lisle has done a good job, but it should really have remained a home. *Our* home. Did you notice the Deverill motto carved in stone above the door? The Count's father, Count Cesare, covered it with the Barberini bees, but when JP moved in, he took them down and displayed the Deverill motto again. Those bees have more prestige than those words in Latin ever could.' She drained her teacup. 'I would have been a superb hostess. I would have filled this castle with the highest in the land and made it great again.'

Margot smiled. 'It's full of people now and, in a way, it *is* great again. It's still relatively new, but I'd say it has the potential to be one of the best hotels in the world.'

'It will never belong to a Deverill again. That era is over. The Deverills are over.'

Suddenly, the temperature in the room dived and a shiver

rippled across Margot's skin. The Countess frowned irritably and turned towards the windows to see where the draught was coming from. The windows, however, were firmly shut. The two women looked at each other in puzzlement, words caught in their throats, as if sensing something strange was about to happen. A vibration shook the air – an invisible force, but they both felt it, the chill and the movement. The flames in the grate spluttered then flared.

'The Count has always maintained that this place is haunted,' she whispered.

'It's not haunted,' said Margot firmly, but she was beginning to doubt her conviction. 'I don't believe in the supernatural.'

'Neither do I, but ghosts are not supernatural. They're part of life. People who have passed and have not found their way into the next world. Lost people. Sad people.' The Countess lifted her chin and inhaled through dilated nostrils.

'I think you're probably right that the Deverills will never own the castle again, although that family has a talent for rising out of the ashes, doesn't it,' Margot continued, trying to regain her composure.

'There will be no phoenix this time. JP is lost, lost in the bottom of his whiskey bottle. Such a shame. You know he was handsome and dashing in his day. But he's weak. He lost his wife thanks to his weakness.'

'Infidelity does seem to run down the male line, doesn't it.'

'Indeed, it does,' the Countess agreed. 'His father with a maid. He with the governess.' Margot did not reveal her surprise. She just nodded and gave the Countess space to elaborate. 'If you're going to have an affair you don't do it on your own doorstep. You do it far away and preferably with someone who has as much to lose as you do. The governess, indeed. Those children adored her. What a betrayal. I wouldn't be at

all surprised if Colin doesn't end up an alcoholic as well. You
see, they're toxic. All of them.' She shook her head and looked
at Margot steadily, holding her gaze. 'You have been making
notes, haven't you, Miss Hart?'

'I have,' Margot reassured her. 'I also have a very good
memory. May I ask, is it common knowledge that JP's affair
was with the governess?'

'Of course not,' said the Countess, giving Margot a sly,
conspiratorial smile. 'I have my sources, so you can trust me
not to mislead you. People suspected an affair. But I know
for certain.'

'This governess, where is she now?'

'I'm afraid you'll get nothing out of her. She moved to
Canada. I wouldn't even know where in Canada she is.'

'I see.' Margot was disappointed. She'd like to have
spoken to her.

'She was a young Englishwoman from a good family. A
country girl. She was not fast. It was not a case of her seducing
her boss. Far from it. But a case of him seducing her. Like you
said, infidelity runs down the male line in that family.'

Margot imagined JP turning to the governess out of unhappiness and a need to be comforted. 'There are always two sides
to every story,' she said.

'But each side does not necessarily carry the same weight.
I pity poor Alana, JP's wife. I'm not surprised she divorced
him. What a mess.'

'It seems to me that the castle hasn't brought anyone much
happiness.'

'If you're implying that it's cursed, you are wrong. It's the
Deverill *family* that is cursed, not the castle. Or perhaps it is
karma. The castle should never have been left to JP and in the
end he paid for that wrongdoing.'

'I don't think karma works like that. If it was a wrongdoing, it was not his but his mother's.'

The Countess gave her head an impatient little shake. 'It was wrong, *punto*.' She watched Margot write something down. 'You must keep me in touch with your research. If you need any further help, do call me. You know where I am.'

'But you travel so much, between all your various homes,' said Margot.

'We will be in Dublin for the foreseeable future. I will be happy to come again. I do so love to spend time in the Count's ancestral home, even though it gives me pain each time I visit.'

'And how does the Count feel?' Margot asked.

The Countess's face hardened. 'He will never forgive his mother, or his half-brother. JP should have shared his inheritance. But he didn't. He kept it all to himself. Shameful! Put that in your book. I hope it's not going to be full of fluff and puff, Miss Hart. I hope you're going to write a proper history of the truth.'

'That is my intention.'

'Good.' The Countess stood up. 'Well, it's been a pleasure meeting you. I hope I have been helpful.'

'You have, very helpful.'

'I'm so pleased. My husband is much too dignified to speak about the injustice he has suffered, but I am not. That is not to say that I am not dignified, you won't find a more dignified woman in the whole of Ireland, but the truth means a lot to me and I cannot abide injustice anywhere. I have to speak out. It is in my nature to be honest.'

'It's important to have both JP and Leopoldo's side of the story,' said Margot.

The Countess flinched as Margot used her husband's first name without his title. 'I'm sure the Deverills have erased the Count from their history,' she said with emphasis on the word 'Count'. 'I'm glad I had the opportunity to set the record straight. Now, where is the manager? I need to let Roach know that I am ready to depart. I do hope that fog has lifted.'

Kitty

I am furious. I am completely and utterly consumed by fury. How I despise that pretentious, lying woman! How dare she suggest that Leopoldo should have inherited the castle. How dare she! Leopoldo's father, Count Cesare di Marcantonio, was a fraud. He had no money of his own and the title was invented by his scoundrel of a father who lived a dissolute life on the back of it, fooling everyone he met that he was a wealthy Italian aristocrat. Leopoldo is as related to the Barberini family of Rome as I am to the Pope! And his father was murdered by Michael Doyle, caught red-handed running off with Bridie's money and his lover. Bridie's brother Michael was never going to allow that to happen. He dealt with the Count in the way he knew best. A horrible death. But Michael specialized in those.

However, the Countess has enlightened me on one thing: that JP had an affair with his children's governess. No wonder Alana was angry and hurt. But I am not one to cast judgement after the way I behaved in my life. Perhaps Margot and the Countess are right that infidelity runs in the family, although not just in the male line. I have sinned in loving Jack, but I do not regret it. Not for a moment. I am only sorry that we hurt people. I will never be sorry for my love.

Three days go by and Margot does not visit the Hunting Lodge. JP is restless and irritable. The house descends once more into silence. The only sound is the regular, mournful ticking of the grandfather clock, which is an affront to Mrs B now that she has rediscovered the radio. 'Has Miss Hart called?' JP asks her hopefully each time she passes the library. 'We mustn't let that room get cold.'

'No, m'lord. I've heard nothing,' Mrs B replies.

JP's shoulders drop in disappointment.

Someone else is disappointed too. Colm. He turns up daily, claiming to be interested in the family history, but JP does not bother to light a fire in the games room for *him*.

'Where's Miss Hart?' he asks his father casually one evening, having taken Hermione Deverill's diary into the library to peruse beside the fire.

'Busy researching, I suspect,' his father replies from the armchair where he is reading the *Irish Times*.

'She hasn't been here in days.'

'Three,' says JP, who has been counting.

'She hasn't finished with these yet, has she?' Colm asks, holding up the diary. 'I mean, it doesn't look like she's even halfway through those boxes.'

JP grins. 'I've been distracting her. Keeping her from her work. She likes to talk. She's good company. I've been rather starved of good company.'

Colm does not allow his father to make him feel guilty for being an inattentive son. As far as he sees it, JP alienated his family all on his own. 'You took her out riding,' he says.

'Indeed. She's a surprisingly good horsewoman.'

Colm raises his eyebrows. He did not expect that. 'Confident, isn't she.'

JP stares into his whiskey glass, astonished that it emptied so quickly. He seems not to remember having drunk at all. He pushes himself off his armchair and makes his way slowly across the floor to pour another. 'What do you mean? She's a modern woman, that's what she is. Independent. Has a mind of her own, and opinions. Lots of opinions. She's certainly no wallflower.'

I sense a sucking in of energy around Colm as they discuss Margot. He resents her inveigling her way into JP's confidence to prise out secrets which shouldn't be aired. But he's clever enough to know that distancing himself from the two of them will only make an island out of them and encourage collusion. He needs to get close and see if he can influence things from the inside.

'I was wrong about her,' he says.

His father has refilled his glass and is now ensconced back in his armchair. 'I'm glad you're decent enough to admit that, Colm,' he replies.

'She's just doing her job, after all. I suppose I should accept that our family was once great and be flattered that someone wants to write about us.'

'I'm only surprised that no one's wanted to write about us before. Of course, there have been small pieces here and there. Short accounts in the odd book about the Anglo-Irish and castles. But this is the Deverill family history from the beginning. From the moment the castle was built and our family name built with it. It'll be very interesting to read. I suspect she's a clever girl.'

'I gather she wrote a book about Eva Perón of Argentina. I might see if I can get my hands on a copy.'

'Good idea.'

'Although, I think I'd rather read about the woman's husband,' says Colm.

'Don't tell *her* that,' his father adds. Colm glances at him. When he sees the jocular twinkle in his eyes, he grins. It has been years since *they've* colluded.

That evening, when Colm goes to O'Donovan's for his usual glass of stout, he finds, to his surprise, Margot perched on a stool at the bar, talking to Seamus as he serves drinks behind it. Colm has made it clear that he does not like her. However, I sense that it's the job she's doing that he dislikes, not the person she is. He cannot help but be intrigued by *her*. He is a man, after all, and she is an attractive woman. *I* was an attractive woman in my day, beautiful even, and I know well that look on a man's face when he is interested. Colm is interested. Margot is less easy to read. In fact, she's closed as tightly as a clam.

'Do you mind if I join you?' he asks, taking off his cap and running his fingers through his hair. He has thick hair like all Deverill men – thick hair, good looks and a talent for making life difficult for himself.

'If you like,' she replies. That's not exactly an invitation, but Colm sits down anyway and places his cap on the bar.

Seamus fills a pint glass with stout. He watches the two converse and I sense him bristle with possessiveness, like a territorial dog sensing a rival stepping into his domain.

'I've been at Dad's,' Colm tells her. 'He's missing your company.'

'He does seem rather lonely,' she replies.

'He needs to get out more.'

'He needs to quit drinking,' she says seriously.

'That too,' Colm agrees, averting his eyes. There's an awkward pause. Colm does not want to go into his father's drinking problem. He is aware that anything he says might go into her book. Seamus slides the glass of stout across the bar. Colm changes the subject and asks Margot about herself. 'How did you like your ride?'

'I adored it.' She smiles. She is lovely when she smiles. One could be fooled into thinking that she hasn't a care in the world. I'm beginning to realize, however, that she has many, she's just good at hiding them. 'There's something very special about these hills. I've travelled a lot, but there's something deep and magical about this place that I haven't found anywhere else.'

Colm smiles back and he's not pretending. He is genuinely pleased that she senses the enchantment in the land that we Irish have always known is there. 'I'm glad you feel it too.'

'I felt a great relief out there. A weight lifted. A rush of wildness, of recklessness.' Her eyes sparkle at the memory of it. 'It was wonderful.'

'My grandmother told me you have Irish blood in you?'

'I do. My grandfather was Anglo-Irish, if that counts.'

'It counts. My aunt Kitty always referred to herself as Irish even though, technically, she was *Anglo*-Irish.'

'I don't think I can claim to be either.'

'But that wild and reckless streak is there, undeniably. Inherited from your grandfather, no doubt. Maybe you unleashed it in the hills.'

'Perhaps. I'd like to do it again.'

'Dad would too. He said you're a good rider. He'd jump at the chance to ride out with you again.'

'Then I'll ask him. Maybe, if I do it enough, I'll discover my inner Irishwoman.'

'Anything is possible.' Colm is grinning in spite of himself.

'My grandfather would have loved that. To him, the good old days hunting with the Deverills were the best days of his life.'

'So they were good friends, he and Harry?'

'They were. Grandpa died not long ago. But I remember all the wonderful stories he told about your uncle Harry and his father Bertie.'

'I'd like to hear them.'

As Margot shares her grandfather's anecdotes, I sense a warmth growing between them. Colm does not *want* to like her and Margot is aware that he resents her writing about his family. Yet, in spite of that they settle into an easy conversation as Seamus serves his regulars with one eye on the job and the other on the two of them. Margot doesn't look at Seamus. She feels no sense of obligation towards him just because she is sleeping with him. It is obvious that she is a woman who takes her pleasure where she finds it and thinks nothing of it. Seamus, coming from a small Irish town like Ballinakelly, is not used to women like her. The priest would call her sinful, others might call her a slut – but it's the 1980s, perhaps she is just modern – nonetheless, the fact that Seamus can't hold on to her makes him want her all the more.

'Where's home for you, Miss Hart?' Colm asks.

She shrugs. 'I don't really have a fixed abode, Mr Deverill.' Her eyes are full of laughter, which prompts him to say:

'That just sounds silly, doesn't it? The Miss Hart, Mr Deverill part.'

'If you're going to sit on the bar stool beside me and talk to me as a friend, then I'm Margot.'

He takes a sip of stout then wipes the foam off his top lip with his sleeve. 'So, Margot, if you don't have a home, where do you hang your hat?'

'My mother is French and lives in Paris. My father lived in Dorset but he died when I was a teenager, so I haven't considered that home in years.'

'I'm sorry.'

'Don't be. Life isn't a bed of roses for anyone. The trick is to live in the moment, isn't it.'

'That's the idea, but it's not so easy when you have things in the past that hurt.'

'I don't think about them.' Margot shrugs and makes it clear with a dismissive sniff that she does not want to think about them now either.

'You're a nomad, then?'

She grins, liking the sound of that. 'I have an English passport and a small flat in London. I return every now and then to open post, bills mostly, and make sure it's still there. Otherwise, I like to move about. I find travel invigorating.'

'You never get lonely on your own?'

'Sometimes. But I've made friends all over. Look, I've only been in Ballinakelly a few weeks and I've already made a new one.' She smiles at him, a charming, guileless smile.

He's not sure how to respond, but he raises his glass all the same. 'To new friends,' he says.

'New friends,' she repeats and clinks her glass against his.

Margot returns to her tower feeling lighter having shared a drink with Colm. She no longer feels like the enemy. She kicks off her shoes and lies on the bed. Then she telephones

Mrs Walbridge. She speaks to her most evenings, updating her on the latest developments. They talk for a long time and Margot tells her about her drink at O'Donovan's with Colm. Margot laughs at something Mrs Walbridge says and I sense a real affection growing between these two women.

Margot does not call her mother. I begin to wonder about her roots – or her aversion to them. I question why she goes through life avoiding lasting ties with people, moving from city to city, country to country, never staying very long in any one place. On the outside she appears contented, charming, carefree and uncomplicated. I'm beginning to realize that that is just a front. A disguise. A decoy. Who is Margot Hart and what is *her* story?

Chapter 9

At the beginning of February snowdrops began to poke their delicate white heads out of the earth and the castle gardens were imbued with the sweet scent of *Daphne odora*. The days felt longer, the light a little brighter, the sun bolder in its attempts to rid the land of the dark winter mornings and the chill. Margot was now feeling at home in Ballinakelly. She was making progress with her research and enjoying her excursions into the hills on horseback with JP and her forays between the sheets with Seamus. She would run into Colm at his father's house, where he was slowly being sucked into the fascinating abyss of his family history. He seemed to have forgotten his animosity towards her. Perhaps he was beginning to realize what a remarkable story his family's was and no longer resented her for wanting to write it.

Most evenings she found entertainment in O'Donovan's. There was usually live music, a folk or pop band or a lone musician with an accordion singing romantic ballads with tears in his eyes. Everyone knew the songs and the evening usually ended with the entire pub joining in. She was beginning to get to know the locals. Tomas and Aidan O'Rourke, who worked for Lord Deverill, were eager to play her at darts. Mr Flannigan to talk to her about ghosts and try to put his hand on her bottom – she avoided him as best she could, especially after he'd knocked back a few pints. Seamus was always there, busily drawing pints, keeping a possessive eye on her when Colm made her laugh, telling her funny tales of his adventures as a vet. She liked the gentle, slightly sleepy atmosphere in the pub, the fug of cigarette smoke and the open fire, the fact that people were slowly warming to her and no longer staring at her suspiciously when she walked in on her own.

One Sunday she decided to go to Mass. She wasn't Catholic. She wasn't really anything. Her mother had been brought up Catholic by her strict French parents, but her father had been Church of England until the war robbed him of his faith in God. How could God exist, he'd argued, in a world where there is such hatred and violence? He had been thirty-five when Margot was born and hadn't stepped into a church in eighteen years. He'd married in a registry office and Margot was neither baptised nor confirmed. She went to Mass in the Catholic Church of All Saints in Ballinakelly out of curiosity, not because she had any desire to pray or to listen to a priest whose sole mission seemed to be to make everyone feel guilty for being born. But churches were exotic, mysterious places for Margot on account of having been denied them. They were pungent with the vibrations of prayer, supplication and hope, heady with the smell of incense and tradition, and bitter with contradiction. Margot wondered at the conflict between the spiritual teachings of Jesus, which in essence were about love and forgiveness and the life after, and the club mentality of religion, which separated people from each other and made enemies of them. She sat on her chair and took in the beauty and harmony of the ancient building and yet she couldn't reconcile that beauty, which was spiritual, with the dogma, which wasn't.

At the end of Mass she remained in her chair while everyone filed out. She noticed Jack and Emer O'Leary and Colm, and various locals from the pub. Róisín was there with her parents and siblings, the younger children eager to get out into the sunshine, delighted that Mass was over for another week. Once most of the congregation had filed out, and more specifically Jack and Emer O'Leary, who she didn't think would be pleased to see her, Margot stood up. It was then that she noticed Mrs B, lighting votive candles on the table at the front of the church, to the right of the nave. She looked small there, alone with her prayers, passing the glowing taper from wick to wick. She was dressed in a long black skirt and shirt, a black shawl draped around her head and shoulders. There was something old-fashioned about her. She could easily have stepped out of one of those Victorian photographs Margot had been looking at in the Hunting Lodge. She wondered how old Mrs B was and decided that, although she looked younger due to her plumpness, she was likely to be in her seventies.

After a while Mrs B stood in front of the altar and genuflected. Then she turned and walked slowly down the aisle towards the doors. Margot went to greet her. 'Hello, Mrs B,' she said.

Mrs B raised her eyebrows in surprise and smiled. 'Why, this is the last place I would think I'd find you, Miss Hart.'

'I know. I'm not Catholic. I'm nothing. I just wanted to come and soak up the peace and quiet. It's a beautiful church, isn't it?'

'Indeed it is very beautiful.'

'It's a nice place to come and reflect on things.'

'Oh, it is. I come here to reflect a lot. I feel it's a place where God hears what I have to say.'

'Do you talk to God often, Mrs B?' Margot asked as they

walked towards the door and the sight of the gravel path and graveyard bathed in sunlight.

'Don't *you* talk to God, Miss Hart?' she asked.

'Not really.'

'Well, you should. You should show your gratitude for your blessings and pray for those you love, both alive and deceased.'

'I feel a bit silly talking to someone I can't see.'

'Then close your eyes.'

Margot laughed. 'I don't know why I didn't think of that.'

Once outside, Margot asked Mrs B where the Deverills were buried.

'Most of the family are buried alongside their fellow Protestants down the road. They had no airs and graces, you know. There's no grand family mausoleum or crypt. Some are scattered like Kitty and Arethusa. They wanted to be taken by the wind. They were free spirits, you see. You'll not find headstones for them.'

'Is your family buried here, Mrs B?'

'Indeed they are.' She walked slowly across the grass, past ancient headstones blackened by age, the words carved into them corroded by years of wind and rain so they could barely be read. Some leaned precariously, others stood proud. There were all sizes, from the small and modest to the large and showy, and some were coated in green moss and lichen. Mrs B stopped. 'This is where my brother lies buried,' she said softly.

Margot joined her. She read the words inscribed on the simple stone. *Rafferty Brandon Carbery 1906–1923.* 'He died young,' said Margot.

'Indeed, he did. He was only seventeen, God bless him.' Mrs B took a deep breath for it still shocked her to see his death so blatantly displayed in those two sets of dates carved into the stone. 'He was killed in the civil war. Irishman against

Irishman. Brother against brother. The young man who killed him was only a boy himself. They'd been at school together. They'd shared the same table, the same bread.' She shook her head incredulously and her eyes stung. Memories, like roses, have thorns.

'How old were you?'

'Thirteen. It was only the two of us. Me and Raffie. And I worshipped the ground he walked on.'

'I'm so sorry,' said Margot. 'You must carry the weight of loss with you always.'

'I do, Miss Hart. It's a load I'm glad to carry. It's me Garden of Gethsemane.'

Margot took her hand. Mrs B flinched. She wasn't used to being touched. In fact, she couldn't remember the last time someone had held her hand. But Margot's was warm and soft and the gesture was sincerely made. Mrs B felt the comfort in it and dropped her shoulders.

'I don't imagine one ever recovers from losing a sibling,' said Margot.

'The ache is always there,' Mrs B agreed. 'It's a quare thing, but there's a part of me that still can't quite believe he's gone. If I close me eyes and picture him, he's as real to me as if I close me eyes and think of *you*. Yet, I'm seventy-five. He's been gone sixty-two years. In me mind he's still the golden-haired youth who'd only just started shaving. If he had lived he'd be as grey as me by now.'

'I bet he was handsome.'

'Oh, he was, Miss Hart. A handsome devil, he was. He knew it, too. He got away with everything because of his looks, because of his smile.'

'I bet he loved his little sister.'

At that Mrs B hiccuped. She put a hand to her mouth,

stifling the sob that followed. Margot saw her face cave in with sorrow. She squeezed her hand, which released something inside the old woman for she began to cry. Margot remained beside her. She wanted to wrap her arms around her, but she didn't think Mrs B would feel comfortable with such a modern display of affection. Instead, she held her hand tightly and waited for her grief to work its way through her. At length she let it go. Mrs B reached into her pocket for a handkerchief and blew her nose. 'I'm sorry,' she said. 'I don't know what came over me.'

'It's okay,' Margot reassured her. 'Grief takes you by surprise, sometimes, doesn't it.' Mrs B nodded. 'Does it help, talking to God?' she asked.

'Oh, I wouldn't have survived had it not been for my faith,' she replied.

'I'd like to have faith,' said Margot suddenly.

'You don't have to go to church to find Him, Miss Hart. God is in beauty and there's beauty in everything. Music, nature, light. Next time you're in a beautiful place, up there on the hill with Lord Deverill, for example, look for Him there. I'm sure you'll find Him. He's love and you have a big heart, Miss Hart. He's already within you, just waiting to be recognized.'

'You know you can call me Margot.'

Mrs B smiled and wiped her eyes. 'You can call me Bessie. But not when we're in the Lodge. Then you have to call me Mrs B like everyone else. We might embarrass his lordship and the locals would think I was uppity.'

'Very well,' Margot replied. 'I like the name Bessie. It suits you.'

'Thank you. I like it too.'

'Are you heading back to the Hunting Lodge now?'

'Indeed I am.'

'Would you like a lift?'

'That would be grand.'

'Thank you for showing me your brother's grave.'

Mrs B put the handkerchief back in her pocket. 'Thank you for listening, Margot,' she replied.

That afternoon Margot put aside her research and went in search of JP. He wasn't in the library, although the fire was lit and his book and reading glasses were in their usual place on the table beside his chair. She called his name, but there was no reply. At length, she found Mrs B in the kitchen, listening to the radio while she prepared stew for supper. It was heartening to hear music instead of the ticking of the grandfather clock and the silence. It suffused the house with life, as if it was able to seep into the cracks in the floorboards and restore the very bones of the building to health. Mrs B smiled when she saw her. The music had revived her too and her cheeks glowed with a faint blush. When Margot enquired after Lord Deverill Mrs B said she had seen him wander into the garden. 'He's begun to take an interest in it suddenly,' she informed her with a frown. 'He used to love to be in nature, but that was before . . .' Her voice trailed off, leaving details of the divorce and his alcoholism unspoken in the air between them. 'But he seems to have found a new lease of life recently,' she said, and she was certain she knew why. However, she felt it might embarrass Margot to attribute his renaissance to her and added simply, 'It's been a long time in coming.' She picked up her wooden spoon and began to stir the stew.

Margot went out into the sunshine. Swathes of snowdrops

covered the ground in puddles of white and dark green daffodil shoots were already emerging out of the earth. Birdsong filled the air and inflated Margot's spirits with pleasure, for spring was ushering in longer days, brighter light and a warm, sugar-scented breeze that gently roused the trees and shrubbery from their long winter sleep. As she walked across the lawn she was sure she could feel a deep stirring beneath her feet, before dismissing it as fancy. She smiled at her lunacy. She'd been in Ballinakelly for just over a month and she was already going mad. If she wasn't careful she'd be seeing leprechauns next!

JP was in the border cutting back a viburnum whose winter flowers were now over. He was in a pair of yellow corduroy trousers and V-neck sweater, with a stripy scarf about his neck. Margot called to him as she approached. 'Well, look at you!' she said, smiling broadly.

He paused his work and returned her smile with a cheerful one of his own. 'It feels good to be outside.'

'It's a lovely day. Would be a shame to waste it inside.'

'Do you want to make yourself useful?'

'Sure, although, I confess I'm not at all green-fingered.'

'I used to be, a long time ago. It's coming back to me slowly. There's another pair of secateurs in that bag. You can help me cut back these shrubs.'

'Why do you prune them now?'

'It encourages growth, prevents disease, keeps the shape. Come, I'll show you how to do it properly.'

She laughed and burrowed in the brown canvas bag for the secateurs. 'Funny, I'd never take you for a gardener,' she said.

'I was many things once, Margot. I was funny, dashing, handsome – though I know that's hard for you to believe – and accomplished.'

'And now you're finding yourself again,' she added, joining him in the border brandishing the pair of secateurs.

'Something of me. The handsome and dashing bits I fear are gone for ever.'

'They're not important.'

'You don't believe that. Not a pretty girl like you.'

'Oh, they're perceived to be very important in the young, but when you're old, don't they become irrelevant? I'd like to think that when I'm old I won't care anymore. I'll eat cake without feeling guilty.'

'I don't think you'll ever stop caring. When you're used to being beautiful it must be hard to give it up.'

'We all grow old eventually. It's life's great leveller.'

'Some grow old more gracefully than others,' JP added. 'I've grown old rather *dis*gracefully, I'm afraid.'

'Well, you've kind of brought that upon yourself, haven't you?' Margot ventured boldly. 'You should quit smoking, you know.' She wanted to add that he should sober up as well, but somehow that subject felt too sensitive to mention.

'You're right, I should. But one step at a time, eh?'

She frowned at the implication that he had already taken one. 'Which step are you referring to, exactly?'

'I'm happy to inform you that I've already taken two,' he told her with a lofty smile.

'Oh, really?' She grinned cynically. As far as she could tell, his breath still smelt of whiskey as well as cigarettes.

'I've taken up riding again and now I'm gardening. Little by little reclaiming the old me. One step at a time, right?' She couldn't argue with that. He held up his secateurs. 'Now, let me show you how to prune a viburnum.'

It was already dark when Colm found the two of them in the library, drinking tea. Mrs B hastened into the kitchen to fetch another cup, a small but perceptible bounce in her gait. For years Colm and his father had barely spoken, the froideur almost tangible between them like a wall of ice, yet now the wall had thawed and the atmosphere was growing warm, even, as they rediscovered each other. She wondered whether Colm was better able to understand his father and his failings now because he was a man. No longer the boy who had watched his parents' marriage collapse. The boy who knew nothing about love, loss, disappointment and grief. Perhaps he was able to stand back and judge him with detachment rather than passion because he had experienced something of the vicissitudes of life himself and had learned empathy. She wasn't sure, but she hoped that this would be the start of a reconciliation between Lord Deverill and all his children. Perhaps eventually with Alana too.

She took the crockery down from the shelf and returned to the library, her happiness fragile due to habit, half-expecting to find them fighting like they used to. What she heard was laughter. In the midst of the laughter was Margot's feminine tone relating an anecdote about JP, imitating his voice irreverently. Mrs B entered the room to find Colm lounging on the sofa, tears of mirth running down his face, while his father smiled with amusement and pleasure in his armchair. Margot was standing in front of the fire with her hands on her hips, committing wholly to her imitation, but carrying it out with affection. Mrs B did not want to interrupt, so she stood in the doorway while Margot finished her impression.

'What do you make of that, Mrs B?' said JP with a chuckle when it was over. 'I think Margot would make a fine actress, don't you?'

'Oh, yes, indeed she would,' Mrs B replied. She smiled at Colm. 'I remember when you were a little boy, Master Colm, and you used to put on plays with your sisters.'

'Aisling always took the best parts for herself, if I recall,' said Colm.

'I think you fared better than Cara,' added his father.

'Poor Cara usually played a cat or a mouse,' said Mrs B, remembering with delight those innocent, carefree times before the castle walls had closed in on them.

'At least you had siblings to play with. I was always alone,' said Margot.

'Well, you have a good audience in us,' said Colm.

She gave a theatrical bow. 'Thank you.' And sat down. 'What else did you do, besides putting on plays?' she asked him.

'We used to play billiards. Most of the time we played rabbits.'

'What's rabbits?'

'Ah, rabbits!' sighed JP with nostalgia.

'It's a game played round the billiard table. Usually with lots of people. The idea is to keep the white ball moving by hitting it with the black ball, which you can only roll from either end of the table. One person after another grabs the black ball, runs to the end of the table and rolls it across the velvet to hit the white and keep it moving. If the white ball stops moving, you lose.'

'In my day, if you lost you had to remove a piece of clothing,' said JP.

'That's the whole idea, Dad,' said Colm.

Margot laughed. 'Sounds like a lot of fun. Let's play!'

'What, now?' said Colm.

'Yes, now.'

'I'm not sure I want to remove my clothes,' said JP, looking uncertain.

'We'll play for points,' Margot suggested. 'It's too cold to remove one's clothes anyhow.'

'I'll go and put another log on the fire,' said Mrs B, leaving the room.

'I'm excited,' said Margot, sitting down beside Colm. 'Rabbits sounds like my sort of game.' Then she grinned at Colm. 'The traditional way.'

Colm held her gaze. 'I've never played with two.'

'Perhaps you should find out if it works.' She smiled and Colm frowned. He wasn't sure whether she was propositioning him or simply making a joke.

'Oh, I have no doubt it will work,' he replied, deciding to take her comment lightly. 'I imagine it will be over rather quickly though.'

'I'm intrigued. Hurry up, Colm, or your father will fall asleep.'

'What! Me? I'm as awake as a sentry on duty.'

Margot noticed that JP was drinking tea. The whiskey decanter remained on the drinks tray, untouched. *One small step at a time*, she thought to herself.

While the fire crackled in the grate and the electric lights glowed warmly, Colm and JP demonstrated the rules of rabbits to Margot on the billiard table cleared of Margot's research. Being young, Colm was quicker around the table than his father, but less skilful. Years of experience had taught JP all the tricks. Colm threw himself about the room, keen to show Margot his prowess. JP was reminded of his youth and remembered with bittersweet nostalgia the times he had raced across the room with Bertie and Kitty, and then later, when Colm was just a boy and they had played rabbits at the billiard table in the castle. Margot watched both men with fascination as their affection for one another, dormant for so long, rematerialized in the jostling for the ball and the resurgence of old, familiar patterns. 'Ah, I remember that move!' exclaimed Colm in delight. 'But don't think you're going to out fox me, Old Fox!'

'Age will win the day every time. It's in the slow roll,' said JP, letting the black ball glide across the table, just out of Colm's reach, to brush the white one with a kiss, halting it and winning JP the point. 'Out foxed, Young Fox!' he declared, triumphant. Margot realized that those must have been the nicknames they had once had for each other. She wondered how long it had been since they'd used them.

'You ready, Margot?' said Colm, eyes gleaming with competitiveness.

'Absolutely,' Margot replied, rolling up her shirtsleeves.

'You start, seeing as it's your first time.' He handed her the black ball then placed the white one in the middle of the table. 'Okay, ready when you are.'

Margot took aim then rolled the ball across the velvet, hitting the white ball at an angle. Colm grabbed the black and walked calmly to the other end to hit the white ball with ease. His father hurried round to hit the white ball firmly, in order to give Margot more of a chance. 'You'll regret that,' she laughed, reaching for the black ball and releasing it to merely scrape the edge of the white.

'Ah, you know what you're doing!' JP roared. 'Then I won't be so kind next time!'

They raced around the table, scuffled at the ends, laughing all the while. It grew hot in the room. JP took off his sweater. Colm's shirt-tails escaped from his jeans. Margot tied up her hair with a band. Their cheeks shone, their breathing grew short, the competition intensified. When Mrs B appeared to ask if they'd like supper, she stood a moment in the door frame, watching them. She never thought she'd see the likes of this again. But here they were, father and son, playing rabbits, just like the old days.

After supper, when Margot announced that she had better be getting back to the hotel, JP lifted the crystal decanter off the table and offered his son a glass of whiskey. 'Care to join me?' he asked.

Colm looked at his watch. It was late. 'Why not?' he replied and took the armchair opposite his father's.

'Good man,' said JP. 'Margot?'

'Thanks, JP, but I think I'll leave you both to it. I'll see myself out.'

'Drive carefully,' he said, watching her go. He turned to his son. 'Tell me, Colm, how's the business?' He filled his glass and handed it to him. 'From what I hear, you're doing rather well.'

'Well enough,' Colm replied. He took a sip. 'Though I'm never going to be a rich man.'

'But you're doing what you love and that's the key to happiness, I believe.'

'It certainly is one of them.'

'I won't pry into the other keys. I'll leave your mother to do that.' JP raised his eyebrows, hoping his son would tell him anyway.

Colm lowered his glass. 'About Mum,' he said. 'I don't suppose you know that she's flying over in a few days.'

JP dropped his gaze into his whiskey. 'No, I didn't know,' he replied dully. The mention of Alana had deflated his enthusiasm. It was now gone, evaporated into the air. 'I suppose she wants to see you, and her parents. Jack isn't getting any younger, is he?'

Colm was sorry to have ruined the evening. 'Perhaps I shouldn't have told you,' he said regretfully. 'I've spoiled your day.'

JP smiled bitterly. 'You could never spoil my day, dear boy. It's been rather magical, hasn't it? We're both here now, you and I, and we're talking just like we used to. No, Alana can't spoil anything, at least, not unless I allow her to. Drink up. The night is yet young. Let's talk about keys to happiness. Any nice girls to tell me about?'

Colm grinned and took another sip of whiskey. 'You said you wouldn't ask.'

'I lied.'

'Ever the Old Fox.'

JP chuckled and his eyes sparkled. 'I'm glad you still see me that way.'

Chapter 10

Margot gazed out over the horizon, to where the sea melted into the sky in a mesmerizing haze of blue-grey, and wondered whether the God that Mrs B talked about resided there, at the Gateway to Heaven, if he existed at all. A blustery wind blew off the water, racing up the bluff and through the long grasses where yellow coltsfoot and gorse grew wild, and thick grey clouds screened the sky overhead, obscuring the sun. 'You're very quiet,' she said, looking across at JP. The two of them sat on their horses at the edge of the cliff. Below, waves crashed against the rocks, covering the water with foam.

JP lit a cigarette and sighed. 'Alana is due to arrive in a couple of days.' He shook his head and blew a jet of smoke into the gale. 'Colm told me last night after you left. It's rather taken the wind out of my sails.'

'I bet it has. Will she want to see you?'

'I doubt it. She never does. We have nothing to say to one another anymore.'

'But the thought of her being in Ballinakelly makes you uneasy.'

'Decidedly.'

'When was the last time you saw each other?'

He shrugged. 'I can't remember. Years ago. Maybe two,

maybe three, and only in passing. I avoid going into town when she's here and I'm sure she avoids me just the same.'

He turned to face the sea again and Margot saw the tension in his profile and decided to say something positive. 'It was fun last night,' she ventured brightly. 'Nice to see you and Colm getting along so well.'

'Yes, that was a welcome change. I'm not sure what inspired it, but I won't look a gift horse in the mouth.'

'Perhaps you just needed to spend time together.'

'I thought I'd lost him. But last night showed me that it's possible to reconcile. That no relationship is beyond repair if one really wants to put things right.'

'Sometimes enough water goes under the bridge to allow one to let go of old grievances. Life's too short to bear grudges.'

'Fourteen years is long enough, you'd think.'

'Since your divorce?'

'Yes.'

'Why don't you try and repair your relationship with Alana? That way you'd repair it with the rest of the family too. I sense she's the doorkeeper to your children and in-laws.'

His face twisted with aversion. 'Fifty years wouldn't be long enough for her,' he said. 'I doubt she'll ever forgive me, in this world or the next.'

'I'm sorry. It was silly of me to suggest it. I'm sure you've tried.'

He looked at her, his eyes darkened with disillusionment. 'In the beginning we fought. Then we sulked and refused to speak to each other. Then we separated and communicated only through our lawyers. After that, it seemed we forgot how to talk to one another. A canyon opened between us and it was too large and perilous to even attempt to bridge, so we let it remain, getting wider and wider. Now she's on one side and I'm on the other and that's just the way it is. I suspect it will always be.'

'Has she found someone else?'

'Not that I know of.'

'Have you?' Margot knew that was a silly question. He was lonelier and more alone than anyone she had ever met.

He grinned bitterly. 'Who'd want to be with me, Margot?' She frowned, appalled by his self-pity. 'I have nothing to offer anyone.'

'That's not true.'

'You're very kind, Margot. But I'm not the man I once was. I'm a totally different person now.'

'You can be anyone you want to be, JP. It's takes will-power, for sure, but, like you said, one step at a time. You've taken up riding again and gardening, why not try to change your state of mind next? Stop seeing yourself as a victim, then other people will stop seeing you as one too.'

He chuckled. 'You're too young to understand what it's like to lose everything. I envy you, Margot. You're young and beautiful. Not a care in the world. You can go anywhere you like. You have no ties, no commitments. You can write your book in any place you choose. Your world is full of light. It's a breeze. You have no concept of what it's like to be me.'

Margot looked away sharply. He was making massive pre-sumptions about her. He had no idea whether or not she had suffered. He knew nothing about her life at all. He was so consumed with his own troubles that he believed himself to have a monopoly on suffering.

Her attention was diverted by the sudden appearance of light falling in shimmering beams onto the water at the point where the sky merged with the sea, the place she imagined to be the gateway to Heaven. The sight of it was spellbinding and at once her irritation dissolved, as if the distant light was drawing her out of herself and away from her cares. 'Look, how beautiful,' she murmured. 'God's giving us a glimpse into the next world.'

JP lifted his chin and watched it. Little by little, the tension eased in his jaw and he too was drawn out of himself and into the light. He took a deep, involuntary breath. 'Ireland is in a class of its own when it comes to beauty. I don't know what it is, but it's magical.'

'I imagine all the immigrants must have taken visions like this with them when they started their new lives in America and wherever else they settled. They must have missed it with all their hearts.'

'I'm sure they did, and still do. I wonder whether Alana ever pines for home. She loved Ireland as much as I do.'

'She didn't have to leave.'

'She did if she wanted to get as far away from me as possible.'

'Interesting that Colm didn't go with her to America, that he stayed with you.'

'Correction, he stayed with his grandparents. He couldn't bear the sight of *me*. He blamed me entirely for the divorce.'

'How's your relationship with Aisling and Cara?'

'They were less judgemental than their brother. When they were teenagers they used to come and stay during the school holidays. I used to see a lot more of them. Our relationship was good. They didn't take sides and their mother didn't try to make them. I give her credit for that. For not trying to turn them against me. Now they're grown-up with husbands and children of their own it's harder for them to find the time to come over. The irony is that I see much more of Colm and he's always been the child who has resented me the most.'

'Isn't that typical of sons, though? They side with their mothers. They feel, being men, they need to protect them.'

'I don't know. Our story is probably one big cliché. Divorce seems to be the same in most cases, doesn't it? But nothing is ever black and white. There are always two sides to every story, and both husband and wife believe themselves the victim of wrongdoing.'

'I only know your side of the story.'

JP looked across at her and grinned. 'If you cosy up to Alana, you might get her to tell you hers.'

'That would make me feel less like a writer and more like a family therapist!'

'I think you'd easily qualify as a therapist.'

'Well, I've read enough self-help books to be quite knowledgeable about human nature.'

He looked surprised. 'You? Self-help books? Why would *you* of all people need those?'

Margot dismissed his question with a shake of the head. She couldn't even begin to answer it. 'Come on, let's gallop. I'm getting cold up here and the horses are restless.'

His face brightened. 'I'll race you.'

She laughed at the challenge and squeezed her horse's flanks. 'Catch me if you can!'

Colm had had a busy morning. The practice had been full of animals that needed treatment, among them a limping Labrador, a cat with an upset stomach and a terrier that had eaten a sock. He took a break over lunch and closed his office door, leaving his partner to hold the fort. While he sat at his desk eating a sandwich, he opened Margot's book that he had bought that morning. He was curious to see how she wrote. He hoped it would give him some indication of how she was going to write about *them*. He had been determined not to like her, but now he realized how foolish that had been, to judge someone without knowing them. The fact that she was researching a book on his family didn't make her a bad person. He had been wrong to dismiss her so swiftly. After all, if he wasn't a Deverill he'd have found her likeable from the start. The truth was his intentions had been shattered by her charm, which was unexpectedly winning. Sure, she was lovely to look at, but so were many other girls in Ballinakelly. What Margot had was different. She had warmth, an independent spirit, intelligence and a sharp wit. On top of that she was elusive. She never talked about herself. It was as if she wanted to keep people at arm's length. As if she didn't want to get close to anyone. That quality only made him want to get closer. He began to read the first page and, as he did so, he could hear her voice as if she were reading it aloud to him in his head. He wasn't in the least interested in Eva Perón, but he found, as he turned the page, that he was becoming increasingly interested in Margot Hart.

That afternoon when Margot returned to the hotel she noticed at once a change in the atmosphere. It was electrified. The staff stood to attention like soldiers, backs straight, shoulders square, faces alert, as if at any moment their colonel-in-chief might bellow a command. No one loitered, or chatted, or lingered. They moved with purpose and energy, as if the entire place had been given some sort of shock. Therefore, it came as no surprise to Margot to find a handwritten invitation waiting for her in her room, requesting her company for a drink in the private sitting room at six. The formidable Mrs de Lisle was in residence.

'So, my dear, how are you getting on with your research?' Mrs de Lisle, in a scarlet double-breasted jacket and pencil skirt, kissed her on both cheeks, enveloping her in a cloud of Rive Gauche. 'I hope my staff are looking after you.'

'I'm being treated like a queen,' Margot replied. 'Your hotel is beautiful.'

'I'm so pleased you like it. It's the jewel in my crown. Come, sit down. What would you like to drink? A glass of wine perhaps? A gin and tonic?'

Margot sat on the sofa where she had sat with the Countess di Marcantonio and took in Mrs de Lisle's stiff red hair and glossy red nails and thought how American she looked. Englishwomen didn't manage to attain that level of polish. 'A glass of white wine would be lovely, thank you,' she replied.

Mrs de Lisle gave a flick of her hand at the member of staff hovering by the door. Heavy gold bracelets jingled at her wrist and a large diamond ring flashed on her finger. When she gave him the order she did so briskly, in the manner of someone accustomed to bossing people around, of someone who considers pleasantries a waste of time. But she could be charming when it suited her. She took a seat on one of the upholstered chairs and folded her legs tidily to one side, one ankle on top of the other, patent crimson stilettos paired. Then she looked at Margot with intelligent, gun-metal grey eyes and smiled, displaying a perfect set of dazzling white teeth. 'Tell me, my dear, how are you getting on with your research? I'm dying to know.'

'Well,' Margot began, 'Lord Deverill has been surprisingly helpful in allowing me to go through boxes of family records.'

Mrs de Lisle raised thin, overplucked eyebrows. 'That *is* surprising. I thought you'd encounter resistance there.'

'So did I. I'm not sure the rest of his family are as enthusiastic to help.'

'If you have *him*, you don't need anyone else, do you?'

'Well, the Countess di Marcantonio came to see me.'

Mrs de Lisle nodded knowingly. 'I thought she would.'

'She believes that *she* should be mistress of this place.'

'She has a point.'

'And she wants me to include the drama in the book.'

'And so you should. A good journalist explores every angle. Besides, you need a bit of tension, a bit of spice, if you want the book to sell.'

'Oh, it'll sell all right. There's enough spice in that family's history to out-spice an Indian market. Have you met Leopoldo?' Margot asked.

'No. I don't think he's set foot on the property in years.'

'But the Countess visits from time to time?'

'Yes, I think she enjoys bringing her friends here and showing off her husband's ancestral home.' Margot laughed at the use of the word 'ancestral'.

The young man reappeared with two drinks on a tray. Margot thanked him as he handed her the wine glass. Mrs de Lisle simply put out a hand.

'She's a very determined woman,' said Margot, choosing her words carefully.

'As tough as old leather,' Mrs de Lisle added with less restraint. 'Aristocratic men always attract ambitious, socially upwardly mobile women like her. From what I understand Leopoldo was a playboy in his youth and squandered vast amounts of money gambling, entertaining lavishly and basically pleasing himself. It's not really surprising that his

mother left the castle and most of her fortune to JP Deverill.
The irony is, had Leopoldo inherited it, his wife would have
probably whipped him into shape and run this place with
great efficiency.'

'And you'd never have had the opportunity to buy it.'

Mrs de Lisle laughed. 'Lord Deverill did me a favour. You
see, what sets this place apart is the history. That's what people
love. How many hotels can boast three hundred years of one
family's ownership? Barton Deverill built it and JP Deverill
lost it. The years in between are full of scandal, tragedy, loss
and love. It's a marvellous tale and you, my dear, are going to
write the most brilliant book and it's going to sell all over the
world and send people flocking here in droves.' Her grey eyes
gleamed with ambition. 'I've pumped serious money into this
project, Margot, because I know its potential. America loves
Ireland. So many are descended from here. We have a special
affection for the Irish. The hotel has only been open for five
years but our reputation is solid and glowing. You see, the
fact that Lord Deverill fell on hard times and had to sell up
only makes people love him. He's not the remote, heartless
aristocrat who exploited his poor tenants, sending them to
their graves during the famine, or across to America in coffin
ships, but a man who struggled beneath the burden of his vast
ancestral home and was forced to let it go. It's a story with such
pathos. His tragedy is my gain. People want to come here to
taste something of the privileged life of these aristocrats and
they don't resent them, they pity them.'

'I think Lord Deverill would hate to know that.'

'Better than loathing him. He should embrace it. We'd love
to have him come and speak to our guests. We could charge
a fortune for dinners. He could stand up and tell people what
life was like when he lived here. They'd be fascinated. It

might make him feel better about the whole thing if he was still part of it.'

'Have you ever asked him?'

Mrs de Lisle wrinkled her nose and shook her head. 'I don't think he's in any position to speak to anyone. As far as I know he's lost himself at the bottom of his whiskey bottle. Shame, really. He could earn good money. I paid him handsomely for this place but money doesn't last for ever. I'll wait until he can no longer pay his bills and then I'll strike a deal. With your book and Lord Deverill speaking at my dinner parties, I'll be turning people away!'

There was something distasteful about her ambition that made Margot fear for JP.

Alana Deverill arrived home, to the house by the sea where she had been born, with mixed emotions. Little had changed. The house itself was the same, with its grey-tiled roof and whitewashed walls, as was the bay and the glittering waves that peaked and plateaued on the surface of the water. She was reminded of the many times she had walked up and down the beach as a child, searching for crabs in the sand and urchins in the rock pools. She had laughed into the wind playing chase with her siblings and sobbed in the rain when they had fought, as all children do. However, she had sobbed the hardest when she had discovered love letters from Kitty Deverill in her father's veterinary bag. She had vowed then that she would never forgive him for betraying her mother, only to learn later that her mother had known all along and waited patiently for the passion to die away. Alana had finally forgiven Jack, for who was *she* to hold a grudge when her mother held none.

Alana had never imagined that *she* would be betrayed in the same way, but she had sobbed again on that beach when she had learned of JP's affair with the governess. Unlike her mother she had not accepted it, or tolerated it, or waited for it to blow over. She had wailed and cried and flung every object within reach at his deceiving head and declared that this time, when she made a vow never to forgive, she would keep her word. It had been fourteen years since the divorce, yet now, gazing out over the sea, the unchanging sea, it could have been yesterday when she had thrown her shattered dreams onto the water.

She sat at the kitchen table with her parents, older and frailer now, and her son Colm, who got more handsome with the years, and shared her news. When she was home Alana always felt as if she had never been away. It was so comfortably familiar. So sheltered. She wondered why she had dashed across the Atlantic to make a life there when she could have stayed in the place she knew and loved. But she couldn't have remained in the same town as JP, fearing bumping into him every time she went to buy the groceries. Bolting to New York was what the Irish did and the Americans had certainly made her and her daughters feel welcome. Hadn't her mother been born there and her father, for a short time, made his home there too? America was in her veins as well as Ireland. And yet, sitting now at that table, the very same table at which she had eaten, studied and gossiped for the first two decades of her life, Alana felt an unmatched sense of belonging as well as a regret for having lost it.

The four of them enjoyed a hearty lunch of potatoes and stew. Emer had baked an apple pie for pudding, making from scratch the custard that Jack so loved. She resisted buying things in packets when she could cook them herself.

'There's something we need to tell you, Alana,' said Emer, putting down her spoon and fork.

Alana knew it would have something to do with JP. 'What's up?' she asked, a familiar feeling of dread clamping her stomach.

Jack polished off the rest of the custard straight out of the jug with a spoon. 'There's a Writer in Residence up at the castle now,' he said. 'And she's writing a history of the Deverills.'

He didn't believe in wrapping harsh truths in cotton wool.

'JP has given her access to the family records,' Emer added.

Alana shrugged. 'Which is his right. After all, he's a Deverill. What's it got to do with me?'

'It'll have plenty to do with you when she gets to the last twenty years,' said Jack.

Colm remained silent. He felt like a traitor in their midst. He didn't want to admit that he had not only befriended the writer, but his father too. He knew how much his mother counted on him for support. He had always taken her side. Now he wished he'd never taken sides at all.

Alana looked at her son. 'Have you met this woman?'

'I have,' he replied.

'What's she like?'

Colm hesitated. He lifted his water glass and held it in front of his lips. 'I don't know, clever, I suppose, and—'

'She's beautiful,' Jack interrupted. 'Beautiful and cunning as a fox. She's got JP wrapped around her little finger.' His gaze lingered on his grandson. 'I suspect she's got *you* wrapped around her little finger too,' he added. 'Men are putty in the hands of the likes of Margot Hart.'

Alana frowned. 'Are you telling me that JP is spilling all the family secrets?'

Colm was quick to his father's defence. 'I think he's helping her research the distant past. They were discussing Hermione Deverill last time I was there.'

Alana's eyes darkened. 'If he's going to use this book as a way of taking revenge on me, then I need to know.'

'There's no telling what he'll do,' said Emer.

'In my experience, there's little more dangerous than a drunk with a loose tongue and a heap of secrets,' said Jack.

'Margot's writing a history book, not a kiss and tell,' interjected Colm. He felt the heat prickle beneath his collar and wondered why it had suddenly got so hot in the kitchen. 'She wrote a biography of Eva Perón. I'm reading it now and it's good. She's a historian not a scandalmonger.'

Jack grinned. 'Well, you've changed your opinion, Colm,' he mused. He thought of Kitty Deverill then. Some women were just impossible to resist. He scrutinized his grandson's face and realized, as he did so, that he'd seen that expression before – on his own face in the mirror.

'I'm going to talk to JP,' said Alana. 'I'm going to find out what's going on. He can't be allowed to speak about me, about us and our relationship, on the record. I'm not going to allow him to publicly humiliate me.'

'I'm sure he wouldn't do that,' said Colm.

His mother looked at him, incredulous. 'Are you?' she retorted. It wasn't like Colm to defend JP. She pushed out her chair. 'I'm going to see him now.'

'I'll go with you,' Colm suggested.

'No, I'll go on my own,' she replied. 'This is between me and your father.' She sighed. 'It's always been between me and him.'

Kitty

Trouble is brewing in the castle and for once it has nothing to do with me. It is Mrs Carbery who is doing the haunting. Mr Dukelow has employed a new girl from Kinsale called Annie Dineen, a sweet, mousey creature with lank brown hair and dull brown eyes and a small, timid mouth out of which nothing interesting is ever said. She is unremarkable in appearance and goes about her duties making beds and cleaning rooms in a quiet, efficient manner, never drawing attention to herself. In fact, the other staff barely notice her at all. However, she is remarkable in one thing: she is an intuitive. She is one of those rare people who sense the finer vibrations of which most are unaware, but unlike my grandmother and me – who in life were very nonchalant about our gift – she is afraid of it. She blocks it out by humming to herself when she feels the temperature drop in the room, or senses a presence behind her in the hairs that lift on the back of her neck. Were I alive I would explain that there is nothing to fear. There are no evil spirits here, only gentle beings watching over their loved ones who come and go in the hotel, or those, like Mrs Carbery and me who are in the In-between, either by choice or by default. Yet, Annie knows not the difference between ghosts, earthbound spirits and spirits and I am in no position to tell her.

She believes in ghosts in white sheets and headless phantoms
who might do her harm. I would like to whisper in her ear
that perhaps Castle Deverill is not the ideal place of work for
her, but she needs the money and is willing to put up with the
creaks and groans that accompany her daily duties. However,
Mrs Carbery in the linen room is quite another matter.

Mrs Carbery is slowly coming to terms with the idea that
she is dead. After having spent decades living in a dreamlike
state, going about her usual routine in the reality she has created for herself, she is beginning to wake up. The illusion is
trembling and petering out like reflections on water. She is
starting to inhabit the same realm as me, and she isn't liking
it one bit. 'Castle Deverill is a hotel, you say?' she asked me in
confusion when I tried to explain the truth. 'Get away with
you, Miss Kitty. I suppose with all his lordship's guests it might
sometimes feel like a hotel. Although what would I know? I've
never stepped inside a hotel before.'

'The castle no longer belongs to a Deverill—' I began.

At this she crossed herself, a horrified expression on her
face. 'Then what has become of Lord and Lady Deverill, I ask
you? God save them and protect them from all harm.'

'They died a long time ago. You remember the fire, don't
you, Mrs Carbery?'

She frowned, a troubled look darkening her face. 'The
fire . . .' she muttered, fishing out the memory from somewhere deep inside her. For sure, she had buried it, along with
the death of my grandfather Hubert, who was her master.

'And you remember my grandmother, Adeline, going mad
in the western tower, the only part of the castle to survive the
fire? You remember her death, surely?'

The furrows on her forehead quivered as she fished out that
memory too, from the silent, still waters of her subconscious

mind. I realized then that the fire, the deaths of my grand-parents and her own beloved son had caused her to lose her mind and, in death, to somehow create and inhabit this illu-sory world.

She looked at me then with terror in her eyes as the fog cleared and images surfaced one by one to reveal the truth that she had wilfully concealed. 'I remember the fire, indeed I do,' she whispered, astonished that she could forget it. 'I remember forming a human chain and passing buckets of water, but they were useless against the flames. The whole building was burning and there was nothing we could do about it, but watch it destroy the place we loved.' She put a hand to her mouth. 'What happened after that? I don't recall ... I can't ...'

I knelt beside her chair and took her hand. It was like she was awakening from a coma and having to face head-on the trauma that had put her there. 'You stayed at home, Mrs Carbery,' I told her gently. 'Your daughter Bessie looked after you. You remember Bessie, don't you? She was only a child but she took care of you like a little mother.' Mrs Carbery narrowed her eyes, straining her mind to retrieve and confront those painful recollections.

'Bessie, yes, I remember my Bessie. Where is she now?'

'She is still living.'

'But my son was killed.' Her eyes dimmed. 'My son was taken from me.' She pressed a hand against her lips again, smothering the sob that came with the pain.

'Your son died in the civil war and you died shortly after.'

She sighed, resigned. 'So, it's true. I really am a goner.' She shook her head in disbelief. 'I don't feel different. My heart still hurts.' She took her hand from her mouth and put it to her chest. 'It still hurts, here. Should it hurt now that I'm dead?'

'The heart is your soul, Mrs Carbery. Your soul can never die.'

'Oh, if this is death then I don't want it,' she wailed. 'What about Heaven, then? What about that?'

And I couldn't help her. She knew she was dead but the light didn't come as I thought it would. I expected to know very well how to send her on her way, but I didn't. I couldn't. She gazed at me in horror. 'Heaven is where you'll go—' I began, but she didn't believe me.

'I've been bad. I must have been bad,' she mumbled.

'You're not bad, Mrs Carbery. You're just lost,' I told her.

'And you?' she shot back. 'What about you?'

'I'm lost too,' I replied, and for the first time I doubted myself. I had refused to move on. Was it possible that when I decided I was ready I wouldn't find my way home?

Now Mrs Carbery is creating havoc. Poor Annie Dineen refuses to go into the linen room. She says it's haunted. It's cold, she complains, and is inhabited by a furious woman who shouts at her to leave her in peace every time she goes in to fetch clean linen for the beds. Now that Mrs Carbery knows she is dead, she is determined to make everyone as miserable as she is. If I rattled the odd doorknob to frighten people, she is banging all the doors like a madwoman. Fortunately for the hotel, she is unable to make herself heard most of the time. Her mind is unfocused and she has no understanding of how it is done. I am not going to enlighten her. But for poor Annie Dineen, who can see her, Mrs Carbery's fear is a real problem. I overheard Mrs de Lisle talking to Mr Dukelow and giving him strict instructions to sort out these alleged hauntings. 'I don't want my staff frightening the guests,' she said firmly. 'Do something about it at once!'

I'm not sure how he can.

I am drawn to the Hunting Lodge where Alana has turned up unexpectedly to speak with JP. When Mrs B opens the door JP's ex-wife does not wait to be invited in. She greets the old housekeeper warmly but briskly and marches right on in before Mrs B can think of something to say to stop her. She watches in alarm as Alana strides up the corridor towards the library. She knows where to find JP.

He hears her approach before he sees her and his energy contracts. If he had a shell like a tortoise he would retreat inside it. He freezes at his desk, pen poised above the letter he is writing, eyes wide with anticipation. He knows it is her. He has been expecting, no, *fearing* this. And he is in no doubt why she has come.

A moment later she is in the doorway. He lifts his chin. 'Hello, Alana,' he says coldly.

She puts her hands on her hips. Her anger is a miasma around her that I can see as clearly as mist. 'We need to talk,' she says.

He gets up stiffly and walks round to the fire. He lifts a log out of the basket and throws it into the grate. He is making time. But he can only delay the inevitable. 'Do you want a drink? Some tea?'

'I won't be staying long,' she replies tersely. I think she feels she has more power standing, so she doesn't take a seat. She is not here as a guest, after all. It is over twenty years since she stood in this library as a guest, when my parents lived here. They were happy then. We were *all* happy then.

'I hear there's a Writer in Residence up at the castle,' she says. 'And she's writing a book about your family.'

'That's true,' says JP. He stands with his back to the fire. The log crackles and sizzles behind him as it becomes engulfed in flame. He lights a cigarette with trembling hands.

'I understand you've allowed her to go through your family records. That's very generous of you.'

'I have.'

'Why would you do that?' Alana's face pinches with fury. 'I don't understand why you would allow the enemy into your home and give her free rein to rake through your family's history. Why would you do that?'

'I think she'll do a good job of it,' he answers. He takes a drag of his cigarette. The fingers on his other hand twitch in agitation. I know he is desperate for a drink. If he had known Alana was coming he would have downed half a decanter of whiskey in preparation. As it is, he is sober and struggling.

'You don't know anything, JP.' He makes to speak but she interrupts him. 'How well do you know this woman? You don't. You've just met her. You don't know what she's going to do with the information you give her. Certainly, she'll want to write a book that sells. Scandal sells, JP, and she's going to want to fill her book with it. Does she know about Kitty's affair with my father? Is that going in the book?' I have been so focused on the disintegration of JP and Alana's marriage and the selling of the castle that I have not considered my affair with Jack. But Alana is right. If Margot finds out about that, poor Emer will be hurt all over again. Even though I am dead, I'm sure the wound his betrayal inflicted on her heart has never fully healed. How could it? Alana is looking out for her mother.

'And what about Archie's suicide?' she continues. 'Celia

is still alive. Have you thought of her? She won't want that tragedy unearthed and written about for all the world to read. And your half-brother Harry's homosexuality? If you think this woman is going to leave all those things out of the book, think again. If she does her job well she'll dig it all up. There are plenty of people around who will give her the gossip. Make no mistake. She's not your friend. She'll just be your friend for as long as she needs you. Then she'll disappear back to England and you won't see her for dust. She'll make a mint out of the book and you'll be left looking stupid. And what about us? Do you want everyone to know why our marriage broke down? Do you really? Because *I* don't, JP.'

JP stares at her. He is searching for words, but they don't come. She has left him pink-faced and floundering like a fish washed up on a beach. 'For the sake of our children, JP, cease all contact with her at once.' Then her expression changes. She looks at him steadily and I see real compassion in her eyes. 'I did not marry a fool,' she says softly. 'But I'm afraid that is what you have become.'

'You have no right to come in here and tell me what to do, Alana,' he exclaims and I think of a cornered dog and how it might snarl and growl, with its back to the wall and nowhere to run.

'I do have a right, because I am the mother of your children. I have every right to protect them. And I am protecting you, too, not that you'll ever thank me for it.'

'Protecting me from what?' he asks with a bitter chuckle.

'Yourself.' He glares at her. 'I have nothing else to say,' she adds.

'Mrs B will see you out.'

'I'll see myself out,' she corrects and leaves the room. His eyes linger on the place where she stood as if she has left an imprint there. He sways a little then makes for the drinks tray. He pours himself a large glass of whiskey and downs it. Ash from his cigarette drops onto the carpet but he doesn't notice. He pours himself another drink. He is riddled with guilt. Sure, he wants Margot to tell his side of the story, but it is clear to me now that he also wants to inflict pain. He is a wounded creature lashing out at those closest to him, hoping that they will suffer too, as he is suffering. That's what unhappy people do.

He takes the decanter and his empty glass to the armchair where he sits and stares into the fire. He refills his glass, leans back and sighs heavily.

Alana is right, she did not marry a fool. How did it get to this?

Chapter 11

That afternoon a storm blew in, battering the cliffs and whipping up the sea so that it rose and fell in waves as high as buildings. Fierce winds whistled around the castle walls and rain thrashed against the windowpanes like thousands of little claws scratching to get inside. There was an uneasy feeling in the hotel. The bones of the building creaked and groaned and everyone spoke in hushed voices, as if nervous of some unseen presence that stalked the corridors. Margot had decided to remain by the fire in the castle's drawing room and read through some of her notes. A pale-faced maid came in to draw the curtains, shutting out the darkness and the storm. Margot lifted her eyes off the page and watched her. She knew most of the hotel's staff by now and was considered very much part of the furniture. The girl smiled at her, but knew not to chat. However, Margot sensed, by the weary look on her face, that something was amiss.

'Is everything all right, Evie?' she asked when the maid came to chuck another log on the fire.

Evie glanced around to make sure she wasn't going to be overheard. 'It's Annie again,' she whispered. 'She's having a right old meltdown, she is.'

'Ghosts again?'

'I think it's the storm. Storms always put the wind up people. We Irish are a superstitious lot.' She gave an impish smile. 'Trouble is, an old place like this is always going to be haunted, isn't it.'

'It's really not that old,' Margot corrected her. 'Celia Deverill rebuilt it in the 1920s.'

'But that's the thing. It's on the site of the old castle, and that was built in the seventeenth century. It doesn't matter how many times it's rebuilt, the energy of the original building is still the same, like a blueprint. Beneath all of this is some very ancient magic.'

Good Lord! Margot thought to herself, but she refrained from rolling her eyes. 'You're not afraid of it, then, this ancient magic?'

'Of course not! I find that sort of thing fascinating. I mean, how much is out there that we can't see? I haven't seen a ghost yet, but I swear I sometimes feel like I'm being watched.'

Margot thought of her friend Dan Chambers. Why was it that every time someone mentioned a ghost she thought of him? She closed her notebook and stood up. Perhaps there was a way of harnessing these so-called ghosts, of taking advantage of them for the good of Mrs de Lisle's business. If everyone believed the place to be haunted, why not profit from it?

She found Mrs de Lisle in her private sitting room having a meeting with Mr Dukelow and Mrs de Lisle's PA Jennifer, who was a polished young American woman with flawless olive skin and glasses. The meeting seemed to be informal. They were drinking tea and Mr Dukelow, at least, was making his way through a plate of biscuits. Jennifer perched on a chair, notebook open, fountain pen hovering. Mrs de Lisle herself was in the armchair, teacup in one hand, saucer in the other, looking as if she was simply enjoying a pleasant afternoon with friends.

'Can I disturb you a moment?' Margot asked from the doorway. She figured that, if they hadn't bothered to close the door, they wouldn't mind being interrupted.

'Please come in,' said Mrs de Lisle with a smile. 'We're just discussing the storm. I'm glad I'm not flying out this evening.'

'It'll have blown over by tomorrow,' Mr Dukelow reassured her.

'The forecast is good for tomorrow,' Jennifer added earnestly. 'In fact, it says the cloud will clear by early morning and the sun will come out mid-morning.'

'I've got an idea that might interest you,' Margot began.

'Take a seat, Margot,' said Mrs de Lisle. Margot sat on the sofa, beside Mr Dukelow, who reached for another biscuit. Margot sensed he was nervous. He did not have the figure of a man who gorged on biscuits. 'So, what's this idea of yours, Margot?' asked Mrs de Lisle, head on one side, an interested frown pinching the smooth skin between her eyebrows.

'Well, it seems to me that there are many who think the castle is haunted,' she replied. 'And lots of people love the idea of ghosts. Perhaps that's something you could exploit.'

Mrs de Lisle narrowed her eyes. 'Go on.'

'I have a friend who's a medium. He's extremely in demand. I went to one of his events a few years ago at the Royal Geographical Society in London and it was standing room only. I'm a sceptic myself, but even I was amazed at the information he was given by spirits in the afterlife. I mean, I'm quick to find explanations for that sort of thing, but I can truthfully say on that occasion I found none. It was extraordinary.'

Mrs de Lisle thought about it for a moment. Whether or

not she believed in the spirit world was neither here nor there. If she could make money out of it, she'd believe in anything. 'That's not a bad idea. Instead of trying to deny the strange sightings, we could make a feature of them. Good thinking, Margot. I like it. We could invite this friend of yours here. We could have a Medium in Residence.' She smiled with cunning. 'Perhaps, if he's really good, he can get rid of the less appealing ghosts who seem to be upsetting my staff.' She laughed and Mr Dukelow and Jennifer laughed with her.

'What's he like, this friend of yours?' she continued.

'He's called Dan Chambers. In his late sixties, I would guess. Handsome, debonair, charming. Just the sort of person who will enhance your hotel. He's like a light to moths. People love him.'

'How did you meet him?' asked Mr Dukelow, trying to regain some ground.

'We met about seven years ago in Montana of all places. I was doing a profile on Ralph Lauren and he was hosting a retreat out there. He's a good person. If anyone can convince you that spirits are real and present, it's him.'

Mrs de Lisle turned to Jennifer. 'Get his number from Margot, will you? Find out if he's available to come over for a week in the spring. I agree with Margot.' She smiled at her. 'We could turn these so-called hauntings to our advantage.'

At that moment there was a knock on the door. It was Róisín. 'Excuse me, Mrs de Lisle, but there's a phone call for Miss Hart. The woman says it's urgent.'

Margot couldn't imagine who it could be. It wouldn't be her mother and it was unlikely to be Dorothy, for they had spoken the evening before. 'Where shall I take it?' she asked, getting up.

'I can put it through to this phone,' Róisín suggested.

But Margot knew she'd get little privacy in here. 'I'll take it at reception,' she said, excusing herself and following Róisín into the corridor.

When she put the receiver to her ear it was Mrs B's quivering voice that rushed in a panic down the line. 'Oh Margot, it's me, Bessie. It's his lordship. He's in a terrible state. I don't know what to do. I tried to telephone Master Colm, but I got his answer machine. I left a message but I can't be sure he'll get it and I really need help. His lordship's been at the bottle, Margot. He's upset. I don't know what to do. I didn't know who else to call.'

'It's okay, Bessie. I'll come over now.'

'I'm sorry to drag you out on a night such as this, but he's in a terrible state.'

'A bit of wind and rain doesn't faze me, Bessie. Stay with him and I'll get to you as soon as I can.'

'God bless you, Margot.'

Margot hurried to her room to retrieve her coat and hat and change out of her shoes into a pair of leather boots. She felt a familiar sense of foreboding as she made her way back down the stairs into the hall. A clenching of the stomach and a tightening of the throat. Yet, she knew she had to go to JP's aid. She couldn't leave poor Mrs B to deal with the drama alone. She knew very well what *that* was like. And a part of her wanted to go to his rescue. *Needed* to go, even.

She headed out into the gale. With her head down and her woolly hat pulled low over her forehead, she fought her way to the car. It was bitterly cold and the night was as dark as ink. She put the key in the lock and climbed inside. The headlights lit up the rain and the nearby shrubs and trees that were bowed into submission by the wind. It wasn't a night to be out, but she had no choice. Margot was not lacking in courage and there was nothing like a distress call to propel her into action. She was a woman now, not a girl. This time she had a chance to make a difference.

She drove out of the gates and into the lane. Twigs and soggy leaves were strewn all over the tarmac and puddles glistened in the headlights and splashed loudly as she motored over them. She took care to drive slowly, keeping an eye on the trees that lined her route in case the wind tossed a branch into her path. It didn't take her long to get to the Hunting Lodge. She parked as close to the front door as she could. Mrs B must have been waiting for her in the hall because no sooner had she stepped out of the car than the front door opened and her pale, round face appeared anxiously in the crack.

Margot hurried inside. 'What a terrible night!' Mrs B exclaimed, helping her out of her coat and hat. 'You're soaking wet, dear.'

'I'm fine, thank you. Where is he?'

'In the library.'

Margot almost ran down the corridor, her heart thick in her throat with anticipation and dread. She expected to find JP slumped in his chair in a drunken stupor, but what she found was far more alarming.

The room was a mess, as if he had taken everything within reach and thrown it onto the floor. Books, ornaments, lamps, pictures. Only the fire had been left untouched. It glowed calmly in the grate, golden and crimson flames gently lapping at the logs and ash as if it were just another quiet winter's evening. In the middle of the room JP sat slumped on the carpet with his back against the sofa, feet outstretched, chin on chest. In his hand dangled an empty whiskey bottle.

Margot crouched down beside him and gingerly patted his shoulder. 'JP,' she said, hoping to revive him. She shook him. 'Come on, JP. Wake up.' Mrs B now joined her. 'What happened?' Margot asked her.

Mrs B's lips pinched. 'He had a visit from Mrs Alana, that's what happened.'

'I see. I suppose they fought.'

'I don't like to earwig, Margot, but I couldn't help over-hearing some of it.'

Margot looked at her steadily. 'I imagine it was about me and the book I'm writing.'

Mrs B nodded. 'It was, I'm afraid. Mrs Alana was very upset.'

'What a pair!' She sighed. 'This was bound to happen. I imagine she sees his cooperation with me as a terrible betrayal. I don't blame her. I'd be the same. You know, I'm not intend-ing to hurt anyone in writing this book, Bessie,' she added. 'I don't want to drive the family apart.'

'You couldn't make it worse than it already is,' said Mrs B, but Margot knew that wasn't true.

A gust of wind blew down the corridor and into the library as the front door was flung open and closed with a slam. Margot looked at Mrs B and frowned. But Mrs B knew who it was and wasn't at all surprised when, a moment later, Colm came striding into the room. 'What's happened?' he demanded. Mrs B stood aside to let him through.

'He's passed out,' Margot told him.

Colm knelt beside his father and felt for his pulse. He shook his head and sighed. He did not articulate his disappointment but it was clear from the expression on his weary face that he was sorely tried. 'Let's see if we can get him upstairs and into bed,' he said.

'Has this happened before?' Margot asked.

'Not that I know of,' he replied.

'Not like this,' Mrs B added softly. 'I've never seen him this distressed before. It's as if he suddenly lost the will.'

Colm knew what had sent him to the very bottom of the bottle. He gave Mrs B a knowing look. She smiled back with understanding and compassion – a smile that held within it all the love and loyalty she had felt for him ever since his boyhood. A smile that, while everything else in his life had been swept up in the turmoil of his parents' marriage, had remained constant.

'Are you feeling strong, Margot?'

'I'll give it a go,' she answered.

They put JP's arms over their shoulders and half-dragged, half-carried him up the stairs. With the force of movement he awoke, but the drink had filled his head with fog. He tried to speak, but the words were incoherent and slurred. At least he tried to walk, which was a help as Colm and Margot struggled to get him to his bedroom.

Once he was lying on the bed, Margot left Mrs B and Colm to remove his soiled clothes and get him beneath the covers. She went downstairs and began tidying up the library. A sick feeling churned in the pit of her stomach, like a puddle of tar that had begun to bubble. It was as if it had always been there beneath a skin of denial, like a dormant volcano just waiting for something to trigger an eruption. Here she was, once again trying to save someone who most likely couldn't be saved, and making someone else's problems her own.

Margot began to cry as she slowly put back the books in the bookcase and the ornaments on the tables. The fire had died down to embers that glowed comfortingly in the grate. She put another log on and watched for a while as it smoked and crackled and finally caught fire. It was there that Colm found her, staring sorrowfully into the flames, fighting a horrible sense of déjà vu. 'Thanks for coming, Margot,' he said, running his eyes over the room with a helpless, sinking feeling. How could he mend someone who was so broken?

Margot wiped her eyes and turned to face him. 'He's not okay, is he?' she said.

'It's not your problem. Why don't you go back to the hotel? I'll clear this up with Mrs B. You've done enough.'

'No, I'll help. I've got nothing else to do. Besides, I feel somewhat invested in your father.'

'You're not invested in him at all. He probably shouldn't have been so quick to invite you into his home. I'm not really sure why he did. My mother's gone mad.'

'I thought so. I'm sorry about that.'

'It was inevitable.' He didn't add that she had made him promise he wouldn't see Margot.

Mrs B appeared looking pale. 'It's the worst I've ever seen him,' she said, eyes damp with sadness. She lifted a lamp off the carpet and replaced it on the table. She looked about for the shade. 'I don't know what to do. It's so painful watching him self-destruct, knowing the man he used to be.'

Margot closed her eyes for a second. This would be the moment to walk away, she thought. Colm had told her to leave them to it. A wise person would do as she was told. It really wasn't her problem. But something inside her prevented her from abandoning JP. 'I tell you what you do,' she said firmly, hands on hips, taking the plunge from which there would be no turning back. 'You get every bottle of alcohol in the house and pour it down the sink. Then you tell him the truth about what alcohol has done to him, and shame him. And most importantly,' she added gently, 'you give him something to get well for.'

'He has nothing,' Mrs B said despairingly.

'He doesn't have nothing,' Colm replied, lifting his chin. 'He has me.'

Margot put a hand to her lips and felt tears welling again. 'I'm sorry,' she mumbled. She turned away and found some broken china on the floor that needed clearing up.

'Would you make us some tea, Mrs B,' Colm asked. Mrs B nodded with understanding and quietly left the room. 'Are you all right, Margot?'

She took a deep breath. 'My father had *me*,' she told him squarely. '*Only* me.'

Colm walked over and relieved her of the broken china. 'Come and sit down. We can clear this up later.' He watched her wipe her nose on the back of her hand. 'If I had a handkerchief I'd give it to you.'

Margot smiled. 'If you had a handkerchief I wouldn't take it because I much prefer my sleeve.' He chuckled at her joke and went and settled into his father's armchair. Margot sat cross-legged on the carpet in front of the fire. For a moment they sat in silence, listening to the soothing sizzle of the fire, wondering how to proceed.

'So that's why you care so much about my father. Because your own father was an alcoholic,' he said at last, choosing his words carefully in case she should want to close the subject.

She nodded and, instead of keeping it to herself as she

always did, she found herself telling him everything. Perhaps it was the fire that drew it out of her, or maybe it was Colm and the way he put his head on one side and really listened. Few have the ability to listen. Whichever it was, Margot began to talk. 'My father was an alcoholic for most of my life,' she told him. 'I was fourteen when he died. It was me who found him one morning when I was about to head off to school. He'd died in his sleep. It was the gin that took him. It was always going to be the gin. My mother had long given up on him and left to live in Paris with her lover, a sleazy musician seven years her junior. Dad and I were alone. I tried to save him.' She stared into the flames and sighed. 'But you can't help someone who doesn't want to be helped.' She turned and looked at Colm. Her eyes were shiny and full of hurt. 'JP reminds me very much of him. Dad wasn't a mean drunk. Sure, he had his moments, but on the whole he was a pathetic drunk. He'd just subside in his chair like your father does. It's pitiful and sad and such a waste. I constantly emptied bottles into the sink but he was clever at hiding them. I'd find them in the strangest places. He even floated them in the loo cisterns. I mean, it was crazy. When I wasn't trying to save him I was at school, falling behind in my work and finding it hard to make friends because I could never invite anyone home. I was ashamed of him and felt somehow tarnished because of him.' She chuckled bitterly. 'So, I made up stories. I told people he was an amazing father. That he spoiled me and indulged me, that we were like two peas in a pod, but the truth was he cared more for his gin than he did for me. In the end, I don't think he saw me at all. I was a nuisance. The obstacle to his pleasure. The villain. And all I wanted was for him to be well, like other people's dads.'

'What was his profession?'

'He was a journalist and a good one too. He had a column on a national newspaper and was highly respected. For a long time he was what you'd call a functioning alcoholic, rather like JP. But then it just took him over. The minute I saw your father I knew exactly what he was. I thought I could detach, research the book and not get involved. But I can't turn my back on a man who needs help like he does. Like my father did. I couldn't save Dad, but perhaps I can save JP.' She laughed bitterly, knowing how ridiculous that sounded. Saving JP wouldn't bring her father back.

'I'm not sure that's possible, Margot,' Colm said gently. 'It's a noble thing to want to do, but I don't think he's capable of turning his life around now.'

Margot swivelled round to face him, her gaze suddenly blazing with passion. 'You see, that's where you're wrong. In the last few weeks there's been such a transformation. He's been out riding, he's been in the garden. He's been taking an interest in life and liking the person he was becoming. It was all going so well. You can't pretend that the other evening, when we played rabbits, he wasn't his old self again.'

'That's true. I did notice. There was certainly a change in the way he and I were getting along.'

'Then your mother arrived on the scene and, while I don't know what she said to him, I have a pretty good idea. He's now hating himself so much and feeling guilty, that all the progress he's been making has been lost in one terrible binge. But he's never stopped drinking, Colm. Not for a moment. I think it's time you told him what he is and forced him to quit. There's no halfway for an alcoholic. I know that from experience. It's either all or nothing. It *has* to be nothing.'

Mrs B appeared with a tray of tea. She'd deliberately taken her time so that the two of them could talk. She put the tray down. 'Now so, I have something to tell the pair of you. 'Tis bottled up inside me long enough and needs to come out. Me poor auld mother always said that it is better to have an empty house than a dirty lodger.' Mrs B took off her pinafore and folded her hands in front of her stomach and twiddled her thumbs. Colm and Margot looked at her in surprise, wondering what secret she was about to reveal. Then her pale eyes settled on Margot and softened. 'Lord Deverill is very fond of you, Miss Hart. I don't want to speak out of turn, but ever since you came to meet him in January he's looked forward to your visits like a childeen at Christmas.' Margot's face flowered into a smile as she recalled how much trouble he had taken to make her feel welcome. How he was drawn out of himself by this new visitor who brought light and warmth and compassion and, most importantly, companionship. 'The fire always had to be lit in the games room whether you were coming or not,' she told her. 'He had a horror of you getting cold. He wanted you to be comfortable and to feel at home. He used to pester me to make cakes and buy biscuits and to draw the curtains early to keep out the draught. God help us, if you only knew what he was like before, you'd realize what a change you made to him. Glory be to God, his face always lights up like the Fastnet Lighthouse when you arrive, and when you don't come, he wanders around in a trance like a cork on the ocean. I could go as far to say that without realizing it he's a bit in love with you, but I don't think it's a romantic type of love. I think it's because you're sunny and kind and you are interested in him. You're the only person who has listened to him in years and God knows he has had a lot of misfortune and tragedy. As me poor auld mother said, we all have our own cross and our own Calvary. And no, Master Colm, I don't count myself as I'm like a piece of furniture,' she added, turning to him. 'If anyone can get him to give up the drink, it's you, Miss Hart. The heart is crossways in me in case he goes off on another bender. After this one, I doubt if he would survive and to tell you the truth, I don't know how I would survive without him either.'

Margot was astonished. She had no idea JP had grown so fond of her. A small spark of hope ignited in her heart and the sick feeling in her stomach subsided. 'We can club together, the three of us, and help him,' she said excitedly. She looked at Colm. His expression was full of doubt. 'It won't go in the book, I promise,' she reassured him. 'You have to trust me.'

He sighed, giving up all resistance. 'Very well, I have no choice but to trust you, Margot. Please don't let me down.'

Colm sent Mrs B to bed and he and Margot remained, tidying up the room and dispensing of every trace of alcohol that they could find in the house. They emptied the decanters into the sink and carried the bottles of whiskey, wine and other spirits in boxes to Colm's car, battling the wind and rain as the storm showed no sign of abating. It was midnight when they finished. The library was almost completely restored to its original neatness, apart from the odd shattered ornament and broken glass that could not be mended. A good vacuum would give it its final polish. By now the fire had dimmed in the grate, only the embers glowed quietly as the final pieces of charred wood were gradually reduced to ash. 'I can't thank you enough,' said Colm. He looked weary and anxious as he escorted her down the corridor to the front door. 'I'm going to stay over, so that I'm here in the morning when Dad wakes up. You're welcome to stay if you like. There are plenty of bedrooms. It's not a night to be on the road.'

'Thanks, but I'll be fine. It's only a short drive to the castle and my car is tougher than it looks.' She put a hand on his arm, moved suddenly by the raw emotion in his eyes. 'I'm so sorry, Colm.'

He knew now that she meant it. 'It's a real help to have your support, Margot.' He sighed. 'Since Mum and my sisters left for America, I've had to deal with Dad on my own and it hasn't been easy.'

'Well, you're not on your own now. You have me.' She smiled sympathetically.

His eyes lingered on her face. They seemed to be delving inside her. She did not look away. She had revealed too much of herself tonight to be coy now. 'Listen, I'm sorry I misjudged you,' he said softly. 'I realize now how wrong I was.'

'I understand why you did, Colm,' she replied. 'I didn't think about your family when I set out on my project. But I'm thinking about them now.'

He nodded. 'I know you are.'

He pulled her into a fierce embrace. She hadn't expected him to and for a second she felt as if a line had been crossed. They were no longer journalist and subject, but two people united by a common pain. Two people who needed each other. Margot closed her eyes. It felt good to have his arms around her, to give up her resistance and yield. She was too tired to resist tonight. Colm held her close for a long moment and Margot realized how very tired she was, not because of lack of sleep or even because of exhausted emotion, but because of holding on to the armour plating she'd wrapped around her heart. She realized too that *he* needed this embrace as much as she did. She put her arms around his waist and rested her head against his chest. She had told him everything. She had nothing left to hide.

Then his lips found hers and he kissed her. He hadn't planned to and she hadn't expected it. But it felt warm and arousing and, as the kiss deepened, Colm's anxiety lifted and Margot no longer felt tired. It felt natural to hold each other like this, to kiss each other like this, as if they had been destined to come together in this way since their very first meeting.

Caught up in the moment, neither thought of the many reasons why they shouldn't.

Chapter 12

It was only in the morning that Colm and Margot thought about the reasons why they shouldn't have kissed.

Margot had driven back to the hotel shortly after, braving the storm in spite of Colm trying to persuade her to stay. All the way back she had smiled to herself and held on to the feeling of his lips on hers, savouring the memory of it, making it last. However, when dawn trickled weakly through the gap in the curtains of her tower bedroom, bringing with it a sharp sense of reality, she realized that she shouldn't have let him. How could she possibly write the book if she was intimate with one of the protagonists? It would look like she was taking advantage of him to get the inside story. And if he *were* to give her the inside story, would she be able to write it? She slept with men to whom she knew she wouldn't get attached. *That* was what suited her best. But Colm Deverill was not that sort of man. Margot could feel it in her gut. If she allowed him in, he'd be there to stay.

Better not to let him in, she thought as she got up and dressed. She hoped he had come to the same conclusion. After all, from his family's point of view, she was the enemy. And it was a foolish man who slept with the enemy. She'd be moving on in a few months. She didn't want anything to keep her from leaving.

Margot ate breakfast in the dining room, at a small table on her own, and read the *Irish Times*. The IRA had launched a mortar attack on the Royal Ulster Constabulary base in Newry in Northern Ireland, killing nine officers and injuring nearly forty others. She wondered whether the Irish Question was ever going to be resolved. But she had problems of her own to think about. She closed the paper, drained her cup of coffee and looked at her watch. It was time to go to the Hunting Lodge and face JP and Colm.

Colm knew he should not have kissed Margot. As he lay in bed, watching the bedroom slowly emerge into the light, he realized that, although he knew he should not have, he had very much wanted to. He didn't regret it. Not for a moment. He lay on his back and stretched as fragments from the evening before surfaced in his mind, giving him pleasure all over again. He had wanted to take her to bed, but she had slipped out into the stormy night and disappeared into the darkness. He held on to the images now solidifying in his imagination. Their skin had had that rare chemistry, when two people have a powerful sexual connection, like a chord played in perfect harmony. He wondered if she had felt it too. She had left him in the hall, aching with desire and yet, in spite of the traumatic events of the evening, happy. He knew how his mother would feel were she to find out. He imagined, too, how his father would feel were *he* to know. If Mrs B was to be believed, JP was a little infatuated with Margot himself. But Colm pushed those obstacles to his happiness out of his line of thought. He didn't have to dwell on them now. He imagined bringing Margot to his bed and making love to her. He closed his eyes and savoured the fantasy. He was a grown man in his late twenties; it really didn't matter what his parents thought.

At length he dressed and went downstairs for breakfast. Mrs B was not surprised to see him. She had noticed his car still parked in the forecourt when she had opened her curtains that morning. She assumed he'd stayed over so he could keep an eye on his father. Lord Deverill was still sleeping. Mrs B had peeped around his bedroom door on her way downstairs and he was breathing gently, the agony of the night before lost in peaceful slumber.

'What'll you have for breakfast, Master Colm,' she asked when he came into the kitchen.

He smiled broadly. Mrs B hadn't seen him smile like that in a very long time and her suspicions were raised. 'I like the music, Mrs B,' he said, referring to the radio.

The old housekeeper smiled back, feeling better about the night before on account of Master Colm's heightened energy, which was infectious. 'It's grand, isn't it? It puts a spring in my step.'

'It's putting a spring in mine.' Colm laughed and Mrs B laughed with him. How attractive he was when he laughed, she thought. 'I'll have eggs and toast, Mrs B. Thanks.'

'Will Miss Hart be coming in today?' She watched Colm carefully.

'She's going to help sort out Dad. Like you said, she's probably the only one who can.'

'I think the two of you together will be a powerful pairing, Master Colm.' She picked out a couple of eggs from the basket on the sideboard and poured a little oil into a pan. 'I pray to God that he allows you to help him.'

'I think we need more than prayers, Mrs B,' Colm replied, looking doubtful.

He ate his breakfast. Mrs B had bought the newspapers as she did every morning, stopping at the church to light votive candles for her loved ones on the way to the shop. However, he couldn't concentrate on the words. His mind was on Margot and the challenge they were going to face together. He listened out for her car, suddenly nervous about seeing her again. He wondered how she felt this morning and hoped she didn't regret it.

Mrs B cleared away his plate. 'I've lit the fire in the library,' she said. 'He'll be down in a minute, I suspect. Knowing him, he'll have forgotten everything about last night.'

'Margot and I will gently remind him,' Colm replied, putting his napkin on the table.

The sound of a motor alerted them both to Margot's arrival. 'I'll go,' said Mrs B, leaving the room.

Colm took a deep breath and followed her out. 'Show her into the library, Mrs B, and bring us some tea, would you?'

Margot drew up in front of the Hunting Lodge. The wind was still high, but the rain clouds had moved on in the early hours of the morning, leaving widening patches of blue sky. She got out of the car and noticed twigs and sodden leaves strewn all over the gravel as well as a tree that had come down over the river. Mrs B opened the door. Margot hurried in out of the cold. 'Good morning, Mrs B,' she said, rubbing her hands together. 'Is he up?'

'Which one?' Mrs B asked.

'Lord Deverill.'

'Not yet. Master Colm is in the library, waiting for you.'

'Great. Thanks. I'll go and find him.'

Margot walked down the hall, anxious about what she was going to say to him. She should never have kissed him. It had been rash. An 'in the moment' thing, which is so often regretted.

Colm was standing at the window when she entered, looking out over the lawn much like his father had been when she had first met him all those weeks ago. He smiled at the sight of her. A smile of joy tempered by hope, which was both endearing and charming. In fact, it was so attractive that it caught her off guard. Suddenly, her regret was less certain. 'Hi,' she said.

'Hi,' he replied. They looked at each other, searching for affirmation.

Margot didn't know what to say. She had been so sure that she had made a mistake, but now, seeing him there, handsome and cheerful, she doubted herself. She had never doubted herself before. She had always known exactly what she wanted, and more precisely, what she *didn't* want.

Colm wanted to kiss her again to dispel the awkwardness, but suddenly his father was in the doorway behind Margot, looking as if the night before had been just another evening spent by the fire with a book and a glass of whiskey, and he had to turn his attention away from Margot. 'Hello, you two,' said JP in surprise. Besides a ruddy complexion and glazed, rheumy eyes, he didn't look too worse for wear, considering the devastation he had caused to the library as well as to himself.

Colm and Margot looked at him in astonishment. Neither had expected to see him so hearty. They glanced at each other. The kiss would have to wait. 'Good morning, JP,' said Margot.

'Would you like breakfast?' He spoke to both Margot and Colm. 'Mrs B can whip up anything you like, within reason.'

'I've just eaten,' Colm replied. 'But we'll have a cup of tea, or coffee, won't we, Margot, to keep you company.'

'Sure. I could really do with some coffee,' she replied.

JP shuffled into the corridor towards the dining room. 'There was a terrible storm last night,' he said, as if they didn't know. 'I looked out of the window just now and saw that a tree has come down over the river. Luckily, not a precious one. Just an old ash. Probably on its way out anyway. Those ash are having a hard time fighting disease. We're losing them all over the country. I'll get the boys to chop it up for firewood.'

Margot followed him. She felt Colm's presence behind her and knew that he was thinking the same as she was. How were they going to broach the subject of his alcoholism when he had no recollection of what happened the night before?

JP took his usual place at the head of the table. Margot and Colm sat either side of him. Mrs B gave a little shrug when she saw him. She knew it would be this way. It had always been this way. Selective amnesia was what she called it. She brought in JP's breakfast, accompanied by a pot of tea. Margot and Colm made conversation, keeping it light, drinking their coffee as if it were simply a normal morning. JP didn't ask what Colm was doing there at this time of day. If he knew his son had slept over, he didn't let on. Margot supposed that if he acknowledged the unusual sequence of events, he would have to acknowledge what he'd got up to last night, and she knew he'd avoid that at all cost. Just like her father used to do. As they talked about the weather and Margot's research, she and Colm did their best not to catch eyes lest JP sense their collusion and grow suspicious.

'So,' said JP with a sigh, putting his napkin on the table and picking up his cigarette packet and releasing one. 'What's on the agenda for today, Margot?' He lit the cigarette, blowing smoke across the table.

Margot smiled sweetly and Colm realized that she was

going to drop the bomb, right now, at the table. He stiffened. 'Today, JP, is the first day of your sobriety,' she declared.

It took a moment for her words to register. 'Sorry, Margot, what did you say?'

'You're going to give up drinking, JP. Colm and I are going to help you.' She put a hand on his. He stared down at it, uncertain whether to remove it or leave it there. Colm dared not speak. He knew that there was a danger of his father exploding into a rage if he joined in.

JP frowned, teetering on the edge between indignation and calm. A moment passed that seemed like minutes and then he forced a smile. 'I'm not sure what you're talking about, Margot. But it's very funny. *You're* very funny.' He withdrew his hand. 'Now, I suspect that Mrs B has already lit the fire in the games room.'

Colm braced himself and plunged in. 'Dad, she's not being funny. Do you remember anything about last night?'

JP's face hardened. He turned to his son. 'Last night?'

'Do you remember what happened?'

Now there was fear in his eyes. 'Nothing happened. I don't know what you're talking about,' he snapped. 'What are you saying, Colm?'

'You got drunk, threw everything you could reach onto the library floor and passed out.'

He was about to deny it. The anger rose into his chest, boiling and spitting with offence. How could his own son accuse him of such a thing? Yet, slowly the memory materialized out of the fog like an ugly creature, or perhaps it had always been there, only he'd chosen not to see it. His face dropped with shame. What was the point in refuting it, when he knew very well that it was true? 'And you put me to bed, I suppose. That's why you're here at breakfast,' he said in a quiet voice.

'Margot was here too,' Colm added.

JP looked at Margot, horrified. 'I'm sorry you had to see me like that.'

The wounded look in his eyes caused her heart to flood with compassion. 'It's okay, JP,' she reassured him gently. 'I grew up with an alcoholic father. I've seen it all before. I'm beyond shocking.'

'Look, that's never happened before. I was upset,' he began, turning back to Colm. 'Your mother came round. We both said some terrible things. I reached for the bottle. It's normal.' He chuckled, dismissing it as a rare and minor occurrence. 'I know I drink too much. I smoke too much too.' He looked at the cigarette between his fingers and shrugged. 'No one is perfect.'

'You're an alcoholic, JP,' said Margot. 'And if you don't get well, you're going to die.'

JP patted her hand. 'Let's not be over-dramatic.'

'She's right, Dad. You know she's right.'

'It won't happen again. I'm sorry I worried you.'

'You *did* worry us,' said Colm.

JP's looked at his son in surprise. '*You* were worried, Colm?'

'Of course I was worried. You're my dad.'

JP searched for words, but failed to find them.

'When I saw you on the floor, I thought you were dead,' Margot added. 'You gave me a real shock.'

'I'm sorry. I'll drink less in future.' He pushed out his chair, signalling the end of the conversation.

'No, you're not going to drink at all,' said Colm firmly. He stood up. 'There's not a drop of alcohol left in the house.'

JP's face reddened. 'You've cleared out my house?' he exclaimed. 'Are you out of your bloody mind, Colm?'

'It wasn't just Colm, JP. It was me too,' said Margot. 'We did it together. Because we want you to get well.'

'This is unacceptable!' he said, raising his voice. He didn't look at Margot. He was unable to direct his anger at her. 'Who do you think you are coming in like thieves and stealing my property? You can't just take what you want without asking.'

'Dad, you have to face up to the fact that you have a problem. We're not the enemy. We're here to help you.'

JP's nostrils flared. He looked from one to the other like a bull backed into the corner by a couple of matadors. 'I want you to leave,' he said. 'I want you both to leave, this minute.' If ever he needed a drink, it was now. He felt panic rising into his chest.

'We're not leaving, JP,' said Margot gently. 'Let's go into the library and talk about this calmly. It's nice and warm in there.'

JP didn't argue. He stubbed out his cigarette in the ashtray beside his place. With his shoulders hunched and his hands in his pockets, he wandered slowly down the cold corridor to the library where Mrs B had lit a hearty fire. He sank into his armchair. He knew there was no whiskey in the room but his eyes searched for it all the same. Colm took the other armchair and Margot the sofa. JP fumbled for another cigarette and lit it. 'So, I'm all ears. Say what you want to say. I know I'll not be rid of you until you do.'

'Until you acknowledge that your drinking is out of control, JP, you're not going to get better. We can't help you unless you want to help yourself.'

'I don't need help, Margot,' he retorted crossly.

'Shall I enlighten you on how bad it was last night?' said Colm. 'That we found you covered in vomit and—'

JP put his hand up, glanced at Margot then back at Colm. 'All right, all right. I get your point. I was not a pretty sight,' he snapped. 'Good Lord, am I to have no dignity?'

'You lost your dignity last night. It's not the first time, Dad. You're not the same man you used to be.'

'We all age, Colm. It'll happen to you, too, then you can see how you like it!'

'It's got nothing to do with age and everything to do with alcohol.'

Margot leaned forward. 'You remember you told me that you lamented the loss of the man you once were?' she said, her voice soft and full of kindness. He grunted, wary of agreeing to anything. 'He's still there, JP, inside you. He's still handsome, charming, witty and clever. You can be him again, if you want to. But you have to want to, because no one else can do it for you. My father never wanted to get better. For him, he chose to die young *with* alcohol rather than to grow old *without* it. It was his choice. I was fourteen when he died. I lost the man I loved more than anyone else in the world. But really, I had lost him years before when he ceased to put me first. No one was more important to him than his gin. Not even me, his child. I could have been drowning and he would have rather reached for the bottle than put out a hand to save me.' Margot wiped away a tear with her fingers. JP was staring at her, his face crumpled with compassion. 'The thing is, JP, I don't think you're anything like as far gone as my father was. You wouldn't reach for the bottle if Colm was drowning. You've ridden out with me and taken pleasure from the light bouncing off the water and the little flowers growing in the grass. You've begun to work in the garden, planting things and waiting eagerly for them to grow. Daddy took no interest in nature. He took no pleasure in beauty, because he no longer saw beyond his next drink. But you're not like that. You can give it all up today and, with our support, find the old JP again. Your old friend, the one everybody loved.'

JP's lips twitched with self-pity. 'Do you really think I can get him back, the old JP, I mean? Is it possible?' When he looked at them both his eyes were no longer blazing with fury but shiny with regret.

'You can, Dad, because, as Margot says, he's still there.'

'Very well,' he replied, his voice buoyant with intention. 'I'll start today. My first day of sobriety.' He gave Margot a small, contrite smile. 'One step at a time, eh?'

'One step at a time,' she repeated.

She stood up.

'Where are you going?' Colm asked.

'I'm going to take a walk around the garden. You two are going to talk.' They both looked at her in confusion. Colm shuffled uncomfortably in his chair. 'You, JP, are going to tell Colm why your marriage broke down and why you sold the castle. You, Colm, are not going to interrupt, or get heated, but you're going to listen with compassion and understanding, because at the root of JP's story is the reason why he started to drink. You're going to be honest with each other, knowing neither of you will be judged. I would stay, but it's not appropriate. You need to be able to talk to each other in private, knowing that whatever is said will remain within these four walls.'

JP looked at Colm. 'Shall I ask Mrs B to make us some tea?'

'That would be a good idea,' said Colm.

Margot left the room. She passed Mrs B in the corridor. 'I think we're getting somewhere, Bessie,' she whispered.

Mrs B crossed herself. 'By God's grace,' she replied solemnly.

'I think I'd make a good therapist,' Margot added with a grin.

But Mrs B was wiser than all of them put together. She patted Margot's arm. 'I think *you* need the therapy as much as they do,' she said and continued on down the corridor towards the library. Margot watched her go, but couldn't think of anything to say, except that she was probably right.

Margot set off across the lawn. Sunshine found its way through the tears in the cloud and cast long shadows across the grass. She felt a cautious sense of optimism. JP wasn't out of the woods yet, not by a long way, but he had taken his first step. Hadn't he said, on their first meeting, that he wanted to tell his side of the story? Hadn't he complained that no one ever listened to him? That they didn't care to hear what he had to say. Well, she hoped he was now telling it and that Colm was listening.

She put her hands in her pockets and watched her breath mist on the damp air. Her mind turned back to the kiss. She sighed deeply as the weight of the dilemma settled heavily upon her shoulders once again. As reluctant as she was to get attached to someone, she had really liked kissing him. They were already colluding, what would it matter if they got a little closer in the process? Since when had she become so sensible? She'd enjoyed many men; Colm was just one more, wasn't he? Margot thought of Mrs B and smiled to herself. She wondered what, in her uncanny wisdom, she would say about *this*.

Kitty

Alana and her father are on the beach. Small figures against the vast expanse of sea, beneath the enormous sky, buffeted by winds that sweep in damp and cold off the water. Angry grey clouds churn above them, as if Alana's fury and pain have materialized into vapour, shutting out the sun, darkening the day, advancing the night before it is time.

She is crying. Jack puts his arm around her as they amble against the gale. She is like a child again, leaning into his embrace. Relying on her father to make things right. But not even Jack, with all his wisdom, can do that. 'What happened to the man I fell in love with, Da?' she asks. We'd all like to know the answer to that. 'What happened to the laughter and the mischief, to the fun?'

'Life,' says Jack. 'Life happened, that's what.'

Life happened to us too, didn't it, Jack?

'Things were less complicated when we were young.'

'They *seem* less complicated when you look back on them from a distance, but at the time, your problems were as big as they are now, only different.'

'I don't remember problems at all,' she says.

'Because the problems you're facing now have eclipsed them. You look back on the past through rose-tinted glasses.

But life wasn't rose-tinted. It was tough and it taught us all some hard lessons.'

Alana walks on in silence. Jack has triggered a dark memory that stirs from its slumber and bares its teeth. I know they are both thinking of me. 'You're right,' she agrees. 'I called off my engagement with JP because of your affair with Kitty Deverill. I remember that.'

'You did, indeed.'

'I didn't want to have anything to do with the Deverills. I thought they had bad blood. I should have stuck to my guns. I went ahead and married one and look where it got me!'

'And what of *me*, Alana? Shouldn't *I* take some responsibility for my affair? Do I have bad blood too?'

'It's different.'

'No, it isn't. I was just as much to blame for breaking my marriage vows as Kitty was for breaking hers. JP broke his and hurt you, just like I hurt your mother. There's very little difference when you boil them both down.'

'I am half the woman Mam is,' says Alana and her voice is heavy with defeatism.

'That's because half of you is me. Hot-headed and stubborn like all O'Learys tend to be.'

'I'd like to be more like Mam,' she says.

'Indeed, she's a good woman,' he agrees. And he's right, she is, a better woman than I ever was.

'You know I promised not to tell Mam about the letters from Kitty that I found in your vet's bag? Well, I broke my promise and told her,' she confesses.

'You did?' says Jack, although he doesn't care about it now. It was over thirty years ago, after all.

'Do you know what she said?'

'What did she say?'

'That she had always known you loved Kitty.'

He stops walking and looks at her in surprise. 'She said that?'

'She did. She didn't blame you or have it out with you. She just waited patiently for the infatuation to die, which it did in the end, didn't it. I promised I'd never tell you.'

'So you broke both promises?'

'I suppose I did.'

'Some promises are meant to be broken for the higher good.'

'Where's the higher good in these broken promises then?'

Jack sighs, no doubt casting his mind back to the time when he had to make a choice between me and his wife, and he chose his wife. But our love never died, as Alana thinks it did, we just had to honour those we had vowed before God to love and cherish. We had to fulfil our commitment to *them*. Our affair had reached the end of the road and had nowhere else to go. We had to do the right thing. 'You said you wanted to be more like your mam. Well, your mam knows when to let go,' he says. 'You need to forgive and let go, too, Alana.'

She doesn't like the sound of that. She inhales through her nostrils and draws her lips into a thin line. There are few, like Emer O'Leary, who have the ability to rise above their egos. Alana is hurt. She is cross and she is disappointed. And JP is collaborating on a book about her family that she fears will expose all her secrets into the light of public scrutiny. 'I am not ready for that,' she says quietly. 'He does not deserve my forgiveness.'

'I did not deserve your mother's.'

'Mam is a better woman than I.' She is a better woman than both of us, Alana.

'Because of the choices she makes,' Jack adds wisely.

'I stand by my choices. It was not my choice that my husband slept with another woman.'

'But it's your choice to hold it against him. It's been, what, fourteen years since you divorced? Are you going to allow one slip to stand between you for the rest of your lives?'

Alana raises her voice. 'It's not *my* choice that he turned into a hopeless drunk. It's not *my* choice that he's helping that writer research her book on our family. And it was not *my* choice that he sold the family home. None of it was *my* choice.'

Jack looks at her, his face is full of compassion and love, but also pity, for he can see her frailties, which she is unable to see for herself. 'Until you take responsibility for the part you played in all of those choices, Alana, you will never be happy.'

And there it is, wisdom spoken by a man who truly understands the meaning of humility and the value of forgiveness.

Chapter 13

Margot was in the games room pacing the floor when Colm came looking for her. She had been trying to work, sitting in the armchair beside the fire, reading, but her mind had kept going back to the library, hoping that Colm was allowing his father to say his piece and that they were both being empathetic. He pushed the door open a crack.

'Can I come in?' he asked.

'Of course. I only had the door closed to keep in the warmth,' she replied, moving closer, eager for a debrief.

'Come for a walk with me? I need to get out of the house. I need some space.'

Colm looked grave and weary, which wasn't a surprise as he and JP had been talking for over three hours.

They set off down the path that shadowed the river, past the fallen ash that bridged it and the evergreen shrubs that wore beads of rain like fine jewellery. Colm inhaled the cold air in loud breaths as if he needed the oxygen to restore his strength. Margot walked behind him in silence, giving him the space he'd said he needed, until the path widened enough for them to continue side by side.

'You're a bold girl, Margot,' he said. 'I couldn't have confronted Dad without you.'

'I'm glad I could help.'

'You might not have managed to save your father, but you're certainly helping to save mine.'

'I don't imagine anyone could have saved Daddy. The difference being that JP *does* want to get better. That makes all the difference in the world.'

'I think he was most ashamed of being seen in that state by *you*.'

'I'm sorry we had to tell him that, but shame was the only way to make him want to change. We can't do it for him. He has to take the steps himself.'

'I also want to thank you for encouraging us to talk, about the past, I mean. We've never really processed it. It's hung between us for years, alluded to, but never discussed. I think we needed to talk about it.' Colm looked down at her. 'It was hard.'

'Did it help to hear his side of the story?'

'It did, but it also helped for him to hear *my* side of the story.' Margot hadn't considered *that*.

'It's interesting how many sides there are to the same event,' he continued. 'We all see the same thing in different ways. It was important for Dad to appreciate that it wasn't just his and Mum's drama, it became mine too, and my sisters'.' Margot wanted to ask why his sisters had maintained a good relationship with their father while Colm hadn't. But she didn't want to look curious. The book she was writing was always in the back of her mind. She imagined it was in the back of his mind too.

They headed through a gate in the drystone wall and continued on up the hill towards the cliffs. She could hear the distant rumble of the sea and the desolate cry of a gull. They followed a well-trodden snake path that meandered across the land. Small yellow flowers flourished in the long grasses with wild garlic and heather, and the sun, ever higher in the sky, warmed the earth as spring edged in to dispel the land of winter. The wind toyed with Margot's hair and she began to feel that sense of exhilaration she felt when she rode out with JP. Was it that ancient magic buried deep in the soil, she wondered, rising up to intoxicate her again?

'I want to show you something,' Colm said.

'What?'

'It's a surprise.'

'I love a mystery,' she replied.

'Then you'll love this.'

She laughed. It felt good to laugh after the emotional events of the last twenty-four hours. 'I'm intrigued.'

'I sense that, beneath your cool exterior, you're a romantic.' He grinned down at her.

She thought of their kiss and blushed. She was not normally a blusher. 'Is that a compliment?'

'It's certainly meant as one,' he replied.

'I don't think I've been at all cool in the last couple of days.'

His eyes lingered on hers and they were full of knowing. 'But you *have* been romantic.'

She stole her eyes back and laughed. A defence mechanism she used to deflect awkward moments. 'Is what you're about to show me romantic then?'

'It's the most romantic place in Ballinakelly.'

She felt her blush deepen. She knew he was also thinking of their kiss. Was he perhaps thinking of doing it again?

As they came over the crest of a knoll a circle of giant stones rose up in the distance, like a coven of witches in dark grey cloaks, hunched against the wind. Beyond them the glittering sea stretched out to the horizon. Margot had visited the most famous of stone circles at Stonehenge as a schoolgirl and been fascinated by the mystery of its origins and purpose, which still remained unsolved. She was riveted to discover that Ballinakelly had its very own stone circle. 'This is our local mystery. We have a few, like the swaying Madonna,' Colm told her.

'The swaying Madonna?' Margot had never heard of that.

'It's a famous statue beside the Ballinakelly Road that sways all on its own.' He arched his eyebrows.

'Have you ever seen it sway?'

'No.'

'Does it really sway?'

'Apparently so.'

She laughed. 'And this? Does anyone know what it was built for?'

'No, it's a mystery too. There are seventeen stones and they're supposedly over a thousand years old. Legend says that they are women cursed to live as stones by day but come alive at night.'

'Nice. Who cursed them?'

'A man, obviously.' He grinned. 'It's always a man, isn't it?'

'A wizard perhaps,' said Margot, sensing the beginning of a good story. 'A very possessive wizard who had seventeen daughters. Afraid that they would marry and move away, he cursed them to remain here as rocks. But his power wasn't strong enough to turn them to rock for always, only during daylight hours. So, when the sun sets they are restored to life, only to return to their sad stone formation at the first blush of dawn.'

'You should be a writer,' he joked.

She sighed. 'I think I'd have an easier job of it were I to write *The Cursed Daughters of Ballinakelly*. Let's go and take a closer look.'

They walked towards them. 'My mother told me that this was her and Dad's secret place when they first met,' he said. 'They'd steal up here in order to be alone together.'

'I bet they weren't the first, or the last.'

'You're probably right. It's an ideal place to steal a kiss.'

Margot didn't dare look at him. She didn't dare mention their kiss, either. There were so many reasons why they shouldn't. Only one good reason why they should. 'These stones hold many secrets,' she said, striding over to touch one. She placed her hand against the hard, cold rock. 'If only they could talk.'

The wind raced around the stones as it had surely done for hundreds of years, playing with them, trying to rouse them from their sleep, or from their enchantment. And yet they remained silent and still and watchful, observing the secret trysts that took place in their sanctuary and listening to the plots and intrigues whispered in their shadows. Margot imagined how much they had witnessed over the hundreds of years of Ireland's turbulent history and how much they could tell if only they were able. Ireland was a country steeped in war. As a lover of stories the stone circle fascinated her not only for its romance but also for the plotting and scheming that must have taken place there.

She turned to Colm, who was leaning back against one of them, watching her with a wistful look on his face. 'It's very beautiful up here,' she said.

'That's why I brought you. I knew you'd like it.'

'And you needed some air.'

'I needed to be alone with you,' he corrected her. 'Far away from the house. Far away from everyone. Just the two of us.' He walked towards her. 'I liked kissing you last night,' he said. And there it was, out in the open, exposed, and Margot didn't know what to do with it.

'It was rash,' she began.

'I know.'

She sighed deeply. 'Look, I'm not a good bet, Colm, and I'm writing a book about your family. It's just a bad idea on so many levels.'

'You're right. It's a terrible idea. I still resent you for writing that book.'

'I still resent you for asking me not to.'

'My mother would be furious if she knew I was even talking to you.'

'Your father might be a little put out, too, if he knew you'd kissed me.'

'But you kissed me back.' He smiled.

She couldn't help but smile with him. 'I did.'

She felt the hard stone against her back. He stood before her, blue eyes gazing down at her and into her, as if he was going to allow nothing to come between them, especially not logic. 'I like you, Margot. God help me, but I can't help liking you.'

She frowned. 'I like you too, but . . .'

Then he was kissing her again. Pressing her against the stone, his hands sliding beneath her coat and around her waist, pulling her into his arms, holding her tightly. And she was returning his kiss without inhibition, eyes closed, every nerve in her body electrified, sinking into the moment without resistance. And the stones kept their silent vigil, enfolding them into their sanctuary as they had done for hundreds of lovers before Margot and Colm. *How little love changes*, they would have said if they could speak. *Always secretive, urgent, passionate and fearful*. High up on the hill with no one for miles around, the stone circle gave them the gift of the moment, placing them fully within it.

At length, they sat together on the grass, sheltered from the wind at the foot of one of the megaliths, and talked about JP.

'Dad and I have kept a secret for years,' Colm told her. 'We never discussed it. But it stood between us like a rotten thing. You gave me the courage to bring it into the light.'

'You don't have to tell me what it is, Colm.'

'Margot, I can't be with you if I'm unable to trust you. So, I'm going to trust you and hope that I'm not an eejit for doing so.'

'You're not an eejit,' she reassured him. 'You have to trust that I have the sensitivity to know what, and what not, to put in the book.'

'I won't mention trust again, I promise.' He pulled her towards him and kissed her temple. 'I was twelve years old. Mam was out with my sisters and I was hanging around the river with my friend Paul. Paul and I had a fight. I can't remember what it was about. But I ran off and went home. I wasn't expected until dinner. I thought I'd go and whinge about the fight to Rosie, our governess. She wasn't really a governess, more like a glorified nanny or a big sister. She was only twenty, or thereabouts. And I thought the world of her. She was pretty and funny. I suppose I was soft on her. She was the first woman who aroused feelings in me.' Margot would have laughed at that if she hadn't sensed already what he was about to tell her. 'I went to her room. Padding up the corridor, all eager to tell her my woe. She had a bedroom on the first floor with a sitting room next door. We often played board games in there because it was warm with the fire lit. I didn't just find Rosie. I found Dad and Rosie, in bed together.'

'God, that's terrible,' said Margot, envisaging the little boy's face full of horror and disbelief.

'I knew next to nothing about sex, but I knew what they were up to all right.'

'What did you do?'

'I ran for it. I hid in my room and sobbed my heart out.'

'Oh Colm, that's awful. And you never told anyone?'

'Not a soul.'

'Rosie never mentioned it?'

'She couldn't look me in the eye after that, and Dad just pretended nothing had happened.'

'How did your mother find out?'

'She grew suspicious. Small things at first, I think. Like the smell of Rosie's perfume on Dad's clothes. Then she looked out for it and, when you look out for something with that sort of dedication, you usually find it. Mum caught them kissing. Rosie was dismissed. I think she went to live in Canada. We never heard from her again. I was hurt. She never said good-bye, not to any of us.'

'So, you lost the woman you trusted, all because of your father's carelessness.'

'That's putting it politely.'

'And then the marriage broke up and you lost your family too.'

'Mum went to live in America. Aisling and Cara chose to go with her. I stayed here, with my grandparents. I didn't want to live with Dad. He was already drinking heavily and turning mean.'

'I bet he was mean because he felt guilty that you saw him like that. You were just a boy.'

'I blamed him for everything. It's only now, as a man, that I can judge him with more perspective. Still, the sense of betrayal and hurt remains.'

'You told him that?'

'I did.'

'What did he say?'

'He said he was sorry. He was sad and sorry. We should have talked about it before. It makes a big difference to hear those words, especially when they're sincere.'

'Did he tell you why he found comfort in Rosie?'

'Yes. As I've learned, there are many different ways of looking at the same thing. We human beings are a complicated lot.'

She turned to look at him. 'Your father's drinking stems from a severe dislike of himself, Colm. That dislike probably goes right back to that moment when you found him and Rosie together. JP is a decent, honourable man. It must have killed him to have been exposed as dishonourable. Because that's not who he really is. He was driven to it by unhappiness. But he let himself down as well as everyone else. I'm sure you've put him on the road to recovery by talking about it.' He nodded. She put her hand to his cheek and ran her thumb over his cleft chin. 'And you needed to talk about it too, Colm. The little boy in you needed to let it out and let it go.'

'Life's a battle and we're all left scarred by it, in one way or another,' he said, winding his fingers around her neck, beneath her hair. He breathed in, his thoughts turning to more present matters.

'You should be a writer too,' she chuckled, noticing the change in his expression and feeling once again a flutter of nervous anticipation in her stomach.

He inclined his head, his blue eyes intense and full of purpose. 'I'm not sure that was very original, but it sounded good.' He smiled and kissed her again.

When they returned to the Hunting Lodge, JP was in the garden, shovelling manure into the border. His cheeks were pink from the cold and exertion and he seemed to be working with a new vigour, as if each strenuous movement of the spade was a deliberate step in the direction of recovery. Margot's spirits lifted when she saw him. He had the backbone her father had lacked. A strong willpower and determination to make a change in his life that Jonathan Hart couldn't find. Where *he* had given Margot a sense of helplessness, JP gave her a sense of optimism. She knew the best way to get better was to keep busy, preferably outside in nature. He would need their support more in the evenings, when the habit of sinking into his armchair by the fire would make him want to reach for the whiskey decanter. She and Colm would have to take it in turns to stay with him. It wouldn't be fair to leave him on his own. She glanced at Colm as they strode across the grass towards JP and envisaged the three of them playing cards in the library. Strangely, that image was not an unpleasant one.

'I suppose I'd better get back to work,' said Colm, putting his hands in his pockets and smiling at his father.

JP stuck his spade into the earth and smiled back. 'All right, son. I'll see you later, perhaps?'

'You will. Margot and I are going to be around a lot to keep an eye on you and to give you support. You're going to get pretty sick of us, I'm afraid.'

JP laughed. 'I'll never get sick of the two of you.'

'I'm going to work a bit here, then head back to the hotel at teatime,' Margot added. 'I need to show my face around there or I'll be sent back to England in disgrace.'

They set off up the lawn, leaving JP to his toil. Colm's Land Rover was parked on the gravel at the front of the house. He took her hand and pulled her behind it. 'We can't be seen by Dad, or Mrs B, for that matter.'

'Or your mother,' Margot added with a grin. 'In fact, we can't be seen by anybody.'

'God, it's like being a teenager again.' He slid his hands around her neck, beneath her hair.

'There's more at stake than being grounded,' she reminded him.

He laughed. 'Better not take any risks.' He pressed his lips to hers and for a moment they were both distracted. Margot felt her body grow warm and wished they could sneak up and use one of the bedrooms in the Lodge.

Colm read her thoughts. 'I want to make love to you, Margot,' he mumbled into her ear.

'I want you to,' she whispered back. The very thought of it made her catch her breath.

He hesitated a moment, deliberating. 'Come this evening,' he said. 'We can have dinner with Dad and then ... I don't know, send him to bed early.'

'Sounds good to me,' she agreed and watched him climb into the Land Rover and drive off.

After the morning she'd had, Margot wasn't sure she'd be able to concentrate on her work, but she went to the games room all the same. Mrs B had lit a fire. Outside, the sun had come out and was flooding the lawn with light. She could hear the birdsong and it made her think of spring, bluebells and daffodils, longer evenings and lighter mornings. She looked at the piles of ledgers and papers neatly stacked on the carpet and recalled their game of rabbits. In her mind's eye she saw Colm racing around the table, his face full of laughter and his wavy hair falling over his forehead.

She was disturbed by a knock on the door. It was Mrs B. 'Would you like a cup of tea, Miss Hart?' she asked.

'I'd love one, Mrs B, thank you so much.'

There was a pause while Mrs B lingered in the doorway. 'It's good to see Master Colm about the house,' she said at length. 'Good that the two of them are talking.' Margot nodded in agreement and smiled. 'You're a bold girl, Margot,' the old housekeeper added suddenly and her gentle eyes were full of gratitude. 'You have a rare gift.' Margot didn't know what to say, but Mrs B did not need a reply. 'I'll go and wet the tea,' she said and softly closed the door.

Margot settled down to work. She opened the final box. It was the smallest of the lot, which was why she had left it until last. Inside was a miniature crimson chest made out of wood. It looked old, early nineteenth century, she guessed. She carefully lifted it out and attempted to open it. To her frustration, it was locked. The little keyhole begged for a key and yet, on further inspection inside the box, there was none to be found. She gave it a shake. It rattled. There were things inside – treasures, she hoped. Reluctantly, she put it to one side. She'd ask Colm to help her later. It was just the sort of thing he'd probably be able to do with one of his veterinary instruments.

She pulled out a pile of letters instead, bound together with a blue silk ribbon. She'd gone through loads of letters already. Some were of interest, others just satisfied her curiosity but would not serve for the book.

She gently untied the ribbon and pulled out the first letter. It was written in neat, slanted handwriting, the ink faded to a light brown but still legible. The envelope was addressed to a Mrs Jane Chadwick in Lancashire, England. Margot wondered who this Jane Chadwick was and why letters addressed to her should find their way into the Deverill archives. She pulled out another one. To her astonishment it was addressed to the same woman. As Margot flicked through all the envelopes she realized that each one was addressed to Jane. Her interest piqued, she opened the first letter and scanned the page until she found the signature at the bottom. Now she was truly intrigued. The letter was signed *Your loving sister, Frances*. Hurriedly and with mounting excitement she turned the page over in search of the date. *12 July 1821*. Frances was none other than Frances Wilson, married to Tarquin Deverill.

Margot curled up in the armchair beside the fire and began to read. The letters, besides being full of mundane news, were full of love for Frances's disabled little boy, Gabriel. Frances had five other children – Peregrine being the eldest and heir – who were robust and healthy, and she had lost three in infancy. Gabriel was her youngest and a source of great worry to her. The letters were increasingly about him. Not only was he born with a twisted spine, which made one leg shorter than the other, but he was mentally retarded. Frances described him as 'loving', 'full of laughter', 'uncommonly affectionate' and 'slow'. *He will always be a child, I fear, even as he grows. His father cannot abide him and will not have him in his sight, but has him hidden away in the tower so as not to embarrass him. It breaks my heart to see him treated in this way. Tarquin gives more affection to the dogs.* Margot wondered whether this poor child was kept in *her* tower. She lifted her eyes off the page a moment and envisaged Gabriel gazing out of the window onto the lawn below where his siblings played on the grass, perhaps even with their father, while *he* had to remain isolated and imprisoned in his bedroom. With a heart racing with indignation, she read on.

Tarquin referred to his son as 'a monster', 'a freak of nature' and 'a beast'. He refused to have him educated with his other sons, so that his mother had to teach him to read herself, which was almost impossible due to his retarded mental development. So great was Tarquin's dislike for the boy that in public he claimed only to have five children. Once, when Frances reminded him of the sixth, he struck her face with the back of his hand, tearing her skin with his signet ring. She never dared do that again.

Mrs B came in with a pot of tea and some cake but Margot barely stirred from her chair, except to mumble a quiet 'thank you' before returning to the letters. More than once did Frances fear for the boy's life. *My husband's loathing for the child is such that I am filled with terror at what he might do while my boy sleeps. I have taken to climbing into bed with him in the night to keep him safe.* And then the letters reached their terrible climax. Frances's handwriting became more erratic. Margot sensed her distress in the fitful striking of the quill across the page. Tarquin had done an extraordinary thing. He'd taken the child into the garden on his birthday to show him the flowers. This he had never done before. Frances was consumed with anxiety. She knew her husband and what he was capable of. And then the unthinkable happened. The boy, Tarquin claimed, was reaching for the fish in the ornamental pond and fell in. By the time his father reached him, he had drowned.

In despair, Frances wrote to her sister: *I do not believe a single word of it, Jane. God forgive me for casting blame, but I believe my husband meant for my beloved boy to die in this way, on this day, to relieve him of the burden of having an imperfect child. Although my beautiful boy was no burden to anyone. Just a source of God's light and love embodied in an innocent and crippled child. He is at peace. But I am in an eternal Hell, dear Jane. I see no release for me.*

Margot wiped away a tear and took a breath. She dropped

the letter onto her lap. She knew what happened next. Shortly after, poor Frances Deverill died, Margot guessed of a broken heart.

She presumed the letters were in the family archive because Frances's sister wanted Tarquin to be held accountable for his crime. That never happened, of course. But somehow these letters found their way into the castle so that, at least, history would record the terrible thing that he had done. Margot gazed into the fire, at the dancing flames of golden light, and wondered what happened to souls like Tarquin's, if there was indeed life after death. Was there such a thing as Hell for the likes of him? If justice was not carried out in his lifetime, was it carried out after?

More than ever before Margot felt a sense of purpose in writing this book. It needed to be written for those like Frances and Gabriel whose stories had never seen the light. She rested her head against the chair and closed her eyes. She thought about the ghosts in the castle that so many people seemed to believe in and suddenly wished that she believed in them too. Countless evil people escaped justice on earth. What a consolation it would be to know that they would, in fact, be held accountable for their actions, in some dark and miserable place *after* death.

She opened her eyes and looked at the small crimson chest sitting on the billiard table. She wondered what secret thing lay inside.

Chapter 14

Margot told JP about the letters over lunch. 'I'm afraid some of my ancestors were not very nice people,' he said, looking sheepish. 'In fact, when Alana accuses me of having bad blood, I think she's probably right.'

'That's not true,' said Margot. 'Their sins are not your sins and besides, if she accuses you of having bad blood then she accuses her children too, which I doubt she means to do. It's just a way of making you feel guilty. But there are two sides to every story and, as far as I can see, she has as much to feel guilty about as you do.'

JP looked at her with tenderness. 'You're very loyal to me, Margot, considering we haven't really known each other for very long. Do I remind you, perhaps, of your father?'

Margot frowned. 'There are similarities. But to be honest, I like you for you, JP. My father was a hopeless case. You, on the other hand, fill me with hope. I know you can get better. I'm counting on you to get better.'

He reached out and patted her hand. 'I'm grateful to you for your belief in me. I won't let you down.' Then he grinned. 'I rather look forward to showing that ex-wife of mine a new, sober me. That'll give her something to think about.'

Margot smiled back in surprise. Who'd have thought that

the person who'd inspire JP to get better would be very person
who had caused him to be unwell?

Margot returned to the hotel in time for tea. She was surprised
to see the Countess sitting at a round table in the middle of
the dining room, holding forth to a group of six enraptured
American tourists. Elegant in a pussy-bow blouse, her hair
swept into an elaborate up-do and large diamond earrings
glittering at her lobes, she looked every inch the blue-blooded
countess – at least, Margot thought, to tourists who knew no
better. 'You see, when my husband the Count lived here,'
she was saying in her thick Austrian accent, '*this* was where
the family ate their meals, at a long table, served by footmen.
One servant for each person, you know, standing to attention
behind the chairs. That was the way it was back then. It was
perfectly normal to live like that. Of course the servants had
to pretend they weren't hearing the conversations, but you
can imagine, they must have heard everything. The guests
were important people, nobility, politicians . . .' The Countess
inhaled and gave a small, self-satisfied smile. 'Even royalty.'

Margot rolled her eyes. She didn't believe poor Bridie had
ever breathed the same air as a member of the Royal Family.
As she made her way across the hall towards the stairs she
was met by Mr Dukelow, striding purposely towards her, on
his face a self-satisfied smile similar to the Countess's. 'Hello,
Miss Hart,' he said, rubbing his hands together. 'I have news.'

She waited for him to tell her that they were, at this very
moment, being graced by the distinguished presence of the
Countess. But he did not mention her. 'I have been speaking
to your friend, Mr Chambers,' he said.

'Ah,' Margot replied, surprised.

'I've booked him in for the first week in May. I haven't asked for references. Your referral is all I need. I'm sure he will be thoroughly entertaining.' He lifted his chin. 'Although, as I've said many times, this castle is not haunted. Not in the slightest.'

'I don't think it's the castle ghosts he'll be contacting.'

Mr Dukelow frowned. 'Then, which ghosts *will* he be contacting?'

'The dead loved-ones of the people in the audience.' Mr Dukelow looked horrified. 'Have you never seen a medium at work?'

'No, I haven't. And it would not have occurred to me to invite one to the hotel if the boss hadn't insisted.' He gave a shrug. 'What Mrs de Lisle wants, Mrs de Lisle gets.'

'I think you'll be surprised how many people are interested in the paranormal.'

'Good. Mrs de Lisle also mentioned asking Lord Deverill to be an after-dinner speaker.'

Margot's stomach twisted. 'I don't think he'd want to do that.'

Mr Dukelow rubbed his thumb and forefinger together. 'He might when he hears how much she'll pay him. He would be a big draw. Lord Deverill himself, speaking about his family's history in the very castle where it all took place.'

'You can certainly ask him.' Margot reminded herself that JP was not her responsibility. Who was she to say whether or not he would agree to work for Mrs de Lisle?

'I will. Mrs de Lisle has asked me to.'

'And if he declines, you could always invite the Countess.' She gave a playful smile.

'The Countess is already giving speeches for free.'

'Angling for a job, perhaps?'

Mrs Dukelow did not look amused. 'Of course not. That would be beneath her,' he replied.

'At least she looks like the real McCoy, even if she isn't really.'

'I did mention her to Mrs de Lisle, but she slammed me down,' said Mr Dukelow.

'I'm sure she did. From what I know of the formidable Mrs de Lisle, she likes things to be authentic. Leopoldo is not a Deverill and he only lived in the castle for fourteen years. I'm afraid, your guests would feel short changed if he, or his wife, were to give after-dinner speeches. If you're going to do it at all, it has to be a Deverill.'

'Or *you*,' he added, raising his eyebrows as if he had only just thought of it.

'I might have a good understanding of the family's history, but if there's a choice, I would definitely go for Lord Deverill. I think he would be a massive draw.'

'How is your book going, by the way?'

'I've nearly finished my research.'

He rubbed his chin a moment. 'Perhaps, Miss Hart, seeing as you're now such a good friend of Lord Deverill's, *you* could ask him about being an after-dinner speaker.'

Margot laughed. 'I'm afraid not, Mr Dukelow. If you want him to work for you, you need to ask him yourself.'

Margot was about to take the stairs to her bedroom when she changed her mind and wandered into the drawing room instead. Lured by the dark magnetism of Tarquin Deverill, she stood beneath the portrait and stared into it with a macabre fascination. Now that she'd read his wife's letters, the man was no longer a flat interpretation in oil but a person, living and breathing with veins full of blood and an energy that radiated into the room, giving her a strong sense of his menacing personality. As she was drawn deeper into the picture, he seemed to slowly turn his face and look her dead in the eye. The cold, resentful stare of a man who does not like to be scrutinized. She caught her breath and stared back in shock. She blinked. Then blinked again. It was scary how powerful the imagination could be, she thought, as the portrait reverted back to its original state. Now he was no longer looking at her, his gaze was fixed on some object beyond the frame, or perhaps lost in some unpleasant thought. For there he was, full of arrogance and show, his chest puffed out, his chin up, his lips set in a sneer, as if nothing pleased him. She wondered how a person became so dissatisfied with life to descend into cruelty, for a satisfied person could never be cruel. Happy people are by their very natures kind and generous spirited. She thought of Frances and Gabriel and wondered once more about justice. Tarquin Deverill had died peacefully in his bed at the age of seventy-eight. That didn't seem fair.

She went up to her bedroom and looked out of the window. She put her hands on the stone sill and wondered whether Gabriel had put his little hands there too and watched the seasons change through the glass. What had he made of it all?

When Margot returned to the Hunting Lodge it was late afternoon and almost dark. She parked her car and let herself in. She was immediately struck by a stark change in the atmosphere.

The house felt warmer, not just in temperature but in energy. Classical music floated down the corridor, like blood coursing through veins, restoring the place to life. JP and Colm were not in the library, but sitting in the drawing room, in their riding clothes. The fire was lit, the curtains drawn. Their faces were flushed from the wind, their spirits high.

'Margot!' JP exclaimed. 'Come and join us.'

'We've had a grand afternoon riding out on the hills,' said Colm, reminding her of their kiss at the stone circle in the conspiracy of his smile.

'And here you are, using this beautiful room,' Margot said, enjoying the rousing music coming out of the speakers in the bookcase. She assumed there was a record player hidden in the cupboard below.

'It was my grandparents' favourite room,' Colm told her. 'They lived in here, playing cards and entertaining friends. It's about time it was restored to its former glory.'

'One more room for poor Mrs B to clean,' said JP.

'I don't mind,' said Mrs B, walking in. 'The house is happy when all the rooms are in use, is it not? No house wants to languish under dust sheets and in silence. Isn't the music grand, Miss Hart? I do love to listen to music.' She stopped a moment and smiled. 'Just grand.'

Margot sat down on one of the sofas.

'I've been going through my old records,' said JP. 'I have quite a collection, you know. This is Richard Strauss.' He lifted his hand and moved to the rhythm as if conducting a small orchestra. 'Doesn't it make one feel good?'

'How was your afternoon?' Colm asked. The way he looked at Margot now was intimate, reminding her of the depth of his kiss and the touch of his hand. How quickly the energy changes between two people whose mutual attraction has been laid bare, she thought, and averted her eyes for fear of betraying her feelings to JP.

'I want to show you something,' she said, getting up. She left the room, returning a moment later with the locked chest. 'I opened the last box this morning and found this.'

Colm held out his hand. 'What is it?'

She gave it to him. 'It's locked.'

'Ah, and no key.'

'Can you pick it?'

He laughed. 'What do you take me for? I'm a vet not a thief.'

'I bet you have something in that vet's bag of yours that will unlock it.'

'I don't have my bag with me, I'm afraid. But I think I can do better than that.' He pulled a penknife out of his pocket. 'All good Boy Scouts carry one of these.'

'Are you a good Boy Scout, Colm?' she asked.

'Never was, but this penknife has come in handy many times.'

'Who did that chest belong to?' JP asked. 'Do you have any idea?'

'I think it might have belonged to Frances Deverill, Tarquin's wife. It was in the same box as letters she wrote to her sister,' Margot replied.

Colm used the tiny pair of scissors to pick the lock. 'Are they interesting, the letters?'

'Very. Their disabled son died by drowning and she blamed her husband.'

Colm looked up from his work, horrified. 'Really?'

'He drowned in the ornamental pond on his tenth birthday. His father turned a blind eye. Tarquin was a brutal man.'

'That's a terrible story, Margot,' said Colm, moving the scissors carefully in the hope of turning the lock.

'I'm afraid it is. I'm hoping that chest contains something interesting.'

'All these treasures, locked away for over a hundred years, and I never thought to look at them,' said JP in wonder.

'Why?' Margot asked. 'Why would you not be curious about your own ancestors?'

'I don't know,' JP replied with a shrug. 'I suppose it's like living in a city full of culture, you don't bother visiting the museums because you take them for granted. I've never been interested in my family's history, until now.'

'I'm glad I've inspired you.'

'Ah,' said Colm. 'I've done it!'

Margot hurried to his side. He handed her the chest. 'Go on, you see what's inside.'

She held her breath. Carefully, she lifted the lid. Inside was a simple wooden cross and an oval object. She took out the oval object and turned it over. When she saw what it was, she was injected with excitement. It was a miniature portrait of a mother and son, set in a gold-and-glass case. 'It must be Frances and Gabriel,' she whispered. 'What a find!' The woman's face was full of tenderness and love as she held her little boy against her bosom. 'She was so pretty,' Margot exclaimed, taking in her long flaxen hair and gentle brown gaze. 'And look at little Gabriel. Blond, like his mother, with big, curious brown eyes. What a shame to die the way he did.' She handed the miniature to JP. 'You must read the letters,' she said to both men. 'Then you'll know the whole story. They were sent to someone in the castle, I imagine, so that the truth would come out. But I don't think it ever did because Tarquin was never accused of neglecting his son.'

'It's a miracle they weren't destroyed,' said Colm.

'Which is why I doubt Tarquin ever read them,' Margot replied.

'Then who did?' JP asked.

'That's a mystery we'll never solve,' said Margot. 'But some-one put them in this box for safekeeping. They were meant to be read and Tarquin's crime was meant to come out. Well, it will now. A hundred and sixty years late!'

While JP studied the portrait, Colm ran his fingers over the skin on Margot's forearm. She remained there a moment, not wanting him to stop, and yet, at the same time, mindful that they were not alone.

'An intriguing find,' said JP, holding out the miniature. Colm withdrew his hand. Margot took the portrait and put it back in the chest.

She stood up. 'I'll go and fetch the letters, JP. They make heartbreaking reading,' she said and left the room.

She returned to the games room feeling aroused. She put a hand to her cheek. Colm's touch had been enough to cover her face in blushes. She took a breath and mentally told herself to calm down. He had only touched her arm. She leaned back against the billiard table and waited for her heartbeat to slow down. The fire had nearly died, leaving only grey ash and the afterglow of warmth. The curtains were closed, her research neatly stacked in piles on the floor. She had finished going through the boxes. It was now time to start writing the book.

Suddenly, Colm strode into the room. He closed the door softly behind him. Then, with a look of purpose, he went straight up to her, pulled her into his arms and kissed her. She returned his kiss with urgency, running her hands through his hair that smelled of horse dust and the salty wind. 'Dad's gone upstairs to bath and change,' he said, answering her unspoken question before pressing his lips to hers and kissing her again.

His hands slipped beneath her sweater and shirt and found the soft skin of her back. Margot felt herself growing hot. Her whole body ached for him. He lifted her onto the table.

'Let's make love, Colm,' she murmured.

'And get caught by Mrs B? That's not a good idea, Margot,' he laughed.

She cupped his face and held his gaze with hers. 'This is driving me mad, Colm. We're adults.'

'With a duty to Dad,' he reminded her.

She rested her forehead against his and sighed. 'Later then. Once he's gone to bed.'

'You enjoy taking risks, don't you?'

'I just know what I want, Colm.'

'So do I,' he replied seriously. 'And that's you, as soon as possible.'

After dinner, Mrs B cleared the table and washed up, then went upstairs to her bedroom. She took the radio with her because she liked to listen to music as she lay beneath the covers and read before going to sleep. There was always something nice to listen to. Now Lord Deverill was playing his old records, the house had at last shaken off its shroud of silence and vibrated with life once again. Even the grandfather clock seemed to have a spring in its chime. It was as if everything in the house had changed colour, from a dull grey to a vibrant palette of pretty shades. Indeed, when the sun had spilled in through the drawing-room windows today the whole room had been bathed in a beautiful amber pink.

She was grateful to Master Colm and Margot. The two of them had inspired Lord Deverill to change and, to give him his due, because it was very hard to change one's ways as he was doing, he had been ready and willing, which is half the battle, or so she'd been told. She sensed something brewing between the two young people, however. Not that Lord Deverill had noticed. He was much too busy fighting his cravings to catch the subtle little signs they gave to one another. But *she* had noticed. Women tended to be more observant, she believed. It was in the way they looked at each other and spoke to each other. There was an intimacy there that hadn't been there before, even though, God love them, they were trying very hard to conceal it. She wondered how Lord Deverill would feel were he to notice too. She knew he had a soft spot for Margot.

Mrs B struck a match and lit the little votive candles in front of the photographs of her parents, husband and brother Rafferty. She whispered her prayer and, as she gazed into her brother's serious face, she felt the tenderness flow into the wounds in her heart where her loss would never heal. However, she felt a sense of positivity and optimism that she hadn't felt in a long time and that certainly helped lift her out of her grief. Grief wasn't something one got over, it was something one learned to live with. Music and laughter resounding through the house was certainly helping her live with hers.

She bathed and changed into her nightdress then knelt beside her bed. One day at a time, she thought with a sigh, pressing her palms together and closing her eyes. She muttered a prayer for Lord Deverill, Master Colm and Margot, for Mrs Alana and the girls. She prayed that they'd be reunited as a family, because she knew they'd all be happier that way.

Then she climbed into bed, turned down the radio, and opened her book and began to read.

JP retired to his bedroom. It wasn't easy abstaining from alcohol, but it made it a lot easier with Colm and Margot to distract him. They made him feel cherished. He hadn't felt cherished in a long time. He changed into his pyjamas and went to the bathroom. He stared at his reflection in the mirror. It had only been a couple of days but he already felt he was looking better. Healthier. Was that possible? Surely not.

He was determined to change. That evening in the library had been a horrible wake-up call. He hoped Margot hadn't seen the worst of it. He cringed to think that she might have. He turned his thoughts to Colm staying in the house. It was nice having him here. Nice not to be alone. Of course Mrs B was upstairs in the attic, but that wasn't the same as having his son around. How he regretted the past. He regretted it bitterly. Yet, shedding light onto it had dispelled some of the fear. Talking about it with Colm had started a powerful healing process. A simple idea, really, to talk something over, and yet difficult to do in practice. It had been hard to find the words. Painful, as if they were wrapped in thorns. Yet, as soon as he'd said them out loud the thorns had loosened. The more they'd talked, he and Colm, the looser they'd become.

The most powerful of all the words he'd said was *sorry*. What a simple little word that is, he thought. *Sorry*. Five letters. Yet, how hard to say with sincerity. But he really did mean it. He'd felt it fall out of his heart and to his surprise the saying of it had taken away some of the pain – for both him and Colm.

As JP slipped beneath the sheets he felt a light, happy

feeling spreading through his chest. He hadn't felt that in a long time, either.

Downstairs in the games room, Margot suggested a round of rabbits. 'The traditional way,' she said with a grin.

'You know you can't beat me,' Colm replied. 'You'll be naked before I've even unbuttoned my shirt.'

'We'll see,' she laughed, taking the black ball in her hand and positioning herself at one end of the table. 'I'll go first,' she told him.

He placed the white ball in the middle of the table. 'When you're ready,' he said.

She aimed then pushed the ball slowly over the velvet. It sent the white ball rolling to the left. Colm quickly grabbed the black and gently let it go to graze the side of the white. Margot snatched the black ball and raced to the end of table where Colm was now deliberately blocking her from taking aim. A scuffle ensued. 'That's obstruction!' she exclaimed as the white ball drew to a stop.

'That'll be one item of clothing, Miss Hart.'

'Very well,' she replied. 'I can play dirty too.' Slowly she unbuttoned her blouse as Colm watched her, both amused and aroused.

'You know you could take off a shoe or a sock,' he said.

'I've never been coy.' She undid the final button and let the blouse float to the floor.

'I like that,' he said. He moved towards her.

She put out her hand. 'No touching. It's against the rules. You can look, but you can't touch – and the winner takes all.'

'All of what?' he asked.

'The loser.'

'I *really* like the sound of that.'

'So do I.' She laughed. 'I'm feeling particularly greedy tonight.'

'Very well. As you lost, I start.' He released the black ball.

A moment later, Margot was lying across the table, blocking Colm's view, and gently brushing the white ball with the black. 'Ah, how embarrassing to be beaten by a woman in a bra,' she crowed as the white ball rolled to a stop.

'The sight is somewhat distracting,' he said.

'Like I said, *I* can play dirty too. So, how coy are *you* going to be, Colm?' she goaded.

'Like for like,' he replied, unbuttoning his shirt. A moment later he stood naked from the waist up. She wished she hadn't introduced the no-touch rule. His body was broad and muscular. She wanted to run her fingers through the hair on his chest and over the down on his belly.

'My turn to start,' she said.

This time she lost. Without wasting time she removed her trousers, socks and shoes. 'You're getting less coy by the minute,' he laughed. 'That's like five points lost in one go.'

'I'm not sure I can last too much longer,' she said, standing before him in her panties and bra. Her hair was falling in tendrils over her shoulders, her pale skin glowed softly in the electric light. He ached with desire and once again made a move towards her.

'Are you sure about the no-touch rule?' he asked, eyes tracing the contours of her body with longing.

She walked up to him and stood a couple of inches away. 'If *I* can restrain myself, then so can you,' she said, but it was all she could do not to reach out and touch him.

They raced around the table. Margot had the black. She

let it go to lightly stroke the white. Colm reached for it but, as he aimed, Margot lay down in between, smiling at him triumphantly. The white ball came to a halt behind her. She laughed throatily. 'Like for like,' she said, arching an eyebrow.

Colm discarded the ball and climbed onto the table. 'I've had enough of this game,' he murmured, taking her wrists and pinning her down. 'Let's call it a draw,' he said, pressing his lips to hers in a kiss.

Kitty

A dark presence has begun to shift in and out of the Hunting Lodge. While the house looks lighter and brighter for those on the earth plane, for me in the In-between, this odious creature is all too apparent. It does not stay for long. I sense it is male and of a lower vibration than myself, coming perhaps from some lesser plane, but why, I do not know. I am used to the coming and going of other spirits, but this entity is different. Disgruntled, angry and resentful, its shadowy form lingers in the drawing room, lowering the temperature and the energy, as well as my mood, which is growing increasingly impatient. It gets lonely here in this limbo with no one to talk to except Mrs Carbery.

I never felt lonely before. I was fired up with fury, but that fury is gradually diminishing. I suppose one cannot be furious for ever. Even spirits run out of juice. Mrs Carbery has thrown me, I admit. I thought that, once I'd woken her up to the fact that she is dead, she would find the light and make her way home. She did neither. Her illusory world collapsed and she now knows exactly where she is and isn't at all happy about it. Maybe I should have left her where she was, in blissful ignorance.

Because of her, one uncomfortable question lingers in my

mind. If the light did not come for *her*, does it mean that it will not come for *me*? Am I to remain here like her? And for how long? When I am ready to leave, will I find that I cannot?

Mrs B and JP are unaware of the Presence. Except for the lowering of the temperature, which they put down to the draught slipping in through the windows that are old and rickety, or down the chimney. They light the fire, heap on the logs, but as long as the Presence remains, the room will not warm up. Still, JP likes to use that room. It's the music, I think, now he's rediscovered his old records. Perhaps the Presence likes the music too, although I suspect it's too mean to have a place in its heart for beauty.

JP is improving every day. The Deverills might not make life easy for themselves with their uncontrollable passions, but they have wills of steel. Once JP decided he would abstain from alcohol, that was that. Margot and Colm held up a mirror so that he could see himself and what he had become, and he made a conscious decision to change. I admire him for that. Perhaps, once he is fully recovered, he might work towards recovering the castle, although I'm not sure how he'll do it, now that it is in the hands of the ambitious and avaricious Mrs de Lisle. I don't like that woman, not one bit.

They have decided to employ a medium to entertain their guests. When my grandmother Adeline was alive, she and her two sisters, Hazel and Laurel, used to hold seances to contact the dead. I remember the table trembling as Barton Deverill, the old curmudgeon, used to sabotage their efforts with mischief. I think *I* can create a little mischief of my own. My fury might have lost its force, but it doesn't require much strength to be mischievous and I really am dreadfully bored.

Colm is in love with Margot. I should have seen that coming. He has the passion of both the Deverills and the

O'Learys, and I should know. They think the Fairy Ring is their special place, but it was mine and Jack's, Alana and JP's, and plenty of other love-struck souls' before they came along to claim it for themselves. The land on which those stones were placed five thousand years ago has a very special energy, buried deep in the soil when the earth was created. Historians and archaeologists debate the mystery, claiming the stones were arranged to view the sun and the moon, or the planets and stars, to commemorate the dead or sacrifice the living, but they never look *down*. In the very depths of the earth beneath their feet is a magnetic pull. A supernatural energy that affects the ground above it and all those who step onto it. Even in death I am drawn to it. I bathe in its radiance and feel profoundly the connection of my soul to its source, somewhere out there, beyond the far distant horizon.

Jack is drawn to it because of the memories. It is among those stones that I often find him with his dog, staring at the skyline as if I am to be found there, in the mist. It is there that I find him now. I sense the heaviness in his heart – the weight of love that has nowhere to go. His mourning is my consolation. His regret mine too. While he is here, within the circle of stones, he belongs to me. He remembers the passion and the pain, and I come alive in his memory. If only he knew that I am with him still. He is searching for me at the point where the sea meets the sky and yet I am right here by his side, reliving the memories too.

Then, to my surprise, his wife appears. She steps into the circle and draws him away from his reverie. I am affronted. This is *our* place. She has no right to be here.

'What are you doing up here, Emer?' he asks. I would ask the same question, if I could.

She smiles in that serene way of hers. She has always smiled like that, without vanity or passion, and I feel myself bristle because she is like the calm, quiet bottom of the sea while I have always been like the waves, changeable, moody and erratic. 'I came to find *you*,' she replies.

'Is everything all right?'

'Alana is packing. She'll be wanting to leave soon.'

'Aye, I'm aware of the time.'

She stands beside him and they turn into the wind, taking pleasure from the gusts that blow salty and damp off the water. She sighs and puts her hands in her coat pockets. 'I wish she didn't have to leave.'

'So do I,' he agrees. 'But she's made her life in America now.'

'I shouldn't complain. I was born there. It's where you and I met. America's a fine country to live in.'

'She belongs here, as do we. I settled in America as a young man but I pined for home.'

Emer takes his hand. 'I'm grateful for the life we built here together. I've been very happy, Jack.'

He settles his blue eyes onto her face and he cannot help but return her smile with tenderness. They built their life together, but it was *she* who was the cement that prevented it from falling apart when our love affair was discovered. One word from him and I would have left Robert and gone anywhere in the world. I was ready to drop everything. Yet no word came. Nothing. I was too late. Jack was wiser than me. You cannot build happiness on the unhappiness of those you love. You simply cannot.

'I know you mourn Kitty,' she says suddenly.

'I know you do,' he replies.

'I understand. She was your great love. I don't want you to feel guilty about it. It *is* possible to love two women at the same time, in different ways.'

He frowns, gazing down at her as if he is struggling to make her out, this creature as serene as the bottom of the sea. She sighs, not in a weary way, but gently, consoling. 'I know that you have struggled with this for all of our married life,' she says.

'Not all of it,' he corrects her.

'Most of it.'

'I fell in love with you in America, good and proper,' Jack tells her firmly, and I know he is telling the truth. I had refused to leave Ireland; I don't suppose his memories of me were so tender back then.

'But eventually we came here and, well, there she was. No one could rival Kitty Deverill in looks or character. With her flame-red hair and those stormy grey eyes, she was like no other. And she was a part of your childhood. You'd grown up together. I couldn't compete with her beauty or the roots that connected you.'

'You didn't have to, Emer. You were always mine.' Jack frowns again and squeezes her hand. 'What's brought all this on?'

She shrugs and looks wistful. 'Life is short. We're old. There are things that need to be said. Things that I need to say.'

'Has Alana said something?'

'She still loves JP, you know.'

'I suspect she does.'

'She wouldn't be so hurt if she didn't still care.'

'JP's a mess. He doesn't deserve her.'

'No, he doesn't. But he did once and they created a beautiful family together. It makes me sad when I think what could have been. It makes me sad now to think of her leaving.'

'Is that why you're coming out with all this nonsense?'

She laughs. 'I just want you to know that I don't judge

you, Jack. I also want you to know that I understand why you're unhappy sometimes. You can mourn her without guilt. I'm not jealous. I wasn't jealous when she was alive and I'm not jealous now she's dead. And you can talk to me about her.'

Jack looks at her in bewilderment. 'You're a better person than I could ever be,' he says and his voice is full of regret.

'You must never beat yourself up for loving, Jack.'

'I beat myself up for disrespecting you.'

'Stop that now. Let's celebrate your love, and Kitty. We stand among her ashes. Let's not be bitter about the past, let's honour it instead. It is what it is, after all, and nothing can change it. I love you. You're my husband and my friend and the journey that's got us to this point has made us into the people we are today. We've done all right, haven't we? We've survived.'

'Only because of you, Emer.' Jack pulls her into his arms and holds her tight. 'I'm sorry if I ever hurt you, or didn't see you, or took you for granted. You're right, we're old. There are things that need to be said.'

'I forgive you, Jack,' she whispers, and I am deeply moved.

I stand aside as these two people make peace with each other, and I realize, to my shame, that it takes courage to say sorry and courage to forgive. I fought in the War of Independence; I carried on after Michael Doyle raped me in his farmhouse; I put aside my own desires in order to bring up JP as my own; I thought I, more than anyone else, had courage, but I was wrong. It takes courage to forgive and I have none.

I am drawn to the Hunting Lodge. JP is in the drawing room with Colm and Margot. They have finished dinner and are at the card table, playing Monopoly. I immediately sense the Presence. The fire is lit and yet I feel the chill. Margot has wrapped a shawl about her shoulders, Colm wears a jerkin over his sweater and JP keeps warm with a velvet jacket even though it is early March and velvet is traditionally a winter fabric. Classical music resounds from the record player in the cupboard. It is an uplifting sound. The Presence lingers close, a shadowy figure who, as I focus, becomes more defined. I cannot make out his clothes, for he is dark and blurred, but I can make out his size. He is a big man, with long hair and some sort of jacket, for the buttons gleam. His energy is so dense and heavy it is hard for me to reach him. But I speak to him nonetheless and hope that he can hear me. Speaking to spirits has never frightened me. In that I have courage enough.

'Hello,' I say. When nothing happens I try again. 'Hello.' The Presence doesn't move. It remains by the cupboard as if it is drinking in the music. Can it really be here because of the music? I wonder. 'Do you like what you hear?' I ask. 'It's beautiful, isn't it?' I feel the prickly sensation of its attention as it turns its focus away from the music, onto me. I continue bravely. 'It's Richard Strauss, I believe. Do you like Strauss? I have always loved music. It is balm for the soul.' I feel as if the Presence is now seeing me, and is surprised to find that it is not alone. I wonder whether it can see JP, Margot and Colm. I somehow think not. It comes towards me, a towering man with a fearsome energy, as brown and heavy as mud.

'You see me?' I hear. His voice is deep and gruff like grinding pebbles on a desolate beach.

'Of course I see you,' I reply with confidence. 'You are a spirit like me. Why would I not see you?'

'Are you here for the music, too?'

'No. I'm here because I used to live here. Are you here for the music?'

'Yes, I was in a dark, miserable place and then, suddenly, I was here. It is the music that does it. I have worked that out now. It is the music I am here for. Then I am back in my hovel and the music has gone. There is no music where I live.'

'Where do you live?'

'In a horrible place. I used to live in a castle.'

'Castle Deverill?' I ask.

'The very one,' he replies.

'I used to live there too,' I tell him.

He steps closer and I feel the stinging sensation of his scrutiny. 'I do not recognize you.'

'Nor I you,' I reply, lifting my chin and standing my ground. 'I am Kitty Deverill. Who are you?'

'I know no Kitty Deverill,' he growls, his voice full of accusation, as if he takes me for a liar.

'Then you cannot have lived in the castle.'

'I did not just live in the castle. I *owned* it.'

My interest is now well and truly piqued. 'You are not Barton Deverill, nor are you Egerton Deverill, for I have come across both. Nor are you my grandfather Hubert or my father Bertie.'

He sighs as if my listing of names is a bore. 'I am Tarquin Deverill,' he states impatiently. 'Which must make you . . . too many generations past to count.'

Chapter 15

With spring came a renewed sense of optimism. Beneath the warm sun the landscape burst forth with purple heather and yellow gorse. Wild orchids and thyme flourished among the long grasses and the earth itself gave off the sweet scent of regeneration. The clamour of birds heralded the dawn in the early hours of the morning, filling the air with their uplifting twitter as the sky cracked and slowly leaked liquid gold onto the horizon.

The feeling of renewal was infectious. JP laboured in the garden, his heart full of wonder at the awesome sight of nature and his own miraculous recovery, for a miracle it surely was. He had relinquished the drink and in its place discovered a new vigour and an exhilarating sense of purpose. With a clear mind and a steady focus he had realized what he wanted, or rather *who* he wanted. It was an outrageous desire, but wasn't it true that the limitations in our lives are only the ones we impose upon ourselves? Our lives are, in fact, full of potential waiting to be realized. The trick was to have the courage to manifest it. JP kept his secret to himself, however. He didn't want Colm to put him off and he didn't want to ruin the fragile relationship they were gradually rebuilding. Mrs B would simply shake her head and tell him that those kinds of dreams cannot be manifested, however hard the heart longs for them. The only person who would understand was Margot. Kind, compassion- ate, sweet Margot who had set him on the path of recovery in the first place. But he wasn't ready to tell her. Not yet. He wanted it to be a surprise and he wanted to be himself again. Of course, the person he'd fear telling the most was Alana. But she'd gone back to America and it would be a while before she returned. That gave him time. Time to find the old JP.

Every morning he rode out in the hills, sometimes alone but often with Colm or Margot. With each ride he began to feel himself again. When he galloped over the grass his mind was wrenched out of the past and placed firmly in the moment. It was in the moment where he found, albeit fleet- ingly, the young man he once was, defined neither by time nor experience, but by his keen and exuberant heart.

Little by little his reflection began to change in his bath- room mirror. First it was the skin tone that improved, from blotchy to even, then it was the whites of his eyes, from the colour of old parchment to a bright, healthy white, finally it was the fat around his jawline and the bloat in his cheeks that left him looking years younger and handsome, even. This transformation spurred him on and brought him closer to his goal. It was possible, after all, for his old and battered heart to fill again with love. The feeling was intoxicating. How had he survived so many years of bitterness and resentment, he wondered, when love had always been there, patiently waiting to be rediscovered?

Margot had started writing the book. Her gratitude towards JP for allowing her access to those boxes of family records was immense. She realized, as she pounded away on her electric typewriter, that she couldn't have begun to bring these Deverill characters to life had it not been for the letters, diaries and ledgers hidden in those seemingly dull boxes. She was excited. A gripping tale was slowly unfolding, for this family was indeed dogged by tragedy, drama, scandal and success. From the moment Barton Deverill built his castle on land stolen from the O'Leary family, a terrible seed was sown. A seed that sprouted into the beanstalk that spawned generations of titans and endless suffering. JP had been right. He was the Jack of the fairy tale who cut it down and brought an end to the Deverill legacy. If her theory – that the obsession with the castle had only brought the Deverill heirs unhappiness – was correct, then the freeing of their ties should have brought JP release, yet it hadn't. It had brought him pain, shame and a crippling sense of loss. JP's sorrow undermined her entire argument.

However, she did not focus on the ending, but concentrated on what she was currently writing. The words came easily, she had never suffered from writer's block, but she was distracted. Every time she lifted her eyes off the page she saw Colm.

On a practical level, it was hard keeping their relationship secret. They spent so much time in JP's company and it was difficult not to reach out and touch one another, to avoid jokes only the two of them understood, impossible to hide the intimacy in the way they looked at each other. But for Margot the fact that no one knew about it gave her breathing space. For a woman shy of commitment, the secret prevented her from feeling penned in. For Colm, the secret nature of their relationship was frustrating. He was falling in love and he wanted to tell everyone about it.

Their moments together were snatched. Late at night after

JP had gone to bed. In the afternoons, when Colm was able to take time off work and spirit her into his house on the edge of the town, and at the Fairy Ring when they rode out together, stealing kisses behind the giant stones where they were certain no one would find them. Ballinakelly was a small community. Gossip spread like fire through straw. They couldn't afford for JP to find out or, for that matter, Colm's grandparents Jack and Emer for they would tell Alana. Margot stopped going to O'Donovan's. She didn't want to bump into Seamus and have to explain her absence. She didn't feel good about the way she had treated him, but she'd left countless disappointed hearts in her wake over the years. Seamus's was just one more.

And what of Colm's heart? Margot knew he was different. She knew because of the way she felt when she was with him, and she knew because of the way she felt when they were apart. She just knew, and the knowing frightened her. In the early hours of the morning, when the dawn chorus stirred her from sleep and she opened her eyes to find that he wasn't there, she felt a sense of loneliness that she had never experienced before. It was that feeling that frightened her the most, the feeling of loss before she had lost.

'I want to wake up with you in the morning, Colm,' she told him one night when they lay entwined on the sofa in the library, long after JP had retired to bed. The antique clock on the mantelpiece above the fireplace showed 2 a.m. The fire had burnt down to an orange glow. 'I want to open my eyes and your face to be the first thing I see.'

Colm smiled at her tenderly. That was the most romantic thing she had ever said. His heart swelled with affection. 'I want your face to be the first thing I see *every* morning,' he said, curling her hair behind her ear. 'I don't want to have to hide away like this.'

'How long are you going to sleep here, in your father's house?'

'For as long as Dad needs me to.'

'He's doing well, though, isn't he?'

'I never believed I'd get my father back, but I have. Miracles sometimes do happen.'

'Don't you think he can be left on his own now? He has Mrs B to look after him.'

'I'm not worried that he'll go back to the drink if I'm not here. I worry that he'll be lonely. He's used to me now.'

'I want to be used to you, too, Colm.' Margot smiled at him, tracing his jawline with her fingers. 'I want to have you for the whole night, not just the beginning. I don't want to creep away like a thief in the small hours.' *I've done that enough in my life to know that I don't want it anymore*, she thought to herself. If only he knew what a momentous thing it was for her to want her lover to stay.

'Soon,' he told her. 'Soon the whole night will be ours.'

Mrs B felt revived as well. She picked daffodils and placed them in a jug on the kitchen table. They brightened up the room and gave her pleasure while she cooked. The music resonated from the radio, lifting her spirits and making her smile. In fact, from time to time she caught herself staring into the half-distance, a small smile playing about her lips, as the music transported her to a happy time in her childhood before the civil war had snatched her joy. But it wasn't just the music and the arrival of spring that had put a bounce in her step, it was the atmosphere in the house. It, too, had shaken off its winter chill, a chill that had covered it in a layer of invisible ice for the best part of nine years. Lord Deverill was a different man. Mrs B had grown so used to the morose and sombre soul who had lurked in a shadowland of his misery that she had forgotten how jovial and charming he used to be. She was reminded now because he stood before her once more, not as young or handsome as he had once been, but with the old twinkle in his eyes and the playful, witty remark. He was good-natured again, laughing with abandon, seeing the beauty in the world and appreciating it with joy expressed in superlatives. Master Colm seemed to have moved back in and Margot was a frequent visitor. They were like a happy family, the three of them. Mrs B did worry, however, about Master Colm's growing attachment to Margot. How would Lord Deverill feel were he to find out? she wondered. Mrs B knew that he was old enough to be her father – Lord Deverill knew that too – but the heart feels what the heart feels and there's no helping it.

She just hoped that if and when they decided to go public with their relationship Lord Deverill would not be badly hurt.

April brought cherry blossom to the castle grounds, dog violets to the meadows, the cuckoo's call – and the Countess di Marcantonio. It seemed to Margot that she was in the castle most afternoons, dressed in her finery, entertaining lavishly and holding forth about her husband's 'ancestral home'. Margot took great pains to avoid her, but Mr Dukelow insisted that she spend time in view of the guests because, he reminded her, what was the point of having a Writer in Residence if no one ever saw her? It was a fair point. After all, she was paying for nothing and, as the saying went, there was no such thing as a free meal.

It was unavoidable, therefore, that she would bump into the Countess at some point. That point came one rainy afternoon when Margot had settled herself at the desk by the window in the drawing room. The fire was lit, the lights blazing, the lawn outside dark beneath low-hanging grey clouds.

'My dear Miss Hart,' the Countess exclaimed, wafting into the drawing room in a bright red jacket worn over the black polka dot dress she had worn the first time Margot had met her. Large gold jewellery shone in every possible place, from her earlobes to her fingers, and her nails were painted a vivid crimson. She smiled enthusiastically, as if Margot were a beloved friend. 'I've been thinking about you so much,' she continued in her clipped Austrian accent. 'Wondering how you are getting on with the book. You haven't contacted me, so I assume that you have completed your research.'

Margot stood up and shook the Countess's bony hand. 'I'm writing the book now,' she told her. 'The research is all done.'

The Countess arched a thin eyebrow. 'I do hope you took on board what we talked about, Miss Hart, and you are going to give the di Marcantonios their due importance. It is only right that the Count should be acknowledged. After all, he had to step aside and watch his half-brother steal his inheritance.' She laughed, the kind of mirthless laugh designed to cushion her intimidation. She gave a little sniff. 'But you are the historian, not me. Far be it from me to tell *you* how to write your book.'

'I will include all the relevant facts,' Margot replied cagily.

The Countess chuckled, once again wrapping her menace

in false laughter. 'Don't leave any of the scandal out, will you? Those are the best bits. The Deverills are a study in indiscretions and scandal.'

'Trust me, the living Deverills have nothing on their ancestors.' Margot turned her eyes to the portrait of Tarquin Deverill. 'I'm less interested in the antics of the present Lord Deverill, to be honest. He's much too benign to make good copy.'

The Countess's smile faltered and her eyes took on a steely intensity. 'Don't belittle my husband's pain,' she hissed. 'If you knew how much the betrayal hurt him you would not use the word "benign" for JP Deverill. But . . .' She paused, composing herself and her smile. 'You're the historian. It's up to you which type of historian you want to be. One who tells the truth or one who doesn't. Simple, really.'

Margot could have told her a thing or two about truth, but she refrained. It was always prudent to take the high ground and not allow oneself to be dragged down by unscrupulous people. She pretended that the Countess's words had made no impression on her at all and, once she had left the room, returned to her work. However, she was fuming. How dare that woman threaten her like that, she thought angrily. She had previously thought her simply pretentious and narcissistic, but now she knew better: the Countess was nasty.

At the end of April Margot and Colm sneaked off to Dublin in Colm's Land Rover for a weekend away together. The drive was beautiful for the weather was fine, the sunshine dazzling and the hills a vivid green after so much rain. Margot felt like a schoolgirl playing truant, nervous at first that they might get caught, then exhilarated when they didn't. They arrived in Dublin to find it blooming with pink and white blossom, daffodils and tulips. Everywhere Margot looked there were hanging baskets and window boxes bursting with flowers. After the bleakness of winter the sight of so much colour was arresting.

They stayed in a small hotel in an unfashionable street. They lunched in a little restaurant in the centre of the city, sharing a bottle of wine and taking their time, holding hands across the table, relishing the feeling of being able to show their affection for each other freely and openly, without caution. No more snatched moments, secret kisses and nervous vigilance, at least for this weekend. After lunch, they walked around St Stephen's Green as ordinary lovers do and no one gave them a second glance, save the odd wistful old person who was reminded of their youth and the transience of such passionate young love.

That night they ate close to the hotel then returned to their room. Their lovemaking was slow and sensual. Tonight there was no rush. No leaving like a thief in the small hours, no longing. When Margot put out her hand at dawn, Colm was there beside her. She pressed her body against his, her stomach aligned with his back, and slipped her arm beneath his. She didn't feel lonely and she didn't sense loss. She closed her eyes and drifted back to sleep, knowing that when she awoke in the morning he would still be there. She had never wanted that to happen before.

Margot had always been an early riser. Colm was still sleeping when the first shaft of sunshine streamed through the gap in the curtains. She got up and showered. When she came out of the bathroom he still hadn't stirred. She decided to go out and buy some pastries to eat in their room. It wasn't the kind of hotel to offer room service.

She left a note on the pillow to let him know where she'd gone, then quietly crept out. They'd passed a café the day before with a mouth-watering display of cakes and scones in the window and it was there that she went. The smell of freshly baked bread and ground coffee hijacked her senses as she opened the door. She inhaled deeply and with satisfaction, savouring the fact that here she was, in Dublin, with Colm. Just the two of them. As soon as she returned to the hotel, she'd wake him up and make love to him the entire morning.

A man with fluffy white hair smiled at her from behind the counter and bade her good morning in a broad Dublin accent. A waitress in a pink-and-white uniform was refilling an old man's coffee cup in the corner. He was reading the *Irish Times* quietly on his own. Besides him, there were no other customers. Margot went up to the counter to choose some things to eat. 'These smell fresh,' she said, sweeping her eyes over the rows of buttered barmbrack slices, scones and currant buns.

'All freshly made at dawn,' he told her.

'How delicious! It's quiet here this morning,' she said, glancing at the old man. He looked dishevelled and lean, as if he hadn't had a good meal in a long time.

'He's one of our regulars,' the man replied in a low voice. 'It'll get busy in a small spell and I'll be meeting meself coming back. They're all enjoying a sleep-in as it's Saturday and the Holy Marys are still at early Mass. No rest for the wicked tho',' he added with a grin.

Margot chose a currant bun for herself and a scone and barmbrack for Colm. She hesitated before paying. She didn't imagine Colm would be up for a while and the smell of ground coffee beans was too good to ignore. She ordered a cup and sat at a little round table and nibbled on the bun. Shortly, the old man in the corner folded his newspaper and got up stiffly. He waved the paper at the man behind the counter before shuffling off. Margot noticed that he had a stoop and his trousers were hanging off his hips. He might have been a sorry sight, she thought, had it not been for his smile, which was the smile of a man who required little in his life to be content.

'I bet he's been coming here for years,' said Margot.

'God knows, he's been coming here as long as I've been here,' the man replied. 'And that's since I was a garsún in short trousers. You'd never know he's a count by the look of him, would you? And a *famous* count at that.'

Margot froze, coffee cup poised midway between the table and her lips. She didn't imagine there were many counts in Dublin. 'Next, you're going to tell me that he's Count Leopoldo di Marcantonio,' she said.

'The very man,' he replied and frowned. 'In the name of God, how do *you* know who he is?'

'I'm writing a book on the Deverills of Ballinakelly,' she told him. 'Leopoldo grew up at Castle Deverill.'

The man looked impressed. He put his hands on his hips and chuckled. 'Well, ma'am, isn't that grand, it is so. Two famous people in my café in one morning. Wait till I tell the quare one. That's me Mrs.'

'I met his wife the Countess,' said Margot, hoping to extract more information. The man did not seem to shy from sharing the gossip.

'Did you now. She never darkens the doorstep here,' he said and pulled a face. 'We're not swanky enough for her.'

'I think she might be on the swanky side,' Margot agreed.

'But *he's* a pure gentleman, he is. No éirí in airde or airs and graces about him. No, ma'am.'

'I thought they spent most of the year travelling between their luxury houses.'

He shook his head, as if the idea was preposterous. 'The Count is here every morning come rain or shine. Has been for years. They have a place round the corner. Nothing grand. I had to make a delivery there once. Nothing special.'

At that moment the door opened and a couple of elderly ladies shuffled in. Margot drained her coffee cup and got up. 'Thanks for the coffee. I think it's the best coffee in Dublin,' she said.

The man grinned. 'You wait until you taste my barmbrack!'

Margot returned to the hotel to find the bedroom curtains open and the bed empty. The sound of the shower and singing was coming through the bathroom door, which had been left ajar. She smiled and put the bag of goodies on the table. Hurriedly, she took off her clothes and slipped naked into the bathroom. Colm was in the shower cubicle, singing an Irish ballad that Margot had heard the band playing in O'Donovan's. When he saw her, he stopped singing and grinned. 'Good morning, you,' he said, running his gaze over her appreciatively. 'What a grand sight first thing in the morning.'

She laughed. 'Is there room for two?'

'There most certainly is.'

She opened the glass door and stepped inside.

Kitty

I am drawn to Tarquin Deverill. There is pain in his darkness that pulls at my heart, and, in spite of his rudeness, I sense that I can help him. I cannot help Mrs Carbery. I thought I could, but I cannot. Perhaps I am a fool to think that I can help Tarquin. A fool to think that I'm in any position to help anyone. I'm not even sure that I can help myself. But I am unable to resist. It is an urge so deep and insistent that it is impossible to ignore. I find myself in the Hunting Lodge more often than the castle, waiting for the music to lure him out of the shadows.

He comes and goes and neither of us knows how he does it. He has no control over his whereabouts as I do. It is as if an invisible force is guiding him, bringing him to this place, giving him a brief respite from the miserable landscape in which he dwells. He tells me it is a hovel. The people are nasty. There is no colour, no affection, no nature, no light. It is dark, he says. 'Dark beyond your imagination, and barren.'

But over the weeks that he comes I begin to notice a gradual change. At first he was resentful and mean, outraged by my presence, as if I was an intruder and had no business to be there. Then he started commenting on the music. How there was nothing of any beauty where he dwelt. How his

soul yearned for beauty like a man dying of thirst yearns for
water. He'd linger by the cupboard, absorbing the notes, his
entire being trembling with emotion as the music touched
something inside him – the tender place deep in his heart
where the darkness had not reached. And that tender place
began to grow. Like a seed, it began to sprout a stalk of light.
Slowly and tentatively at first, but then with more momentum,
it grew. The light expanded and I realized then, in a flash of
inspiration, that God is love and love is beauty and, as beauty
stirred his soul, it gently began to awaken the love inside him
that was already there – are we not, all of us, sparks of God?

Then, to my surprise, he shows the first signs of regret.

'I suppose I could have lived my life better,' he tells me.

'How might you have done that?' I ask.

There's a long pause as he circles the truth, afraid to step
into it and face the monster that he is. 'I had a son. Gabriel
was his name. He was a cripple.'

'What happened to him?' I ask.

'He drowned.'

'I'm sorry.'

'He drowned on his tenth birthday.'

'That's terrible. You must have been devastated.'

His energy contracts. It becomes like a tight shell around
him, hard and impenetrable. 'I could have been kinder to my
wife,' he says grudgingly. 'I was not very kind to my wife.'

The next time he comes, there are daffodils in the room.
Bright yellow daffodils that Mrs B has picked and put in a
glass vase. 'There are no flowers where I live. Nothing grows,'
he grumbles.

'These are beautiful, aren't they?' I reply. 'I've always loved daffodils. They're a sign that spring has arrived.'

'Ah, spring,' he sighs. 'What I would give to be in a meadow in springtime.' He sighs again then and I sense that burgeoning shoot of light in his heart growing a little stronger. 'I never appreciated flowers when I was alive.'

'What did you appreciate?' I ask.

He searches for the answer. When he finds it, it does not satisfy him. He ruminates on it for a while, wondering whether or not to divulge it. I sense his shame. It is hard for spirits to hide their feelings when they don't have bodies with which to conceal them. 'This is a beautiful room, isn't it,' he says, as if seeing it for the first time. 'The colours are beautiful.' He sighs again, a heavy sigh full of longing. 'It would be nice to have some colour where I live. I wouldn't have to have much. Just a vase of flowers, like these daffodils. Or some colour on the walls. My soul grows sick of the dark.'

'Tell me about Gabriel,' I ask. I know that Gabriel is at the core of his pain.

'He was a cripple,' he tells me again.

'How did that make you feel?'

He turns on me then. 'How do you think it made me feel?' he snarls. 'He was unnatural.'

'Unnatural?' I retort. 'Nothing that God creates is unnatural.'

'He brought shame on my family name,' he growls and I realize that he is not yet ready to see the error of his ways.

'Did he like flowers?' I ask.

Tarquin stares at the daffodils and the little shoot of light flickers slightly. 'He loved flowers,' he says quietly. 'He loved nature.' Then he turns again and the light dies. 'But he put his hand in the pond to stroke the fish and he drowned. The idiot!'

When he comes again I decide to be a little tougher on him.
'Why do you think you dwell in a miserable place with no
light or colour?' I ask. 'Why aren't you in Heaven?'

'I don't know,' he replies. 'Don't you think I'd do something about it if I knew?'

'Might it not have something to do with the life
you lived?'

He turns his attention away from the music and stares at
me. 'I lived in a fine castle. I had great wealth and power. I
had people who worked for me, people who depended on me.
My clothes were made of the finest silk and velvet. My horses
were the most superior beasts in the land.'

'But you had a son who was a cripple,' I remind him. 'How
did he fit in to your world of fine clothes and horses?'

'Why do you bring him up again?' he demands.

'You had other children, I assume. Did they bring you
shame too?'

'Of course not.'

'Your eldest, Peregrine, inherited the castle. I bet he was a
perfect reflection of you.'

'He was everything a son should be,' he replies.

'Perfect in body, just like your stallions, I imagine.'

'I know what you're doing, Kitty Deverill. You're trying
to shame me into admitting that I was wrong to treat the
cripple badly.'

'*Did* you treat him badly?'

He looks away. 'I didn't want him in my sight.'

'Because he was an embarrassment.'

'He wasn't fit to be seen.'

'Of course he wasn't, not in your lavish home, with your lavish furnishings and important friends.'

He knows how that makes him sound and he doesn't like it. 'He was slow. Slow in mind,' he adds, in order to excuse himself. 'Only his mother could abide him. They spent all their time in the tower, reading, or walking in the garden. Always together, the two of them.'

'Did you resent her for that?'

He pauses as once again he searches for an answer that, when found, does not satisfy. 'She was no wife to me,' he replies at length. 'She was too soft-hearted. She only had eyes for the boy.'

'She loved Gabriel,' I say.

'Yes, she did,' he concedes. 'She loved her helpless little boy.'

'And you resented her because you did not.'

He turns away. 'I *could* not.' And there it is, the pain in the guilt now seeping into his heart. His conscience is slowly awakening.

'Did you ever look into his eyes, Tarquin?'

'Why would that have made a difference?' he asks.

'Did you?'

'No.'

'If you look into a person's eyes, you see beyond the body, into the soul. To the person they really are. Gabriel was a beautiful soul, Tarquin. Your wife knew that.'

'I couldn't look at him.'

The music reaches a sublime climax. Tarquin is stirred by it. I seize my moment. 'He was just a boy,' I say. 'An innocent boy just wanting to be loved.'

He cannot speak. He remains listening to the music. But I noticed his energy soften. I sense regret. He puts a hand on his heart. I know there is nothing more for me to say. I leave him there, his hand trying to smother the light that is now flooding into his heart, for it is painful, that light. It brings with it realization. It cannot be avoided. His evil deeds are slowly emerging into his consciousness in all their horrible truth.

Perhaps he is realizing now that the hell in which he is living is of his own making.

Chapter 16

In May Dan Chambers arrived at the hotel with Dorothy, having by coincidence taken the same flight from London. Margot was thrilled to see them and embraced them both warmly. 'We've had such an interesting conversation in the taxi,' Dorothy told her as they waited at reception. 'Dan sees dead people all the time, fancy that?'

'Not all the time,' he corrected her with a smile. 'I'm able to switch it off when I need to.'

'Like a television,' said Dorothy. 'Isn't he clever!'

Dan was tall and elegant, with thick greying hair, intelligent pearl-grey eyes and a kind, noble face. He was a dapper dresser, in a beautifully cut pale grey suit, pink-and-grey-striped Hermès tie and black lace-up shoes that shone like mirrors. With a quiet charisma and easy-going nature, he was the sort of man who charmed everyone he met and Dorothy was no exception. 'He's handsome, isn't he?' she whispered to Margot. 'Although I'm old enough to be his mother.'

'Only just,' Margot replied. She caught Dan's eye and they both grinned.

'Can you see anyone yet?' asked Dorothy keenly.

Margot frowned. 'I thought you were afraid of ghosts,' she said.

'Dan has reassured me that they're friends not foe. However, I still don't want to see one in the middle of the night.'

'This place is full of spirit energies,' he said to Margot. 'I'm going to have my work cut out for me here.'

'Well, you'll have lots of people to deal with too. It seems that all the locals believe they see ghosts. I've never known so many superstitious people in one place,' Margot replied.

'They're not wrong. It's busy,' he said, running his eyes around the hall. 'Beautiful place, though, isn't it?'

'Very,' Margot agreed. 'I've been enjoying living here since January.'

'You fall on your feet, don't you?' he said with a chuckle.

'It's not always as good as this.'

'Of course not. Make hay while the sun shines, is my philosophy.'

'Mine too,' said Dorothy. 'It's lovely to be back. Just lovely.'

Margot followed Dorothy to her bedroom on the first floor, near the stairs that led up to Margot's tower. It had a four-poster bed, blue floral wallpaper and matching curtains. There were seats in the window recesses and outside the windows was a view of the box garden, which was cultivated into a maze. 'Tell me, my dear, how is the book coming along?'

Margot sat on the bed as Dorothy unpacked. 'It's going to be really good,' she said. 'Thanks to JP's boxes of records, I've been able to bring all his ancestors to life.'

'They're an extraordinary family,' said Dorothy, hanging up her coat in the wardrobe.

'I think it'll do very well for the hotel.'

'Mrs de Lisle is no fool. That's why she invited me here.'

'Of course. Shrewd is the word I'd use.'

'And why she introduced me to the Countess di Marcantonio.'

'I suppose she wants the book to be as spicy as possible. Scandal sells, after all. You only have to look at our tabloid newspapers.'

'In that case, I don't think she'll get what she wants. It's not going to be that sort of book.'

'Quite right, Margot. Still, it'll bring people flocking to the hotel, especially Americans. They love the Irish and I suspect they enjoy an English title too.'

'They want JP to give talks here.'

'What does he say about that?'

'I haven't mentioned it.'

'Is he up to it?'

'If you mean, has he relapsed? No, he hasn't. You wouldn't recognize him, Dorothy. He's a changed man.'

Dorothy was surprised. 'How wonderful. A real credit to you and Colm for supporting him through it.'

'Colm and his father are getting along very well.'

Dorothy looked concerned. 'Does his mother know about this?'

'I don't think so. Why? Don't you think she'll be pleased?'

'I think she rather enjoyed the fact that Colm supported *her*.'

'Colm is JP's son too. He belongs to both of them. It's a good thing that he's made up with his father. It's a *really* good thing that he's encouraged him to clean up his act. She'll be very surprised when she next sees JP. It's taken a lot of willpower for him to do what he's done. She should celebrate it. She should also encourage reconciliation. Colm loves both of them. It would be nice if they could all get along.'

Dorothy closed her empty suitcase. 'So, you're still seeing a lot of Colm, are you?'

'A fair bit,' Margot replied breezily.

Dorothy was not fooled by her nonchalance. 'I always knew you two would like each other. He's handsome, isn't he?'

'What? Like Dan?' said Margot with a grin.

'Dan bats for the other side,' Dorothy replied, a knowing look in her eye. 'You, on the other hand, are very much Colm's type.'

'How do you know what Colm's type is? How do you know he's *my* type?'

'Because you look much too well for someone who's been locked away writing a history book.'

'I've been riding out with JP.'

'You've been riding out with Colm, too.'

Margot sighed. 'Okay, Dorothy. You win. I like Colm. I like him a lot. But I can't let anyone know that I like him.'

Dorothy sat on the window seat and folded her hands in her lap. 'I see.'

'As you know, Dorothy, it's complicated.'

Dorothy nodded sympathetically. 'I understand just how complicated it is.'

'You're the only person I can talk to.'

'I'm flattered, Margot, that you should feel you can talk to me and share these things. But what about your mother? Do you confide in her?'

'My mother and I haven't spoken in years. She probably wouldn't recognize me if I walked through her front door. She's never been interested in me. In fact, I'd go as far to say that I'm an inconvenience. The last time I saw her, which was about six years ago, she couldn't wait for me to be gone. She has a young lover so I suspect having a daughter of my age betrays her own age, which she probably tries very hard to hide.' Margot shrugged then lowered her eyes because the compassion in Dorothy's was too sincere.

'I'm sorry to hear that,' Dorothy said softly.

'I'm over it. I look out for myself.'

Dorothy sighed. 'You know, you're much more complex than you look,' she said.

'I know. But I try not to define myself by my past and the people who brought me into the world. And, you know what? I'm doing fine.'

'You most certainly are.'

'Shall we go downstairs and have some tea?'

'What a good idea.'

'If you're lucky, you'll see the Countess in there, spouting lies about her husband's ancestral home.'

'I do hope so,' said Dorothy with a smile. 'She sounds very entertaining.'

Margot sighed and stood up. 'You have *no* idea!'

They did not find the Countess in the dining room, which was disappointing, but they did find Dan. He was standing in the entrance, waiting to be shown to a table. 'Mind if we join you?' said Margot.

Dan smiled, pleased to see her. 'What perfect timing,' he replied.

'So, Dan, when is your first session?' Margot asked when they were sitting down and enjoying their tea.

'Tomorrow,' he said.

'What will happen?' Dorothy asked a little anxiously. 'Are we going to see anything?'

'Unlikely,' Dan replied. 'I do the seeing for you.'

'And you'll see ghosts?'

'Spirits, earthbound spirits and ghosts. I'm sure I'll see a bit of everything.'

Margot looked bewildered. 'What's the difference between them? I thought a ghost was a ghost.'

'There are very important differences,' he said. 'Most people are ignorant of what sets them apart, but let me tell you.' He settled his grey eyes onto Dorothy who gazed eagerly into them. 'What you saw in your bedroom was likely to be an earthbound spirit.'

'The cleaning ghost?' said Margot, grinning at Dorothy.

'Not a ghost,' Dan corrected her. 'Ghosts are simply energy trapped here on the earth plane. Rather like a two-dimensional film of a person or an event that has happened in the past. For example, Anne Boleyn haunting the corridor of the Tower of London is not her. She's long gone. It's her energy that is stuck because of trauma, repeating itself over and over again. In time it will fade. You hear stories of people hearing the sound of battle in places where there was once horrific conflict. The Somme and the Battle of Hastings are just two examples. The soldiers aren't still there, fighting on in spirit. It's the trauma that's stuck and somehow repeats itself on a loop.'

'What's my housekeeping ghost then, if she's not a ghost?' asked Dorothy.

'She's an earthbound spirit. A person who has died yet doesn't move on into the light.'

'Why wouldn't she move on?'

'There are many reasons. Fear of where she's going. A strong desire to remain where she is. Sometimes, people don't realize they are dead. They exist in a strange, dreamlike state where there is no time.'

'How do they find their way to Heaven, then?' asked Dorothy anxiously, hoping very much that she wouldn't wind up as one of those.

'They eventually do. Mediums like me step in and help move them on. They have guides in spirit who eventually get through to them. Some spirits are happy to stay, believing that what they already have is Heaven enough for them. If they knew what awaited them in the next life they wouldn't be so keen to remain here.'

'And spirits?' Margot asked, surprised at her own, genuine interest in a subject that had previously bored her.

'Those are the people we love who have moved on into what you'd call Heaven, coming back to be near us. To guide us, help us in our daily lives or simply to enjoy being with us. Those you love never leave you. We are all connected by love.'

'Does that mean my loved ones are with me sometimes?' asked Dorothy with a tender smile.

'They most definitely are, Dorothy,' said Dan and the certainty with which he said it was deeply reassuring.

'That's nice,' she said. 'I like to think of them paying me visits every now and then.' Suddenly her smile faltered. She bit her lip and her eyes betrayed an old sorrow from long ago. 'It's nice to think that those we love and lose are never really lost.'

Margot hoped it was true. She, too, liked to think of her father supporting her in spirit, although he'd never supported her in life. She wanted to ask Dan why he'd be any different up there. If he hadn't cared for her during his lifetime, why would he suddenly care for her now that he was dead? But she didn't. Perhaps he hadn't loved her. Perhaps that was just the way it was.

'When you mentioned Heaven, you said, *what you'd call Heaven*. What do *you* call it?' Margot asked.

'There are many levels to go through before we reach Nirvana,' Dan replied. 'Heaven is a blissful place, full of love and light and beauty, but it is not the end of the journey. It's just another step along the way.'

'I think I'll be tired when I get there,' said Dorothy, taking a breath and brushing away the emotion that had, without warning, crept up on her. 'I think I'll stay at that level for a while. I'm not bothered about reaching the end of my journey. If it's a nice place and I'm with the people I love, what's wrong with staying there for eternity?'

Dan laughed. 'I suspect the soul yearns for more,' he said.

'Sounds exhausting, if you ask me.' She reached for a sandwich. 'I hope my soul doesn't yearn for more and gives me a rest! I'll settle for a place of love, light and beauty, thank you very much.'

Margot was pleased that Dan and Dorothy had arrived. She felt she now had allies in the hotel and not just in the Hunting Lodge. She hoped Dan's events would be successful so he'd be asked back. It was she who had recommended him. If he wasn't any good, Mr Dukelow would be very unhappy with her.

Margot met Colm later at his house, which was really a small cottage on the edge of town, positioned up a short driveway and hidden behind a thick beech hedge. He had moved back to it at last, giving them the freedom to meet whenever they felt like it. She liked the cosiness of his sitting room and his bedroom under the eaves. She relished it being just the two of them. In Ballinakelly, it seemed that they had an awful lot of time. It didn't matter that she returned to the hotel in the mornings. She was at liberty to come and go as and when she pleased. Even Mr Dukelow's raised eyebrows did not faze her.

She was falling in love. She had never allowed that to happen before.

The following day Colm went off to work and Margot went to the Hunting Lodge to see JP. She found him at the round table in the corner of the sitting room, mending what looked like an old model ship. Music resonated from the cupboard and, for the first time since winter, the fire was not lit. Sunshine, warm and bright, tumbled through the glass windowpanes with the enthusiasm of early summer, warming the room and filling it with an uplifting sense of optimism.

JP raised his eyes from his work when he saw her. 'Good morning, Margot,' he said with a smile. 'I made this when I was a boy. With the help of my father, of course. I thought I'd resurrect it.'

'You made that?' she asked, taking a closer look. 'It's amazing.'

'Well, I wouldn't go quite that far. It's pretty amateur, really. But I had fun making it. I had a thing about boats when I was a child. I used to sail out with my father in his little sailing boat, and fish. We'd also sail around the coast, looking for caves. I used to love hearing stories about smugglers.'

'I didn't know you sailed.'

'I don't. I did, but I don't now. Haven't for years. Since Colm and the girls were children, I suppose.'

'Perhaps that's something else you should resurrect.'

JP unscrewed the lid on the bottle of glue and dabbed it

onto the model. 'I don't know. I found my riding legs, but I'm not sure I'll find my sea legs again.'

Mrs B wandered in, duster in hand. 'Good morning, Miss Hart.'

'Have you seen this, Mrs B?' Margot asked, pointing to the model ship.

'Oh, yes. It's a wonder, isn't it? Lord Deverill has always been very talented.'

JP chuckled. 'What would I do without you, Mrs B, blowing my trumpet for me?'

Mrs B laughed and put her hands on her hips. 'Get away with yourself and your codding, m'lord,' she said.

Margot sat on the sofa as JP stuck pieces onto the ship with steady hands. It wasn't so long ago that those hands had trembled, she thought, as she observed him concentrating on his work. 'My friend Dorothy Walbridge has returned to the hotel,' she told him.

'Mrs Walbridge? She's a friend of Emer O'Leary's,' said JP. 'You know her?'

'Not very well. Nice lady, if I recall. English. Wears brown lace-up shoes like Miss Marple.'

Margot laughed. 'Yes, she does.'

'Her husband died in a car crash.'

Margot was astonished. 'That's terrible! Did they have children?'

'They had a daughter who died. Leukaemia, I think it was. When she was young. You know she lived in Buenos Aires?'

'Yes, she told me that.'

'I think she has a son who married an English girl, that's why she moved back to the UK. They're Anglo-Argentine. She's one of those stoic women who just gets on with it. They don't mope about and feel sorry for themselves. They carry on.

It was women like that who built the Empire.' He chuckled. 'I didn't know she was your friend too.'

'I met her the day I arrived at the hotel. She introduced me to Emer. That was before they discovered what I was here for. I'm not exactly flavour of the month in the O'Leary household.'

'That makes two of us.'

'If they knew Colm was a friend of mine too it would make us a group of three.'

JP paused his work and looked at her. 'If they knew what a good person you are, they'd see beyond the book, Margot.'

'Like Dorothy, *she's* never judged me.' Margot sighed, feeling an expanding gratitude for her new friend. 'I guess the O'Learys are just going to have to read it before they see me as a good person.'

'*I* look forward to reading it,' he said.

'You, JP, will be the very first.'

He smiled. 'Thank you.'

Mrs B walked in with a tray of tea and cake.

'I have another friend who has arrived at the hotel,' Margot continued. 'He's called Dan Chambers and he's a well-known medium. He's staying the week and doing lots of events and workshops. It's Mrs de Lisle's way of profiting from the castle's ghosts,' she added with a cynical chuckle.

Mrs B put the tray down and began to pour the tea. 'He'll find plenty of ghosts there, as sure as there's an eye in the needle,' she said darkly. 'God help us, I could feel them around me when I was doing a bit of cleaning. I wasn't a bit worried about it because I always had a miraculous medal pinned to me vest and a little bottle of Lourdes water in me pocket. Sure the poor holy souls are only the same as ourselves, some are happy and contented and others are troubled and agitated.

God guard us, some of them would cause trouble in an empty house. We are all one, the living and the dead, with only a thin veil between us.'

'You should have heard Kitty talk about spirits,' said JP, rolling his eyes. 'Goodness, she was always going on about them, as if she had a direct line to the afterlife. Still, if your friend's a good medium, he's come to the right place. Mrs B is right. The castle is riddled with them.'

'His first event is tonight,' said Margot. 'I was wondering whether you'd come with me.'

JP frowned. 'To see a medium?'

'To see the *hotel*,' she replied with emphasis.

'Ah.'

'How long has it been since you've been up there?'

'I haven't been back since the day I moved out.'

Margot was astonished. 'Really? Not since then?'

He shrugged. 'I had no reason to.'

Mrs B placed his teacup on the table beside him. She looked down at him, her face now grave with concern. She of all people knew how much the selling of that place had wounded him. 'I'd let sleeping dogs lie,' she said quietly.

'Which dogs are those, Mrs B?' asked JP.

'Your own ghosts, m'lord. The ones that hounded you out of the castle in the first place.'

Margot took the cup Mrs B offered her. 'I don't agree,' she argued. 'I think it could be very healing for you to go back. It's only by letting the light into dark places that you banish fear.'

'I'm not afraid of the castle,' said JP cheerfully. 'Of course I'll come with you.'

Mrs B cut the porter cake slowly. She'd like to have gone to the hotel too, but she was anxious. She didn't think she'd be happy to see the Deverill home converted into a hotel, however sumptuous it was. Nevertheless, if Lord Deverill himself saw nothing wrong in visiting it, then she shouldn't either. She'd wait and see what he thought of it and then, perhaps she'd be persuaded to go up there. She'd always been curious about those who claimed to communicate with the dead. Her brother's face floated into her mind then and her heart felt soft and warm. She wondered whether the medium would be able to contact *him*.

That evening Colm and JP drew up outside the hotel in Colm's Land Rover. They were silent. The sight of those stone walls and tall towers caused their chests to tighten with anguish and they were unable to find the words to express it. The family motto, carved into the stone above the front door, was now an affront because the castle was no longer the Deverills' kingdom but the Deverills' shame. It taunted JP as he climbed out of the car and stepped onto the gravel where Deverill feet had stepped for over three hundred years. He faltered a moment and put his hand on the vehicle to steady himself. He swept his eyes over the castle where memories shimmered on every glass window like reflections on water. Pictures from his past, both sad and happy, and each one pulled at his heart. He could hear Kitty's voice begging him not to sell. He could hear his own response that he had no choice. He even heard Alana: *How could you? How could you, JP?*

Margot had been waiting in the hall. When she saw them draw up she hurried outside. JP's face was ashen. Colm was also solemn. Both were visibly unsure. For a fleeting moment she wondered whether she had done the right thing in making JP come.

'This is not going to be easy,' she said, taking JP's hand. 'But we're here with you.'

He drew his eyes away from the windows and managed to give her a small, grateful smile. 'I'm not going to be done in by this,' he replied, pulling back his shoulders. 'I'm going to face it head-on.'

'You all right, Dad?' Colm asked.

'All right, son,' JP replied. 'Let's see what ghosts come out of the shadows for us!'

The doorman, in a long coat and top hat, greeted the esteemed guests with a smile and a nod and opened the door with a white-gloved hand. JP walked into the hall where Mr Dukelow was waiting to meet him. This was clearly a momentous occasion for the hotel manager. He stood to attention in his best navy-blue suit, pink-faced, wide-eyed, his most charming smile upon his lips. Lord Deverill betrayed none of the doubt he felt inside and extended his hand like a prince, with confidence and graciousness. He had none of the pomposity of the Countess, but was quietly spoken and polite, praising Mr Dukelow for the wonderful job he was doing, for didn't the hotel look splendid? Then he introduced his son and Mr Dukelow shook Colm's hand with vigour. Margot watched the manager fawn over JP, rubbing his hands together and thanking him for gracing them with his presence. To Margot's cynical eye, it was too much. Mr Dukelow was unable to contain his excitement and used JP's title in his speech as much as he used the Countess's. Yet, Margot was wrong to think the flattery excessive, for JP seemed to get taller with every compliment, as if Mr Dukelow's ill-concealed admiration was restoring to him a little of his damaged prestige. He hadn't been out much over the years and, Margot imagined, he had most likely pictured a hostile public of gossiping, disapproving people. But here was Mr Dukelow telling him how honoured they were that he had come to their small event. He had set aside three seats in the front row and, if his lordship would like, he'd be happy to show him around the hotel afterwards so that he could see for himself the respect with which Mrs de Lisle had treated his former home. 'She wanted it to retain the feeling of a home and not feel like a sterile hotel,' Mr Dukelow told him. 'It's advertised as the Deverill family seat. I hope, when you look around, that you will agree that she has done a terrific job.'

'I'm sure I will,' said JP.

'This is so good for Dad,' said Colm to Margot as they followed Mr Dukelow through the castle to the ballroom, where, in bygone years, the Deverill summer balls had been the highlight of the Anglo-Irish calendar.

'I worried that I might have been wrong to have persuaded him to come,' she replied. 'But doesn't he look great in his suit? He looks every bit the Lord Deverill of Ballinakelly.'

'I'm proud of him,' Colm said. 'I never thought I'd ever say those words. But I am, really proud of him.'

Margot wanted to take his hand. She wanted to squeeze it to show him that, with every step they both took, she was right beside him. But she did not.

The ballroom was full of people. Margot caught her breath when she saw it. Rows and rows of chairs and barely an empty one in the house. It was like a theatre, for a stage had been erected at one end. Mr Dukelow showed them to their seats in the middle of the front row. Margot and Colm sat side by side. As JP was about to sit down, a woman in the row behind him stood up to greet him. It was Dorothy. 'Lord Deverill,' she said. 'You probably don't remember me, but . . .'

'Mrs Walbridge,' he replied with a smile, sandwiching her hands in his. 'What a pleasure to see you again.'

Dorothy was taken aback. She had not imagined him to look so well, or to appear so lucid. From what Emer had told her JP was a sorry drunk, wallowing in self-pity. But here was a man in command of all his faculties. A man with charisma and confidence and the loveliest twinkling blue eyes. He even smelled of lemon cologne. She couldn't wait to tell Emer.

Margot felt something touch her hand. She looked down to see Colm's little finger brushing hers. It was a tiny gesture, hidden from view, but it meant a great deal to Margot. She turned her attention to the stage and smiled. As the audience welcomed the medium with loud clapping, Colm knew that her smile was for *him*.

Kitty

I am surprised and, dare I admit it, moved to see JP in the castle again. My half-brother whom I raised as my own son and loved as much as any mother who has carried her child in her belly for nine months, sits in the front row of the ballroom where once we danced beneath glittering chandeliers to the finest orchestras in the land, and I am overcome with emotion. My home, my beloved home, is once again restored to a Deverill, if only for one evening. But it feels right to see him there. It's as if everything that has been out of kilter in this castle is now in balance once again. Sure, it is still a hotel, but with JP sitting in the front row of the grand ballroom, I feel that the missing piece has been replaced. With Colm by his side I feel the universe is sending me a sign. The Deverill legacy *will* live on. It will continue after JP with Colm and, in time, with Colm's son. The castle will be restored to them, I just know it will. The only question is how. That, I don't know.

I stand on stage as Dan Chambers greets his audience. He is an elegant man with a gentle nature and a generous spirit. I cannot tell whether or not he is a medium, however. I wait with excitement and, I'm ashamed to admit, cynicism, because in my life I was a gifted medium and proud of it too. I'm doubtful that anyone is as good at communicating with the dead as my grandmother Adeline and I were.

A part of me wants to hijack this meeting. Oh, the mischief I could make if he really can talk to spirits. I could give him wrong names and make him look like a fool. It's dull where I am, after all. Sure, there are periods of interest like talking to Tarquin Deverill or watching Mrs Carbery spook the living, but for the most part it is uneventful here, like watching actors in a boring play that never ends. At first my anger kept me busy, my hauntings entertained me and the novelty of being privy to people's secrets was exciting. But now I'm used to existing without a body to limit my movement and my anger has diminished somewhat. If the truth be told, I'm weary of being furious. It is an emotion that feeds on itself, like a snake that eats its own tail. The only person it hurts is me. I'm not sure why I didn't see that before.

The medium stands quietly and takes a moment to tune in. I know what that's like. I used to tune in, too, when I was alive. It's like turning the dial on a radio to find the right frequency. I stand beside him and whisper into his ear. 'Santa Claus.' I see the expression on his face. It is one of disbelief and horror. So, he is a medium, after all. A moment's jubilation is replaced by a feeling of guilt. How can I, a woman who brought so much comfort to the grieving because of my gift of passing on messages from the deceased, play with a man who is only trying to do good? I am suddenly filled with shame.

I am about to put it right by whispering *my* name, but then I notice a bright light to my left. I turn and see a child. A radiant child. She is dazzling. Her hair is golden and all around her is a halo of light. She exudes such a powerful feeling of love that I am humbled. I shrink back, my shame cloaking me in shadow, and watch as her energy hovers beside Mrs Walbridge. The old woman feels nothing. She's watching and waiting like the rest of the audience, a little anxious now because the medium has been standing on the stage for a while now and he has said nothing.

He looks at Mrs Walbridge and smiles. 'Did you lose a little girl?' he asks.

Mrs Walbridge's face flushes pink. She looks behind her, unsure whether or not the medium is speaking to her. Then, realizing that it is indeed her, she looks back and nods.

'She's showing me a lily,' he tells her.

Mrs Walbridge puts a hand on her mouth. 'She was called Lillie,' she gasps.

'She passed when she was thirteen,' he continues. 'Was it leukaemia?' Again Mrs Walbridge nods. 'She's showing me a house in a hot country with a garden full of flowers. I'm understanding South America. Argentina. She's showing me a club where lots of elegant people are playing golf. She's telling me that she loved to collect the balls, for they were hidden in the long grasses all over the grounds.' Then he laughs. 'Was there an ostrich who used to eat them?'

Mrs Walbridge's eyes are full of tears. She nods, then she laughs with him. I feel the love flowing between this bright spirit and her mother and am awed by the power of it. Awed that such a seemingly young spirit can have such an intense radiance.

'She wants you to stop feeling guilty for leaving her remains in Argentina,' he says. 'Because she's not there. She's where *you* are.' There's a sigh from the audience who are as moved by what he is saying as I am. 'Whenever you see a robin behaving strangely, know that your daughter is sending you a message to remind you that she's with you.' Mrs Walbridge wipes her eyes with a tissue. Her hand is trembling. Her daughter bends down and kisses the top of her head. I notice a shiver pass through her mother. 'She has just kissed you,' says the medium.

I notice now that the room is aglow with hundreds of spirits. They are not dull like me and Mrs Carbery, who are earthbound. They come from Spirit and they are made of light. Pure white light. They are all eager to communicate with their loved ones. I know what they want to say. Spirits are all the same in that regard. They just want to reassure them that they are not dead, that they live on and that they love them. It is really very simple. With the room full of souls like this it is hard to believe that there are people who believe that death is the end of life. If only they could see what I see. How much easier life would be if people could be certain that those they love and lose just move on into another dimension, another state of being, and never leave them. That *that* is the fate of the majority of people, at least those who have love in their hearts. Those who are cruel should fear death very much.

The medium has to concentrate hard to distinguish each spirit. He does a fine job of it. Every person who receives a message is uplifted. Those who don't are moved, carried on this enormous wave of love that is flooding the room. And that's what strikes me the hardest: the love that these people feel for those who have moved on, and the love that the spirits feel for those still living. Love is an unbreakable bond that ties them to each other. I look at JP, sitting there quietly, lost in thought. Is he thinking about me? Or our father, Bertie, perhaps? His face is very serious. His brow furrowed. But I cannot read his thoughts, I can only read his energy and there is too much of that in this room right now to read anything other than love.

The two hours pass very quickly. The medium cannot impart all the messages, but he reassures those in the audience who were hopeful of communication that he will be holding more of these events during the week. The spirits fade away, the people stand up and talk excitedly to one another. Margot embraces Mrs Walbridge, who cries onto her shoulder. I doubt she will be afraid of ghosts anymore.

And then I see the 'housekeeping ghost' Mrs Carbery. She is on the stage, looking bewildered. A drab little shadow of a woman, like a mouse, watching in amazement as the room slowly empties of people.

Then it is just her and me and a young woman walking through the chairs, picking up leaflets and tidying up.

'Almighty Jesus, what was that performance all about?' she asks me.

'He's a medium. He talks to dead people like us and passes on messages to those still living.'

'Like a kind fortune teller?' she says.

'Sort of but not exactly.'

'The priest used to tell us that people like that are limbs of the devil and to give them a wide berth, God save us.'

'No,' I reassure her. 'They just have special gifts.'

'Well, in that case and me being dead, do you think he would carry messages from me?'

'Who would you want to get in touch with?' I ask.

'I think I have a daughter still alive.'

Of course she does. 'Bessie,' I say.

'Bessie. My little girleen who I had to leave behind. Bessie who looked after me and brought me back from the jaws of death after Rafferty was killed. When he didn't come home,

I went into deepest black. In all the years since, I never wore a coloured garment. God help me, me poor heart was in so many pieces that only St Anthony himself would be able to find them and put them together. After that, me life was a Garden of Gethsemane. Where is Bessie now?'

'She's in the Hunting Lodge. She still works for Lord Deverill.'

'And Rafferty? Is he in Heaven?'

'I don't know,' I tell her.

Mrs Carbery begins to cry. 'I believed that once I died, I'd see my boy again. It was one of the reasons I welcomed death and went halfway to meet it. What have I done to deserve this purgatory? I went to Mass every morning and was a daily communicant. I never touched a bite of meat on a Friday and I went to Loch Derg and Knock every second year. What did I do to earn this? What more could any living Christian do? It's all a fine bit of blackguarding, it is. They tell you that you'll go to Heaven if you lead a humble and devout life, but it's a downright lie to keep us from rearing up. There is no Heaven. There's only this old foggy existence. God almighty, I'm neither fish, fowl nor red herring. I'm like something that was flung together in a hurry!'

I don't know what to tell her. I can only watch helplessly as she leaves to aimlessly wander the castle's corridors and frighten those who happen to sense her there.

I am drawn then to the Hunting Lodge where JP, Colm and Margot are having dinner in the dining room. Mrs B has cooked them a feast. I notice how she lingers, keen to hear what this medium was like. She has a strained look on her face, as if she is struggling to reach a decision about something important. I wish I could tell her that her mother is in the castle and wishes to communicate with her. It is easy for me to frighten people but impossible to bring them comfort.

'What an extraordinary evening that was,' says JP. He is buoyant, his spirits lifted by the friendliness in the hotel. He thought he was a pariah but he was wrong. He is Lord Deverill of Ballinakelly whose family lived in the castle for over three hundred years. He has realized that that is something to be proud of. 'Your friend Dan Chambers is truly gifted.'

'I'm a sceptic,' says Margot. 'But, I have to admit, tonight has left me wondering.'

'It's a great comfort to know that the people you love who have died never leave you. I mean, you only had to look at Mrs Walbridge's face to see how much joy the communication with her daughter gave her,' says Colm.

'Terrible to lose a child,' says Margot sadly. 'You know, she's never mentioned Lillie to me, or that her husband died in a car crash. She's had so much sorrow in her life and yet, you'd never know. She's such a lively, happy person.'

'It's a gift,' says JP. He has had his fair dose of sorrow too and is gradually learning to let it go.

'Dan would say that that's what life is about,' Margot tells them. 'That we're here to grow through our suffering. If life were a bed of roses we'd all be selfish and complacent. Suffering teaches us compassion and appreciation. I think he's probably right about that.'

'When is his next meeting?' asks JP. 'I'd like to go and see him again.'

'Tomorrow evening,' Margot replies. Mrs B cannot linger any longer. She leaves quietly, her hands full of dishes.

'Who would you like to come through for you, Dad?' asks Colm with a chuckle. 'Kitty?'

JP pulls a face. 'Lord no! She's furious with me for selling the castle. I think if she came through we'd all feel the chill!' They laugh. But he is right, I am furious with him for selling the castle. However, I am humbled by the love communicated by the spirits in the ballroom tonight. Not one came through with a stony heart. Not one spoke in anger. There was only love. Does that mean that when *I* move on I will leave my resentment behind? Will I want to? Is it such a bad thing to love the castle so?

After supper they move into the drawing room and JP puts on a record. The sublime music fills the room and, as I anticipate, Tarquin Deverill is drawn from his murky realm. I notice at once that he is different. He has changed. He is cowed. His energy is less dense and softer in texture, and he is in despair. I sense his desolation in a heavy cloud that spreads throughout the room and I feel immense pity for this tortured soul.

This time he does not seek the music. He seeks *me*.

'I need to confess,' he says as soon as he sees me. 'My soul is in anguish and I cannot take it anymore.'

'What has inspired you, Tarquin?' I ask.

'I am in turmoil. I cannot endure another minute down there in that horrible place. I cannot. There is no colour, no light, no kindness, no music or flowers or ...' He gasps and clutches his chest. 'But it is no more than I deserve. If I never see a single thing of beauty again it is what I have earned, but I pray for forgiveness.'

'From whom do you seek forgiveness?'

'From my son. From Gabriel.'

'Tell me, Tarquin, what did you do?' In truth, I do not wish to hear the terrible thing that he has done, but I know I must push him to see the error of his ways and to allow the light into the darkness in his soul. It is the only way that he can redeem himself.

He falls to his knees and drops his chin onto his chest. 'I murdered my son,' he whispers. I catch my breath. I had not expected that. 'What did you do?'

'I lured him to the pond on his tenth birthday. I told his mother that I would take him into the garden to look at the flowers. I had never taken him out before. I showed him the fish. He lay on his belly and put his hand in the water to touch them.' He pauses. I sense his regret. It twists inside his heart like a shard of glass. He shakes his head, but there is no dispelling the memory of what he did. 'I pushed his head into the water. I held it down until the life had gone out of him.'

He stands up suddenly. 'I was wrong to ask forgiveness,' he says. 'How can I expect my son to forgive his father for such a heinous crime? I cannot. It is beyond the capability of any human being. First, I robbed him of his joy, then I robbed him of his life. It is unforgivable and I must suffer in Hell for eternity. It is what I deserve. I will leave you now, Kitty, and return to the place I created for myself. You were right, after all. The life I lived on earth fashioned the life I live now. One cannot escape justice. I only have myself to blame.'

My heart swells with pity. I want to reach out to him, this tormented creature who has at last seen the light. He begins to withdraw.

The room is at once filled with a blinding radiance. I shield my eyes, for it is too bright for me. I sense Tarquin recoil. He also hides his eyes from it. It is too intense for us both. Little by little it dims and at last we are able to see the unearthly being now standing before us. At first I think it is an angel but I quickly realize that it is not an angelic being but a beautiful soul of great love and purity.

He looks upon the anguished creature trembling before him with compassion. 'Father,' he says.

I am astonished. Is this magnificent being the spirit of the crippled child?

'Gabriel?' Tarquin's voice is a rasp. He cannot believe it, either. But I know that it is true. If he had looked into the boy's eyes he would have seen what his mother saw: a beautiful, perfect, unblemished soul.

'I have always been with you, Father,' he says. His smile is full of joy, his eyes shining with love. 'I never left you.'

'But I ... I ...' Tarquin fights his emotions. He cannot articulate the words. He is too full of shame.

'Even in the dark place where you have been dwelling I have been with you. Only, you couldn't see me. Now that you have acknowledged that you hurt people terribly, you have allowed the light into your heart and I am able to reach you. I am here to take you home.'

'Home?' Tarquin gasps. 'But why would you care? No, better to leave me in disgrace.'

'Come.' His son holds out his hands. 'I forgive you. Now you must forgive yourself.'

Tarquin is trembling. His entire energy is oscillating with a faint though unmistakable light. It is spreading through him, like a growing flame. He takes the hands and I watch in awe and humility as this very advanced soul leads his father into the next world. The light disappears and the room is restored to its usual tone. JP, Margot and Colm are sitting around the table, playing cards. They have no idea of the extraordinary event that has just taken place in their midst.

I realize then that it really is true. The way we choose to live on earth creates the life we go to when we die. And it is a choice. How many of us choose unwisely!

Chapter 17

Dorothy felt as if a great weight had been lifted off her shoulders. Lillie was still with her. Tonight had confirmed it. How could Dan Chambers know about the robins? How could he have got Lillie's name and what she died of had she not been there, telling him? Lillie was not a ghost. She knew that now, having spoken to Dan. Lillie was a vibrant spirit. The same loving person as she had been when she was alive, only without her sick body. She hadn't changed, sprouted wings or become pious. She was free, happy and full of mischief. Really, those robins were extraordinary. Never again would she fear spirits, although she'd prefer not to see the housekeeping spirit again. There was something about waking up in the middle of the night and sensing someone in one's room that was very disconcerting. She'd rather that didn't happen.

Dorothy was in her nightdress and dressing gown on the point of climbing into bed when there came a knock on the door. Wondering who it could be at this time of night, she called out a little anxiously, 'Who is it?'

'Me, Margot,' came the reply.

Dorothy assumed something must be wrong for Margot to need her at eleven o'clock at night and opened the door. But Margot did not look like a woman in distress.

'I'm sorry it's so late,' she said. 'But I wanted to come and check on you. I mean, it's been an extraordinary evening, hasn't it.'

Dorothy opened the door wide, suddenly keen to talk about it. 'Come in,' she said enthusiastically, stepping aside.

Margot walked into the room. 'I've always been a bit of a cynic myself,' she said, sinking onto the bed. 'But tonight Dan really threw the cat among the pigeons.'

Dorothy sat down on the small sofa by the window and folded her hands in her lap. 'He's a very gifted man. I mean, how could he have known about the robins?'

'Exactly. It was amazing.'

Dorothy smiled. 'There were so many people in the room, but my Lillie came through for me. She always was a determined little thing.'

'It's nice to know that she's with you.'

'It's made all the difference,' said Dorothy. 'The one thing I always worried about was leaving her alone in Buenos Aires. That's why I stayed for as long as I did. Much longer than I wanted to. Because *she* was there. Silly really. Of course I knew she wasn't in her grave. I believed she was in Heaven, but still, that's all I had left of her, her plot with her name on the plaque. It was a wrench to leave it. It still pains me sometimes to think of her there without anyone to visit her.'

'You don't have to feel like that anymore. She really isn't there. She's here.' Margot smiled affectionately. 'She's probably here right now.'

'That's a nice thought,' Dorothy agreed. 'It's also encouraging to know where I'm going to end up when I die. You know, when you get to my age, you think about death quite a lot.'

Margot looked horrified. 'Oh Dorothy! You're not going anywhere yet.'

'I hope not, but still, I'm edging closer to the end of my life, aren't I?' She chuckled. 'No one gets out of here alive.'

'You have a good many years left in you, and besides, I need you.'

'Well, I'll hang around as long as I'm able to,' said Dorothy. She had only known Margot a short time, but it was nice to feel needed. And it felt good to support Margot who hadn't a mother she could count on. 'You can count on me,' she said and she was touched to see that her words meant something to Margot.

'Thank you,' said Margot, her cheeks flushing pink. 'That's one of the nicest things anyone has ever said to me.' In the past, the only person Margot had been able to count on was herself.

After Margot had gone, Dorothy lay in bed and prayed. She thanked Lillie for communicating with her and she thanked whichever power it was that had facilitated it. She sent a prayer out for Margot, too. Had it not been for her, Dan would never have come to the castle. It was good that he was here. He would bring relief to so many grieving people. It was impossible to avoid death. At some stage in everyone's life they would be touched by it and eventually death would greet them all. How much easier would it be if they could be certain that it wasn't an ending, but a transition?

The following morning she paid Emer O'Leary a visit at her house by the sea. The day was blustery but sunny. Fat clouds bumbled across an azure sky and beneath, the waves rose and fell sharply, challenging the fishermen who were out in their boats in pursuit of the daily catch. She took a taxi, which the hotel organized for her, and drew up outside the O'Leary home at ten. Emer greeted her warmly at the door. Jack was in bed with a bad cold, she told her.

'Nothing serious, I hope,' said Dorothy.

'It's been a hard winter,' said Emer, closing the door and accompanying her into the sitting room. 'Jack's out every day with the dog, come rain or shine, and he's not getting any younger.'

'None of us are,' said Dorothy. 'One foot in the grave and the other on a bar of soap.'

They sat and shared their news. Then Dorothy told Emer about JP. 'He must have quit the booze,' she said. 'He's looking very good. Bright-eyed and bushy-tailed my father would have called it.'

'What's come over him?' Emer asked pensively. 'Do you think he's in love?'

'Possibly. I can't imagine a transformation happening like that for no reason.'

'But who with? Who does he see besides Margot Hart?'

'I don't honestly know. Perhaps Colm has convinced him to clean up his act.'

Emer shrugged. 'He's said nothing about it to us.' She frowned. 'Was he there last night, as well?'

'Yes, it was JP, Colm and Margot. The three of them.'

Emer thought about it for a moment. 'Margot's young enough to be his daughter,' she said, a note of disapproval in her voice.

'Oh, I don't think he's in love with *her.*'

'Why not?'

'Because he's not a fool.'

'She's very beautiful. Men behave foolishly when it comes to beautiful women.'

'I don't think he's in love with her. They're friends,' said Dorothy firmly. She couldn't tell her that she and Colm were lovers. She couldn't betray Margot's confidence.

'Margot is not JP's friend. She's using him. Surely he can see that?'

'I really don't think so.'

'You're very naïve, Dorothy.'

'Am I?'

'Oh, yes. Margot is a sophisticated, cunning and ambitious young woman. She's a journalist as well as an author and you know what they're like, don't you? They have no scruples. She's playing with JP like a cat with a mouse, I tell you. Once she's finished the book she'll be off and he won't see her for dust.'

'Do you really think so? I'm not so sure. She's got a good heart.'

Emer shook her head. Dorothy was confused. It wasn't like her to speak ill of someone. 'Maybe they're using each other,' said Emer. 'JP's helping her with the book to hurt Alana, and Margot's using him to get all the information she needs to make the book as juicy as possible.'

'I think she'll be tactful,' said Dorothy in Margot's defence.

'Oh, you do, do you?'

'I've got to know her a little and my gut tells me that one can trust her.'

Emer laughed. 'Then you've fallen for her charm as well.'

'I hope you're wrong,' said Dorothy in a small voice.

'So do I, for Alana's sake.'

Then Dorothy understood why Emer had so vehemently taken against her. She was like a lioness protecting her cub. But what if Emer was right? What if Margot was playing them all? What if she was playing Colm? The old lady gazed into her teacup and frowned, a sick feeling brewing in her belly. Surely Margot wouldn't be so callous?

Margot sat writing at her desk for the entire day. Her motto was *Get it written, then get it right.* Once she'd got the story down she could go back to the beginning and polish it to her heart's content. The hard work was getting the facts onto the page. As entertaining as it was writing about Barton Deverill, it still required discipline and effort and a great deal of concentration. By teatime she realized that she needed to get out. To walk around the garden, get some fresh air and stretch her legs. She left the growing pile of A4 sheets of paper beside her typewriter and headed downstairs. It came as no surprise to see the Countess being escorted into the hall by Mr Dukelow. He was rubbing his hands together and smiling as he delivered compliments in extravagant superlatives. Margot dived behind a pillar in order to avoid them.

'Might I offer you Mrs de Lisle's sitting room for some privacy?' he was saying as they passed her.

Margot noticed the Countess put her hand on his forearm. 'You are too kind, Mr Dukelow. You think of everything. No wonder you're the manager of the hotel.'

'I do my best to make sure important guests, such as yourself, are well taken care of.'

'You most certainly do.' She sighed. 'What would Mrs de Lisle do without you?'

Margot watched them leave the hall, then came out from her behind the pillar. There was something very out of place in the way the Countess had put her hand on his arm. Margot's suspicions were raised. She knew when something was up. The older she got, the sharper her intuition became.

She made her way outside. Róisín waved at her from reception. The porter greeted her at the door. Everyone in the hotel knew her well by now. The sun shone and birdsong filled the air. She inhaled the fertile scent of the soil and took pleasure from being outside after a whole day at her typewriter. She stretched her legs, taking long strides over the lawn. Then she glanced at the castle. She knew, from having looked out of the window of Mrs de Lisle's private sitting room, where that room was located. She bit her lip. She knew it was imprudent, as there was a high chance of being spotted by the gardeners, but she felt a strong desire to spy on them through the window.

She looked about her. No one seemed to be around. The lawn was quiet, the borders silent and still. A solitary pigeon cooed from the castle roof. She hoped the gardeners were busy in the vegetable garden and greenhouses. Trying to look nonchalant, she strolled towards the castle. She pretended to look in the flowerbeds, to sniff the odd plant, to appreciate the views. Then she sidled up to Mrs de Lisle's sitting-room window. She glanced about her once more. She really did not want to be caught snooping. She leaned back against the stone and peered into the bottom corner of the window.

The sight burned her eyes. She gasped. The Countess and the hotel manager were in a passionate embrace against the bookcase. They were kissing, their bodies moving together in a heated frottage. Margot tore her eyes away and hurried back onto the lawn, heart racing. Just as she set off towards the trees one of the gardeners drove out on a quadbike, pulling a cart of turf. He waved at her. Margot waved back. She sighed with relief. If she'd remained a moment longer at the window she would have been caught.

She put her hands in her coat pockets and processed what she had just witnessed. Was the Countess after Mr Dukelow for his body or for something else? Sure, her husband was old and decrepit and Margot knew that women had their needs, but Mr Dukelow? It didn't add up. As preposterous as the Countess was, she was a few rungs higher on the food chain than Mr Dukelow! Margot quickened her pace. She couldn't wait to tell Colm.

Mrs B took a seat at the back of the ballroom and put her handbag on her knee. The room was full of people. Lord Deverill, Margot and Colm were in the front row, but she had wanted to come on her own so she hadn't told them she was attending. She was glad she'd got there early because if she'd arrived any later she would not have found a seat at all. People were standing behind her and more were coming in. Word had got out about Dan Chambers' extraordinary gift and they wanted to witness it for themselves. Mrs B looked around timidly. She imagined everyone here had lost some-one. It was impossible to go through life without losing loved ones. *We all go eventually*, she thought to herself.

Dan Chambers walked onto the stage. She was surprised by the sight of him. She thought he'd be more flamboyant. More like a wizard. But he was a tall, slim man – willowy, would be the right word, she thought, with a lovely face. Yes, indeed, it was lovely: gentle, wise and unassuming. The face of someone with a big heart and lots of love to give. She perked up. If Rafferty came through with a message, she was glad it would be delivered by a man like Dan Chambers. She felt she could rely on him to tell the truth. As he began to speak, she sat up. Her heart began to beat a little faster, a little harder, and her palms started to sweat. She told herself not to be nervous. But it was of no use. She wasn't nervous because there was a chance she might hear from her brother; she was nervous that she *wouldn't*.

One by one the spirits came through and every time the recipient was moved to tears. The feeling of love in the room was overwhelming. Mrs B was moved. The spirits gave evidence first that it was really them, evidence that satisfied the bereaved in the audience and caused them to gasp in amazement. Then they sent their love. That was all it was really.

She waited for Rafferty, but he never came.

At the end of the two hours, which had felt like ten minutes, Dan took a sip of water. 'I'm sorry if some of you are disappointed. There are so many spirits in the room, I'm unable to channel all of them. I'll be back tomorrow evening, so do come again. They're very persistent, these spirits, and they all want to pass on their love to you. I will do my best to acknowledge them all during the week that I am here. But for those of you who don't receive a message, don't despair. Your loved ones are with you, I promise. Love connects you to them and that is a bond that can never be broken.'

Mrs B dabbed her eyes and put the ball of tissue in her handbag, then she got up and went back to the Hunting Lodge, her heart a little heavier, her sorrow more acute. *I know you're with me, Rafferty, and I'll try not to be disappointed. I'll go back again tomorrow. I'm sure you'll come to me then.*

The following morning Margot was joined at the breakfast table by Dorothy. She seemed a little pale. 'Are you all right, Dorothy?' Margot asked, pouring them both cups of tea.

Dorothy sighed. 'I'm fine, thank you, dear. But I've got something on my mind which I need to talk to you about.'

'Of course. Go ahead.' By the anxious look on Dorothy's face, Margot knew it wasn't anything good.

'It's about the book you're writing. I'm worried that it's going to hurt people,' she said.

Margot was relieved it was only that. She was confident she was writing the book with enough tact to avoid hurting anyone. 'You really don't need to worry,' she said.

'Don't I?' Dorothy gazed at her searchingly. 'Are you sure?'

'You know you can trust me.'

'I don't really know that. After all, we haven't been friends for very long.'

'But what do your instincts tell you?'

'To trust you,' said Dorothy firmly.

Margot thought a moment. She imagined her friend had been talking to Emer O'Leary. 'Look, if it makes you feel better, you can read the first draft,' she suggested. 'Before I give it to anyone else. To be honest, I'd really value your opinion.'

Dorothy's eyes brightened for surely, if she couldn't be trusted, Margot would never have allowed her a preview. 'That would put my mind at rest,' she replied gratefully.

'It's a history of the family, Dorothy. The recent past is only a tiny part of it. I will choose what to put in and what to keep out with sensitivity. It's not an exposé.'

'I know. You're right. You are the master of your pen. I'm sure you'll be tactful.' Dorothy's mood now lifted. The colour was restored to her cheeks and she was as chirpy as a chaffinch. She swept her eyes around the room. 'It's busy, isn't it, this place?'

'It's doing well. Like her or not, Mrs de Lisle has done a very good job of it.'

'A splendid job. Tell me, what did JP think of it? Was it the first time he'd been back?'

'It was the first time both he and Colm had been back. They were both impressed. I think JP was surprised at how nice everyone was to him. I think he felt the world was against him.'

'Not the world. Only his ex-wife,' said Dorothy with a sorry smile. 'I'm glad he's made up with his son. There's nothing as important as family.'

Margot reflected on the fact that she had no family. 'I'd say there's nothing more important than *friends*,' she said with emphasis and smiled at Dorothy.

Dorothy smiled back. How could Emer have suggested Margot was playing them all? If she knew Margot like *she* knew her, she'd realize what a sweet person she was

Margot was talking to Róisín at the reception desk when the Countess glided into the hall. She was met by Mr Dukelow, who shook her hand in a formal greeting. Margot searched for a hint of the intimacy she had witnessed in Mrs de Lisle's sitting room, but found none. The Countess moved gracefully into the dining room where she was seated at a table of six American tourists. They stood when she entered and she gave her hand to each one in turn, smiling graciously and repeating their names as they introduced themselves so she would not forget them. They looked thrilled to see her, electrified, as if she were royalty.

'The Countess seems to be spending more and more time here,' said Margot to Róisín.

Róisín grinned. 'It's good money, I suppose,' she replied with a shrug.

Margot was stunned. 'Is she being paid?'

'Oh yes,' said Róisín, lowering her voice. 'Mr Dukelow pays her for entertaining the guests. They're delighted, of course, to be in the presence of someone connected to the castle.'

'I wouldn't imagine she needs the money,' said Margot, knowing from the sorry sight of her poor husband that she did.

'I wouldn't know. Perhaps it's more of an ego trip for her, being lauded by tourists. She can pretend she's the chatelaine of the castle. She'd like that, she would.' Róisín gave a little snort. 'I'll admit to you, and only you, that I don't like her one little bit.'

'I think I agree with you,' said Margot. 'But Mr Dukelow is rather taken by her,' she added, throwing a line into the water and hoping to hook a salmon.

'He's bedazzled by her. But that's typical of Mr Dukelow, he gets overexcited about important people. The trouble is, sometimes he can't tell the difference between really important people and those who are pretending!' Róisín pulled a face. 'But I mustn't speak ill of my boss or I'll go to Hell!' She laughed. 'It would be better to invite Lord Deverill to speak to the guests. He's the real deal, isn't he? That would put the silly Countess in her place.'

That evening Mrs B took a seat in the ballroom and placed her handbag on her knee. Once again the room was full and once again she silently reached out to Rafferty and asked him to come through. Dan walked onto the stage and a hush came over the room. The air seemed to thicken and still. Mrs B's heart-rate quickened again. She almost forgot to breathe. Might her dear brother come through for her tonight?

Kitty

I stand behind the medium and observe the room before him, filled with both the living and the dead. I see spirits shining with love and notice a few shadowy earthbound spirits who have been drawn into the room to watch the spectacle. Among them is Mrs Carbery. She blinks in bewilderment at the sight, such as she has never seen before. In comparison to the spirits, she is like a little brown hen. She runs her gaze over the people for I'm not sure that she can see the spirits like I can. Their light is too bright for her. She could not endure it, I don't imagine.

When she recognizes her daughter, Bessie, she is stunned. Her small face opens into a beautiful smile. I have never seen her smile before. She has always been miserable, her mouth downturned, her eyes lacklustre and sad. But now they acquire a light of their own and gleam. 'My Bessie!' she exclaims. 'My little Bessie!' She tries to get her attention, but her efforts are fruitless. Bessie sits with her handbag on her knee, her hand trembling as she dabs her eyes with a tissue. She is hopeful, yet expectant of disappointment.

Mrs Carbery is desperate. She is now standing on the stage, right beside the medium, but I can tell that he does not hear her. I realize then that *I* have the power to do something and

I *must* do it. I must attract the medium's attention. If I cannot help her find the light then at least I can help her communicate with her daughter.

With all the will I can muster I send a ripple through the air and the tissue in Bessie's hand flies out and floats off like a dove. The people sitting next to her gasp too and a murmur of voices interrupts the medium's concentration. I send another ripple out and the jug on the table beside the medium falls over, spilling water onto the stage. The murmur grows louder. The medium narrows his eyes. 'I believe someone is trying to get my attention,' he says. He puts up his hand. 'Fear not,' he adds. 'It is a friendly spirit. A spirit desperate for communication, I believe.'

Mrs Carbery speaks. 'I want to talk to Bessie,' she says. But the medium still cannot hear her.

I am now in a rage. It's just not fair that poor Mrs Carbery, a lost and earthbound spirit, is not able to pass on a message to her daughter. I send out a thought to those higher beings who I know must be there, asking for help. Mrs Carbery's light dims and she retreats into the corner of the room. She is so small now, and subdued, that it is almost impossible to make her out from the shadows.

Bessie's mouth is still agape. She is alert, her eyes jumping about the room, anticipating something. She knows the tissue didn't fly out of her hand on its own. Perhaps she senses that someone in Spirit is wanting to communicate with her. Or maybe she is just hopeful. I cannot bear for her to be disappointed. Her pain is visible in the aura around her body. I can see it and I want so very badly to heal it. I send out another request for aid. *If anyone is out there who can help, for God's sake, do something!*

And then my prayer is answered.

A light, brighter than all the lights in the room, appears on the stage. It is the radiance of the crippled child who came down to rescue his father, Tarquin Deverill. With him is a handsome boy. He must be about seventeen. His hair is blond, his eyes are bright blue. He has a sweet expression on his face. The medium stops talking. He cannot ignore or fail to sense this advanced soul who now stands before him.

Silence descends on the room. There is no movement. Not even a cough or a sniff. Nothing. It is as if everyone here senses the presence of this beautiful soul.

The medium narrows his eyes. He tunes in.

'I have a young man here called Rafe or Rafferty,' says the medium.

Bessie lets out a moan. The name strikes her in the heart. She puts a hand there. She is too astonished to speak.

'Is there anyone here who lost a young man called Rafe or Rafferty? He was a quiet young man, thoughtful. He liked to sing ballads. He had a little sister called Bessie or Bess.'

Mrs B lets out another moan. The woman beside her puts up her hand. 'I think it's this lady here,' she says, pointing to Bessie. 'It *is* you, isn't it, dear?'

Mrs B nods.

The medium looks at Bessie with compassion. 'He says he was killed in the civil war. But he has forgiven the man who killed him, for he took no pleasure in it.'

Bessie is now crying. Fat tears are running down her face. She is too stunned by what the medium is saying to brush them away.

'He's telling me that you light a candle for him and your parents every night and say a prayer: *Until we meet again, may God hold you in the palm of His hand.*'

I am moved to see the joy that is now glowing in Bessie's

chest. It is like a flame that is burning away the pain, purging it, restoring her broken heart with love. She nods, but she is still unable to speak.

'He wants you to carry his love throughout the rest of your life, not the memory of his death or the ache of his absence. Life is for living, he is telling me, and he doesn't want you to miss a moment of it. He will be with you when you pass. He will take your hand and lead you into the light.'

Bessie can no longer see for tears. She is overwhelmed, but full of happiness.

And then an extraordinary thing happens. Mrs Carbery comes out of the shadows. Her son Rafferty reaches out his hand. She sees him, this shining soul, and her face is aglow with love. I too am overwhelmed. I watch, rapt, as she puts her hand in his and the three of them, the crippled child, Mrs Carbery and her son, disappear into the light.

She found it at last. Heaven.

She has found her way home.

Chapter 18

As summer approached, Colm and Margot's hold on their secret relationship relaxed and they grew complacent. They rode out into the hills after work, lay against the stones in the Fairy Ring and sat on the beach, sheltered from the wind by rocks, enjoying sundowners brought with them in flasks. They made these places their own, without realizing that countless other lovers in the past had already claimed them.

JP no longer needed constant supervision. He was happy, and busy – in the garden, on horseback and, as it transpired, in talks with Mr Dukelow about the possibility of giving after-dinner talks about his past to the hotel guests. Contrary to what Margot had thought, this idea did not faze him in the least, and the money was certainly a temptation. Mrs de Lisle would pay handsomely for a Deverill – far more handsomely than she was paying for the Countess!

It had been weeks since Margot had ventured into O'Donovan's. She hadn't seen Seamus and, she assumed, Seamus had no idea about her burgeoning relationship with Colm. Usually, she left men in her wake and never looked back. But as she was still here in Ballinakelly, that wasn't possible. She hoped that Seamus was the sort of man who didn't look back either.

The pub was full on this Saturday night. A band was play-ing. The atmosphere was exuberant. She and Colm found a small table in the corner and Colm went to the bar to buy drinks. He had a word with Seamus, who glanced over at Margot. She gave him a smile. He smiled back and Margot immediately read the confusion in it. She knew what he was thinking. He was no fool. She could see his mind working it out. He then turned back to Colm and began to pour the drinks. The two of them chatted away, seemingly noncha-lant, but Colm's face suddenly darkened and he shot a look at Margot. Margot felt her skin prickle with uneasiness. She wondered what Seamus had said to him, but she didn't have to wonder for long, because Colm returned to the table, put down the drinks and sat on the chair opposite. 'So when were you going to tell me you'd been to bed with Seamus O'Donovan?' he asked quietly.

Margot's instinct was self-defence. 'I wasn't. It's not rele-vant, is it?'

Colm put his glass of stout to his lips and knitted his eye-brows. 'Oh, so you weren't going to tell me, is that right?'

'I didn't need to, did I?'

'I'd rather have heard it from you than from Seamus.'

Margot shrugged. 'It was at the beginning of January, Colm. That's four months ago now. I slept with him the odd time. It meant nothing.' She sighed. 'Not very gentlemanly of him to tell you.'

Colm looked at her with concern. 'Is this what you do, Margot? Sleep with people and then discard them?'

'It's what most *men* do, if I'm not wrong. Why should women be any different? Sure, I've enjoyed brief encounters, haven't *you*?' She knew he wouldn't like that – most men didn't – but she wasn't going to hide who she was.

He wasn't sure how to answer her. He knew her argument was sound – she had every right to sleep with as many men as she liked, but it made his stomach clench to think of it. 'Seamus is none too pleased about it,' he said, trying to focus on this particular lover and not on others she might have had.

'We enjoyed a brief fling and it was fun. But it was never going to be anything more than that.'

He frowned again. 'Is that what *I* am, Margot? A brief fling?'

'You know you mean more to me than that, Colm.'

'For all I know, you'll leave when you finish the book and I won't see you for dust.'

She reached out and touched his hand. 'I want to be with you. You know that.'

He glanced to his left and right, then took her hand and squeezed it. 'I'd like to go public,' he said. 'This skulking around is doing my head in.'

'So would I.'

'Then let's do it.'

'Do we need to worry about your father?'

Colm sighed. 'I don't know. I don't want to cause a relapse.'

Margot rolled her eyes. 'He likes me, but he doesn't *love* me, Colm. That's Mrs B reading into things. I make him laugh and we're good friends, but I assure you he's not interested in me like that.'

'Have you not seen the way he looks at you?'

'With fondness.'

'No, let's keep it quiet for the time being,' he suggested, letting go of her hand.

'Seamus knows,' she said, seeing Seamus glance their way. 'He's watching us.'

'That's because you weren't very kind, Margot,' Colm replied reprovingly. 'You should have told him.'

'About us?'

'No, that you didn't want to sleep with him anymore.'

'I don't do that,' she said dismissively. 'It's awkward.'

'When you decide you don't want to sleep with *me* anymore, I'd appreciate the heads-up.'

'Colm, that's ridiculous!'

'Is it?'

'Yes.' She grinned. 'I think I'm always going to want to sleep with you.'

At last he smiled too. 'You think?'

She nodded. 'Come on. Let's go back to yours so I can show you just how sure I am about that.'

It was well past three in the morning when Mr Dukelow led the Countess into the castle via the old servants' entrance at the back. This entrance was never used these days and he had to brush away the ivy that concealed it. The night was black and deep. There was no moon, only the small light from the torch he carried to show the way. The two of them sneaked down the corridor and up the old servants' staircase. This part of the hotel had not been decorated in the sumptuous style of the public areas. There were linoleum floors, white walls and naked light bulbs hanging from the ceiling, a thick layer of dust and heaps of crisp brown leaves that had once blown in and been left to wither. It was also cold. But this did not deter them. They did not speak, but crept like thieves, quietly and in silence, deeper into the castle until they reached the bottom of the staircase leading to the little suite of rooms at the top of the western tower.

Here they hesitated a moment. 'Are you sure she's not up there?' the Countess whispered.

'Absolutely sure. Like I told you, she's at Colm Deverill's house.'

The Countess curled her lip in disgust. 'She's sleeping with him, is she?'

'She is,' Mr Dukelow confirmed. 'She thinks no one knows.'

The Countess smiled, her thin lips disappearing into a line. 'How very satisfying.'

They were careful to tread softly. When he reached the top, Mr Dukelow lifted the latch and gently pushed open the door. It was pitch black inside. He shone the torch around the sitting room. The curtains had not been drawn, which was a clear indication that the occupant was not in residence. He stepped inside with confidence, followed by the Countess, who lifted the hood of her cloak and sighed. Mr Dukelow strode into the bedroom and shone his torch onto the bed. It had not been touched since the morning when housekeeping had made it. The beam of light revealed what they were looking for. The pile of A4 paper neatly stacked on the desk beside the typewriter.

The Countess fell upon it with a gasp. She turned the pile of paper over and lifted the final sheet. She beckoned him closer. 'Shine your light here,' she demanded. He did as he was told. Her eyes scanned the lines greedily.

'What does it say?' he asked.

She tutted in frustration. 'She is writing about silly old Hubert and Adeline. Well, we will have to come back in a few weeks' time when she has written more.'

Mrs B wasn't the same woman she had been when she had sat in the ballroom, handbag on her knee, a muddle of anticipation, hope and dread. She was lighter and, most surprisingly of all, *jolly*. That was a word one would never have used to describe Bessie Brogan. But jolly she was. Jolly, cheerful and full of joy.

Lord Deverill had noticed immediately. When Mrs B had returned to the Lodge that evening, her eyes wet and dreamy and her heart brimming with emotion, he had sat her down in the library and listened attentively. Mrs B had cried all over again during the retelling of it, but after that she hadn't once reached for her tissues; not once.

She continued to light the votive candles in her bedroom and repeat the prayer, as she did every night, but now she closed her eyes and felt her dear brother beside her. She knew he was there. He had said so, hadn't he? He was right beside her and would be, until her time ran out and she too was called home.

Mrs B danced to the music on her radio. She tapped her feet, swayed her hips and moved her shoulders as she cooked and prepared meals and when she washed up. She hummed too. She listened to ballads as well and sang along with gusto. Her heart was full and she needed to express it. Music allowed her to do this, without inhibition because, now Master Colm had returned to his own home, no one ever came into the kitchen.

The Hunting Lodge had emerged out of the shadows into the light, just as the land had been lifted out of the hard cold and damp of winter into spring. The place felt warm, not just because it was early summer, but because it was happy. Mrs B knew that was what it was. The house was happy and she and Lord Deverill were happy in it.

One evening at the beginning of June, Margot, Colm and JP were sitting outside on the terrace, enjoying drinks before dinner. The air was balmy and warm, the amber light soft as the sun slowly sank behind the horse chestnut trees. It was a perfect summer's evening, the kind of evening one would look back on with nostalgia when the cold autumn winds came in October to chase the summer away. The garden was at its best, the plants still young and tender, the shrubs trimmed and the Himalayan roses in full flower, climbing rabidly to the very top of the sycamore tree. There was a feeling of optimism, a sense of things changing for the better. Mrs B watched the three of them laughing and chatting as the pigeons cooed from the rooftop and the sky turned pink. She had just brought out another jug of lemonade, when JP announced that he had some news to share.

'By the look on your face, I'd say it's good news,' said Colm.

'I *hope* it's good news,' JP replied, putting his glass on the table beside the bench. 'At least, I hope you'll think it's good news. I have a job.'

'You're going to be a speaker at the castle,' Margot declared. 'I think that's brilliant!'

'Yes, I've been talking to Mrs de Lisle. She's very keen and she's going to pay me very well. Exceedingly well, I should say.'

'I think that's a grand idea,' said Colm.

JP looked at Margot. 'But there's more. I have an idea, you see.'

'And what's that?' said Margot.

'How about you and I put on an act together? You tell some stories of past Deverills and what they got up to and I talk about what it was like living in the castle. Together, we'd make an entertaining duo, I think. What do you say?'

Colm glanced at Margot. Margot had anticipated this. She thought about it for a moment. What was there to lose? JP was right. They would make a brilliant pair, complementing each other with a combination of history and personal experience – it was just the sort of pairing Mrs de Lisle would love.

'Did you suggest it?' Margot asked.

'Not yet. I wanted to ask you first.'

'I think it would be fun to do something together. Why don't I have a chat with Mr Dukelow and see what he says.'

Mrs B felt a twinge of concern. Lord Deverill still didn't know that his son and Margot were in a relationship. She knew how fond he was of her, a fondness that would only grow deeper if they started working together, she suspected, and she worried that when he learned the truth he'd be hurt. Sure, he was old enough to be her father, but that never stopped the heart feeling what it felt. There was no controlling that. She wondered when the two young people were going to come out of hiding. They couldn't keep their relationship secret for ever, could they?

Mr Dukelow visibly trembled with excitement when Margot suggested that she and Lord Deverill do some after-dinner talks together. He immediately telephoned Mrs de Lisle.

'I have a brilliant idea,' he began. When he told Mrs de Lisle about it, she was ecstatic.

'You see, *that* is why I employ people like you, Mr Dukelow,' she gushed. 'You know exactly what we're doing here. It's a very strong idea. I like it a lot. I always thought the Countess was a bit of a fraud, although the tourists bought it. Still, you can tell her that we don't require her services any longer. We have the real McCoy. A Deverill is what we need. What we've *always* needed, and you, Mr Dukelow, have pulled it off. Margot and Lord Deverill will be a sell-out. I'll get the marketing team on to it right away.'

Mr Dukelow was not happy about having to let down the Countess. She was not going to be at all happy about it. 'Are you sure we shouldn't keep the Countess on for the tea parties? They're very popular, you know.'

'I never liked her, Mr Dukelow. But she was good for business. She's no longer good for business, so, just do as I say, understood?'

'Of course, Mrs de Lisle.' He clenched his jaw to restrain himself. He'd have liked to fight harder for the Countess, but Mrs de Lisle was a woman who did not like to be contradicted. 'We'll have to pay Miss Hart something,' he added.

'Of course we will. We'll pay her well. After all, she delivered us Dan Chambers and what a success he turned out to be! She's dynamite, and wait until the book comes out. It'll send people flocking to the hotel. To think they'll get to shake hands with Lord Deverill himself. Dynamite. That's what it is.' Mrs de Lisle sighed with satisfaction. 'I always knew the castle would be the jewel in my crown.'

Mr Dukelow waited until the Countess had given her final tea party before he told her the bad news. She stared at him in horror. 'I don't understand,' she replied. 'You are firing me?' Her white face stared at him in disbelief.

'I'm afraid Mrs de Lisle no longer feels it's—'

'Angela de Lisle! She cannot treat me like this. It's disgusting! It was *she* who begged me to give her guests a taste of aristocracy and history in the first place. I don't believe it. It can't be true.'

'I'm afraid it is, Countess. I spoke to her this morning.'

She smoothed down her skirt and folded her arms. 'I have never in my life been treated with such disrespect. Wait until my husband, the Count, finds out about this. He will be furious. There is no telling what he might do!'

'I did fight for you, I promise. But she wouldn't change her mind.'

'Is she forgetting who I am? My husband grew up in this castle. It should, by right, be mine. I should be hosting private dinner parties and lunch parties and garden parties and . . .' She took a breath, overcome suddenly with emotion. 'It should be *me* firing Angela de Lisle, not the other way round.' She glared at Mr Dukelow 'I am the closest person to the history of this place that she will find. If I am not going to give the hotel guests a taste of history, then who is?' She smiled triumphantly.

Mr Dukelow rubbed his chin. Well, she would find out about it in the end anyway. 'Lord Deverill,' he replied.

'Lord Deverill? That old drunk!' She laughed scornfully. 'Now I've heard everything.'

'Actually, he's sober now,' he told her, watching her face fall and gaining no satisfaction from it. 'He's going to give talks with Margot Hart.'

The Countess didn't know what to say. 'Well, don't come crying to me when it all goes horribly wrong. I won't be back!' She pouted her lips and sighed like a petulant child.

'I'm sorry, Countess. I really am. If I had my way, you'd be hosting dinner every night.'

'You couldn't afford me,' she hissed. Then, remembering suddenly that she still needed Mr Dukelow for the other small matter of Margot Hart's book, she ran a crimson nail down his cheek. 'I shouldn't blame you, Terrence,' she said in a low voice. 'I know this must have been very hard for you too.'

Relieved that she wasn't going to storm out of his life, Mr Dukelow dropped his shoulders and took her hand. 'You know how much I adore you, Countess.' He planted a kiss on her pale skin. 'If there's anything I can do to make it up to you . . .'

She smiled. 'There is,' she replied without hesitation, 'one small matter still unresolved.'

Margot and JP came up with a format for their talk whereby she would introduce the family with the story of Barton Deverill and the building of the castle, plus the odd amusing anecdote about subsequent descendants, then she would step back and give JP the floor. He would tell guests about his grandparents Hubert and Adeline Deverill and how he came to inherit the castle from his mother, Bridie, Countess di Marcantonio, who had started out as a maid. It was a great story.

The first event was scheduled for the end of June. In the run-up, they practised on the terrace, refining their speeches until they were able to deliver them confidently and without hesitation. Margot was used to public speaking but JP was a novice. However, the preparation paid off, for the dress rehearsal in front of Colm and Mrs B went without a hitch. They even answered the most impertinent questions Colm and Mrs B could think of without a moment's pause.

However, it is one thing to give a talk to friends and family, but quite another to be in front of a room full of strangers.

When the day arrived JP was understandably nervous. He kept busy in the garden, trying not to glance at his watch, as time ticked along in its usual fashion, bringing him closer to the event that he was now beginning to dread. 'What do you think, Mrs. B? Have I been a little rash in agreeing to do this?' he asked when he came in for lunch.

'Get away with yourself, m'lord. In the whole of Cork, there isn't a man, woman or child knows the castle like you do. You'll never see the day that you will get the castle back. For good or ill, those days are gone for ever. But it doesn't mean you can't have a bit of fun lording it around in there once in a while. For the honour of God, m'lord, what harm can it do?'

JP sat down and put his napkin on his knee. 'I don't think I'd want the castle back, even if I could have it,' he said pensively. 'There's something about the lack of responsibility and freedom that appeals to me now as I get older. I like it here, in this house, Mrs B. It suits me.' He smiled at her as she placed a slice of soda bread in front of him. 'Thank you for looking after me all these years, Mrs B. I do appreciate you, you know.'

'Thank you, m'lord,' she said quietly, pink staining her cheeks. She picked up the dish of leek and potato soup from the sideboard and brought it over. 'Has it never occurred to you that you've looked after me too,' she added. 'I'm one of the luckiest women ever born to have been a part of your family.'

The smile in JP's eyes deepened with tenderness. 'You could say, we've rescued each other,' he said, and she nodded.

'God works in mysterious ways,' she replied, watching him ladle the soup into his bowl. 'There's always a plan only, most of the time, we don't see it. As me poor auld mother used to say, every auld stocking finds an auld shoe. I'm beginning to see it clearly now.'

'So am I,' he agreed.

'Get on with yourself now, m'lord, and go out tonight and enjoy yourself. You've earned it.'

With that intention, JP stood in front of one hundred guests in the castle's dining room and introduced himself as Jack Patrick Deverill, the eighth Lord Deverill of Ballinakelly, the one who lost the castle his great ancestor, Barton, built in 1662. 'The King stole land that belonged to the O'Leary family and gave it to the Deverills. Nearly three hundred years later, I married Alana O'Leary and moved into the castle, thus restoring it, in a small way, to the O'Leary family. I like to feel that, with that union, something of that terrible wrong was put right. Perhaps it was karma that caused us to lose our home, who knows? But,' he said, sweeping his blue gaze over the room, 'there is something very satisfactory about seeing you good people now sharing in the history and magic of Castle Deverill.' The audience was enraptured and JP rose on a wave of goodwill and delivered a fascinating and humorous speech. Margot watched him with pride, this broken man she had helped put back together. She caught Colm's eye and saw the pride glowing in his face too. When she had arrived in January she could never have predicted that her life would come to this.

At the end of the talk there were questions. Nothing that JP and Margot couldn't handle.

Then the Countess, who had been sitting on the table at the far end of the room, keeping an uncharacteristically low profile, put up her hand. JP recognized her at once and bristled.

'Lord Deverill,' she said. 'You imply that you lost the castle because of karma. The land was stolen so, in the end, as payment for that crime, it was taken from you. There is a certain justice in that, to be sure. However, my husband, Count Leopoldo di Marcantonio, would say that the castle should have been left to him, as the only son of your mother Bridie and Count Cesare di Marcantonio. Do you not see that you lost the castle because of that more recent wrong? Do you feel regret, or any sense of injustice on my husband's behalf?'

JP lifted his chin. 'Thank you, Countess, for coming tonight. It is a pleasure to see you here at Castle Deverill. To answer your question, I do sympathize with your husband's predicament. He expected to inherit the castle, yet it was left to me. We cannot undo what has been done in the past, we can only let it go. I have learned, through many hours of soul-searching, that contentment comes from letting go of old hurts. The castle is now a beautiful hotel. I celebrate it. To do otherwise would be detrimental to my health and peace of mind. I suggest that you and your husband do the same. Nothing will come of resentment but unhappiness.'

The Countess's face blanched as the audience erupted into a wild applause.

Margot watched her warily, surrounded as she was by a dark miasma which set her apart from everyone else in the room. Something cramped in her stomach. A feeling of unease that, as she graciously received the praise and congratulations from those seated at her table, did not go away.

Kitty

I stand by Jack's bed. He is sick and fading fast. Alana has flown over from the States with her daughters, Aisling and Cara, and her siblings, Liam and Aileen, have come from Connemara and Co. Wexford to be with their father in his last moments. Colm arrives. They gather with Emer in Jack's bedroom, around his bed, as Jack lies still with his eyes closed, his cheeks sunken, waiting for death. If you ask me, he looks dead already, but his chest gently rises and falls in defiance. 'I'll not go until I'm ready,' I hear him whisper soundlessly. He always was a stubborn man.

As night falls, he puts out his left hand. Emer takes it. His eyes open and they are full of peace and acceptance. They are the eyes of a soul already halfway to Heaven. 'Forgive me, my darling Emer, for all the wrongs I have done you,' he says.

Emer's eyes sparkle. 'There is nothing to forgive, my dear,' she replies softly, pressing her lips to the diaphanous, speckled skin on the back of his hand. 'We forgave each other long ago, did we not?'

'Alana.' He turns his head slowly and finds her, hovering on the other side of the bed. He gives her his right hand. 'Make peace with JP,' he says. His voice is a whisper now.

Alana blinks and the tears are released. She nods. It is no time to deny a man his dying wish.

He has a word to say to each of his children and they receive it with gratitude and reverence; Jack is already closer to God than they are.

He turns to Colm. 'You've been a good grandson, Colm,' he says. He manages a small smile. Then he mumbles something so quietly that Colm has to lean in to hear. He has to put his ear to his grandfather's lips so that the words can be heard. But that is exactly what Jack wants, for Colm to get so close so that no one else but him can hear what he has to say. 'Don't let her get away,' Jack whispers.

I am overcome with emotion; on his deathbed, Jack is thinking of me.

It is not long before he takes his last breath. With his family by his bed he silently slips away. There is no death rattle, no struggle, nothing but peace. I see his mother in Spirit. A being of light and love. She puts out her hand and he takes it. He rises up, leaving the body he no longer needs lying like an old coat on the bed, and together they depart. He does not see me.

It is then that I am gripped by an urgent and passionate longing: I want to go home.

I want to go home *now*.

But there is no one to take me.

Chapter 19

JP was sorry when he heard the news about Jack. Colm drove over in the morning to tell him. He'd been up all night, keeping vigil at his grandfather's bedside, as was tradition. The wake would last the day. Friends would come to pay their respects, drink Guinness and eat snacks in darkened rooms aglow with candlelight. Jack's dog lay by his side, refusing to move.

JP embraced his son and held him for an extended time. He knew how close he had been to his grandfather. 'Let's go for a stroll around the garden,' he suggested. 'The fresh air will do you good.' The two men set off across the lawn.

It was a beautiful morning. Birdsong filled the air, the breeze was silky and warm, the sun radiant as if it hadn't noticed Jack O'Leary had died. 'Dad, I need to tell you something,' Colm said, putting his hands in his pockets.

'All right, go on,' JP replied.

'It's about Margot.'

JP looked alarmed. 'What about Margot?'

Colm hesitated. 'I'm in love with her,' he said at last, then winced, expecting his father's face to betray his hurt.

'So am I,' he laughed. 'I think everyone's a little in love with Margot Hart.'

'You misunderstand me. She's in love with me too. We're in a relationship.'

JP stopped and looked at his son with different eyes. 'Really? Since when?'

'We wanted to tell you, but we didn't want to upset your recovery.'

'Now, why would telling me good news like that upset my recovery?'

'Well, I thought you might be a little in love with her yourself. Like you just said—'

'My dear boy, I don't mean I love her like *that*.' JP laughed at the absurdity of the idea. 'I'm old enough to be her father!'

'I know that, which is why—'

'I'm tremendously fond of Margot,' JP interrupted. 'We're friends. Good friends. If it hadn't been for her I don't think I'd have had the courage or the will to get better. She saved me and I'll always be grateful to her for that. But I'm not in love with her. Not at all.' He patted his son's back and they walked on. 'I'm glad you've found each other, Colm. She's a good girl. I must admit, I never suspected a thing. You've been very good at hiding it.'

Colm was relieved. 'It hasn't been easy.'

'I don't suppose you're going to tell your mother.'

'That's the other thing I want to speak to you about. I want you to go and talk to Mum. I don't mean have a row, I mean talk to her nicely. She's really cut up about Grandad.'

'Colm, I'm the last person she wants to see.'

'I don't agree. What's the opposite of love?'

'Hate.'

'No, it isn't. Indifference is the opposite of love. Not caring at all. You both must care for each other a little bit if you still have enough energy to hate.'

'Hate is a very strong word, Colm. I've never hated your mother.'

'Then talk to her, Dad. For me. For the three of us.'

Dorothy was in a terrible state when she arrived in Ballinakelly. She had come as fast as she could, dropping everything and getting the earliest flight to Shannon Airport. Jack was dead. Jack O'Leary, the man she had admired above all others, was gone. It was unthinkable. Of course, she had never let on that she had secretly loved him. Emer was her friend and besides, Jack had never encouraged her, not for a moment. He had probably never known how she felt. After all, she hadn't shown it, or shared it, with anyone. It had been her secret and she had guarded it closely.

Even at eighty-eight he'd held her heart captive. Fancy that! An old man still having the power to make an old woman in her eighties grow hot under the collar. But that was Jack O'Leary. He'd always had a twinkle in his eye and the sort of charisma that doesn't dim with age, but shines on regardless. And, of course, she had known him when he was a young man, full of fight. How dashing he'd been. How full of magnetism and vigour; now he was gone.

Dorothy thought about death often these days. The years ahead of her were far fewer than those behind her. Was there really a life after? she wondered. She had faith, having been brought up as a church-going Protestant, but she doubted now, as the end drew close. She doubted out of fear. It almost sounded too good to be true, and experience had taught her that things which were too good to be true often were; it was a fact. Dan Chambers' events remained vivid in her memory and yet, she doubted that too.

Had her daughter really come through? Had Dan pulled a name out of his mind and simply got lucky? Lillie wasn't an uncommon name, after all. It had seemed very real at the time, but now she wondered whether she'd believed because she so wanted to believe. Had her longing clouded her judgement?

Where was Jack now? Where was his consciousness? It was strange to think that he knew the answer. Of course, he wouldn't even be aware of the question if he no longer existed. That thought chilled her the most.

After a brief stop at the hotel Dorothy took a taxi to the wake at Emer and Jack's house. People had crammed into the small space, there was no room to sit down. Emer embraced her fiercely, grateful that she had come. 'I won't know what to do with myself now that Jack's gone,' she said hoarsely. 'I'll be like a dandelion on the wind.'

'I'll stay with you for as long as you want,' Dorothy reassured her.

Emer's eyes filled with tears. 'You mean that, Dorothy?'

'Of course I do. I'll stay at the hotel until Alana and the girls have gone and then I'll move in and keep you company for a while. Now Jack's gone, I'll stay as long as I like.'

Emer laughed sadly. 'Oh, you are funny, Dorothy. But I can tell you now that you were right, Jack really didn't like people staying.'

'I knew it!'

'He wasn't a sociable man. Most of the time it was the just the two of us. I liked it that way.'

Emer was distracted suddenly. She turned her eyes to the door. To her surprise, JP was standing there, unsure whether or not he'd be welcomed in. He was in a tweed jacket, holding his hat in his hands, an anxious expression on his face. 'Would you look who's turned up?' said Emer to her friend.

'There's nothing like death to bring out the best in people,' Dorothy replied, surprised to see him there too.

'I'd better go and welcome him. After all, it's kind of him to come.'

'And brave,' Dorothy added.

Emer smiled cautiously when she greeted JP. He had hurt her daughter, after all, and she was still sad about that. But she was a gracious woman who did not like confrontation or hard feelings and it was impossible for her not to be polite. 'Thank you for coming, JP,' she said, amazed to see him looking so bright-eyed and clear-skinned. It was like he was a younger, fitter version of himself. Closer to the dashing, insouciant man Alana had fallen in love with and married all those years ago. He expressed his condolences in a few, carefully chosen words and Emer received them with gratitude. 'Why don't you go on in and pay your respects.' She did not imagine her daughter would want to see him and hoped he'd be in and out before she realized he was there.

The mourners spoke in hushed tones in the room where Jack's body was laid out beneath a white sheet. It was dark, but for the candles that glowed golden on the bedside table and dresser. Jack looked peaceful, as if he were sleeping. JP felt sad that he hadn't made his peace with him. After the divorce the two families had stopped speaking to each other. JP was sure that Jack would have blamed him for Alana leaving Ireland. In a way, Jack had lost her too. Life was complicated. It was hard to accept, this froideur, when one looked back to the early days of their marriage, when they'd been happy and without a care.

He felt a hand on his arm. He turned to see Alana standing beside him. She gave him a tearful smile. 'Thank you, JP. It means a lot to me that you came.'

He acknowledged her words with a nod. They looked down at Jack with tenderness, struggling to accept that he was no longer present. It was as if he might open his eyes at any moment and wake up.

They moved into the corridor. 'Would you like to stay for a drink?' she asked.

'No, thank you. I think I'll be getting back. I just wanted to say goodbye. He was a good man, your father. Wise, brave, strong. We were friends once.' He hesitated, then cut himself off with a bland, meaningless sentiment. 'He deserves a good rest.' He sensed he was starting off down a thorny road of nostalgia and regret and now wasn't the time or the place for it.

'He does indeed,' Alana agreed and watched him leave. There must be a woman, she thought with a twinge of jealousy. He wouldn't look as good as he did, or have sobered up so quickly, if it wasn't for a woman. She wondered who she was, this person who had inspired him to pull himself together. Surely not Margot Hart?

The funeral took place the following day in the Catholic Church of All Saints in Ballinakelly and Jack was laid to rest in the graveyard, where generations of O'Learys had been buried before him. The entire town came out to pay their respects for he had been a much-loved, albeit elusive, member of the community.

Colm was heartbroken. He loved his grandfather and now he was gone. It was visceral, this feeling of loss, as if he'd been filleted like a fish. Then he remembered something Mrs B had once told him: *Grief is just love with nowhere to go.*

That night, while Margot slept in Colm's arms, the Countess once again followed Mr Dukelow into the castle via the back door, their way illuminated by torchlight. Again they climbed the old servants' staircase, up into the western tower where Margot's room lay in darkness and silence. The Countess pulled back the hood of her cloak and moved straight to the desk. Her hands grabbed the manuscript and turned it over. She lifted the top page and saw, to her delight, that Margot had very nearly finished the book. Mr Dukelow shone the torch on the words so that she could read them.

Her eyes feverishly scanned the lines searching for Leopoldo's name. Impatiently, she turned over the page and grabbed another one. One after the other she skimmed them, but there was very little besides the occasional mention of her husband. 'There must be some mistake,' she muttered. She started again, this time more slowly.

'Put the pages down and let's read them together,' Mr Dukelow suggested calmly.

'She has barely mentioned Leopoldo,' she snapped. 'This is preposterous and she calls herself a historian!' She laughed bitterly. 'But she's written about Cesare's murder. Of course she's written about that. She's written that he was running off with his wife's money and a young girl he'd seduced from town. Outrageous!' she exclaimed. 'I have a good mind to burn the lot!'

'That wouldn't be a good idea,' said Mr Dukelow. 'Come, let's get out of here.'

The Countess's nostrils flared with anger. 'I took the time and trouble to come and see her and to help her with her research. And this is the way she repays me! I shouldn't have wasted my time.'

'This is a book about the Deverills, Countess. Perhaps she doesn't want to digress.'

'Like an idiot she's swallowed all the lies JP has told her,' she continued, ignoring Mr Dukelow's lame excuses. 'I should have known that would happen. And she's sleeping with his son. Well, she's got all the information she needed, no doubt. As soon as she's done, she'll be off back to England without a backwards glance, I should think. I was a fool to believe that she would write a truthful account. There's no truth in this. Leopoldo is but a footnote! A footnote! How dare she!'

Mr Dukelow didn't quite understand what all the fuss was about. Why should Miss Hart write about Leopoldo when he only lived in the castle for fourteen years? He wasn't really relevant to the Deverill family history. Mr Dukelow wondered whether the Countess wasn't a little unhinged. Years of resentment had surely blown the situation out of all proportion. Now she no longer had a role to play in the hotel's entertainment and had read the almost-finished manuscript, would she require him to sneak her back into the castle? If she didn't, would she still want to see him?

'I have seen everything I need to see,' she said, a calmness descending on her now, like the hush after a storm.

'You'd better make sure the paper is stacked as neatly as you found it,' Mr Dukelow warned.

She tapped her manicured fingers against the pile to ease the paper into a tidy wad. 'There, it is done,' she said. 'She will never know.'

Mr Dukelow led her down the stairs and out into the night. Stars twinkled and the crescent moon hung like a sickle above them. They hurried down the garden path and into the trees, leaving the estate by way of a gate in the castle wall. Mr Dukelow had parked his car in a lay-by. They climbed in and he drove her back to her house in Dublin. It was a long drive, but he was happy to do it. Happy to spend a little more time with her. Anxious that this might be the last time.

'When will I see you again,' he asked as he drew up outside her building.

She turned to him and smiled sweetly. 'I don't think I will ever come to the castle again.'

'We can meet elsewhere. Wherever you want. Just say the word and I'll be there.'

'You're very sweet,' she said, lightly touching his cheek. 'But I think the time has come for us to say goodbye too.' She laughed through her nose, a bitter, mirthless laugh. 'Don't look so sad, Terrence. It was fun. Sneaking around like a pair of thieves. It felt like we were living inside a novel, didn't it? A romantic novel. Two lovers, skulking about the shadows, snatching stolen moments together. But that kind of thing cannot endure. Surely you know that. It's a fantasy and fantasies only work for a short time because reality will always come in and ruin them.'

'We can skulk around Dublin,' he suggested hopefully, although he sensed hope was futile.

She opened the door. 'No, we can't,' she replied. 'It's over. Goodbye, Terrence.'

He watched her unlock the door to the building and slip inside. He remained, staring at it for some time, hoping that she might change her mind and come out. But she didn't. The street was empty and quiet. The Countess was gone. He made his way back to Ballinakelly with a heavy heart, his mind working on ways to get her back. Surely there was something he could offer her?

The day after Jack's funeral, Margot found Dorothy having breakfast in the dining room. She was dressed in an ivory silk blouse and cardigan with a pair of sensible lace-up brown shoes on her feet. 'I'm going into town,' she told Margot. 'I thought I'd walk. Nice to take the air. It's a lovely day, isn't it? Just lovely.'

Margot sat down and placed a brown parcel on the table.

'Is that what I think it is?' said Dorothy excitedly.

'My book,' Margot replied. 'The first draft.'

'Goodness, you *are* quick.'

'It's not hard once you've got all your research in front of you.'

'You're a clever girl. That's what you are.' Dorothy picked it up. 'It's heavy.'

'You don't have to read it all. Just the last hundred pages.'

'I will read it all. Every word.'

'I'm open to advice. Like I said, I don't want to offend JP or his family.'

'I'm sure you've been very tactful.'

'I hope so,' Margot replied.

'I'll start reading it at once.'

'Well, after your walk.'

'Yes, after my walk. Thank you, Margot for trusting me. Do you need it back?'

'Only when you've finished it. I don't want it falling into the wrong hands.'

'It's not your only copy, is it?'

'No. Róisín made me another on the hotel photocopier.'

Dorothy sighed. 'To think Jack is gone. The world feels incomplete now. Off-kilter. I can't imagine how Emer is feeling. I'll pay her a visit this afternoon. As soon as Alana and the girls leave, I'll move in and keep her company for a while. It's hard being a widow. But one does get used to it in the end.'

Margot drove to a secluded beach and went for a walk. She needed to think. The book was written. Sure, she needed to polish it, but the narrative was down on the page. She'd wait until she'd heard Dorothy's opinion before sending it to her editor. It was a fine balance between maintaining integrity as a historian and loyalty as a friend. She hoped she'd satisfied both history *and* the Deverills. It would have been easier had she not grown close to JP and Colm. But she had. The last thing she wanted was to upset them.

She strode up the sand. Grey-bellied clouds scudded across the sky, the wind was blustery but warm, the air sweet with the scent of brine and peat. Ireland really was a beautiful country, she thought, but did she want to stay here? Soon her contract would end with the hotel and she'd be free to go wherever she chose. She'd spent the last decade wandering the globe, the idea of remaining in one place made her feel decidedly uneasy. Yet, she was growing to love Colm. Sure, she'd been in love with him for some time, but that was different to really *loving* someone. 'In love' is the heady, sexual attraction of two people drawn to each other because they like what they see. Loving is what happens when you fall out of being 'in love' – the moment you realize you love the person faults and all, inside and out, in good times and bad times. The moment you realize you can't be without them. Was she there with Colm? Could she stand being without him? She put her hands in her jacket pockets and marched on. She didn't know.

Kitty

I am alone. I am *all* alone and it is lonely in the In-between.

Mrs Carbery has moved on and, although I didn't seek her company much, it was reassuring to know that she was here. Of course, I am aware of other earthbound spirits shuffling around the castle's corridors, but they are unaware of me. Those who are stuck often don't realize that they are dead. They exist in a strange, dream-like state – until someone comes to rescue them. Who is going to rescue *me*?

It used to be fun haunting the hotel, but I am tired of it now. It used to be entertaining watching the living going about their daily lives, but now it bores me. It used to be a thrill to travel by thought, but that too leaves me disenchanted. But what can I do? I am truly stuck. Stuck by my own volition. Even the castle, which held me earthbound because of my obsessive love, is losing its grip on my heart. And Jack has gone. Perhaps it wasn't the castle that kept me here, but Jack; perhaps it was Jack all along.

After all, the castle is just bricks and mortar.

I am drawn to the Fairy Ring. A week has gone by since Jack was buried. He should have been scattered here, with me, but he was interred in the ground. But what does it matter? His body is of no use to him or anyone else now. It is only me and my romantic heart that likes the idea of our mortal remains being set free on the same wind, in the place that we had once made our own.

But it is not only our place. It is Colm and Margot's too, and, by the look of Alana now pacing the grass, waiting for JP, it is theirs as well. Or rather, it used to be. She waits for him nervously and impatiently and, as she stares out to sea, her gaze is pulled into the far distant horizon. The place where all our truths can be found. The more she stares into that mysterious mist, the more she understands herself and her longings. And it comes to her, her truth, in a flash of awareness that causes her breath to catch in her chest.

She turns and JP is there, walking towards her in his tweed jacket and hat. His long strides confident. His face handsome. She is not used to seeing him like this.

She lifts her chin and pulls back her shoulders and the softness in her face hardens again. She does not want to expose herself.

'Thank you for meeting me here,' she says.

He greets her with a cautious smile. He is curious. He wonders why she has invited him to this particular place.

'Do you remember the times we used to come up here?' she says, turning her eyes to the sea once more. 'It was our special place. It hasn't changed. But we have.'

'It's been like this for thousands of years,' he replies. 'Think of the things these stones have witnessed.'

'What I wouldn't give to be able to talk to them.'

He grins. 'You can talk to them as much as you like.'

'You know what I mean, silly.' She smiles in spite of herself. JP used to have the ability to make her laugh like no one else.

'How are you bearing up?' he asks.

She shrugs. 'So-so. It hasn't really sunk in yet. I still

expect my father to be there, around the house. It feels strange without him.' She gazes at JP and puzzlement furrows her forehead. 'You look good. You've sorted yourself out. I have to admit, I never thought you would. What did it?'

'I hit rock bottom. There was only one way to go and that was up. The other way was not an option.'

She frowns. 'But who helped you?'

'Colm and Margot.'

She stiffens. 'I thought so.' She laughs bitterly. 'There had to be a woman behind such a dramatic transformation. I want to say that she's young enough to be your daughter, but it's none of my business.'

'She's in a relationship with Colm,' he tells her.

Now Alana feels foolish. She blinks at him in bewilderment, like a mole emerging into the light. 'She and Colm are dating?'

'I think it's gone well beyond the dating stage.'

'But I thought you—'

'I don't know why.'

'Well, I assumed you couldn't look this good without, well, without a woman inspiring you to get better.'

'You're not wrong. A woman *did* inspire me to get better, but not the one you think.'

Her disappointment is palpable. 'Oh, so, I *am* right. Well, I thought as much. Good for you, JP. I'm happy for you. I am,' she says *un*happily. 'I suppose we should both have moved on by now.' She can barely look at him. 'Who is she?' she asks.

'You,' he replies.

Alana is confused. She does not want to believe what she is hearing. 'Sorry? Me? I don't understand.'

'Of course you don't. Can we walk? I think we'll both find

it easier to talk if we walk. And we don't want those stones knowing our business, now, do we?'

I watch them stroll along the clifftop. The waves swell and foam below them and gulls squawk as they swoop and dive in search of prey. 'We never really talked, you and I. We both nursed our hurts on our own islands, resenting one another. And, as we drifted further apart, the will to communicate grew weaker, until we stopped talking altogether. Margot encouraged me to talk about my feelings. To go back into that dark place and let the light in, was what she said. Once the light was in, I realized the terrible mistakes I'd made and I owned up to them. I shouldn't have sought comfort in Rosie. I shouldn't have resented you for wanting another child. I should have been more supportive when you lost the baby. Alana, there are lots of things I shouldn't have done. But most of all, I shouldn't have let you go. We should have found a way to communicate.'

Alana's eyes are welling with tears. Her chest is so tight she can hardly breathe. She puts a hand there and inhales with difficulty. 'I'm sorry I drove you into Rosie's arms, JP. I have things I need to take responsibility for as well. It's not easy, is it, owning up to things? But Dad's death has made me think and I don't want to leave for America without talking to you frankly. It wasn't all your fault. It was mine too. I pushed you away after losing the baby. I was so furious with you for not wanting another child that when I lost it I blamed you for somehow jinxing it – and for getting what you wanted. I should never have tricked you. We already had three children. I should have been grateful for what I had and not craved for more.'

'We were happy before we moved into the castle, weren't we?' he says wistfully.

'I never realized what a burden that inheritance was for you. What a burden the castle became. You should have told me. I could have supported you.'

He frowns at her. 'Have you been talking to Colm?' he asks.

'No,' she replies quickly, but she looks shifty. 'I've just spent this week thinking.'

'I don't want the castle back,' he says. 'Kitty will curse me for saying it, no doubt, but I'm glad that it's a hotel. I like living in the Hunting Lodge. I'm happy there. I'm free of the burden of having to run the castle, having to pay for it. The good old days of the ascendancy are long gone. No one lives like that nowadays. It was fine for my grandparents, but Margot has a theory—'

'That the castle has only ever brought its inhabitants sorrow and tragedy.'

'You *have* been talking to Colm!' he exclaims.

'There might be some truth in that,' she continues without answering his question. 'Maybe it was cursed. After all, Barton Deverill built it on land stolen from someone else. That's bad energy, isn't it? What goes around, comes around. I'm glad you lost it. I only wish it hadn't hurt you so much.'

'I'm over it now.'

'Good.'

'But there's something missing. *You're* missing.' JP stops walking and looks down at her, his face full of affection. 'I still love you, Alana. I don't think I ever stopped. I'm not asking you to love me back, only that we're friends. It would be a wonderful thing, for all the family, if we could be friends.'

She takes his hand. 'I think we could become more than friends,' she says, a tentative smile on her lips. 'But we need to take it slowly.'

'Of course.'

She does not let go of his hand. They walk on. The atmosphere is lighter, clearer. The sun is bouncing off the water in spangles of light.

'When are you returning to America?' he asks.

'I'm not.'

'Oh? I thought—'

'I was, but now I'm not.'

'Good.'

She smiles at him. She hasn't smiled like this in a long time. 'This is home, after all, isn't it.'

And I feel a sorrow in my soul for this land was once *my* home too, but now it is not. I know where my true home is and yet I have no way of reaching it. For how long will I remain cut off from the light?

Chapter 20

Margot lay in her bed in the tower and stared up at the ceiling. A sliver of moonlight sliced through the darkness, picking out the beams above her and bathing the room in a pale, watery light. She couldn't sleep. Her mind was restless. She'd left Colm's bed for her own, needing to be alone to try to make sense of the growing feeling of claustrophobia that had started as a twinge in her solar plexus, but was now building into a cramp. Why did she have it, this fear of settling down? She trusted Colm. She had never been able to trust her father, but she knew Colm was a totally different animal to him. If this fear stemmed from trust issues she'd had with the first man she'd loved, then her father had a lot to answer for.

She wanted to commit, she really did. But when she thought of staying in Ballinakelly, her whole body bristled with aversion. For years she'd been a nomad, travelling from city to city, following her work. She wasn't afraid of being alone, she was used to it, and loneliness, when it crept upon her, had been dispelled by people she had picked up on her way through. Friends, lovers – strangers she'd talked to in bars or met through her research. She could argue, of course, that these people weren't real friends. They wouldn't be there for her if she needed them. Not like Colm. So why did she have this horrible cramping sensation in her stomach when she envisaged life in Ballinakelly? Why couldn't she be like other women? Fall in love, marry, settle down and raise a family? How could wandering the world aimlessly on her own hold more attraction than that?

Frustrated, she went to the bathroom and rummaged around in her washbag for sleeping pills. She didn't usually need them, but tonight she just wanted to knock herself out. The book was done. The pressure was off. She should be feeling satisfied, but she wasn't: she was feeling restless and confused.

The sleeping pills took effect quickly. Darkness obscured the light as damp clouds covered the moon. The wind began to howl and the sound of rain pattering against the windowpanes accompanied her as she grew drowsy. There was a shuffling sound, but Margot didn't believe in ghosts. She drifted into a deep sleep.

She was awoken by the smell of smoke and the feeling of being unbearably hot. Groggy from the pills, she opened her eyes slowly. At first she thought she was dreaming, but when she started to choke she realized, with a stab of panic, that she wasn't. It was real. The castle was on fire.

Being an old tower, it went up like a box of matches. The crackling sound of burning wood brought her sharply to her senses. Margot jumped out of bed and gazed about her in horror. Her first thought was for the manuscript. She hadn't worked this hard all these months for it to be consumed by fire. She tried to get into the sitting room, but was forced back by the heat. She couldn't see her typewriter, notes or manuscript for the smoke, but the sight of the raging flames told her that it was too late; all her work was gone.

There was no time for self-pity. The fire was moving fast. The instinct to survive kicked in. She hurried into the bathroom, gasping with fear and a terrifying sense of helplessness. She threw a towel and a dressing gown into the bath and turned on the taps. Then she quickly struggled into the sodden gown and grabbed the towel. By now the bedroom was on fire as well and the flames were inching closer, devouring everything in their path. With her heart racing and her chest congested with smoke, Margot held out the dripping towel and fought her way to the window. She threw it open and took a gulp of air. It was pouring with rain. She hoped the rain would put out the fire. She looked down. There was a terrace some way below her window, a narrow walkway edged with a crenelated wall. This was the only way out. There was no other exit. However, it was too far for her to jump safely. She simply couldn't. She'd break every bone in her body.

She turned back. There must be some way out besides the window. But it was hopeless. With the fire behind her and the drop in front of her, she only had one option if she wanted to have a chance of surviving.

Margot's legs were trembling so violently she could barely climb onto the windowsill. She felt as if she had lost control of her body. Her insides had turned to jelly. Where was her courage? She had always prided herself in being strong, independent, fearless, but now she felt small and afraid. She sat down, legs dangling in the air, the narrow terrace a frightening vision beneath her feet. It was then that the fear really hit her. She began to sob. Loud, primeval sobs that were ejected from the deepest part of her. 'Please, God, don't let me die,' she wailed. The rain thrashed against her face, the sodden dressing gown felt as tight as a straitjacket.

She thought then of Colm. How could she have doubted that she loved him? She thought of her mother, but the image quickly dissolved and Dorothy floated into her mind. Her room was not far from Margot's. She hoped she'd managed to get out. She *prayed* she was okay.

The cries of the hotel guests rose up as they spilled onto the lawn. Margot looked to her left and right to see that the fire was spreading rapidly into the rest of the castle. She shouted, but her voice was lost in the roar of the fire. Would anyone see her through the smoke?

Then the flames were consuming the tower. She could feel them almost licking the back of her neck. She smelt something rotten, like a dead animal, then realized suddenly, as a pain shot through the back of her neck, that her hair was on fire. She had no choice. She jumped.

JP had seen the fire from his bedroom window. Something had stirred him in his sleep and he had awoken with dread's cold fist clenching his stomach. He had called Colm immediately. Colm had run out to his car in his pyjamas, but he wasn't alone on the road. By now the whole town knew. Everyone was racing up to the castle as fast as they dared drive in the rain, in the middle of the night. Colm could barely breathe. The one night Margot chose to sleep in her hotel bedroom, this happened. He cursed loudly, hooted at the car in front of him and slammed his hand against the steering wheel with impatience.

It began to rain hard. Big fat drops fell in a torrent, like a tropical rain storm, onto the land. Colm had never seen rain like it. If this doesn't put out the fire, he thought, nothing will.

Dorothy sat up in bed. Her room was filled with smoke and flames were dancing all around her. Her first instinct was to panic. And she did panic, but only for a moment. She realized after a few seconds that she did not need to panic, because she didn't feel the heat or, in fact, taste the smoke, which she was surely inhaling. The flames were now consuming her bed and she couldn't see anything in the room except grey, billowing smoke, and yet she couldn't smell it. It had no scent at all. This was very strange. A calm came over her. She climbed out of bed without the usual stiffness. Why, she didn't even groan. She looked down at her feet, her bare feet, and was surprised to feel not the slightest discomfort from the burning wood on which she was standing. Then she turned her eyes and saw the horrifying sight of herself. Yes, there she was, Dorothy Walbridge, lying in the bed asleep while the fire took her.

She should have panicked at that point. But this calm that had come over her was total. The sight of herself was quite mesmerizing, and she would have watched for longer if she hadn't then become aware of a light far greater than the fire. She turned her attention away from her burning body to see her daughter, Lillie, surrounded by an aura of brilliant white. She was smiling, so *she* certainly wasn't at all worried about the fire. The child held out her hand.

Dorothy knew then that she was dead. A frisson of excitement rippled through her. Dan had been right all along. Lillie *had* come through that evening and here she was now, reaching out. She put out her hand and felt her daughter take it. At once she felt a tremendous love, a love greater than she had ever felt while alive. She was ready to burst with it.

I never got to tell Margot how good her book is, she thought, and with that one small regret, she followed her daughter into the light.

When Colm reached the castle the fire brigade was in the process of putting out the fire. The rain was helping. Indeed, the rain was a blessing. A large number of people had congregated on the lawn, their faces horror-stricken as they stared up at the burning castle in disbelief. Mr Dukelow ran among them in agitation, rubbing his hands together, shouting orders, but achieving nothing. Cars arrived in droves, locals swarmed into the forecourt, everybody wanted to help, but there was nothing they could do but hope. In everyone's mind was the same question: how was it possible that the castle had caught fire a *second time*?

Colm shouted for Margot. He ran through the crowd, desperately calling her name. His chest ached with fear. The more he searched the more he feared that she wasn't there. That she hadn't got out. That she was still in the castle. 'It started in that tower,' said someone, pointing up to Margot's room. 'I believe it's the oldest part of the hotel, so you can imagine how quickly it must have caught fire.'

Colm found Mr Dukelow. 'Have you seen Margot?' he demanded.

Mr Dukelow's face was grey. 'No,' he replied. Then he lifted his eyes to the western tower.

Colm looked at it too. The wooden ceiling had fallen in, but the thick stone walls were still standing. The rain was putting out the flames that remained. However, if Margot was in there, she wouldn't have survived.

The firemen and the rain were doing a very good job of putting out the fire, but Colm wasn't going to stand there helplessly. He had to *do* something. 'Perhaps she jumped out of the window!' he exclaimed. 'We need to get up to that terrace,' he said, pointing at it.

'We?'

'Yes, you and me. Come on, Terrence. I need you to help me.'

'It's dangerous. The firemen—'

'I'm not waiting for the firemen.' He took Mr Dukelow's sleeve and dragged him towards the back of the castle where the flames had not reached. Mr Dukelow found his courage – fuelled by guilt, because he knew, rather, he *feared* he knew, who had lit the match. Colm knew the old servants' entrance well from when he was a child, playing about the castle with his sisters. Mr Dukelow felt nauseous as he pushed open the door, where only a week before he and the Countess had sneaked inside.

The two men hurried up the staircase. Colm jumped three steps at a time in his hurry to get to Margot. Mr Dukelow struggled to keep up. At the top of the stairs the corridor was filled with thick, grey smoke. Mr Dukelow grabbed his throat and began to cough. 'I can't ...' he wailed, turning back. 'My asthma.'

'Come on, Terrence! Don't let me down!' he shouted, grabbing him by the arm. If he hadn't needed him so badly he'd have punched him in the face.

Mr Dukelow stared at him for a long moment, before pulling his arm away and disappearing back down the corridor.

Colm took off his T-shirt and pressed it to his mouth, then, with his eyes watering and his chest filling with smoke, he made his way deeper into the hotel. The closer he got to the western tower the thicker the smoke became. At one point he wasn't sure he'd be able to find the door. But he needn't have worried. By the time he reached it, he saw that the door no longer existed. The wall had collapsed and the roof caved in, leaving smouldering beams and rubble. Margot's tower bedroom above had been completely destroyed. A man's voice shouted to him through the hole in the ceiling. 'Hey, you . . .' But Colm ignored it and fought his way outside.

He saw her at once, lying like a broken doll on the stones. Blood staining her sodden dressing gown red. His heart stopped. He rushed over and knelt beside her, a sob bursting in his chest. Picking up her wrist he felt for a pulse. He thought he felt a faint beat, like the heartbeat of a bird, against his fingertips. Then he was surrounded by firemen. He was ordered to one side. After that it seemed as if everything quickened. The world looked blurred around the edges. Nothing was defined. Ambulances arrived, Margot was placed on a stretcher. Colm demanded to go with her to the hospital.

'Are you a relation?' an official asked.

'I'm her husband,' he lied.

'Very well, then. Follow me.'

Kitty

It was I who caused the rain. I'm not sure quite how I managed it, but I did. Now *I'm* surprised at the things we spirits can do when we put our minds to it. Ah, the power of the mind to work miracles, but sadly the western tower is gone.

Once I would have minded. I would have despaired. That was the oldest part of the castle, the only part to survive the fire of 1921, but now I am impassive. The castle is still a hotel. Sure, it's going to take a long time for Mrs de Lisle to repair the damage, but I gather she is already making plans for the new tower. She's going to call it the Margot Hart Suite.

JP will continue to give talks; I think it has given him a new lease of life. He and Alana are growing close again. Out of the ashes of their marriage, new shoots are growing. It is promising. I realize now that home is where love is. The castle ceased to be my home long ago, I just never understood that. I do now. Everything in the material world passes away. But we souls are eternal and we endure, with the love in our hearts, because that is the meaning of life.

I love JP. I love him fully and unconditionally. I love Colm and Alana and all those I have been watching over these past years. My spirit is so full of love that I no longer care about the castle and what becomes of it. I don't care who set it alight. I will not be seeking revenge, for my heart feels only compassion for a soul so lost and full of resentment. What place have they created for themselves in the afterlife? I can do nothing but pray for them to find their way.

My memories are not in the castle, but carried within me. I soar over the hills, the magnificent hills where yellow gorse and purple heather grow among tiny white orchids and wild garlic. I soar with the gulls and the rooks and the silent barn owls, and I am free. I will not return to the castle now. I am liberated from the obsession that I mistook for love. I have finally let go, and in so doing have unshackled myself.

And I ascend towards the far distant horizon where all my truths lie, waiting for me to recognize them. In that serene, golden light I see Jack. He is not the old man who recently breathed his last in the cottage by the sea, but the young man I fell in love with, knee deep in the ravine searching for frogs. His hair is black and falling over eyes of indigo blue. His smile is wide and full of mischief and delight. His heart is overflowing and, as I take his hand, I know something I have always known, only forgotten. Our lives on earth are as the lives of characters in a play whose love is limited to the stage. As soon as the curtain falls our love is set free. It grows big, like a powerful light that knows no boundaries. Jack loves me, but he loves Emer too, and when it is her time to come home, he will reach out his hand with all the affection with which he now reaches out for me. And I love Emer, too. Why ever did I think I didn't?

Chapter 21

Margot drifted in and out of consciousness. She was aware of people coming and going, but she couldn't make out their features. She didn't know where she was, and, quite frankly, she didn't care. She was in a strange, dreamlike limbo, in her body and yet not particularly attached to it. She didn't feel any pain. In fact, she didn't feel her limbs at all. Neither was she aware of her breathing. But she knew she wasn't dead. At least, she hoped she wasn't, because, though not unpleasant, it wasn't what she'd had in mind for the afterlife.

Time no longer seemed to exist. Sure, she was aware of being conscious and then of slipping out of it, but she had no sense of day or night, hours or minutes. She *was* aware, however, of a dark presence beside her. Dark and solid and somehow reassuring. It wasn't an angel – not that she believed in angels, but she was ready to believe in anything right now – because angels were meant to be made of light and this presence was dark and solid. Like a rock. Yes, like one of those megaliths in the Fairy Ring. It seemed to be beside her every time she emerged from oblivion. She thought of the Fairy Ring and then she thought of Colm. When she eventually opened her eyes, she saw that the dark, solid and reassuring presence was him. Then she felt her hand, warm and safe, in his.

Colm had been by Margot's bedside since she had come out of Intensive Care. She had broken most of the bones in her legs, her hips, her ribs, one arm, her cheekbone and jaw. Her hair had all but burnt so the nurse had cut it off, leaving it sticking up in uneven tufts. She was lucky to be alive. Colm had turned to God and prayed, the same supplication over and over: *Please let her live. Please, I beg you, don't let her die.* His faith was strong, but it had been tested over the last week, when there had been a good chance that Margot wouldn't survive. He realized, as he sat watching her lying silent and still in her hospital bed, her skin waxy and her hair short and uneven, that he loved her deeply.

But now she opened her eyes and looked into his, and he knew that she would pull through. He held her gaze and smiled, revealing his sorrow and his pain only in the tears that caused his eyes to sparkle. 'Hello there, you,' he said softly. She blinked at him, knowing instinctively that she couldn't speak. 'Don't try to talk. Let me do the talking for you.' He stroked her hand with his thumb. She felt it, a rhythmic, gentle caress, and was comforted by it. 'You gave me a fright, you know. Yes, you did. But you're going to be just grand. You're in hospital in Dublin and you're going to be well again soon. The doctors have been great. You're going to be as good as new. And I'm not leaving your side. Not for a minute.'

She closed her eyes, a warm, sweet feeling washing over her like honey. Sinking into oblivion once again. The deep, cool sleep that allows the body to heal and the spirit to rest, in the knowledge of being loved. Somehow, that mattered; it mattered very much.

The Countess di Marcantonio was at her dressing table in a pink silk dressing gown when there came a knock on the front door of the apartment. 'Darling, are you going to get it?' she shouted. No reply. She sighed. She really didn't want anyone seeing her like this, without her make-up on, with her hair in rollers. 'Darling! The door!' She scowled. Where was the Count? She shook her head and put down her make-up brush.

She padded into the hall and pressed the button on the intercom. 'Who is it?' she asked.

'It's me, Terrence.'

'You cannot come up here!' she hissed, panicking suddenly. 'You must leave at once!'

'I'm here with Inspector Coyle. He wants to speak with you.'

There was a long pause. Inspector Coyle? What on earth could the Garda possibly want with *her*? 'Can he not come back another time? I'm not ready to receive visitors.'

'This cannot wait, Countess di Marcantonio.' That was the inspector. The Countess flinched a little at the sound of his voice replacing Terrence's. She didn't want either man to see her like this, but there was no avoiding it. 'Very well. Please come up.' She pressed the buzzer and waited.

The Count shuffled into the hall in a scruffy shirt and stained sweater, looking frail.

'Where have you been?' she snapped. 'Did you not hear the doorbell?'

'Who is it?' he asked.

'The Garda.'

The Count frowned. 'The Garda? What do they want?'

'I don't know. He's coming up now, with Mr Dukelow from the castle.'

'What's left of it,' said Leopoldo. He shook his head and

put a hand on his heart. 'A great tragedy. But thankfully not my problem.'

'He wants to speak with *me*.'

The Count frowned again. 'Why, what have you done?'

'Absolutely nothing,' she replied. 'I have done nothing. I cannot imagine what he wants to talk to me about.'

There was a rap on the door. The Countess took a deep breath, then opened it. She shook hands with Mr Dukelow and then the inspector, who was a stout little man with a thick moustache and plump cheeks the colour of redcurrants. His eyes were large and unsmiling behind his glasses. She showed them into the sitting room, but did not offer them a seat. She did not expect them to stay for long.

'What would you like to speak to me about?' she asked the inspector haughtily. 'I'm really not sure why it couldn't wait.'

'I will not waste your time, Countess.' The inspector took a little pad out of his breast pocket and held the pen over the page. 'Where were you the night the castle caught fire?'

'Well, I was here, of course.' She shook her head testily. 'I don't understand. Are you suggesting it was arson? Did someone set it alight on purpose?'

'Mr Dukelow has confessed to letting you into the castle at night through the old servants' entrance at the back, and up to the western tower, which is where the fire started.' The Countess was careful not to look at Mr Dukelow, and held her chin up and her eyes impassive so as not to give anything away. She did not look at her husband, either. 'He tells me you were unhappy with the book that Miss Hart was writing and you were determined to stop her getting it published.'

'I don't know what you're talking about, Mr Dukelow. I'm really not sure why you would lie.'

'We have a witness who saw you and Mr Dukelow on more than one occasion,' the inspector continued.

'A witness? Who?' demanded the Countess.

'One of the maids.'

'Nonsense. She must have been dreaming. You know that castle is riddled with ghosts.'

This did not impress the inspector. 'You are aware, Countess, that Miss Hart is in a critical condition in hospital and Mrs Walbridge perished.'

The Countess blanched. She put a hand to her mouth. 'That is terrible. Truly terrible. But I had nothing to do with it.' She turned to her husband and narrowed her eyes. Where had the Count been when the castle burned down? she thought. She stiffened her jaw and held her husband with a steely gaze. 'Darling, tell the inspector where I was on the night the castle burned.'

Leopoldo looked at his wife. The woman he loathed with every fibre of his being. Now was his chance to be rid of her for ever. 'I'm afraid I cannot lie,' he said, pressing a fist to his breast and looking crestfallen. 'You were not with me, my love. At least, not for the greater part of the night. I'm afraid I must tell the truth. As God is my witness, I must.'

'Liar! Leopoldo, how *could* you?' She turned to Inspector Coyle, her cheeks smarting as if slapped. 'You should ask the Count where *he* was the night the castle burned down. *I* was in bed, as innocent as a lamb, and *he* was out. Terrence, I didn't do it! I would never do such a thing. I admit I did not want the book to be published. It did not do justice to my husband and his family, but I would never have taken such drastic measures to prevent it.' She looked at her husband in bewilderment. 'Why did you do it, Leopoldo? Your family home . . . I don't understand.'

'Countess Amelie di Marcantonio, you are under arrest on suspicion of arson and manslaughter. You do not have to say anything, but it may harm your defence if you do not mention when questioned something which you later rely on in court. Anything you do say may be given in evidence.'

The Countess put her hand to her eyes and swooned. As her legs gave way beneath her it was Mr Dukelow who reached out to catch her. Leopoldo watched with a certain satisfaction as the hotel manager lifted her into his arms, confirming that his suspicions had been right. They had indeed been having an affair. 'I didn't do it, Terrence,' she mumbled. 'It wasn't me. It really wasn't me.' Then she glared at her husband and hissed at him like a snake. 'I won't let you get away with this!'

Margot cried when she saw the state she was in. How could Colm love her when she looked like this? She ran her good hand through the short tufts of hair and over her swollen face, and sobbed at the ugliness of her reflection in the mirror one of the nurses had given her. Colm came to visit, as he did daily, but this time she turned away. 'Don't come in!' she exclaimed.

'Why not?' he asked, coming in anyway.

'I'm disgusting.'

'What are you talking about?'

'I have no hair,' she gasped. 'My face is a horror. I'm ugly.'

'You're talking nonsense, Margot. You're beautiful.'

'That's a lie. How can you say that when I look like this? I'm monstrous. You don't have to be here. You have no obligation. You're off the hook. Really, I understand. I wouldn't want to be with me, either.'

He sat down and took her hand. She tried to take it away,

but he held on to it tightly. 'Margot, you nearly died,' he said seriously. 'So, you've got a boy haircut and you're all bandaged up, but your hair will grow back and, with physio-therapy, you'll learn to walk again. Do you think I love you for your physical beauty alone? I love you for *you*, Margot.' Her shoulders began to shake as she broke down again. 'I love the way your eyes flash when you're cross. I love your short upper lip and the way your smile turns sweet when you're unsure. You've managed to fool yourself that you're not lonely wandering the world on your own and yet sometimes when I watch you and you don't know you're being watched, your entire being is a picture of loneliness. But you know what, we're good together, you and I. Indeed, I like who I am when I'm with you, and I like who you are when you're with me. I don't want to be with anyone else and I don't think you do either.'

'I should have died,' she replied miserably. 'What a mess I'm in. How will I ever recover?'

'But you didn't die, did you. You're alive and that's a gift.'

'Not for me it isn't.' She felt defeated in the face of the challenges ahead. How would her broken body heal? What if she remained ugly for ever? 'My life will never be the same. It's over, basically, isn't it?'

'It's not like you to be so defeatist.'

'I've never been in this situation before,' she snapped.

There was never going to be a good moment to tell Margot about Dorothy Walbridge, but Colm thought the sad news might focus her mind on her luck rather than on her misfor-tune. 'Margot, I'm afraid Dorothy didn't make it.'

Margot stared at him. 'What? Dorothy . . . died?'

He nodded gravely. 'She perished in the fire.'

'Oh God, no!' Now her tears were no longer for herself but

for the woman who had been more of a mother to her than her own mother had ever been.

Colm held her hand more tightly. He would have liked to embrace her, but she was too fragile for that. 'The tower where your rooms were was totally destroyed, as was a vast chunk of the castle beneath it, where Dorothy's room was. She didn't stand a chance. You did the right thing in jumping. Had you remained up there in your tower, you would have died too. I know it's hard, Margot, but at least you still have your life.'

'Poor Dorothy!' she cried. 'She didn't deserve that. God, I hope she didn't suffer. I hope she died quickly. I can't believe it. I can't believe she's gone.' Margot took a staggered breath and began to sob again. Colm stroked her hand until her grief had passed through her.

'Has she been buried yet?' she asked at length.

'Yes, she was flown back to England and buried in her home village.'

'When I'm better, I want to go there and say goodbye.'

'Of course. As soon as you're better, we'll go together.'

Margot looked at Colm, her eyes shiny and uncertain. 'Are you really sure you still want to be with me?'

'I've never doubted that I love you, Margot. Not for a moment. This is only going to make me love you more.'

'Why? How could it?'

'Because love isn't just about the good times. In fact it's more about the bad times. That's what love is, being there to pick each other up when we're down.'

'I don't deserve you, Colm.' She smiled at him through her tears.

'Then let me teach you to love yourself, then you'll realize your value and that you deserve the very best.' He grinned mischievously.

She managed a small chuckle. 'Are you telling me that you're the very best?'

'I am, Margot. You deserve nothing less than me.'

She laughed then felt a pang of guilt. 'Dorothy wouldn't want us to be sad, would she?'

'No, she'd want you to laugh.'

'I suppose my manuscript was destroyed too?' She sighed. In the light of Dorothy's death, the loss of her book did not seem too great a tragedy. Just a big disappointment. 'I'll never know what she thought of it,' she added sadly.

'But look at the good that came out of it. If it wasn't for your book, we'd never have met. I'd never have reconciled with my father, Dad would never have got well, and my mother would never have reconciled with him, either.'

'They've made up?'

'It's early days, but they're friends again, which is astonishing. All because *you* saved him.'

'That's nice,' Margot said, grateful that something positive had come out of it. 'And I'd never have met Dorothy,' she added, her eyes welling again with tears. 'I really loved her, you know.'

'I know you did,' Colm replied, and he leaned over and gently pressed his lips to her temple. 'You need to get well for her, now, Margot.'

Margot nodded. 'I will, Colm, I'll get well for the both of you.'

Chapter 22

After six weeks in hospital Margot accepted visitors. JP was the first. He came with Mrs B, armed with a porter cake in a tin. 'I light a candle for you every day in front of the statue of St Finbar, Miss Hart,' Mrs B told her, placing a soft hand on her arm. 'God help us, I have me poor old knees worn down with praying and thanking Jesus and His Blessed Mother for saving your life and not taking you in the fire like he took poor Mrs Walbridge. But she's with her little girl in Heaven now and it's a happy day for her. But it wasn't your time, thanks be to God. As me poor mother always said if you're meant to be shot, you won't be hanged. I know you don't have much value on it, but I brought a bottle of Lourdes water for you. What harm can it do?'

JP pulled up a chair and sat at her bedside and told her how the castle was going to be rebuilt. 'Mrs de Lisle is insistent that business continues as usual. She's given interviews in all the papers and shone a flashlight onto the history of my family and the fire of 1921. I think it will be advantageous for the hotel. People love a good story.' Margot thought of her manuscript and suffered a painful stab of loss. But then she remembered Dorothy and reminded herself that she was lucky to be alive, just like Colm said.

The next visitor was Seamus O'Donovan. He came with a bouquet of flowers and a brown paper bag of oranges. 'Who did you think you were – superwoman?' he said with a grin, sitting down.

Margot laughed. 'I won't be launching myself out of any windows for a while, I can assure you,' she replied, happy to see him.

He looked at her seriously. 'You've been the talk of the town. You gave us all a fright, you know.'

'I gave myself a bit of a fright, too.'

'Well, I'm glad you didn't die. I know you and Colm are together now, so, I'm not going to lay claim to you, but I'll say one thing, for what it's worth, you got to me, Margot, and no one's got there since.'

'Oh Seamus, that's so sweet,' she replied, touched. Then her eyes filled with regret. 'I'm sorry for the way I treated you. You didn't deserve that.'

'Water under the bridge,' he replied, his smile turning bashful.

'For what it's worth, we had fun, didn't we?'

'We certainly did.'

She put her hand on his. 'You're a good friend to come and visit me. Thank you.'

'Indeed, I'd like to be your friend,' he said. 'Fancy an orange?'

After that there was a steady flow of visitors to Margot's bedside. She was surprised at the amount of locals, some of whom she'd only met once, who brought her fruit and flowers or simply kind words and encouragement. Mrs de Lisle wanted to know when she'd be up for giving talks again. 'You must rewrite the book,' she insisted firmly. 'It's as simple as that. You've got all this time in bed, what better way to spend it?

You've done the research already, so it won't be too difficult. It might even be better the second time round.' Margot humoured her with empty words of promise, but in her heart she knew she could never rewrite it.

After three months in hospital, Margot was finally discharged. While she had been shut in, summer had passed outside her window. Now the leaves were beginning to turn and an autumn chill was blowing in over the sea, bringing with it a wistful sense of melancholy. She was glad to be out in the fresh air and not stuck in a hospital ward. She looked about her with fresh eyes, appreciative of the smallest, most insignificant things, as if she were seeing the world through the eyes of a child, with wonder and curiosity. Everything looked so beautiful.

JP had insisted she move into the Hunting Lodge until she was able to look after herself, for Colm had to work. Mrs B was ready with the teapot and porter cake and a temporary bedroom had been set up for her downstairs. JP was eager to repay Margot for putting him back together again; *she* had healed *him,* now it was *his* turn to heal *her.*

Up at the castle, the hotel had reopened, although the western tower and surrounding walls were still under scaffolding. There was a new manager called Mr Cavendish who had been poached from Claridge's in London and he was very keen for JP to resume his after-dinner talks. It was just a shame, he said, that Miss Hart's book had been lost in the fire. It would have been wonderful to have had the history of the Deverill family in the library for guests to read, and for the author to speak with Lord Deverill in a double-act. He couldn't think of a single other hotel in the entire world that could boast such a compelling duo.

The newspapers had been full of the story of the fire and the fact that the Countess di Marcantonio had been arrested on suspicion of causing it. However, some said the Count himself had committed the crime and then blamed his wife, who had apparently been having an affair with the manager of the hotel. A housemaid, who had subsequently been sacked, had sold her story to a newspaper. She claimed that she had seen someone sneak in through the old servants' entrance at the back of the castle on the night of the fire, but was unable to tell whether it had been male or female. It was all very seedy and JP wasn't sure what to believe. But the fire had taught him one very valuable lesson. Home is where love is, and he didn't want to be anywhere else but in the Hunting Lodge, where his son came to visit, and his daughters too when they came to Ireland, and, increasingly, Alana. He discovered, to his joy, that Colm had been right: the opposite of love was not hate but indifference. The spark that had caused their anger and pain was, in its core, love. With a little nurturing it had begun to grow.

Margot sat in the garden of the Hunting Lodge, savouring the sound of birds and the warm feeling of sunshine on her face, and thought of Dorothy. She hadn't known her very long, but her affection for her new friend had been deep and indelible. She missed her constantly. While the wounds slowly healed on the outside, those on the inside were taking longer to repair. She suffered nightmares about the fire, of jumping from the window, and of losing her work. She knew it wasn't right to bemoan her lot when Dorothy had lost her life, but it pained her to think of all that research and toil disappearing in the flames. It was proving hard to overcome the trauma.

She was surprised when one balmy evening at the end of September Emer O'Leary came to visit. She hadn't visited her in hospital nor popped into the Hunting Lodge. In any case, they sat on the terrace, drinking tea and talking about Margot's recovery. Then they talked about Dorothy. 'I miss her terribly,' said Emer sadly and her eyes shone. 'It was such a shock. A terrible shock. I'd just lost Jack and then, in a matter of weeks, Dorothy went too. I confess, I have not been in a good place. I'm sorry it's taken me so long to come and see you.'

'Dorothy was a very special person,' said Margot, sharing Emer's sorrow.

'She was your greatest champion, you know. When I doubted you, she stood up for you.' She lowered her eyes. 'I'm ashamed of that now. I should have known better.'

'It's okay. You were only protecting your family.'

'I should have trusted her, and Colm, who tried to convince me to give you a chance. I don't know why I reacted with such suspicion. It was only a history book, after all. What harm could it do, really?'

'Well, it's gone now. I won't rewrite it.' Margot sighed with resignation and shrugged. 'Perhaps it wasn't meant to be published. Maybe Fate saw to it that it would never see the light of day.'

'That's very philosophical of you,' said Emer.

'It's the only way to be. One has to accept things that can't be changed. Isn't that right?'

'It is in theory. But it's hard to do in practice.'

'I'm doing my best.'

'You're doing very well, Margot.'

'I'd like to know what Dorothy thought of it. She was the only person who read it. I gave her the manuscript a week or so before the fire and she was going to give me her opinion. Now I'll never know. The strange thing is, her opinion really mattered to me.'

'You have to look for the positives. If you hadn't come to the hotel you'd never have met her, or Colm. He loves you very much, Margot, and, as you probably realize now, he's not an easy man to please in that department.'

Margot laughed and her eyes lit up. 'He's been wonderful. He couldn't have been more attentive. When I lost the will to get better, he had enough drive for the two of us. If it wasn't for him I think I would have given up.'

'And you've been good for him, too, Margot. Don't overlook *that*. I'm happy to admit when I'm wrong, and I admit it now. I'm sorry I ever doubted you. You and Colm are good for one another. I'm happy you found each other.'

Margot knew that she was right. Colm had shown her, through many small acts of kindness, that she mattered to him. If her father had taught her to doubt her value, Colm had shown her just how much she was worth.

'I'm not sure Alana is too happy about us being together,' she ventured. Alana, although not unfriendly, seemed unable to look her in the eye. 'She's his mother so perhaps she doesn't think I'm good enough for him.'

'Oh, that's not true,' said Emer quickly. 'I can't imagine why she'd think you're not good enough for him. He's hardly a prince, is he?' She laughed her gentle, sympathetic laugh. 'I think she might find it hard to accept that he now has a woman in his life. He's always been a bit of a loner in that respect. She'd always wanted him to settle down – mothers all want their sons to find nice girls to look after them – but now he's found someone, maybe she's taking time to accept it.'

'Maybe,' Margot conceded. 'But it can't be the book, can it, now that it's gone.'

'Give her time to get used to you. It wasn't so long ago that she was upset about you writing it. She mistrusted you and now you're in a relationship with her son. It'll take time. That's all it is. It'll be just grand. Don't you worry.'

But Margot *did* worry. Alana couldn't suspect her anymore of inveigling her way into Colm's heart in order to research the book. So, if it wasn't that, what could it be?

The days gradually shortened and the leaves began to fall from the trees. A blustery wind whistled through the branches, damp and cold, and in October the first frost turned the garden white. The fires were lit once more in the drawing room and the library, and the place smelled yet again of woodsmoke. The house no longer resonated with the desolate emptiness of before, however. JP invited friends for dinner and the house vibrated with the sound of cheerful voices and laughter as they dined and played cards. It was just like old times, when Bertie and Maud Deverill had entertained the county. JP hired a couple of local girls to help Mrs B with the catering, but there was no question of Mrs B retiring. The Hunting Lodge was her home and Lord Deverill her master, and the only way she was ever going to leave was feet first. She had made that very clear.

Margot worked hard at her physiotherapy, determined to restore her body to its former strength and agility, and Colm was ready to give her encouragement every time her resolve faltered. She hobbled about on crutches and enjoyed the simple pleasures of reading, playing cards and board games, and listening to JP's music. Most of all she enjoyed being outside, in nature, watching the landscape slowly change as each day passed. Colm drove her to the pub in the evenings and occasionally, when the weather was fine, to the beach. They sat among the dunes, sheltered from the wind, and talked about everything and nothing, and kissed and laughed and teased. When the light was at its most tender, Margot gazed out over the far distant horizon and thought of Dorothy – and then she thought of her lost book and tried hard to feel nothing but gratitude for being alive and with Colm.

One rainy afternoon she hobbled into the games room. It was cold in there. The fire hadn't been lit in months. It was a long time since anyone had played billiards. She was surprised to see the boxes of research still piled up at the end of the room and was assaulted by the familiar pang of loss. All those hours working through those diaries and letters and ledgers that she'd never get back. The pages of notes written and organized into box files that had been destroyed in the flames. The time she had spent working out how to word things tactfully so as not to cause hurt to family members still living, JP and Alana in particular. She'd done a good job of it, she thought, but now she would never know. She wasn't sure she would ever muster up the energy to write another book. Perhaps all her willpower was being diverted into getting better and that was the reason she felt so uninspired. Maybe when her bones had healed she'd come up with something else to write. But she couldn't think of another subject that inspired her like the Deverills had. Her mind was as infertile as barren scrubland where nothing grew but the odd intrepid weed.

In early December Margot moved into Colm's house. She put her toiletries in the bathroom and her clothes in the cupboard and it didn't cause her anxiety to see her shoes lined up beside his. In fact, it gave her a warm sense of belonging. She hadn't felt that in a very long time.

To keep her busy, Colm started taking her on house visits to see patients who were too big, or too sick, to bring into his practice. Margot loved animals and she enjoyed watching Colm tending to them. He was sensitive and wise and the more she watched him at work the more attractive he grew in her eyes. She also enjoyed getting to know the locals and realized that, having written off Ballinakelly as a small provincial town of little interest, she'd been wrong. It was a vibrant community full of good people who looked out for each other. After Colm healed a sick pig, the owner, an eccentric old lady with a penchant for poitín, brought him round a dish of soda-bread pudding to thank him. As Margot tucked into it at teatime, she realized that she'd never been part of a community before. For the first time in her life she really wanted to be. She decided then that she'd become more involved. The only thing she was particularly good at was writing. So, she offered her services to the local newspaper and began searching for stories. Since the fire she hadn't felt so much as a spark of inspiration, but now the anticipation of writing again ignited a small flame in the place where dwelt her resolve and her creativity. She bought a typewriter and set up at the kitchen table. Then she poured herself a glass of wine, sat back in her chair, and wondered what she was going to write about.

Colm was delighted to see his parents getting along again. He was astonished that after years of acrimony and not speaking they had forgiven each other so easily. He wondered whether Jack's death had triggered a change of heart in his mother, causing it to soften and for her to reach an understanding that before had seemed too great a breach to bridge.

Margot wanted to have a good relationship with Alana but, as she had no relationship at all with her own mother she thought that, perhaps, she just wasn't very good with mothers in general. Colm hadn't noticed there was a problem, for when Margot mentioned her coldness, Colm told her that she was imagining it. 'She's probably still sad about Grandad,' he said, not giving the problem more than a passing glance. But Margot was a perceptive woman. She knew it wasn't that. It was something else, but she couldn't for the life of her imagine what.

Alana should have been happy. She had returned to Ballinakelly to live with her mother, whom she adored, in the house where she'd grown up. Her father was gone, but she'd come to terms with her grief. He'd been old, she reasoned; he'd had a good life. She focused on the golden memories and was thankful that the two of them had enjoyed such a loving and open relationship. She and JP were spending time together and the old feelings of love and attraction were blossoming once again, for they had never truly died, only hibernated during a long and hard winter. There had never really been anyone else for her besides JP Deverill. She saw much of her son, who had remained in Ireland after the divorce, and she was proud that he had grown into such an admirable and attractive man. He'd braved the fire to save Margot, even risked his own life, which was testament to the way he felt about her. If he hadn't found her she would most likely have perished along with Dorothy Walbridge. Their relationship was romantic. He loved her, and that love, so clearly displayed in the light in his eyes, was heart-warming to see. Alana should have been happy, yet, she had done a terrible thing.

At first she thought she could ride out her guilt. She'd done something bad, but relatively speaking, it wasn't so terrible. She could dismiss it, forget about it, and get on with her life. But the trouble with good people is that they have consciences, and Alana's conscience was much too strong to allow her to continue as if she'd done nothing. Every time she saw Margot the claws of guilt drove a little deeper into the lining of her heart. And, as the weeks turned into months, those claws began to shred it. What would Dorothy say? she wondered. What would her father think? If her mother knew, what would she advise her to do? But Alana knew what was right, only she'd left it so long now, she wasn't sure how to redress it. So she did nothing and kept her distance. If she didn't see Margot, perhaps she could forget what she'd done. Or perhaps the guilt would just go away and in time the matter would no longer be important or relevant.

It was Christmas that changed her mind. Margot, who was still walking with crutches, clubbed together with Colm's two sisters, who'd flown over from America with their husbands and children, and put up a fir tree in the drawing room of the Hunting Lodge, decorating it with tinsel, baubles and fairy lights. Cara's small children made the gold star and her husband, Declan, tied it to the top of the tree to much applause. Margot had gone to great trouble to buy everyone presents, even Aisling's and Cara's children, whom she had just met, wrapping each carefully chosen gift in silver paper with silvery green ribbon, tucking a small piece of mistletoe into the knot of the bow. Alana was touched by the effort she had made. Margot had also arranged Christmas lunch and invited Mrs B to join them at the table and for the celebrations afterwards, as she had no family of her own with whom to celebrate. She'd even brought her a present. Mrs B was moved. She changed into a fresh white blouse and wore the gold-and-diamond brooch which had once belonged to her great-grandmother at her throat. She had only worn it once and that was on her brother's seventeenth birthday, a few months before he died. Now she wore it again and knew that he'd be with her in spirit on this special day.

After lunch, there was music and games in the drawing room and plenty more wine. It was the best Christmas they had ever had. They were happy. Every one of them. Alana drank too much. She lay against the back of the sofa and watched JP with unfocused eyes, enjoying the feeling of tenderness that washed over her in waves of nostalgia and gratitude. She watched her children and grandchildren and thought how incredibly lucky she was to be given a second chance at family life. She was home, where she belonged, with the people she loved.

Overwhelmed once more by guilt, which was now warping the joy, she began to cry. Margot, who had been careful not to get too close, gave her an anxious glance. JP went and sat beside her on the sofa. 'It's lovely, isn't it,' he said, taking her hand. 'To be together.'

Alana nodded. Then she wiped her eyes with her sleeve. 'Margot,' she said. 'Can I have a word?'

Margot looked at Colm for reassurance but he just shrugged. 'Sure,' she replied.

Alana got up and walked unsteadily to the games room. They'd lit a fire in there that afternoon in order to play billiards, so it was warm, although the embers had died in the grate, leaving only the residue of heat in the iron back plate. She was nervous. She leaned against the billiard table, as much to steady herself as to give her somewhere to perch. Margot stood apprehensively in front of the fireplace and wondered what Alana needed to talk to her about.

'I have something to confess,' Alana began. Margot listened, not sure what to say. Alana took her time. It was clearly hard for her to articulate this thing she wanted to confess, and judging by the crimson colour of her face, Margot sensed that it was obviously a *terrible* thing. Alana took a breath and decided to plunge in. 'I have the manuscript of your book,' she said.

Margot was astonished. Her mouth opened, but she couldn't find the words. Could it be possible that it wasn't lost, after all? She barely dared hope.

'You see, Dorothy gave it to me to read. She said I needed to see it. I wasn't sure what she meant until I read it.' Alana clasped her hands together. She gazed at Margot with glassy eyes, the lines on her forehead deepening with supplication. 'I'm so sorry, Margot. Please forgive me. It was wrong of me not to tell you. To hold on to it. I'm so sorry. I'm an idiot. Or selfish. Or whatever you want to call me. Basically, I'm horrible. All that work, all those words, lost. But it's not lost. I have it.'

Margot shook her head. 'I can't believe it. I thought it was gone.'

'No. Not gone. In my bedroom drawer, to be precise.'

They stared at each other; Alana, horrified by what she had done – saying the words out loud had made her deed seem all the more devious – and Margot, dumbfounded by

the wonderful surprise. She wanted to throw her arms around
Alana in gratitude, but the crutches prevented such a sponta-
neous gesture.

'Well? What did you think of it?' Margot imagined she
must have been unhappy, for otherwise why would she not
have admitted to having it in her possession? She held her
breath, fearful of her response.

Alana smiled. 'It's brilliant,' she said. 'Gripping, funny,
fascinating and, well, tactful. Some parts were hard to read,
obviously, but I hadn't looked at the situation from JP's point
of view and you gave me that, his point of view. It allowed me
to understand him and . . .' She sighed regretfully. 'To see how
much I had hurt him too.' She put up a hand. 'Oh no, don't
think I'm offended, I'm not. In fact, I'm grateful. You gave a
very balanced account.' Margot smiled sadly as she thought
of Dorothy. 'You were impartial,' Alana continued. 'Which,
considering your friendship with JP, was quite miraculous, or
you're just a very good historian. You didn't take sides. And
you didn't give too much away. You left us with our dignity.'

'Then, why did you keep it?'

Alana swallowed. 'Because I wasn't sure I wanted the world
to read it.'

'And now?'

'It's okay. I don't mind. Because of you, my family is
together again. I should have told you before, but I didn't
know how to. I'd let too much time go by. The longer I left
it, the harder it became. I almost threw the manuscript away.'

Margot gasped.

'But I didn't,' Alana added quickly. 'Something else made
me hold on to it. Dorothy wrote notes in the margins in her
shaky handwriting.'

Margot was astonished. 'What did she say?'

'She loved it. That's why she gave it to me. She wanted me to read it because she knew it was good, but she also knew it would help. The book we all thought would tear us apart brought us together.'

A lump lodged itself in Margot's throat. 'I'm so happy to hear that,' she said. She wiped away a tear. 'You've made my Christmas, Alana. Thank you.'

Alana laughed. 'I've made mine too! I've been feeling so guilty, it's been horrid. So we're friends?'

'We are,' said Margot.

Alana reached out to embrace her. 'I'm a little tipsy,' she said. 'I don't think I could have confessed had it not been for the wine. I think I've had a little too much.'

'It's very good wine,' said Margot.

'Shall we get some more?'

'I think that's a very good idea.'

'Capital,' said Alana. 'That's what JP would say. A capital idea.' Her smiled wobbled drunkenly. 'I do love him, you know.'

'I know.'

'And you love Colm, don't you?'

'I do,' said Margot. She laughed because Alana really was very tipsy.

'Good, because he loves you very much. There's just so much love in this house I can hardly bear it.'

Chapter 23

It was a glorious July day in Ballinakelly. The sky was a gleaming, cerulean blue, the fluffy white clouds like dandelion beards wafting gently across it. The wind was warm and salty, blowing in off the sea, and all was calm and serene with summer's blithe spirit. A honey-scented breeze rustled lightly through the horse chestnut trees and about the leaves on the shrubs and flowers that bordered the immaculately mown lawn at Castle Deverill. It had always been tradition for Lord and Lady Deverill to throw a lavish garden party in July for the hundreds of tenants and workers employed by the Deverill estate. Over the three hundred-odd years that the castle had presided over the town, this party had been the highlight of the local people's year. Today, the party was not for the tenants and workers, but for the launch of Margot Hart's book, *A Deverill's Castle is His Kingdom, a Biography,* and it was much more lavish. Mrs de Lisle had spared no cost. The castle was the jewel in her crown, after all, and she wanted to garner as much publicity as possible, so the world would see what a unique and marvellous place Hotel Castle Deverill was.

The castle could not have looked more magnificent. The grey stone walls stood proud and defiant, having survived the

fire. The towers and turrets, which for centuries had domi-
nated the skyline and given reassurance to fishermen out at
sea, now shimmered in the sunshine. Rooks cawed from the
rooftops and seagulls wheeled above, their gaze fixed upon the
tables of sandwiches and cakes below. The western tower had
been rebuilt and the set of rooms was now called the Margot
Hart Suite. Guests made their bookings months in advance,
for it was the most popular set of rooms in the castle.

Mrs B stood near the tea table in a straw hat, a fresh white
blouse and a long black skirt, even though it was summer and
nearly thirty degrees. Initially, she hadn't wanted to come,
being a little timid of big crowds, but Margot had insisted and
she had relented, as long as she didn't have to stay all afternoon.
She sipped from a pretty china teacup and let her gaze wander
aimlessly over the faces. She recognized some people, for she
had grown up in Ballinakelly and attended Mass every week.
Mrs de Lisle seemed to have invited everyone from the town,
which was a nice thing to do, Mrs B thought. The castle had
always been the centre of the community.

'How are ye, Bessie?' Mrs B turned to see Neil O'Rourke,
Tomas and Aidan's grandfather, standing beside her with a
glass of stout in his hand.

'Well if it isn't Neil O' Rourke himself. I don't ever see you
at Mass.' He'd always been tall and willowy like a bullrush,
with soft brown eyes the colour of peat, but now he had a
stoop and a gaunt look about the face. He grinned and Mrs B
remembered the playful young man he'd once been. 'I haven't
seen you in years,' she said. He'd been an undergardener when
she'd started working for Celia Deverill. She used to sneak
slices of cake to him in the maze garden.

'I don't go to Mass anymore, Bessie,' he said.

Mrs B looked at him reproachfully. 'Almighty God, why

not, Neil? You used to be a daily communicant and the backbone of the St Vincent de Paul Society.'

'I have God in me garden, Bessie. That's where God is. In
me garden with the little birdeens as altar boys and the old
fox as sacristan.'

Her face softened. 'God knows you could be right about
that. Sure isn't God's beauty everywhere.'

He turned his eyes to the castle. 'Do you remember those
days long ago?' he said.

She smiled wistfully. 'Oh, I do, Neil. I remember them
with fondness that I had them and sadness that they are gone.
They were good old times, weren't they?'

'You used to bring me a bit of cake and a basin of tea and
we'd eat it together in the maze garden.'

Mrs B laughed. 'You remember that too?'

'You were a missy, Bessie.'

'I was not, was I?'

'Oh, you were. You were always up to some old antics.'

'I don't think I was.'

He smiled down at her. 'God, 'tis good to see you again,
Bessie. You mustn't go hiding yourself away.'

'I won't now,' she replied, the affection in his smile causing
her to wonder why she hadn't been a little braver in seeking
the company of old friends.

'Do you fancy taking a walk with me around the gardens?
I'd like to see them again. It would be nice to see them
with you.'

'That would be grand altogether.' She put her teacup down
on the table. 'Shall we start with the vegetable garden? Those
greenhouses were full of cannabis in Lady Deverill's day,
Adeline Deverill, that is.'

He laughed. 'The way things are now, she would either be

a millionaire or in Limerick Jail. But don't think she was the only one who made tea with it.' He glanced at her slyly. 'It was still growing in those greenhouses in Celia Deverill's day.'

'You didn't! Neil O'Rourke, shame on you! Was it you who gave it to poor young Eily Sullivan, the junior maid?' she exclaimed. 'She shared a bedroom with me and one night she woke me, roaring that in place of the statue of the Blessed Virgin, she saw a tom cat!'

'Oh, I did. Guilty as charged, your honour.'

'You're a fine blackguard!' she chuckled as she linked his arm.

'How things have changed, Bessie, but not for us. It used to take the master six hours to go from Ballinakelly to Dublin. Now they are going all the way to Ameriky in the same amount of time. 'Tis hard to make sense of it all.'

On the other side of the lawn, sitting on a bench beneath an arch of roses, were JP and Alana. 'Are you sorry it's a hotel?' Alana asked.

JP swept his eyes over his family home. The place that had caused him so much grief. 'No,' he replied firmly. 'It brought me nothing but unhappiness.'

'According to Margot's book, it didn't bring many of your family happiness either.'

'No, it didn't. That was an interesting observation of hers, I thought. She's right, we were all too preoccupied with our status as one of the country's most important Anglo-Irish families, living in this splendid castle, given to us by King Charles II. The fact is, Barton Deverill was the only Deverill who was entitled to feel that way. He earned it. The rest of us just inherited it without lifting a finger. We lived off Barton's prestige. For hundreds of years, the Deverills put the castle above the needs of the people living inside it. That was their mistake. That was *my* mistake.' He smiled at her fondly. 'I'm happy now, Alana. I'm really happy. I don't have to worry about paying the bills, managing the estate, keeping the tenants happy and finding the money to keep it all afloat.'

'And you're going to give after-dinner talks with Margot,' she added with a grin. 'You could say that the castle is now keeping *you* afloat.'

He chuckled. 'You could indeed. We're even talking about doing a book together, she and I. A glossy, coffee-table book about the castle itself. There are plenty of photographs we can include and I can supply anecdotes.'

'That's a great idea,' she enthused.

'We really should change the motto.'

'To what?'

'A Deverill's *family* is his kingdom.'

She took his hand and smiled at him affectionately. 'I agree. Blood is thicker than water, after all.'

'It is indeed,' he agreed, returning her smile with a twinkle in his eye. 'And more important than stone.'

'Walk with me,' Colm suggested, putting out his hand.

Margot took it and retrieved her walking stick with the other hand. She got up from the chair where she'd been sitting signing books. She'd signed so many, her wrist ached. They set off at a gentle pace along the herbaceous border where purple and lilac delphiniums stood tall and bright among hydrangeas and peonies. They strolled hand in hand, away from the party where Mrs de Lisle presided over journalists she'd flown over from

London and influential guests whom she'd personally invited to stay in the hotel. Colm and Margot were pleased to get away. To be just the two of them. It was exhausting talking to people, even though everyone was very complimentary about the book. They paused a moment to look at the castle. Margot's eyes drifted up to the tower. The fire seemed like another life somehow. 'You were a real hero, Colm,' she said quietly.

'I wasn't a hero,' he replied. 'I did what any man would do for the woman he loves.'

She smiled at him with tenderness. 'That's sweetly put.'

'I have a way with words,' he replied flippantly.

'You know, I don't think I ever thanked you.'

'You didn't,' he said.

'Didn't I really?'

'No, you just took my heroism for granted.'

She laughed. 'Well, I'm thanking you now.'

'You owe me one,' he said.

'I don't think I'll ever be able to repay you for saving my life, Colm.'

'You won't.' He grinned. 'But you're going to spend the rest of your life trying.'

Her smile faltered.

He turned to face her. 'I want you to spend the rest of your life with me,' he said seriously.

'Are you asking what I think you're asking?'

'Yes, I'm asking you to marry me, Margot. And before you go all funny on me, I want to add that, once we're married, we could travel round the world, or go and live somewhere else, I don't know, France or Spain or Italy. You can choose, anywhere you like. I know you don't like to stay in the same place for long. The world is your oyster. You just let me know where you want to hang your hat.'

Margot narrowed her eyes. 'I want to be here,' she replied with a satisfied sigh. 'With you.'

Colm beamed a smile. 'Really? Here? In boring old Ballinakelly?'

He put his arm around her and she nestled into him. 'Home is where love is, Colm,' she said. 'I never realized that before. I've spent years running away from attachment, from commitment, from anyone who might have wanted more than I was willing to give. Now I've found you, I want to be well and truly tied down. Colm Deverill, I'd like to hang my hat in *your* hall.'

'That's grand,' he said.

'So, it's a yes. I will marry you, Colm.'

He bent down and kissed her. A long, sensual kiss that sent a ripple of pleasure over her skin. 'If marriage is like this, I think I'm going to like it.'

'It's *just* like this,' he said with a chuckle and kissed her again.

Kitty

I watch Colm and Margot wander back across the lawn to join the party. The sun is bright and in the shimmering rays of light I see that I am not alone. Dorothy is here too. 'I never told Margot how much I enjoyed her book,' she says, smiling wistfully. 'I enjoyed it immensely, you know. I hope she read my scribbles of praise in the margins.'

'It's frustrating not being able to communicate, isn't it,' I reply. 'There are so many things we want to tell them. That there is no such thing as death. That the soul lives on. That love connects us for ever. That we are never far away, but watching their lives from Spirit. And what a beautiful place Spirit is, isn't it! I'd like to tell them that.'

'I'd like to tell them that, too,' says Dorothy.

'There *are* ways.'

'Of course,' Dorothy replies, remembering the little robin her daughter sent. 'I suppose you would know how to do that, wouldn't you, Kitty?'

'Oh, yes,' I tell her. 'I'm an old hand at that.'

'Would you mind?'

'Come, I have just the thing.'

It is the end of the afternoon. The last of the guests have left. Colm and Margot remain on the lawn with a couple of girls from the hotel, putting the books back into boxes. Margot picks up one of the books and looks at it proudly. 'I wish Dorothy were here,' she says to Colm. 'I'd love her to know that I dedicated the book to her. She'd have been thrilled with that. I'd love her to know that it's had really good reviews as well, and that JP and Emer think I've done a good job. She took such an interest in it, writing her thoughts in the margin in her spidery hand. More than anything I'd like to tell her that I'm engaged. I'd like to tell her that I'm going to stay here in Ballinakelly. That I'm happy. Oh Colm. There are so many things I'd like to tell her.'

And then a little robin flies over and lands on the grass in front of her. She sees it and smiles in wonder. 'Look! It's a robin!' she whispers so as not to frighten it away. Then her expression changes and she gasps. 'You don't think . . .?' The robin hops across the ground towards her, then flaps its wings and jumps onto the book. Margot holds her breath. She daren't make a sound. The robin remains very still. It looks at her for a long moment. Margot gazes back until her eyes fill with tears and she can only see a red blur. 'Thank you, Dorothy,' she says and the robin tilts its head to one side as if to say, *Really, those tears aren't for me, are they, dear?* And then flies away.

Acknowledgements

With this book I bring an end to the Deverill series. Well, that's what I said after number four, so I won't make any promises I can't keep. There's a slim chance I might delve into the Deverills' distant past and write about their ancestors in the eighteenth or nineteenth centuries. After all, there's still so much of their history yet to be created. But for now, here it is, the final part.

Once again, I called upon my dear friend and co-conspirator, Tim Kelly, to help me develop my Irish characters. I owe him a huge debt of gratitude for all his help and advice. I really couldn't have embarked on this series without him.

My interest in the esoteric has led me to some wonderful people who I would like to thank here. Simon and Lisa Jacobs, Susan Dabbs, Robin Lown and Avril Price. There is more to this world than what we see with the physical eye and I'm having such a great time learning about it.

I also want to thank my agent, Sheila Crowley, and my editor, Suzanne Baboneau, who are the two most important people in my working life. I don't think I'd have a writing career at all if it wasn't for them. It's not just about the deals and the sales figures, it's about nurturing, mentoring, advising and supporting, and those two magnificent women do all of that and more. Thank you.

I'm also grateful to my film agent, Luke Speed, and to all those at Curtis Brown who work on my behalf: Alice Lutyens, Sophia MacAskill, Katie McGowan, Callum Mollison, Emily Harris and Sabhbh Curran. A huge thank you to Ian Chapman, my boss at Simon & Schuster, and his brilliant team who work so diligently and sensitively on my manuscripts: Sara-Jade Virtue, Gill Richardson, Dominic Brendon, Polly Osborn, Rich Vlietstra and Alice Rodgers.

My love and thanks to my husband Simon Sebag-Montefiore, our children Lily and Sasha, my parents Charles and Patty Palmer-Tomkinson, James, Sos, Honor, India, Wilf and Sam Palmer-Tomkinson and my aunt Naomi Dawson who keep me sane and make me happy.

Santa Montefiore

Stories that stay with you forever

Stay in touch with Santa for monthly updates
on her latest books.

Sign up for Santa's newsletter at
SantaMontefioreAuthor.com

You can also connect with Santa on social media,
or follow her on Amazon for new book alerts.

🐦 SantaMontefiore

📷 SantaMontefioreOfficial

📘 /SantaMontefiorebooks

🅰 bit.ly/FollowSanta

Discover more from *Sunday Times*
bestselling author Santa Montefiore ...

Faced with losing everything, all that matters is ...

HERE *and* NOW

Marigold has spent her life taking care of those around her,
juggling family life with the running of the local shop, and
being an all-round leader in her quiet yet welcoming
community. When she finds herself forgetting things,
everyone quickly puts it down to her age. But something
about Marigold isn't quite right, and it's becoming harder
for people to ignore.

As Marigold's condition worsens, for the first time in their
lives her family must find ways to care for the woman who
has always cared for them. Desperate to show their support,
the local community come together to celebrate Marigold,
and to show her that losing your memories doesn't matter,
when there are people who will remember them for you ...

**Evocative, emotional and full of life, *Here and Now* is the
most moving book you'll read this year.**

AVAILABLE NOW IN PAPERBACK AND EBOOK

**SIMON &
SCHUSTER**

The SECRET HOURS

'*Let the wind take me and the soft rain settle me into the Irish soil from where I came. And may my sins be forgiven …*'

Arethusa Clayton has always been formidable, used to getting her own way. On her death, she leaves unexpected instructions. Instead of being buried in America, on the wealthy East Coast where she and her late husband raised their two children, Arethusa has decreed that her ashes be scattered in a remote corner of Ireland, on the hills overlooking the sea.

All Arethusa ever told Faye was that she grew up in a poor farming family and left Ireland, alone, to start a new life in America as did so many in those times of hardship and famine. But who were her family in Ireland and where are they now? What was the real reason that she turned away from them? And who is the mysterious benefactor of a significant share of Arethusa's estate?

AVAILABLE NOW IN PAPERBACK AND EBOOK

SIMON &
SCHUSTER